THE
ABJECT
GOD

IMMORTAL TREACHERY: BOOK 4

By Allan Batchelder

The monster's roar grew louder, more urgent, and then stopped altogether. Ona and Hjuest rushed to find positions from which they could see what was happening. At the edge of the fire's radiance, a new hill stood, its tentacles thrashing silently and its pincers snapping. "Reaper?" came a small, almost boyish voice that was immediately echoed by a chorus of equally odd voices. "Frog!" the Reaper shouted, now farther off. "How how how are you alive alive alive alive?" Suddenly nearby, Vykers yelled, "You can't kill me, boy. I am the bringer of death!" And, just like that, he was gone again, spirited away on his mercurial horse. The monster shrieked in confusion or fury; no one listening could have said for certain. "Tonight," the Reaper called out from somewhere to Ona's right, "tonight you die!" The creature made a new and horrible sound, a scream of pain, Ona hoped. A small wisp of fire appeared high up on its bulk—a flaming arrow, which was rapidly followed by another and another, until the monster was freckled with fire. The arrows seemed to bother him not at all, but at least they defined the general area of his head for those below. Ona, Hjuest, Ngoro and the rest of Vykers' crew rode out from cover and attempted to position themselves at the Frog's back, the better to attack but also to avoid impeding the Reaper's more-frontal attacks. Vykers appeared in brief flashes, his new axe hacking away at the monster's legs with impossible speed. Was he making any difference though? How does one kill a mountain, exactly?

Dedication

This book is dedicated to the good folks at BestFantasyBooks. com, and, in particular:

Kenubrion
SneakyBurrito
Silvion Knight
TomTB
Darth Tater
Jakyro
Khartun
Derk of Derkholm
Fbones24

And others too numerous to recall. Your support has meant everything to me!

Prologue

He staggered and stumbled through the ice-crusted snow, hour upon hour, day into night and back again. Not that he noticed. An angry wind rasped against his cheeks, and sleet pelted the rest of him. Not that he cared. He just kept pushing onward—not towards, but away. Away and away and away, knowing there were no answers or comfort to be found anywhere. The winter storm raged about him, but it was as nothing to the maelstrom he felt within.

Let me die, he prayed. *Let me die.*

In time, he found himself on the edge of a cliff, overlooking a great crevasse. He wept, and his tears froze in their tracks. Shoving his hands in his pockets, he said a final goodbye and then closed his eyes and leaned out into space.

He was alarmed at how much time he had to think.

Until he stopped thinking.

ONE

Vykers' camp was a whirlwind of activity, as its disparate groups prepared to set out on their separate missions in preparation for war. Though he'd listened attentively to everyone's plans and pronouncements, Spirk was only dimly aware of the details, preoccupied as he was with the sudden disappearance of his friend Long Pete.

It had been less than a day since Spirk had learned that the old Virgin Queen was, in reality, the goddess Alheria. As hard as that was to swallow, it paled in comparison to Her Majesty's claim that Long Pete was her former lover and rival, Mahnus. At first, Spirk had been so overwhelmed and confused by this news that he avoided his friend. Now, in Long's absence, the young Shaper was wracked with guilt.

How could he have turned his back on his oldest friend? And how would Long survive in the wilderness without his crew?

Spirk raced about the camp, looking for the rest of his mates and attempting to rally them in search of their leader. To his chagrin, his friends were mostly uncooperative.

"Look," said Ron, his white-blond hair ruffling in the breeze, "we were lucky to make it this far. If we don't attach ourselves to one o' these larger parties, we won't make it anywhere alive."

Spirk was dumbfounded by Ron's response, but he knew he had no time to debate the matter. Instead, he turned to Remuel Wratch, the actor. "Won't you come with me?" Spirk asked.

"And do what? Recite epic poetry?"

"But he'll die out in that cold, all by hisself."

"Not if he's really a god, he won't," Yendor Plotz cut in with an angry edge to his voice.

There was no point in asking Captain Kittins, Spirk knew, so he made one final appeal to his friends. "Are you lot serious? This is our friend we're talkin' of. We been through the infinite hells together, and you know he'd die for any one o' you!"

"This is different," said Ron. "Before, we were helpin' him find his little one. We all wanted to save her. But now, he's gone and run off on his own."

"But…"

"Enough," Kittins cut in. He'd come up behind Spirk and, as usual, scared the shit out of him. "We'll wait a day, boy. One day to round up supplies and rest our horses. Then we all head south to the capital. Alheria will have a plan for the land's defense."

A day, Spirk sighed. Well, a day was better than nothing. Perhaps Long would return.

Elsewhere in camp, Karrakan gathered his belongings and said a final few words to his king before joining Mardine at the little forest's southern edge.

"It's a good walk," he warned his companion.

"Any walk with my daughter at the end's a good walk," she replied. But her words belied an emotional brittleness at the bittersweet prospect of reuniting with her child even as she excluded her husband from the family.

"And your man?" Karrakan asked, not urgently.

Mardine shrugged. "What else can I do? If he is who the Queen says he is…" Her voice trailed off in uncertainty. "What else can I do?" she repeated.

Seeing her distress, Karrakan summoned his will-o-wisps, and they seemed to ease her suffering as they floated and fluttered around her.

The snow had let up and, since Eyatu's death, the air itself had warmed noticeably. Karrakan took this as a hopeful sign that the trek south would be easier than coming north had been.

Vykers was alone, shaving with a dagger when Aoife approached him at the fire.

"I owe you my life."

He looked up at her, almost smiled. "No you don't. Not me."

So, he wouldn't accept her thanks. "Well, in any case, I'm glad we were finally able to defeat him...my brother."

Now, Vykers did smile. "Ah, that. You mighta told me."

Aoife offered a rueful chuckle. "Oh, yes. And how might I have done that? 'By the way, the End-of-All-Things, the lunatic who's trying to destroy the world, he's my brother?"

The Reaper returned Aoife's chuckle with a merrier one of his own. "That is a little weird, you put it that way. What's the story there, anyhow?"

The Umaena was suddenly demure. "I think," she said softly, "we'll save that for another time."

"Another time, is it?" Vykers asked. "You reckon there'll *be* another time?"

"That," said Aoife, "is entirely up to you."

Vykers looked down for a moment to wipe the whiskers off his blade, and when he looked up again, Aoife was gone. "Damn," he muttered. "We didn't get to talk about the war."

The Emperor, Near the Eastern Shore

The conventional wisdom was that the ocean could not be crossed, that it was too full of monsters, and that it robbed all wizards of their magics. This same wisdom held that the Reaper was dead, had been, in fact, for more than a century.

Now, the world knew otherwise. Treaman Wykkerian had engaged and defeated the Emperor's knights at the obelisk, and the only question was how long it would be before he returned for the Emperor's throne. It had happened before, after all.

Thus, Mendis Staurachia stood near the bow of his ship, leaning over the gunwale on the port side, as if readying himself to leap overboard once the water was shallow enough. In truth, he was only impatient to begin the invasion. In the Emperor's mind, it was a race, now, to see which man would be first to strike at the other's homeland with an army. Mendis wasted no time in rallying his legions and navy, and formulating his plan of attack. Since Wykkerian had proven the ocean could be crossed, Mendis determined to do it himself, and with such numbers at his back that victory was a foregone conclusion.

The cries of gulls overhead caused the Emperor to look up from the waves and consider the shadow of the distant shoreline that stretched across the horizon. *Another land!* Strange to think he'd been Emperor of the world and hadn't seen this part of it. Back home, this land was an abstraction, spoken of in fairy tales and ghost stories but never quite perceived as an actual place, a destination one could visit, populated with peoples and animals all its own.

The Emperor planned to do more than visit, though. Before, during and after his hunt for Wykkerian, he would make himself known to the natives, help them understand that they were now his subjects and citizens of the Empire, and this was good. The Empire was well-run, a place of law and prosperity, and what man alive would not benefit from such? These natives— whatever their cultures—would come to appreciate the fair and organized nature of life under the Emperor, or they would perish.

As for Wykkerian? The Emperor would avenge his great grandfather and give the Reaper the slow and painful execution he so richly deserved. And the man who captured or killed the Reaper would be immortalized for the deed—a suitable fate, Mendis reflected, for both men.

He was not a large man, was the Emperor, and he knew it. But his spirit was large and his destiny stupendous. In a short while, he would be Emperor of the world in title and in fact.

He took a deep breath of salt breeze and studied the sweep of his navy to his left and right. From where he stood, it almost appeared he could walk from ship to ship up and down the length of the coast. There were so many ships at his stern, he felt he could even have walked home across their decks. Wykkerian—or whoever it was ruled this land—was already beaten.

The Abject God

The world was white with snow; the world was red with pain. Everything hurt, but worst of all was the knowledge he hadn't died. He'd thrown himself from a precipice, fallen for an age, and failed to kill himself. *Ha!* Only he could be so inept.

Unless, of course, he *was* a god.

He hadn't quite believed it, didn't want to accept it, but the evidence was certainly piling up.

Slowly, stiffly, the man got to his feet and brushed the ice and snow off his face and chest. Maybe he couldn't kill himself by falling, but there were other ways to die. He pulled his gloves off with his teeth and spat them into the snow. He worked his way out of his overcoat and jacket, undid his doublet and belt, and shucked the lot next to his gloves. He followed that with his shirt, his breeches, his hose and his boots, until he stood naked and unprotected from the elements. But what could he do until exposure took him? He hated waiting.

And so he resumed walking.

Maybe he'd get eaten by wolves; it was no more than he deserved. Or maybe the Svarren would get him.

He was both amazed and disheartened by the ease with which he continued to function. His world had ended some time ago; it seemed unfair that he'd outlived it. He forced his mind back to the earliest of his mortal memories. His 'life,' he felt, had been more punishment than pleasure and continued to be so, even now. Was it this way for everyone? Was this what it meant to be human?

Without warning, his heart flooded with pity for his fellow men, and especially his former comrades. He remembered them shivering in this same cold, starving, suffering from injuries and maladies, fatigue and fear. What kept them going? How had they been able to greet each new sunrise? Oh, yes: their loyalty to him. Bile rushed up the man's throat and into his mouth—a reflection, perhaps, of his own bitterness. He scowled and forced it back down.

When he looked up again, the sun had flown halfway across

the sky. He'd been walking for hours, naked, and was still none the worse for it. Angered, he kept walking. In time, he came to a great flat area, its perimeter defined by stands of trees. This, the man realized, was a frozen lake, hidden beneath the snow. Only a fool would walk onto its ice, now that the air had begun warming.

He walked onto its ice. It made no sound and seemed solid enough near the shore, but the further the man walked towards its middle, the more the ice creaked. Gradually, the creaking gave way to loud cracks, and the man grinned. Maybe this was—

He plunged into the frigid water and made no effort to abate his descent, but instead expelled all the breath from his lungs, so that he sank like a stone. His ears popped, and still he sank. With every foot, the water grew darker and darker, until at last the man could barely see the surface above. In these depths, the water was deathly cold. And yet it brought no death. The pressure was intense. And yet the man felt no need to breathe. His feet sank into the mire at the lake's bottom, and the only coherent thought he had was how good the muck felt between his toes.

Sadly, his death did not seem imminent.

Bailis, Near the Eastern Shore

He'd mustered five thousand men, had Colonel Bailis, but it would not be enough. Not nearly enough. The sea to his east was black with ships—a tide of death, he was certain. But there had to be some resistance, did there not? Her Majesty had sent him here to inform the invaders they were not welcome and would not be tolerated. Bailis wasn't sure they'd get that message even if he'd brought five hundred thousand men with him.

What to do?

If he'd had Tarmun Vykers for company, he'd have felt a damn sight more confident. Or even the old Shaper, Pellas. But five thousand men? They might as well have begun digging their own graves; they'd occupy 'em soon enough.

Bailis brooded. He could attempt to assault the enemy's

landing parties, but they'd likely shower his men with arrows until he had no one left. And, anyway, he could hardly cover the whole coast. A massive landing would envelop him. He might lure a portion of the invaders away, though. Lead them on a merry chase through a swamp or ancient forest until they were utterly lost and helpless. Then he could return and do it all over again.

Sure. And he could shit lava, too.

If only the Queen had given him more men and time. He'd heard some idiot once proclaim, "You go to war with the army you have, not the army you might want or wish to have." Sounded like the wisdom of some parchment-pushing coward to Bailis. War wasn't an option when you were outnumbered a thousand-to-one or more. He had to probe the enemy and get his men the hells out of there until or unless reinforcements arrived.

He glared back out to sea, figured he had a day, at most.

Vykers' Camp, In the North

The Dead One had requested another day to await the return of the man Alheria had singled out as Mahnus. Vykers pretended to be displeased, but in reality he was still somewhat drunk and continued to grapple with questions he felt entirely unable to answer. Another day's rest might do him good. The others in his crew seemed to be emerging from their post-battle daze, but Vykers figured he had more on his mind.

Alheria, for instance, had maintained her cover as Queen of the midlands' kingdom for longer than the Reaper could remember. But she was out in the open now. Everyone who'd just participated in this second battle with the End knew her secret and would probably share that information with friends and family at the first opportunity.

...Unless, somehow, they all died unexpectedly. Vykers wouldn't put it past the Queen to engineer something like that.

He'd been wanting to kill her for some time—had even possessed, in the End's dagger, the means to do it—but something always got in the way—a battle, a crisis, a mutual enemy. And now this Mahnus-cursed invasion. Was it all coincidence, or was there a darker purpose at work?

Vykers' thoughts drifted to Long Pete. He didn't fit any vision of Mahnus the Reaper had ever had, but maybe that was proof enough of Alheria's claim. Maybe Mahnus had been hiding in plain sight all along. Suddenly, Vykers was curious about Long Pete's whereabouts, too. He looked around and saw none of the fellow's companions within shouting distance, and he wasn't disposed to leave the campfire. Off to his right, the mysterious and ancient Historian reclined near the flames. Vykers recalled that he also had questions for the Ahklatian.

"Historian," he called over, "let's talk."

Although the Historian was a Shaper hundreds of years old, it was generally understood that one approached the Reaper and not the other way 'round. If he wanted to talk, you dropped whatever you were doing and went to talk with him. Weary as he was, the Ahklatian was no different. He limped over to a vacant spot on the log next to Vykers and sat.

"Yes?"

"How far out's this fleet again?"

"A few days is what Her Majesty said. As of yesterday."

"Her Majesty," Vykers sneered. "You mean Alheria."

"Alheria, then."

"So now it's a few days, less one or two."

"I would assume immediate arrival."

Vykers nodded. "Makes sense."

"What will you do?"

The Reaper rubbed smoke from his eyes and yawned. "Last time we spoke, you mentioned the Sholdorn."

"I remember."

Vykers examined his friend's pallid visage and jet black eyes. They revealed nothing. "Why'd you want me to go visit 'em?"

The Historian seemed to take stock, to sink into himself, and his voice dropped in volume until it was barely audible. "You know, I am sure, that after the Awakening, there was much violence and destruction."

"Everyone ran around smashing everything to shit."

"That's one way to put it," the Historian said, offering a tepid grin. "Suddenly, no one could read, no one could write, and because they feared what was hidden in the writing they could no longer read, men went mad, destroyed all traces of it."

"Or tried to."

The Historian arched an eyebrow at Vykers. "Just so. The Sholdorn, however, have made it their mission to find and salvage whatever remains. In doing so, they've acquired an artifact or two that may speak to your past...and future."

"That settles it, then. I gotta pay 'em a visit," said Vykers, as he tossed a stick on the fire.

"Now?" the Historian asked, alarm evident in his voice.

"Why not?"

"Well, but we're being invaded, no?"

Vykers stood, smiled. "That's Her Majesty's problem. I'm sure she's counting on draggin' me into this, but I'm also sure she'll come up with some other solution in my absence. I mean, being a goddess and all."

The Historian was aghast. "But...is this wise?"

"The old beldam thinks she can read me," the Reaper laughed. "Let's see how she deals with this!"

Qansip Deda, Eastcliff

Qansip Deda was the most beautiful young woman in the county, and that was not only the general belief, but Qansip's as well. When she gazed into her hand mirror, she marveled at her honey-gold hair and deep brown eyes—an arresting combination, to be sure. And while it was the fashion for the best ladies in Lunessfor to paint the skin of their faces white, Qansip required no such measures. Her skin was flawless and perfectly colored on its own. Her nose was most feminine and her lips were full and lush. But her figure! Oh, her figure! She was tall and lithe with an ample but not overbearing bosom, a slender waist, a firm but not over large posterior and long, willowy legs. There wasn't a man within miles who didn't think of her the moment his eyes were closed of an evening, nor a woman who didn't resent her, and Qansip was fine with either notion. She comported herself as if she were due the world's admiration simply for having been born.

Her father, Driegan Deda, had named her after a princess. Of course, there had never been a Princess Qansip, but no one dared question Driegan's fantasies to his face. What he wanted for his daughter was a name as unique as he hoped she'd one day become. In that regard, at least, both father and child had succeeded. And her beauty meant she might become a princess in fact, one day, if the right prince could be found. After all, she was much too beautiful to be married off to a trades-man or merchant, and Driegan was set on making a sizable profit off his daughter's maidenhead. He envisioned himself as his future son-in-law's primary advisor and right-hand man, and he hoped that son-in-law would someday be king...of something.

Unfortunately, the damned Virgin Queen had been swal-lowing up city-states and smaller kingdoms for generations, and there was nary a nobleman left of sufficient station to merit consideration as a potential husband for Driegan's greatest prize. He contemplated choosing one of the lords of the Great Eight—Lunsford's eight most powerful families—but there'd been so much strife between them of late that it was hard to determine which house was in favor and which was not.

But it was not as if Driegan could bide his time. Qansip grew older with each passing day, and women of a certain age were no longer marketable. To make matters worse, war was coming, and the whole Deda clan—this branch of it, anyway—might very well be forced to flee. If her father dreaded this possibility, Qansip embraced it with youthful excitement. She'd never been out of the county and was rarely allowed off her father's estate without a large escort. To her, the looming invasion offered the chance to see other parts of the realm and perhaps even Lunsford itself; the possibility that tens of thousands of folks might die never seemed particularly real. Oh, she'd heard men fretting over wars her entire life, but she'd never seen or suf-fered one. She expected the same result this time.

Sensing that his daughter did not possess an especially authentic grasp of the situation, Driegan commanded his manservant to fetch her and meet him on the bluff overlooking the shore.

It was an oddly warm winter's day, a welcome change from the previous few months, but Driegan could not help feeling the unseasonable weather was being pushed ashore by the massive fleet now evident on the horizon. Fishermen had brought news of the fleet's approach two days past, but hearing about it and seeing it were two different things. He hoped it had the same effect on Qansip.

"You sent for me, father?" she asked upon arrival.

"I did," Driegan replied, without turning to greet his daughter.

"It's about those ships, then..."

"It is. I was hoping your own eyes could convince you of a danger that your elders clearly have not." Driegan pointed to the distant fleet. "There are tens of thousands of men on those ships, perhaps even hundreds of thousands. They will swarm us like insects, devouring everything in their path. Do you fancy being raped by ruffians?"

"Father!" Qansip cried out in alarm.

"Oh!" Driegan said, pulling a long face, "Does my language offend you? Imagine what those bastards will do!"

"You are right, father, as always. When do we leave for Lunsford?"

"We don't," Driegan scowled. "We're running as far west as the land will carry us. We'll put the whole continent between us and these invaders. That should buy us some time."

"Yes, father," said Qansip. "But wouldn't we do better to head for Lunsford?"

"Lunsford is a trap!" Driegan said adamantly. "If Her Majesty should fail to hold the city, we'd be trapped like rats. No, we're going west." Before Qansip could proffer another objection, Driegan cut her off with a gesture. "You'd best get packing, girl, if you want to live."

The Abject God

Well shit, the man thought, *looks like I can't drown or freeze, either.*

How does one go about killin' a god?

The answer, he suspected, was not to be found wallowing in the icy mud of a frozen lake. With little else to do, the man started trudging along the bottom. Movement was something, at least, even if he had no particular goal or destination in mind.

It was funny, really, how much he'd feared injury and death when he'd believed himself mortal. Now, he feared the opposite, that he could not die. He reflected on all the times he'd been frightened out of his wits, when he might simply have stood fast and proclaimed "I am a god!" and banished whatever it was that had bothered him. But...being a god had cost him his wife, daughter, home and friends. Some thought the gods all powerful, yet he felt anything but.

Just his luck, really, to become the most feeble god in existence. And that was odd, too. Alheria had proclaimed him Mahnus, and the man had always believed Mahnus to be the greatest of the gods. Why did he feel so foolish, so stupid? Where was his ability to Shape, to Jump, or see the future?

A prodigious, bottom-dwelling fish moved past on the man's right. He didn't see it, but rather sensed its presence. Would it eat him? Apparently not. The man noted numerous crustaceans in the area, too. Great, thorny things the size of dogs. These, too, were lost in darkness, and yet the man knew where each was located. Abruptly, he came to a stop and let his mind wander into the blackness. The crustaceans were everywhere, as were the fish. There were smaller creatures, as well, along with shells, decaying branches and logs, and the occasional wreckage of boats. There were bones, too, of animals that had once stepped too far from the shallows and been taken by something. And there were the bones of humans. The man didn't suppose it much mattered whether their owners had been victims of capsizings or tribal justice: they were just as dead. What fascinated him more was his newfound ability to sense such things. Maybe he had Shaping talent, after all. The question was, had this talent emerged because he'd finally acknowledged his birthright, or was he simply growing stronger over time, as his human body adjusted to his divinity? He wondered what else he could do.

He began walking again. As he slogged along, he tried a number of things like creating light, warming the surrounding waters, and propelling himself along the bottom. None worked. Still, his continued existence hinted at more to come, more to be discovered. He kept walking.

At the deepest part of the lake, he sensed something roaring at him—or that's how it felt, anyway. Hours ago, he'd been eager to die, but now he approached the unseen thing carefully. No point in going out in agony. Pressing forward, he came upon another pile of bones so overgrown with weeds and algae that at first he didn't recognize them. A stick jutted from their midst, and the man identified it as an axe haft. Drawing closer, he saw that the axe had been buried in someone's ribcage. The roaring intensified, but he didn't see how the thing could hurt him unless he touched it. Funny: only a short while earlier, he'd been trying to kill himself, but dying was different than suffering, and he'd been trying to end his own suffering, not prolong or intensify it. He bent over to get a better look and saw that the axe head had rusted away in a pile of red flakes, leaving the haft alone in the nest of ribs.

So, it was the haft that screamed at him.

Never been known fer my smarts, the man joked to himself.

And then he reached out and grasped the axe handle.

Vykers' Camp, In the North

Vykers crawled out of his tent, stood, stretched. He still felt a little drunk from the liquor he'd ingested two days earlier and made a point of questioning the one-eyed man who'd shared it as soon as he saw him again. First, though, he wanted to find the Dead One and see if they'd located that Long Pete character or not. Alheria had claimed the man was Mahnus, and, in retrospect, Vykers thought he should probably have paid him a bit more attention. If he truly was Mahnus, and Alheria had in fact tried to kill him, that made him a natural ally.

A shadow appeared at the Reaper's shoulder: the Dead One. Vykers turned to him.

"You got a name besides 'the Dead One'?"

"Nothing as fittin'."

"How 'bout I just call you 'Dead,' then?"

"Bound to happen sooner or later," the man quipped.

"Right," Vykers nodded. "'Dead' it is. Any news o' your friend?"

Kittins cracked a kink from his neck. "I wouldn't say we're friends, and the Shaper claims there's no sign of him. He's flat disappeared."

Like a god.

"Well," said Vykers, "let's see what's to eat and then get everyone on the road. I won't miss this Mahnus-cursed place." *And maybe it really is Mahnus-cursed.*

The Dead One grunted in agreement and went off about his business.

Vykers headed over to the communal fire, where Hjuest already had his meal prepared. There were times the Reaper preferred traveling alone, but the Red Knight and his crew sure knew how to make camp life easier. They handled the acquisition and preparation of food, making and maintaining the fire, tending the horses, and setting up and striking the tents. Vykers was welcome to help—who'd dare to forbid him, after all?—but most of the time, he found his men had matters well in hand without him.

He accepted a bowl of soup and sat in a space on a log evidently reserved just for him. A moment later, the one-eyed man stumbled up with his comrades and plunked himself down near the flames.

"You," said Vykers.

Yendor looked up, nervously. "Yes sir?"

"Your name?"

"Yendor, sir."

Vykers cast an eye over Yendor's fellows. "And the rest o' your gang?"

Yendor worked his way to his feet. "Reaper, sir, I present Ron, Spirk, and Remuel Wratch, actor."

"We met earlier," Rem interjected, bemused that the Reaper seemed to have forgotten.

"None o' you are fighters, I see."

"Is it that obvious?"

The Reaper smirked. "So, what are your roles, then? The young fella's a Shaper, and the actor's an actor...whatever *that* means in a fight...but what are you two supposed to be?"

"Ron's a bowman," said Yendor. "And I'm a drunk."

"Are you?" Vykers asked. "Well, every company's got one. At least you're honest about it. Now, here's *me* bein' honest: you fall, I ain't slowin' down for you. You fuck up, that's your look-out. I got enough shit to deal with. Understand?"

Yendor nodded.

Vykers went on, "But tell me, what was that liquor you shared the other night? Stuff lasts longer 'n a northern winter."

"I s'pose that's the point, eh? Anyways, we found it in a hole in the ground. As deep a hole as I ever hope to see, filled with monsters and darkness and fell portents."

"Sounds like my kinda place." Vykers paused for a moment, and then added, "But, look you, we're leavin' this morning. If you're travelin' with me, you'll have to share mounts with my men. Don't ask me a lot o' questions, and don't waste my time. War is coming."

Wasn't it always? What could Yendor and his friends say in reply? Nothing. Besides, they were all still reeling from Long's exposure and subsequent disappearance. They'd follow the Reaper and obey, because they had nothing else to do that made any kind of sense.

Vykers resumed eating, but Yendor had the distinct feeling the man was watching him and his friends from the corner of his eye.

The Reaper's horses were not natural. They possessed an awareness that Yendor and the others found intimidating to say the least. But they also traveled so quickly that it was difficult for their riders to get a fix on the surrounding scenery as it flew by. Yendor wanted to say something about all of this to Rem and the others, but was worried about looking a fool in front of Vykers. The truth was, he'd nearly pissed himself in his earlier conversation with the legendary Reaper, and he wanted no more dealings with the man until he got a little better grip on himself.

Anyway, the coming invasion gave him more than enough to worry about for the nonce. How would Her Majesty, Alheria, meet the challenge? Would she muster an army? Resort to sorcery? Or would she simply lock herself inside the fortified gates of Lunessfor and wait until the enemy abandoned its cause? Was such a thing even possible?

Weighty as these matters were, Yendor couldn't avoid thinking of his friend Long forever. When he finally did, he was almost overwhelmed with feelings of guilt and regret. Had Yendor's treatment of Long led to the man's disappearance? *Man*? Ha! It was pretty damned obvious that Her Majesty was in fact a god, and if she'd labeled Long one as well…

And yet, Yendor wanted proof, something more tangible than someone else's say-so, even if that someone else was Alheria. He wanted to see his friend perform miracles. Maybe Long even possessed the power to restore Yendor's lost eye.

Only…Yendor had no idea where to find his old friend and couldn't quite figure what he'd say to him if he did. They'd been testy with each other since they'd all fallen down that accursed hole.

Rem, Ron and even Spirk were likewise lost in their thoughts, each wondering what the next few days and weeks would bring for themselves, the kingdom, and for Long Pete. Like Yendor, the other fellows regretted their treatment of the captain, but none could imagine what they might have done differently. It was a most painful conundrum, the kind of problem for which prayer seemed the only suitable response. To whom should this prayer be directed, though? To Her Majesty? To Long Pete? Rem chuckled grimly at the mere thought of it.

Then he directed his thoughts elsewhere. If nothing else, he was due for a long, hot bath and a sumptuous meal. Surely he could fit that much in before he went rushing off to war again. He might even manage to entertain a lady or three.

Alheria, Lunessfor

The view from Alheria's tower window was breathtaking, but the goddess ignored it, staring instead at the backs of her hands as they rested on the sill. How wasted and withered they'd become, those hands. She had the power to change their appearance, of course, but doing so would be self-deluding, and she wanted always to remain aware of the simple fact that time was short, even for her. Indeed, in recent years, time seemed to have sped up, resulting in an almost unending cavalcade of calamities. The Queen clicked her nails on the sill and pursed her lips. The climax of the current age was fast approaching; the only question was who, if anyone, would emerge victorious.

The Emperor was coming in full force, as Alheria had always suspected he might. If things proceeded as she'd foreseen, Tarmun Vykers would once again ride to her kingdom's defense, not because he had any affinity for it, its people or its Queen—he had not—but because he was unable to resist the challenge to his martial supremacy. It was why he had been made. The damnable thing was that Vykers would resist and complain until the very last moment, as if he had any choice in the matter. Alheria was reminded of a line from a play she'd seen once, "They love not poison that do poison need." For the time being, the Reaper remained a necessary evil.

A shuffling of feet at her back alerted the Queen to her Fool's arrival. "You took your time in coming," she snapped.

"Your pardon, mum," Hoosh Bindy replied. "I turned left when I wanted right and ended up somewheres in Outer Delirium."

"You have ever been delirious."

"'Tis so, indeed, milady. But a Fool out of his wits is like a drunkard out of his drink, all too sober and aware of it. "

"Then by your logic, a Fool out of his wits is not a Fool."

"And so am I made invisible. And what's *she*, then, who sees and speaks to the invisible?"

"You'd have me say 'a fool'."

"Better to say than to be, for then I'm out of a job. This castle has room for only so much foolery."

"Enough!" Alheria cried. "Have done! We've weightier matters to discuss."

Hoosh executed a slight bow and regarded the Queen in silent expectation.

"Your brother is dead, at last."

"*Half*-brother," Hoosh corrected. "I'll own no more of the End than I must."

Alheria waved the comment away as if it were nonsense. "The half you share is mine. The shame is mine."

Hoosh quirked an eyebrow at this comment. "Shame? What shame? You're answerable to no one."

Her Majesty spun and faced her son directly. "Mahnus has returned."

The Fool's mouth fell open, and his eyes grew wide with fear.

"Yes," the Queen continued, "he's come back, and once he recalls the enmity between us..."

"Your treachery."

Alheria shot Hoosh a sour look. "My...*actions*...then, he will likely seek retribution."

The Fool pondered this whilst his mother continued to glare at him. "Meantime, the Emperor invades."

"Just so."

"Am I to be lost defending you and the winner takes all?"

The Queen stepped towards her son and put a hand on his shoulder—an uncharacteristically sympathetic gesture from her. "We shall see who takes what. It may well be that the thick-skulled Reaper wins the day."

"Perish the thought!" Hoosh cried melodramatically. "I'd rather be killed by Mahnus."

Suddenly, Her Majesty remembered a line from another play. "There's small choice in rotten apples," she said, a grim smile on her lips.

The Emperor, Coming Ashore

The fleet's tenders rode in on the surf, laden with more sol-diers than they'd been designed to carry, but the Emperor was anxious to get as many men ashore as possible in the shortest amount of time, so as to protect those coming in behind them. His legions, the Emperor mused, mimicked the sea from which they emerged, flooding onto the beach in wave after wave, more than enough to drown local resistance and, Mendis hoped, wash the land free of the Reaper and anyone else who might be an impediment to lasting peace.

Much of the coast was evacuated, and the weather, though damp, was surprisingly mild for winter. Given the challenges his men might have faced, the Emperor was both pleased and confident as the first of his boats touched the shore. Soldiers jumped into waist-deep water and rushed up the beach, eager to establish a foothold from which to defend their fellows and survey the landscape before them. Someone had spotted a single horseman, but the stranger had fled before any sort of pursuit could develop. The man was a scout, more than likely, and was off to alert the natives of the invaders' arrival. In his absence, the Emperor's legions continued to pour out of their tenders and onto the sand. Better still, his wizards were once again on solid ground and able to practice their arts. If an enemy force appeared, the men of the Empire would be more than ready to meet them.

Within half an hour, Mendis' soldiers had secured the beach beyond sight in either direction. An advance contingent had similarly established a defensible vantage point atop the nearest dune, allowing the Emperor's generals an excellent view of the lands to the east. In a short while, plans would be formulated and strategies set for the exploration and conquest of the new land's interior. Even if Wykkerian chose to intervene, he could never hope to stand up to the overwhelming might of the Empire's legions. They had ruled their homeland for generation upon generation; Mendis could not imagine them falling to anyone.

Two of the Emperor's men stood ready to lift him free of the launch and carry him to the beach, but Mendis dismissed them. He was not a ruler to be pampered; whatever he asked or expected of his men, he asked and expected of himself. Thus, he leapt into the sea, planted his feet against the cresting waves, and felt their invigorating cold surround him. He reached into the water, scooped up a generous handful, and splashed it on his face, raking the last of it through his jet-black hair. In the next instant, he strode forward, pushing against the ebbing tide, and made his way out of the surf. He stood well away from his troops to make himself easier to spot for his officers and his wizards. A lesser man might have feared making himself a target for hostile natives or even assassination from one of his subjects, but the Emperor had no such worries. He knew those tasked with protecting him were the best and most subtle of their sort in the world. He was not a tall man, no, but his confidence worked every inch out of his frame, and he seemed much larger for it.

"Magnificence," one of his officers called out as he approached. "We'll have your pavilion in place within the hour."

Mendis nodded regally at the man. There was no need to do or say more.

"Magnificence," said another of his men, "the High Wizard informs me that the nearest enemy force is some miles away and comprised of but a few thousand men. Nothing to worry about."

The Emperor turned on the man abruptly. "I'll decide what I should worry about, Telding."

The alacrity with which Telding fell to fawning was astounding. "Of course, Magnificence, of course."

"And tell the High Wizard I would speak with him in person."

If a man could grovel whilst walking backwards out of the Emperor's presence, Telding had mastered the art. "Your word, your will, Magnificence."

Mendis shook his head, made a sour face in exasperation. He understood that the honorific 'Magnificence' was necessary to instill and command respect for his station, but it annoyed him nevertheless. Had he been born a peasant, he would have been simply 'Mendis,' and that would have been just fine with him. He might even have sported a nickname, something familiar and playful that spoke to his essential self. He supposed 'Magnificence' was meant to do that, too, but somehow it seemed like foppish puffery. Now, Wykkerian had a nickname that truly meant something: The Reaper. He'd earned that name, legend had it, through countless acts of butchery.

Anyone who heard the name knew in his bones what it meant. 'Magnificence,' on the other hand, sounded like something one might say of a queen.

Well, Mendis would make a new name for himself in this strange land, and he'd write it in the blood of its inhabitants.

Vykers' Camp, In the North

The Historian had been gone for more than a day, but he reappeared suddenly as if he'd never been absent. "I must speak with you," he whispered to the Reaper when the group stopped for a water break.

"Huh," Vykers grunted.

"The enemy has come ashore."

"I figured."

"What will you do?"

Vykers adjusted his saddle and offered his horse a handful of grain. "What will I do? Does Her Royal fuckin' Goddess expect me to take on the Emperor's forces without an army? Come to that, what's *she* been doin' about this? Anyway," the Reaper said, "I've already said I'm headed for the Sholdorn. Tell Her Majesty I ain't available, or tell her nothing. It's all one to me."

When the Historian next spoke, his words surprised Vykers. "Sometimes, I envy your self-assurance, your supreme confidence, your decisiveness. I imagine you sleep better than I."

Vykers made a noncommittal gesture. "I fall asleep okay, but my dreams are pretty fuckin' baffling."

"Nightmares?"

The Reaper shot the other man a look of disbelief.

"Of course not," the Historian answered himself. "But strange nonetheless?"

"Passing strange. I wish we had time to discuss 'em, but I've gotta talk to my sergeant before we get goin' again." With that, the Reaper slapped the Historian on the shoulder and went off in search of the Red Knight.

The Historian remained where he was for several minutes, thinking, and then Jumped out of Vykers' company.

Hjuest was no happier than the Historian upon hearing of his master's plans. "But de men! Dey von't go back vidout you!"

"They won't?" Vykers challenged.

"Vell, of course dey vill do vat you say. Of course. But dey von't like it."

Vykers laughed. "So what? They don't like followin' my orders, they're free to make their own ways."

"It is not dat," the smaller man replied. "Most of us feel dere is no...better ting...den vorking vid you."

"Good o' you to say so. Batshit crazy, but still good. Look," said Vykers, "the Queen's gonna need someone who can talk to the Emperor and his men. And that's you. Remember me sayin' you'd make a fine herald? Well, now's your chance."

"But de others..."

"They're grown men, no? They can decide what to do, who to follow once you all reach Lunessfor."

Hjuest wanted to say more, to object, to stall the Reaper somehow, but words failed him. Vykers gave him a quick jab in the upper arm and returned to his horse. The subject, it seemed, was closed.

That night, Vykers waited until everyone had settled into their tents or around the fire before he slipped away. He'd taken the precaution of tethering his own horse just beyond the firelight's range, so that when he wandered off into the bushes ostensibly to relieve himself, he actually climbed onto his mount and led it carefully away from camp. He gave not another thought to his companions—his *former* companions—but focused all his energies and attention on his own journey. It was past time to visit the Sholdorn and make them reveal their secrets.

Sporadically, the night intruded upon the Reaper's thoughts. It had been a good while since he'd last been alone anywhere, especially the wilderness. And he savored the opportunity. The rich combination of scents and sounds evoked something animal within Vykers. Fleetingly, he recalled his chimeras and how efficient they'd been at hunting and killing in the dark.

There were few people he missed much throughout his life, but he missed the chimeras. In many ways—those that mattered—they'd been kindred spirits. Men? What did the Reaper have in common with them? He'd no interest in building a home or running a farm. Commerce bored him. Politics? An endeavor only the stupidly self-important would ever enjoy. Why negotiate with some asshole when it was easier to break him to your will?

Once Vykers and his horse were well clear of the camp, he urged the beast into its preternatural gait, and the night surged by all around. Such a thing would have been dangerous for a normal horse, but his was as far from normal as he. When he was certain his men could no longer find or follow him, Vykers slowed his mount to a stop and prepared to make camp.

It was a dark night, but Vykers was darker yet. He took his time building a fire and almost wished something would dare to attack him. He never felt quite so alive as when he was killing something. He'd had plenty of companions in the past who'd have had something to say about that—Arune, the Historian, Turley, even Aoife—but he was on his own now, answerable to no one, and he liked it that way. *Just let something come near,* he thought, *I need the exercise.*

Nothing appeared, though. Not then, and not the rest of the night, either. Vykers woke up mildly disappointed. He packed up his things, cared for his mount, and inspected his weapons. He had a serviceable if unremarkable sword, a hand axe, and a dagger. And his claws. He'd once killed the End with those claws, but rarely used them otherwise. They tended to alarm folks—not that he cared overmuch. But in the wild? He couldn't wait to tear something in half.

At mid-day, he had to adjust his course. The Sholdorn were located, as he recalled, south and east of Lunessfor, a long way south and a little east. He knew the Emperor's fleet was attacking the eastern shores, but surely it didn't extend that far south. If it did, Vykers didn't see much anyone could do about it. An invasion that large probably couldn't be stopped…

Not that he wouldn't be involved in the fighting, one way or another. It was all he lived for. But he was becoming increasingly

unsure of whom or for what he was fighting. Why save the kingdom? Why save the land? Maybe things would actually be better under this Emperor. As long as he wasn't a god like Alheria,
he might not prove as manipulative, or, if he was, perhaps he
wouldn't be as skilled at it.

Then Vykers remembered the Emperor's living armor, those
giant, solid steel juggernauts that could destroy everything in
their paths. What difference did it make if women and children
were killed by men or these monstrosities? Well, Vykers mused,
the thing was, it wasn't a particularly fair fight. Even a child
could still stick a man with a dagger. But the juggernauts? They
had no weaknesses. There wasn't a man, woman or child in the
world who could withstand their onslaught.

The Reaper was struggling to decide whether he cared. It
was funny how the farther he got from people, the less he concerned he became about their fates.

After a brief stop, he got back on his horse and resumed his
trek, in no particular rush this time, because rushing felt like
taking orders, and he was in no mood for that. Later, he smelled
something following him. Again, he hoped that whatever it was
would be stupid enough to attack. He liked scenery and solitude
as much as the next fellow, but he was getting a mite bored. He
stopped altogether and slid out of the saddle, feigning a need to
piss. Now, he was a seemingly unarmed man, alone in a bush.
If anything was going to happen...

The underbrush around him came to life, shaking, rustling
and rattling. And there was that odor again, vaguely familiar. Out of the corner of his eye, Vykers caught a glimpse of
something shadowy—*several* somethings shadowy—pushing
through the undergrowth. An instant before they burst into the
clear, he recognized them: grebbers. Months and months ago
now, he'd fought an endless horde of them. But then, he'd had
help. If the damnable things came at him in similar numbers
this time...

But this bunch was different, both in appearance and behavior. As before, the creatures were about two feet in height, perhaps two-and-a-half, and possessed only rudimentary facial
features, as if someone had been sculpting them from clay and

lost interest halfway through the job. Unlike their plains kin though, these grebbers were colored like the bushes and trees around them, in mottled greens and browns. They carried crude club and axe-like weapons, and a few had spears and tiny bows. The Reaper might have laughed, except that he knew anything could be deadly in sufficient numbers.

To his back, he heard additional creatures moving to flank and encircle him. That was not going to happen. He took a moment to assess whether or not his horse was at all alarmed— it was not—and decided to fight this one out until he lost interest or killed all of the creatures. With a great roar, he leapt backwards into the mass of grebbers still attempting to surround him. Startled, they scattered like pearls dropped on a table top, yipping and shrieking in their panic. The Reaper had left his weapons on his horse, an unusually cocky decision even for him, but he still had his claws. Too, the grebbers themselves were small enough to use as weapons, if Vykers so chose.

More of the beasties poured into the area around Vykers and his horse. He began to see that the greatest danger might be to his mount and the gear it carried. Still, the eldritch thing showed no signs of discomfort or unease, so Vykers decided to focus on killing as many grebbers as possible. With a strike almost too fast to be seen, he lashed out with the claws of his right hand and gutted three creatures on the spot. Double that number rushed into the void created by their deaths.

Good. This would be a healthy test...for *him*, anyhow.

The grebbers swarmed him, just as their kinfolk had. Vykers clawed, kicked, punched and threw until he'd worked up a good sweat. It was time to switch tactics. He grabbed a creature with each hand, moved his grip to their ankles, and swung them like twin maces at their brethren. This only served to enrage the grebbers further, and they responded by throwing rocks, darts, and spears at him. Those with bows shot at him. Most of these weapons missed the Reaper or did minimal damage...but some of the pointed ones had been envenomed, and Vykers cursed himself for an arrogant fool. He should have expected that.

The wisest option at this point was to race for his horse, mount up, and ride away. But the Reaper had never been known for his wisdom, and, anyway, the poison burning on and in his skin began to enflame his own rage. *The bastards!* It was not enough that they had superiority in numbers; they had to use poison, too. Vykers tossed the ruined meat of the two dead grebbers away and started ripping the heads off any of their fellows who came within his arms' reach. Still, the things came on, and it looked very much to Vykers as if this horde would match the one he'd fought previously. And he had no Aoife, no chimeras, no jester at his side. Soon, tearing the grebbers' heads off was not violent enough. The Reaper darted about in a mist of blood, ripping the creatures asunder by whatever parts he could grasp. He felt more pinpricks, nicks and gougings along his back and sides, but he didn't care.

...Until he began to slow down. His limbs became leaden, and a fog enveloped his brain. He understood that this was unusual, but he failed to understand its cause. Suddenly, he lurched back and forth like a clumsy drunk, swiping at his enemies and missing terribly. For a moment, he was able to regain clarity, and saw himself adrift in a sea of grebbers.

The Abject God, In the North

The axe handle bellowed in fury. It roared. It snarled. It was wrath made tangible.

The man knew a thing or two about anger. He'd spent most of his life, his *mortal* life, angry. That it had all been directed at himself was beside the point: he recognized the handle's rage and even identified with it. There was so much to be angry about, so many people and things that deserved to be punished. The man decided to keep the axe handle, to bring it with him in case a suitable head could be found.

He'd grown weary of walking on the lake bottom, however, and with a thought he was standing on the far shore, tasting the winter air as if it were his favorite wine. He'd never really noticed how pleasant breathing was before. He was glad he could still do it.

But.

He missed his wife terribly, and his daughter even more.

And yet, who was to blame for his current predicament? The gods? He *was* a god! Hard as this was to swallow, recent evidence made it undeniable: he, Long Pete, was Mahnus. It was a curse. And apparently self-pity was a fault not reserved for mortals alone. Pathetic. Disgusting.

There must be some benefits to bein' a god, Long mused. *I mean, besides bein' unkillable.* He'd Jumped up here from the bottom of the lake; that was something. It didn't assuage his loneliness or magically make him like himself any better, but it was a start, a tool that might help him somehow, if only he could reason it out.

He was cold—though not as cold as he should have been—and hungry. He set about finding a suitable spot to make camp—a fire, a lean-to of some sort, a bed of branches. He felt as though his best course of action was *inaction*: a good, long sleep that would blunt the edge of recent woes and allow his better, saner self to reemerge.

At the base of a large hill, he found a tumble of boulders that formed a cave-like recession in which he felt he could rest out of the wind and sleet. He gathered up branches for a sort of nest-bed and also a pile of wood for a fire. On one side of the boulders, he found plenty of moss, which, once dry, would make an excellent cover for his bed. He might also use some for tinder.

Fire. How was he to make it? He'd thrown off all his clothing hours and hours earlier, cast it off like a great serpent shedding its skin. Back when he'd still possessed some vestige of mortality. Back when he'd still held out hope he was human.

But I'm Mahnus, by the gods! Be a pretty piss-poor deity if I couldn't make fire. He discovered it was only a matter of focusing his thoughts on the kindling and demanding it burn. Why hadn't he possessed this ability earlier? In short order, a small but lusty fire brightened both the cave and Long's mood. Now for food. Could he make it appear simply by concentrating on it? He tried and tried for long minutes, but had no success. Perhaps he hadn't been specific enough. He wished for roast duck and red wine. Neither appeared.

Some god.

But he did *hear* a duck somewhere nearby. Grudgingly, he got to his feet and poked his head outside his cave. A large, fat duck stood not ten paces away, staring at him as if waiting for directions.

"What are you doin' up here at this time o' year?" Long demanded.

Quack!

Without losing sight of the bird, Long reached behind himself until his fingers happened upon the axe handle. Part of him wanted to spare the hapless thing, but another part said feeding himself was more important than mercy. And besides, what had ducks ever done for *him*?

"C'mere, then, duckie. Come into my cave."

Incredibly, the bird approached, eager as you please. This was too much for Long, and he suddenly screamed at the duck 'til it backed away. More, it seemed almost shocked to have been used so unkindly. With a quick flap of wings, it was gone.

Yes, some god. Can't even kill a duck without pangs o' conscience.

Long slunk sullenly back to his fire and threw himself down beside it. Well, if he couldn't die from a great fall, or by freezing or drowning, perhaps he could still starve to death. What should he do in the meantime, though? He didn't much relish the thought of sitting in this little cave for the days or weeks necessary for starvation to do its work. In fact, he suspected the experience might drive him mad. Or madder. He pictured himself running wildly through the wilderness, naked and raving. The image made him laugh. Mardine would've...would've had something to say about that.

How he missed her. And would continue to miss her, he knew. But she'd had the right of it: his presence in her life—or anyone's—would only invite danger, once the truth of his real identity was out. He thought of Esmine, and his eyes brimmed with tears. He hadn't even been able to say goodbye, to tell her how proud of her he was, how much he loved her. Thinking on his daughter, however, caused him more pain than he could bear; quickly, he turned his thoughts in other directions.

Her Majesty, for instance, had a lot to answer for. He'd heard in Vykers' camp that she was Alheria, and he'd seen ample proof of it in that last battle with the End-of-All-Things. He could hardly compass it, yet, he'd *seen* it. And if it was as it seemed, and he was Mahnus, as she'd claimed...then what? Weren't Mahnus and Alheria a pair? How was it that they'd been separated?

He had too many questions and too few answers. *As always.* But he intended to find those answers, even if it meant direct conflict with Her Majesty. Infinite Hells, he still owed her for that fiasco with the Great Eight. And, for all he knew, a great deal more besides.

He was thrilled to find that he suddenly had a purpose. He needed to learn more about himself, first, but once he'd gained a better sense of his abilities, his strengths and weaknesses, he was absolutely bent on confronting Alheria.

Bailis, in the Northeast

The invaders' scouts were following. It was time to divide his force, humble though it was, into smaller and humbler units still. It was, Bailis reflected, rather like trying to make a meal of an apple's peel long after its flesh had been eaten, sound in premise but meager in practice. But what could he do about it? He gave a quick tug on his beard and turned to his two captains.

"Derry," said he, "you'll take your half into the hills. Run these foreign bastards a merry chase. When the moment's right, divide again. Lead 'em through bog and bracken, through graveyards and mires, over mountains and down the bottom o' canyons. They've got the numbers, certainly, but we know the land, we'll make 'em hate every inch of it!" He then looked at the older captain, Willes. "You and I'll run our share of enemies down around the lakes. They'll get so tired o' crossin' streams and fordin' rivers, they'll wish they'd never set foot on our shores!"

It sounded good, but Bailis could see his men didn't quite believe it, no matter how badly they wanted to. Well, he couldn't fault himself for trying. "With a little luck," he added, "the Emperor's lackeys will run afoul of some Svarren. Wouldn't *that* be a sight to see?"

There was brief burst of half-hearted laughter that ended when Captain Derry motioned for his men to move out. Bailis nodded to the captain and then offered the same gesture to his own troops. Time to start running...

Which sounds all well and good, but running in armor, even maintaining a fast march, can be hell on the legs and feet right quick. For one thing, there's the chafing. If left untreated at day's end by an A'Shea or a field chirurgeon, the resultant wounds can eventually lead to the kibes, go septic, and from thence to gangrene and death. Thus, care and maintenance of the feet is everything on the march. At least, it was so in Her Majesty's army. Bailis rather hoped the Emperor's men were not so cautious. They'd be crippled inside a fortnight if that was the case. Still, Bailis knew he could run his men only so far and so long before they had to make camp and attend to their feet. Once in a while, you'd find an old campaigner who thought such attentions fussy, who refused to take off his boots. To the colonel, this was a sure sign of a problem, and he usually had four or five big fellas hold the old fart down whilst they inspected his feet. More often than not, he was hiding an infection.

So, the chafing and the feet were problematic. But there was also dehydration and exhaustion. Good soldiers trained with their weapons constantly, but very few took the time to practice running in full gear for great distances and in all weather. It took a special sort of beast to withstand such duress for long, someone like Tarmun Vykers.

Thinking of the Reaper, the colonel wondered where the man was at such a desperate time. If ever his services were needed and welcomed, surely it was now. But there'd been no word of him. And the Queen had been terse on the subject of additional troops, too. To Bailis' thinking, it was almost as if nobody cared about the invaders. Madness! Surely Her Majesty could muster 50,000 men. She'd done better than that when they'd fought the End's horde of thralls. And it had been years since then.

Bailis shook his head in frustration. He'd refused the offer of a promotion to general, and the consequence was that he was left in the dark on most of the Crown's strategies and decisions.

He couldn't be blamed for failure, yet he hadn't enough information to prevent it, either. Sometimes, there was just no winning in the military, no matter what side you were on.

"You hear that, sir?" Willes invaded Bailis' thoughts.

He heard: a great and distant rumbling that could only have come from the hooves of hundreds of horses. Damn these invaders, but they were well supplied. And most of Bailis' men were on foot, too. "Caltrops!" he barked at his captain.

"Yes, sir!"

Willes rode to the back of the column, called upon a few specific men, and, with their help, began tossing the spiked iron balls in the army's wake. Even a single suddenly-crippled horse could collapse the whole front edge of the pursuing force. It was a desperate, nasty trick, but about the only recourse available to Bailis and his men, and if it worked, it would buy them precious minutes in which to continue running. The colonel looked at the sky and calculated the hours until nightfall. If he and his men stayed ahead of the invaders 'til then, they might yet see the morrow.

TWO

Vykers, Alone

Vykers opened his eyes to darkness. Was he blind? He didn't think so. But he was tightly wrapped in some sort of shroud, like a corpse for burial. His legs were bound together; his arms were likewise stuck to his sides. Whoever had tied him up had done a thorough job. He could barely wiggle a finger. His head was covered and secured in the same manner, and the only thing that truly surprised him was that he'd been allowed a small slit through which to breathe.

He listened, heard nothing. He sensed no presence or movement nearby either. He was alone. He should have been angry, bent on escape. To his astonishment, he felt only calm. Since he'd risen from his long-ago sickbed in Lunessfor, he'd known nothing but boisterous activity—running, riding, fighting—and he'd almost forgotten what it was to relax, to pause and take stock. Damned funny time and place to do it, but there it was: Vykers basked in his unlooked-for quietude.

And all the thoughts he'd been pushing aside for weeks and months came tumbling in upon him with a vengeance.

He had countless questions about Alheria and her motives, but answers only came in a thin trickle, like an old man's piss, and Vykers quickly tired of thinking about Her Majesty. He thought next of Arune, of how they'd saved one another, how she'd betrayed him—however much she'd been a pawn of Alheria's—and lastly of how the Shaper had given her own life to save Aoife's. He wondered if some part of Arune was still present and sent his thoughts out to her, halfheartedly, and was not surprised when he felt nothing in response. No, she was well and truly gone this time, without even the bones to tie her spirit down as they had before. Turley had been another casualty of Arune's decision, robbing the poor goblin of his hopes and condemning him to a body he could never accept. The Reaper had rescued Turley from execution by his clan, but had only bought him a few more weeks of life for all that. And, in killing himself, Turley had destroyed whatever was left of Igraine as well. Aoife had often suggested Vykers was only good for one thing—destruction—and he'd always thought that an excellent thing. He'd been proud of it.

The ghosts of his former companions might not share his views.

He extended his claws and began sawing through his bindings, slowly, quietly, so as not to alert his captors. He hadn't made much progress when he was interrupted by the sound of something shuffling towards him. There was a strange, high-pitched croaking, and then he felt a sharp jab in his ribs. He twitched involuntarily, which made the croaking escalate into a noise not unlike laughter. The next time he got poked, he was ready for it and moved not one muscle. Tiny claws latched onto the cloth over his face, accompanied by a brief sawing sound. Soon, the cloth was pulled away until Vykers could feel a draft on his skin and see a small flame from the corner of his eyes. A little, gnarled fist smacked him in the cheekbone, followed by more laughter.

Off to his right, someone or something was hard at work starting a fire, and Vykers got an idea. All he needed was time.

"Why don't you little fuckers show yourselves?"

A small, misshapen head appeared over his face and spat on him.

Vykers bared his teeth. "What, did I kill your dam? I'm sure the bitch deserved it."

Another blow, more spit, nails raking his face.

A miniature stone blade dangled in the Reaper's sight and then disappeared. The grebbers were trying to frighten—

Vykers felt a stinging pain on the side of his head, near his left ear, which was followed almost instantly by a wetness trickling down to back of his neck. The grebber's fist reappeared above his eye, clutching the ruins of his left ear. It was astonishing to think of all the wars he'd been in without sustaining so much as a scar, and now he'd lost his ear to—

They took his other ear, too.

Vykers growled deep in his throat, glanced to his right. The fire was almost ready.

One of his tormentors carried his ears to the fire and tossed them onto the rocks surrounding it. Vykers could hear them sizzle and pop. Then he could smell them, and his guts betrayed him by rumbling with hunger. *Gods!* His eyes darted back to his left, where he saw three little monsters capering with glee at his discomfort. They jabbered at one another in their indecipherable language, and the one with the knife reached for Vykers' nose.

He roared into its face with everything he had. The creature and his fellows shrieked and jumped backwards. When it was clear he could do nothing more, they rushed at him and pounded upon his face and chest. Vykers laughed at them, until they sawed the nose from his face.

He howled with rage, could wait no longer. They'd take his eyes next, he was sure, and those he would not lose. With a great lurch, he heaved himself sideways and rolled towards the fire. He crashed over the hot stones surrounding it and landed smack in the middle of its flames. In no time, his bonds burned through, and he leapt up, still smoldering, free and eager to avenge his injuries.

The grebbers, amused at first that he'd landed in the fire, quickly grew terrified and attempted to flee. But Vykers was too quick for them, as he generally was for anyone. Since he only had two hands, he killed the first outright, and then seized the remaining two. He held them up to his face, so they could see the damage they'd done and how little it bothered him. Then he burned them alive, slowly.

The creatures squealed in agony, but their cries were in vain; nothing and no one came to their rescue, much to Vykers' surprise. Perhaps his escape would be easier than he'd imagined. Once the grebbers in his hands stopped wriggling and twitching, he tossed their blackened remains aside and finally took in his surroundings. He was in a kitchen, of sorts. He'd been lying on a low table and, on a shelf nearby, he saw crude pincers, forks and cleavers. His captors had been planning to eat him, it seemed, bit by bit. He wondered if they, in turn, were edible. The ones he'd roasted didn't smell very appetizing, so he quickly abandoned the idea.

He continued examining the rest of the chamber. It was roughly round, clearly unfinished, and its ceiling was too low for Vykers to stand fully erect. Two grebber-sized holes in the walls marked the only possible exits, but either would require the Reaper to crawl if he wished to escape. They must have dragged him down here on his back, but how and when had they wrapped him up?

Vykers stepped back towards the fire and picked up a remnant of his bindings. The stuff was stringy and sticky, not fabric after all, but a series of ropes stuck together with…what? He tried to tear the stuff but found it unexpectedly strong. Impressive. If only there were more of it lying around, it might prove useful in his escape.

On the far side of the table on which he'd been resting, Vykers discovered a small pile of spears he'd overlooked. These must have been the ones the grebbers had stuck him with earlier. He grabbed one, examined it. The point was covered with a foul-smelling, tar-like substance. Vykers didn't need weapons to kill his way out of this hole, but he tucked the little spear into his belt, anyway. Maybe he'd meet someone who knew what its poison was; maybe he could use that information sometime.

Retrieving a brand from the fire, he got down on all fours and poked the flame into one of the tunnels. It turned out of sight almost immediately. He stuck the flame in the second tunnel, and it ran straight on into darkness. *Fuck it*, he thought, and crawled inside.

By now, blood was running freely down the sides of his head and his face. His movements kicked up dirt and dust as he went. It got into his open sinuses and made him sneeze. It caused the blood on his head to congeal and crust. He was in pain, but he'd endured worse. He dragged himself forward. Other tunnels crossed his path at irregular intervals, and Vykers was reminded of the goblin tunnels below Alheria's castle: they were so much cleaner and better organized. Now, he felt like nothing so much as a giant mole, rooting around in the filthy darkness.

And he thought of Turley.

And then of Arune.

He didn't like to think of or dwell upon anything that didn't involve conquest, especially not his own failings. But he had let the goblin down terribly. *I didn't owe him anything!* He told himself. But he knew it was a lie. Without Turley's help, Vykers might never have recovered his body from Arune.

And the Shaper? She'd betrayed him, yes. But she'd been set up to do so by Her Majesty. Arune had saved Vykers' life on more than one occasion, and he'd been happy to let her die in exchange for Aoife.

Bollocks!

Drinking, wenching and fighting were the most reliable ways to forget one's troubles, and while there was no drinking or wenching to be had, there were plenty of grebbers to fight, if a man could find 'em.

He dragged himself onward.

The Emperor, Ashore

According to his generals, the native force had run for the hills at the first sight of the Emperor's legions. He didn't blame them. If he'd been in their position, he'd have done the same. He'd mustered almost every able-bodied man (and more than a few women) in his homeland for this invasion. He'd twisted arms, forged alliances, blackmailed, and made all sorts of promises to any and all who would accompany his troops overseas. He'd guaranteed endless plunder, but it would be up to those who'd answered his call to secure it for themselves.

From his perch atop the forward observation tower, he watched the Tsundi peel away and head north. They were a sallow, taciturn people, ever-wrapped in heavy furs, brandishing equally heavy weapons, used to colder weather, after all, and best suited to handle its challenges. To the south, Mendis knew, the dark-skinned B'shar were storming onshore in their light armor, carrying javelins and battle whips, eager to race for warmer climes and environments more to their liking. And between those two warlike peoples were Mendis' legions, supplemented by fighters from countless smaller, less significant nations. Everyone wanted a piece of the pie, it seemed. The Emperor only hoped there was enough to go around.

Sleet turned to rain, and rain gave way to relentless drizzle. Mendis didn't care. He'd come at the worst time of year; things could only improve with time. By summer, perhaps, this new land would be his, and he'd celebrate by drinking a local vintage out of Wykkerian's skull. His troops, he'd found, had a penchant for melodrama, and he was only too pleased to provide it.

His plan was to drive his legions straight across the continent, whatever its length, and split the land in half. Those fleeing the predations of the B'Shar would run straight into his legions. The same would be true of those attempting to escape the Tsundi. In either or both cases, his soldiers would flank the enemy, providing the very anvil upon which the twin hammers of the B'Shar and Tsundi smashed the natives and whatever feeble resistance they mounted. Nor was this plan built upon conjecture and surmise, but upon practice and experience. In the Imperial Scrolls and also the Nionian Tablets, Wykkerian was referred to as the Destroyer of Empires. But there had never been an Empire like the one Mendis had built, as powerful as the sea, as relentless as the wind, as inevitable as death. Even if Wykkerian were a god, he could not stop what was coming.

"Magnificence," an officer said, interrupting Mendis' ruminations. "The landing continues apace. Your generals estimate completion by this time tomorrow."

"And our wizards, have they espied the enemy?"

The man's face grew somber. "No, Magnificence. It seems that none approaches."

The Emperor barked out a laugh. "If this be a trap, 'tis the most strange that ere I've seen."

"'Tis that, Magnificence."

"Away, then!" Mendis cried cheerily, "And ask my attendants to bring me supper."

"Your word, your will."

The Emperor was not a madman as the End-of-All-Things had been, but a canny, seasoned veteran of a hundred military campaigns. He'd overseen his legions for decades, and they'd been well-honed by his father before he'd come along. Was Mendis worried by the enemy's absence? Say he was intrigued, but worried? No. They'd show themselves in time.

Eoman and his Kinsmen, the North

The king of the giants and his kinsmen approached their quest with the peculiar excitement of those traveling to meet long-lost loved ones. And who could say? Perhaps those they sought *were* long-lost loved ones, for Eoman and his companions were looking for others of their kind—any and all others of their kind. It had been ages since the race of giants had convened as a whole, as one people with one heritage, one goal and one future. But that was the very thing Eoman had set his heart upon. Well, that and pushing the latest invaders from the land.

Truth to tell, Eoman, Beesmarch and the Brothers had been more than a little disappointed in their battle with the End-of-All-Things. They'd believed that, along the way, they'd have a reckoning with the Svarren, a chance to batter the savages into submission or even extinction. Instead, the foul creatures had simply turned tail and fled whilst the giants stood dumbfounded by the Virgin Queen's revelations. Oh, they might have run after the Svarren, but it didn't seem Tarmun Vykers and the rest of his new allies were disposed to follow suit. And... Karrakan had insisted on leading Mardine to her daughter.

Now, though, the prospect of uniting his people to rebuff the Emperor's forces thrilled Eoman. What could be more magnificent than the giants of legend reappearing at the land's darkest hour and saving all its peoples from slaughter and subjugation? In that event, truly he would be a king. And there was something else, too, something he scarcely dared admit even to himself: he looked forward to the chance to kill humans, and he knew Beesmarch was of the same mind. Oh, the men who'd helped him in his quest for Mardine's killers had been kind enough, but that didn't erase the centuries of distrust and often outright enmity between the two peoples. The Emperor's invasion, then, would be the perfect opportunity to vent.

Of course, some of his kinfolk would die. He might even go to it himself. And yet, what else in the wide world was worth doing? He'd traveled the land from north to south, east to west and back again. He was, he reckoned, too old to sire children, even supposing he could find a giantess willing to bear with and for him. What was left for the king but leading his people in battle and defeating someone of equal might?

Like, say, the Reaper.

Except that he and the Reaper were on the same side, supposedly. And he'd seen how well Beesmarch had fared in unarmed combat with Vykers. Eoman didn't suppose he could do much better, with or without his axe. That damned Reaper was a weapon unto himself.

And a mystery.

Eoman had lived many times longer than the average human, and Vykers, or, more properly, *tales* of Vykers had always been there. The man was then at least as old as Eoman. The impossibility of it hit the giant like a blow to the gut: The Reaper was centuries old. Or more. It ought to have been common knowledge, and yet nobody ever mentioned it.

"Bees!" Eoman called.

The surly, larger giant strode to his king's side. "Eh?"

"What's your earliest memory o' the Reaper?"

Beesmarch was silent for a while before answering with a sardonic chuckle. "Me mum used to frighten me, to spook me into doin' her bidding with warnings the Reaper'd come get me if I dinna behave."

"But no tales? No fireside stories?"

"O' course."

Eoman stared into his companion's eyes. "And did it feel like you were fightin' an ancient when he bested you?"

Beesmarch frowned. "Well, when you say *'bested'*…"

"You're missing the point, Bees: Vykers is much, much older than he looks. Too old, really, for a mortal man."

Without warning, the larger giant crashed into a sitting

position, his right hand lost in his massive beard. "Humph," he muttered, a good deal less emphatically than usual. "That's odd, that."

"Odd's an understatement!" Eoman exclaimed. "It's damned unnatural, but..."

"But?"

"We've just seen the Virgin Queen stand taller than the greatest pine. We've heard her name that rumpled fellow Mahnus. Considerin' we just fought alongside a couple of gods, I guess Vykers' age isn't exactly surprising. Still, it's a wonder nobody talks about it." After a moment's pause, Eoman added, "Would that Karrakan were here. He loves this kind of conundrum."

"As I don't," Beesmarch said emphatically. "Let's keep movin'. This ground's freezing my ass off!"

"Nobody asked you to sit, Bees!" the king reminded his friend. "And I could go the rest of my life without hearing about your ass again."

"If you're the king o' me, you're the king o' my ass as well!"

Eoman extended a hand and helped his massive friend to his equally massive feet. "That's a comforting thought," he quipped.

Vykers' Camp, In the North

Kittins was dealing with questions of his own. "Where the fuck is he?" he roared at the Red Knight who'd served as Vykers' second.

"Avay."

If Hjuest was frightened, he gave no sign of it. Kittins would have been impressed if he wasn't so pissed off. "Away, huh? We're gettin' ready for all-out invasion, and he just up and disappears?" He grabbed the shorter man by his collar and pulled him close. "I wanna know where he went and when he'll be back."

Again, the Red Knight answered calmly. "Do you truly sink de Reaper answers to me?"

Kittins stared him down a good moment longer and then let him go. "I didn't realize it was 'every-man-for-himself.' Maybe I'll take off, too."

Hjuest shrugged. "As you please."

The captain was about to backhand the fellow when Rem intruded on the conversation. "Can I speak to you in private, Captain?"

Kittins turned his death's head stare on the erstwhile actor. "What is it?"

"It's...uh...it's to do with a conversation you and I had a while back..."

The moment to murder the Red Knight apparently having passed, Kittins nodded assent and gestured for Rem to lead him away.

Once they were out of earshot, Rem cast a glance back over Kittins' shoulder at the Red Knight and said, "Did I hear you say Vykers has left the company?"

Kittins grunted, suddenly taciturn.

"Well, I'm sure he'll turn up when the fighting's at its worst."

"That may not be good enough for you and me." Rem was about to ask what the big man meant, when Kittins continued. "I figured with Vykers in our company, Her Majesty'd be less likely to focus on the fact we killed her Shaper. But now that he ain't here to provide distraction, goin' back to Lunessfor might not be our best choice."

Rem was stunned. "You think she's forgotten us? You saw what she did against the End. They say she's Alheria, and I'm prone to believe it! If she'd wanted us dead, we'd have been dead days ago."

The captain grimaced in frustration: this was a thought that hadn't occurred to him, and he wasn't at all sure what to make of it. "Well..." he said at last.

"Well?"

"We might as well continue on, 'til something better presents itself."

Rem laughed. "Better than a hot bath, a fine wine and a nice feather mattress?"

"Bah!" Kittins scoffed. "You sound like a woman."

"Go ahead, old friend: insult me. What do I care? I'm overdue for a little comfort, and I mean to have it."

"Huh. But you said there was something else you wanted to talk to me about?"

"Oh yes!" said Rem. "I think I've remembered the name of this land—the whole land, that is."

"And?"

Rem squinted apologetically. "Well, I've got it down to three choices, three names I think I remember: Esahra, Tdorome, or Ureia."

Kittins shook his head. "'S none of those."

"Well, dammit man, what *is* it then?"

"Fuck if I know. Maybe you can ask Her Majesty next time you see her."

Rem watched the big man stalk off towards his tent. "Maybe I will!" he called at Kittins' back. *If Alheria doesn't know what this land's called, nobody does.*

The Emperor's Legions, Ashore

The Emperor's men came in waves, like the waves they'd arrived upon; they surged over the dunes and salt marshes, like the highest of high tides; they flooded the pastures, the forests, and the coastal villages, but whereas waves ebb and tides withdraw, the Emperor's legions did not. Up and down the eastern coast, the banners of Mendis Staurachia were raised above farmsteads, hamlets and larger villages almost without resistance, and the men of the Empire rejoiced. It had been a hard crossing; for all their numbers, they'd still lost several ships to winter storms and the monstrous denizens of the sea. Those happy men who'd survived to scrub their boots in the sand of the new world's beaches nevertheless had secret fears of all they might encounter. And so it was good to march unopposed across the landscape, good to find game that could be eaten without consequence, good to find wood that burned cleanly and quickly. The men worried little about the reasons for their good fortune; if there was a problem, even a whole passel of them, it was meat for their generals, wizards and Emperor to chew upon. For the men, there was naught to do but march and fight, and, so far, there'd been precious little fighting.

The Emperor thought he spied smiles on the faces of his men as they paraded past his platform, and it made him uneasy. He was used to seeing scowls of grim determination. Indeed, he'd often taken comfort in their stoicism, knowing they'd do their jobs whatever fate had in store. Now, though…He was suspicious. He found and chewed that very meat of worry his troops would not: where was the opposition? With every passing acre, its absence grew more ominous.

"Newak!" he called, only to find the wizard right at his side. The man had startled him. Again. "Henceforth, you'll maintain a ten-foot distance from me, unless I am imperiled."

"Yes, Magnificence," the wizard replied, bowing his head ever so slightly.

"What's the latest on the native forces? Where are they? Why are they so scarce?"

"Apart from those few we met at landing, the rest seem concentrated around the biggest cities, Magnificence."

Mendis looked down as the last of his troops moved past. "An odd stratagem, to let us march so deeply into their land without impediment."

The wizard gestured, ensuring his Emperor made eye contact. "This land has seen more than its share of war."

"And whose has not? Have we not grown our father's empire to unprecedented size and strength? Was that done without bloodshed, Newak?"

"No, Magnificence. I offer the observation for your contemplation, only. Perhaps the natives are weary of it all; perhaps they're exhausted. Or…"

"They might be setting a trap," Mendis cut in. "Yes, that is my worry. Wykkerian is nothing, if not canny. And what of the local royalty? This Virgin Queen, for instance: what keeps her in power?"

Here, the wizard paused, as if uncertain how to proceed.

"What is it?" Mendis demanded.

"Her city is rife with magic, Magnificence, and impenetrable. I've never felt the like."

"But you know its general location, I see. Good. You send your spies; I'll send my scouts. The more we know and the sooner we know it, the more success we'll have in creating a plan of assault or siege." The wizard bowed as if to go, but Mendis stopped him. "And Wykkerian?"

"We hear nothing of him, but there's another here of similar reputation: Tarmun Vykers."

The Emperor seemed to examine the planks under his feet. "Wykkerian, Vykers...assume they're one and the same. Where is this Vykers, then?"

"We're searching for him, Magnificence. He...is difficult to track."

Mendis waved a hand to dismiss his wizard. "Let me know when you've found him." Once the wizard had disappeared, the Emperor called for a page. "Tell General Promartis I'll see him now."

The boy bowed and rushed off, all efficiency.

In no time, the General appeared, a tall, burly fellow with close-set eyes and a slight overbite.

"You've heard the wizards' reports?"

"Yes, Magnificence."

"And?"

"It seems the great cities are preparing for a siege. Or sieges."

"They won't unite against us?"

"One would think so, Magnificence, but..."

"Their actions defy reason!" Mendis snapped. "If this is a trap of some sort, I fail to see how it's meant to work. If we bring all our force to bear on the large city to the south, the Virgin Queen's city, the others won't be able to muster troops in time to relieve her."

"Perhaps there's enmity between the local kingdoms. In fact, I'd be surprised if there wasn't."

Again, Mendis interjected. "And they put pride before survival? That feels too good to be true."

"Nonetheless," Promartis said, "it may be. It is also possible these kingdoms are already so weakened from wars of their own that they haven't enough able-bodied men to oppose us."

Mendis turned away, seemed to talk to himself. "I was expecting resistance or outright surrender. But this...lack of response... baffles me. Well," he added with sudden determination, "we'll take what they'll give us, for now. Eventually, they'll *have* to respond or face starvation."

Mardine and Karrakan, On the Road

The climate—and Mardine's mood—improved with every passing day. Soon, she knew, she'd see her Esmine again, after so much fear, so many tears, so much suffering. Oh, she'd had to say goodbye to Long Pete, and that was excruciating. But it was hard to remain miserable in Karrakan's company. The shaman and his magics were both soothing and reassuring, as was the constant presence of his will-o-wisps. And maybe there'd be a way to send messages to Long, someday, if he still wanted to communicate with Mardine. If nothing else, he'd want to send his love to Esmine.

The giantess wondered if she weren't doing the wrong thing in rushing to her daughter's side, though. After all, Mardine had heard the menfolk talking of war—*more* war—and it sounded as if this next bout could be worse than all the others combined. A full-out invasion by a foreign empire? That might endanger or even kill the few friends Mardine had scattered about the land. To stand by whilst it happened would be...unforgivable. But what if getting involved got her killed, again? She couldn't endure the thought of leaving her child without a mother. Again. And hadn't she done her part in the last two battles?

As much as Mardine loved and was grateful for her friends, she loved Esmine more, and she reckoned a mother's duty to her child was greater than a giant's to her friends. She'd brought Esmine into the world; she meant to keep her there.

"How much farther?" she asked her companion.

Karrakan smiled a patient smile. "A few days. Never fear, my friend. We are making excellent time!"

Mardine returned his smile. She couldn't help it. "Very good," she said. And so it was.

The Svarren, In the Forest

The caravan passed within a few hundred yards of the copse of trees in which he and the Woman stood. They were a bedraggled bunch, Omeyo saw, but still carried things of value to himself and his new people. The former general was torn: he was human and felt some primal allegiance to these desperate refugees. On the other hand, the Svarren he now lived amongst were no less desperate. The question was, would the spoils be worth the losses the Svarren would likely endure? While he was pondering the conundrum, the Woman poked him with a long, gnarled nail.

Why are they running? She wondered.

Omeyo thought about it. She was right: The End was dead at last; he'd watched the fiend die. What cause had these folks to continue their flight?

Best ask.

Yes, he thought back at the woman, *I'll ask.* Leaving her in the shadows, Omeyo strode from the tree line and made for the rapidly retreating column. To his surprise, it was not difficult to catch up.

"Where'd you come from, then?" yelled a short, wide fellow with a large knapsack over his shoulder.

"North," said Omeyo, having no better answer. "And you?"

"You jokin'? They's a foreign army up 'n down the coast! Come from across the seas, they did!"

Omeyo fell into step alongside the man. "A foreign army, you say? Not the End-of-All-Things?"

"Bah!" the man exclaimed. "That's yesterday's news, yesterday's war. These new bastards, now, they's too many ta count."

"How do you know they're from across the sea?"

"I seen their ships, didn't I?"

"Did you try to count them?"

The man laughed loudly. "Try? Ain't nobody can count *that* high!"

"Thanks, friend," Omeyo said, and slowed to a stop, letting the caravan continue its journey without him. In minutes, he was back at the woman's side.

??? She asked.

"Another fucking war," the general said aloud. "An invasion."

She grabbed him by the wrist and pulled him behind her as she sprinted deeper into the trees. Clearly, this was a matter for the whole Svarren people.

Omeyo could hardly stand once they reached the main body of Svarren a quarter of an hour later. But he and the woman had somehow become the tribe's leaders, and he knew she expected him to act the part, strange as it was to him. Accordingly, he stood on a small hillock and yelled to get the horde's attention.

"We have just escaped a war, but another is coming." He believed only one in ten of the Svarren could understand him, but his speaking pleased the woman, so he continued. "We hear that soldiers have come from across the sea, in numbers too great to count." Omeyo looked out across a different sea, a sea of brutish, primitive and in some cases utterly inhuman faces, and saw comprehension. They were listening to every word he said, and they understood! "What we do not yet know is whom these soldiers mean to fight. Will it be the humans, will it be us, or have they come to conquer or kill everyone in our land? Where should the Svarren stand? What is best for us?"

If Omeyo was expecting an answer, he didn't get one. Instead, the woman beamed at him and gently pushed him aside. It was her turn to address her people, and she bellowed and roared in high dudgeon. Omeyo had believed these creatures understood him; now he knew he'd been mistaken, for the woman's bestial oratory had them leaping and howling at the sky like wolves under a full moon. Whatever he'd meant to accomplish, it was his mate, the true Svarra, who had galvanized her people.

But to what end? He'd heard the Svarren words for 'war' and 'strangers,' but nothing else he'd recognized. Based on the horde's behavior, he guessed retreat was not in the plans.

Vykers, the Grebbers' Lair

Vykers wriggled into a bigger, more open space. Ahead of him, several large, undulating shapes glowed with eerie luminescence. If they saw him, they paid him no heed, so the Reaper climbed to his feet. His face and head were throbbing, and the blood lust was upon him. The creatures, whatever they were, were obvious targets. Vykers charged forward and came to an abrupt halt. They were worms, vast, blubbery worms, trailing strands of the same stuff he'd been bound in but a short while earlier, which made them livestock of the grebbers. The Reaper bared his canines in disgust, extended his claws, and lunged for the first worm. It exploded under his blows, emitting a high-pitched squeal as it died, an alarm if ever the Reaper had heard one. The other worms reared their heads—or whatever passed for them—and joined in the chorus. *Good*, thought Vykers, *let's have this out once and for all!* He waded in amongst the foul things and ripped and slashed until there was nothing left but a small lake of offal.

He felt a sharp pain in his left shoulder and realized he'd been hit with another of the grebber spears. Without bothering to verify the source of the weapon, he spun and barreled into an open tunnel mouth, flattening the grebbers who stood there. Enraged, the Reaper forced his way farther into the opening, against a tide of oncoming creatures. For this, he didn't even need the use of his eyes. He simply ripped and ripped and ripped his way forward until at last he met no resistance. Suddenly, he tumbled into another, larger chamber. That he could see its boundaries surprised him, until he discovered that he was glowing. Drenched in the blood of the worms he'd killed, Vykers had taken on their luminescence. He'd lost a bit of it on the front of his body where the grebbers' blood had washed it away, but enough remained to make seeing easier. And what he saw delighted him.

This new chamber was a repository of sorts for all the things the grebbers had stolen from travelers, including weapons. A great pile rose before Vykers, and he dug his fists into it with gusto. The mound bristled with swords and great axes, but he knew he'd never be able to work up a proper swing in such closed spaces, so he chose of pair of matching hand axes, battered, but possessed of enough history to pique the Reaper's curiosity. Also in the pile, he found flattened wineskins, tattered knapsacks, and the feathered ends of countless arrows. Ah, so that was where the tiny spears had come from: the grebbers fashioned them from stolen arrows. The little bastards were not entirely brainless. Deeper under the spoils, Vykers found the rock-hard remnants of breads and cheeses taken from the grebbers' victims. The foodstuffs were well past inedible, but the Reaper ate them anyway. *Won't it be rich*, he thought, *if it ain't a sharp blade kills me, but a sharp cheese?* Grim humor, certainly, but for a newly-earless and noseless man lost in the bowels of the earth, grim's better than nothing. Some there were who claimed grim was better 'n *anything*.

Hefting his axes, he decided it was time to escape.

He chose the largest tunnel, was momentarily awash in a tissue-thin memory of Turley, or the chimeras perhaps, and pushed ahead into the darkness. There was a slight draft, and that seemed to bode well. "Come on, you little fuckers!" he roared. "Let's see what you're made of."

This time, he heard them coming—at first, like a gentle rain, and then like a deluge, 'til the sound of their feet pounding in the dirt was all and everything Vykers could hear. He smiled, felt the gaping wound where his nose had been crack and bleed afresh. Blood trickled down his upper lip and into his mouth. He laughed, a guttural, ugly sound, which, if the grebbers had only been able to hear, would have sent them into frenzied retreat. The Reaper had blood in his mouth, death in his hands, and carnage in his heart.

The grebbers danced on the edge of oblivion and toppled inwards.

Vykers left not a creature alive in the whole colony.

When he reached the surface, he looked a thing of mud and blood alone; only the whites of his eyes betrayed his true nature.

It was daylight, and the forest seemed deserted. Vykers dragged himself into a deadfall and passed out.

Despite the pain of his wounds, there was something very pleasant working its way around his face, a soft and soothing caress. When he opened his eyes, he found Aoife staring back at him with a look of profound sympathy.

"What have they done to you?" she whispered.

Vykers tried to sit up, but she pushed him gently back down, and he allowed it. "You remember those little grey fuckers we fought on our quest to find Her Majesty?"

"Grebbers?"

"That's right: grebbers. Little shits tied me up and carved into my face." While the Umaena digested this, Vykers asked, "What are you doing here, anyway?"

Now, she smiled. "You called me."

"I what? When?"

Aoife began cleaning the mud from his face with a damp cloth. "In your sleep, I suspect. But call you did, Tarmun, and here I am."

He was not unhappy to see her. "There anything you can do about my wounds?"

The Umaena studied them, a bemused look on her face. "They seem…to be healing well enough on their own."

"You mean the bleeding's stopped."

"No," Aoife countered, "I mean your wounds have sealed and new skin appears to be forming in their place."

Vykers stared up at his former lover. "What…?"

She took his chin in her right hand and made certain he was paying attention. "I believe your ears and nose are starting to grow back."

"But that's imposs…" the Reaper trailed off. Was it? Hadn't he once had his hands and feet taken from him, only to see them restored? He'd always assumed that had been Arune's doing, or that of his magic sword. Now, though… "You might be mistaken," said he to the Umaena.

Her laugh had an even more salutary effect upon him than the good news she'd just delivered. "Oh, Tarmun," she smiled, "ever the skeptic." She allowed him to sit up.

"What, now?"

She helped him to his feet. "Nothing important. How would you fancy a bath, a hot meal, and a warm bed?"

He winked at her, actually winked! "Depends what's making it warm."

She blushed and poked him in the ribs. "As if I'd share a bed with an earless and noseless monstrosity."

"It ain't my nose you'll be busy with…"

Again she struck him playfully, and he knew that for all that had passed between them, little had changed. What though it made no sense, the killer and the healer were drawn to one another.

Qansip and Driegan, On the Road

Qansip could not so much as go into the bushes to make water, but her retinue had to accompany her, by her father's order. "It's a dangerous world!" he declared, "And never more so than now."

Qansip yawned. "Oh father," she drawled, "you worry too much!"

"And you, too little!" he quipped as he tucked her back into her palanquin.

"Tarmun Vykers will stop this invasion, if anyone can."

Driegan leaned into her, lightly tapped the end of her nose with his finger, and said, "A big 'if,' young lady, a mighty big 'if.' Meantime, we've got to keep ahead of the tide of refugees this invasion's likely to scare up."

Qansip stuck out her lower lip in her most fetching pout. "But where are we going, father? And why not the capital? I want to see the Queen and her castle! I want to visit all the best shops!"

Lord Deda ground his teeth in frustration. "This is no holiday, girl!" he reminded her. "Indeed, it could become a damned free-for-all, with everyone, everywhere, looking to take and no one willing to give. No, we've got to safeguard ourselves and our fortune and hope that Her Majesty can sort things out."

It was not a long speech, but somehow Qansip had managed to nod off in the middle of it. Driegan scowled at her. What in the infinite hells was he to do with such a child? She was ready for marrying—perilously close to *past* ready, really—but with the land in chaos, as he surmised it soon would be, his options were limited. On the other hand, there were bound to be more suitable candidates for his daughter's hand in Lunessfor than anywhere else in the land, when and if this latest war ever worked itself out. He'd have to provide a dowry, of course, but he could expect to gain titles, land or business in the exchange, for, if nothing else, Driegan had always been a good man of business.

He signaled to the servants who carried Qansip's palanquin to continue, and he returned to his horse. The girl had wanted a coach, of course, and a lavish one at that. But a coach could not traverse some of the secret game trails and goat tracks Driegan intended to use in order to avoid the refugee rabble he knew was only days behind him. No, he and his retinue needed to travel lightly and quickly in order to remain in front of the crush. He had twenty fighting men, eight servants, and his daughter. In a pinch, he and Qansip could escape on his horse, whilst his employees held off whatever threatened from behind.

And if worst came to worst, he could always offer his daughter in trade for his own life.

For he was a planner, was Driegan. He took both pleasure and pride in his penchant for thinking things through to the least likely eventuality. He liked to be prepared for anything, or at least think that he was. And somehow he'd known that a day would come when he'd have to flee his home with all haste, and he'd made provision for it. He looked back down the column at his back and felt tremendous satisfaction. He'd been right, as he was always right.

With his skills, he reckoned he'd make a killing in a war-torn land.

Long Pete, In the North

He tried more Jumping, and his first few attempts were even more awkward than Spirk's initial efforts. Long crashed into trees, fell from great heights, and slammed himself over and over into the ground. If he'd been *only* Long Pete, he knew, all of this would have killed him a dozen times over. After much trial and error, he concluded that he needed to start simply, to Jump a mere ten paces or so. When this strategy brought instant success, Long gradually extended his Jumps until he was leaping leagues at a time. Before he knew it, the sun had set. He'd burned an entire day in experimentation and completely forgotten how miserable, how distraught he'd been just twenty-four hours earlier.

And he'd had reason.

But now…plans began to take shape in his mind, and hope, to rekindle. He might be able to visit his daughter, for instance. Why not? And why say goodbye when he'd the power to visit whenever he wished? Oh, Mardine wouldn't like it, but so what? Wasn't the girl his child as well? Long understood that his hurt had become resentment, even anger at his wife for the choice she'd made. He'd accepted it at first, but now it seemed foolish, even naïve. He was a god! Who better to raise and protect Esmine than him?

He sat down on a boulder, breathed deeply and attempted to calm himself. Were these the thoughts of a reasonable, rational man? And, then again, he wasn't a man, was he? What was reasonable and rational for a god? How *was* he supposed to feel?

Her Majesty came to mind then, Alheria. Long wondered how she managed to maintain her sanity. Or had she? She'd killed him, after all, when he'd been Mahnus. And for what? And why hadn't she done so again instead of unmasking him?

None of it made any sense to Long, and it suddenly occurred to him that he hadn't slept enough to recover from the ordeal of the past few days. Maybe gods didn't sleep, but he certainly wanted to now. Thinking on it, he became aware of a farmstead off in the darkness, a place to which he could Jump with relative ease. In a blink, he was there, and, typical of his luck, he landed in a fresh pile of cow shit, which was when he belatedly recalled that he wasn't wearing boots, stockings, or anything else.

Fine god I am! He berated himself. *Can't even stay clear of the shit!*

Long looked around and saw both a farmhouse and a barn. He briefly imagined the look on the still-unseen farmer's face when a naked and shit-smeared Long appeared at his door. Perhaps the barn was the better choice.

With a sigh, he trudged around the side of the barn until

he found the door, prized it open just enough to admit himself, and stepped into the thick, pungent darkness. A pair of dogs watched him from the shadows. How he knew this without seeing them, he couldn't have said, but he felt their presence just the same. To his surprise, they registered his arrival without concern. Indeed, none of the barn's creatures seemed bothered by his presence, and Long felt, at last, that he'd found a safe haven, someplace he could rest and recover from the horrors of the past few days.

Concentrating, he was able to identify the cow who'd favored him with footwear, three sheep, two pigs, a donkey, a horse, and the two dogs. He chose to bed down with the sheep, reasoning that their wool would provide some warmth and comfort. The dogs, in the mystical way of their kind, decided to join him as well. Long lay down in the hay, between the sheep and dogs, and fell quickly asleep. At some point, an old barn cat found its way onto his chest. Long smiled at it and then wept himself to sleep.

And awoke sometime later to the most awful pain he'd ever experienced, or at least could ever remember experiencing. The sun had risen, and Long could see quite clearly what his problem was: the farmer had shoved a pitchfork through Long's abdomen. Looking up, he saw the fellow staring him down with a look of equal parts anger, fear and amazement.

"D'you mind removin' that thing from my gut?" said Long.

The farmer held it fast. "Do you mind explainin' what you're a-doin' with my animals?"

"I s'pose this does look a little odd," Long replied, as blood from his wound ran down his belly. "A naked man, sleepin' amongst your sheep. Still, you didn't have to kill me, did you?"

"You ain't dead, yet!" the farmer answered. "Fact, you look surprisingly hale 'n hearty, given the circumstances."

Long glanced down at the tines piercing his body. "Yes," he said matter-of-factly. "It's not as bad as I would've figured it'd be. Do you mind if I stand up now?"

The farmer thought for a bit and then nodded. "Suit yerself. But don't be tryin' anything, or I'll give this fork a good twist!" As Long struggled to his feet, the farmer continued. "Tell me you didn't do nothin' to my sheep."

"Look at your dogs," Long suggested. "Do they look like I've been up to no good?"

The farmer allowed as they didn't; still, he remained skeptical, and held onto the pitchfork running through Long's belly. "T'ain't normal, to find a man naked in winter, lyin' in the barn with a man's animals. And besides," said the man, "why ain't you in more pain?"

"Oh, I'm in plenty 'o pain. Don't you worry about that. As for bein' naked, well, I went through a bad spell a few days back, lost my wits for a time."

"Madman, are you? I shoulda guessed!"

"Yes," Long confessed, "I suppose I am a madman, at that. Still, I'd be much obliged if you'd take this thing out of my belly. You can always stab me again if I make any sudden moves."

The farmer squinted at Long and spat into the hay. "Oh, I will, too, and no mistake!" But he yanked on the pitchfork, and Long tumbled free. Blood ran down his legs, front and back, but the worst of it seemed to have passed.

"You wouldn't happen to have an old blanket you'd be willin' to part with, would you?" Long asked. "Might be, I could make it worth your while."

The farmer shook his head in disbelief. "You got some nerve, madman. What'll you want next, a fox fur cloak and a rasher o' bacon?"

Long smiled. "I don't know about a cloak, but I wouldn't object to a bit o' bacon, now you mention it."

"Wouldn't you?" the other man said, beside himself with the oddness of the situation. "Has the whole world gone mad?"

"Long since," said Long Pete. "Long since."

"Well," said the farmer, "you might as well come into the house, then, and have a bath. Missus won't like seeing I stabbed you."

"I know how she feels!"

Inside the farmhouse, the farmer was quick to cover Long's nakedness with a great coat that hung by the door. "I'll dress yer wounds m'self," the man said. "No need to let the missus know..."

"Know what?" a higher-pitched voice called from the next

room, whereupon the farmer's wife appeared not ten feet away, as if by magic.

The farmer blushed and stammered.

"I ran afoul of your dogs," Long lied. "Crossed your property in the dark, not knowin' I was trespassin', and the dogs let me have it. Tore my clothes to ribbons, dragged me around a bit..."

"Ooh, my!" the wife said. "Oooh, my! I'm suh sorry! But Greff 'n me'll set you right!"

The farmer nodded vigorously, and Long knew he'd made something of a friend.

"He needs a bath, first and foremost," Greff told his wife. "And some clothes. I guess I've got somethin' will serve. But can you keep the little ones out o' the way, 'til my man here's dressed?"

Little ones? Long's heart sank. He'd have to tell his hosts about the invasion; no farmstead was safe in the face of a hungry army.

"I hear you, husband," the wife said and scuttled off to attend to her children.

"I don't mean to put you out like this," Long told the farmer. "'Specially not when you've got young 'uns to think about."

"It's no nevermind," Greff replied. "They generally do as they're told." The man offered a shoulder to lean on as he led Long farther into the house and into a back room, where stood the family wash basin.

"How many you got?"

"Nary enough for the work's got to be done 'round here. Three, but I could do with thrice that many."

Long looked at the man, studied him, took his measure, really, for the first time since they'd met. By his age, he should have had seven or eight children at least. "Problems in the bedroom?" he dared.

The man chuckled good-naturedly. "Nah, none o' that, thank Mahnus. I just got started late. Took me forever to find the right woman."

Long understood and nodded as much. Of course, she'd sent him packing recently, but he still loved Mardine.

Greff asked Long to strip to his waist, the better to see his wounds, and both men were astounded to see they'd already closed. The farmer was instantly suspicious again. "You a witch o' some kind?"

"No, no!" Long countered. "Just a man, a regular old man, like yourself. I didn't fight back when you stabbed me, did I?"

"No, you didn't," Greff agreed. "Still, I never seen the like o' this."

Long shrugged. "I'm a fast healer. Always have been," he lied.

"There's fast, and there's sorcery-fast," Greff said, unconvinced.

What could he say to reassure the fellow? "You want me to go, I'll go, but first, there's something I have to tell you."

The farmer regarded him with deepening concern. "Yes?"

"Truth is," Long said, "I've been running from the coast. There's a full-out invasion underway by a foreign army."

Greff sat and fixed Long with his most menacing stare. "Go on."

"I've been in a lot o' battles over the years—mostly recently against the End-of-All-Things," which was true in any sense the farmer took it. "And I've seen what an enemy force can do to the land and its peoples." The other man said nothing in reply, so Long continued. "What I'm suggestin' is, your best bet is to take whatever you value and head south and west as fast as you can."

"Never mind the bath," Greff said. "I think you'd better leave now. You can keep the coat, though."

"As you wish," Long answered. "But do yourself a favor and keep an ear out. Be ready to move if your chance comes."

While the farmer's wife was still boiling the water for Long's bath, the farmer ushered Long out the door and into the morning light.

"Just think on it," Long pleaded, by way of farewell.

Greff said neither yes nor no, but his eyes wandered off down the path leading away from his home. Long took the hint, wrapped himself tighter inside Greff's coat, and concluded, "I'll just fetch my stick from your barn and be off then."

Mendis and the Imperial Army, Yarrow

A sizable line of armed knights approached the little village of Yarrow. Not one of the knights spoke the native tongue, but the villagers took their meaning notwithstanding: evacuate or die. One crazy old bastard chose the latter and rushed at the knights with a dung-crusted shovel. To their credit, they did not laugh or mock the man, but instead quickly dispatched him with a crossbow bolt through the eye. Faced with such indisputable proof of the knights' seriousness, the old man's fellow citizens didn't spare a moment to grieve his death. They packed up what little they had and raced out the other side of town.

This is not to say they hadn't planned and planted a mean booby trap or two—far from it! But soldiers expect such things and sustained fewer casualties than the absent villagers would have liked. And those few fools who succumbed to their trickery were certainly not missed by the other knights, who would just as soon have the weak-minded amongst their ranks rooted out before any significant conflicts occurred. No one wants to fight shoulder-to-shoulder with an accident prone or credulous buffoon.

By moonrise, the Emperor's men had secured Yarrow for their lord and master. It was not an especially strategic location and its lack of fortified walls made it utterly unsuitable as a fortress. Still, it possessed some amenities that a mere field camp did not, including a number of respectable wells, a couple of well-stocked root cellars, and even an abandoned blacksmith's shop, complete with working forge and anvil.

In the morning, the Emperor would arrive and stay until he'd decided on the next course of action. His legions were spread far and wide, and he might travel with any—or none—of them, as his mood and circumstance dictated.

Once the village's perimeter was secured and watch had been established, some of the soldiers naturally chatted amongst themselves.

"It's a strange land," said one.

"Aye," said another, "it is that. But pray, in what particular is it most strange, to your way of thinking?"

The first man barked out a single-syllabled laugh. "Ha! The complete lack of resistance, for starters. Either the natives are utterly craven or they've so much land and wealth that this here village means nothing to them."

"Ah," said the second man, "but it's hardly just this village, is it? They fled the coast, too. All we've ever seen of them is their backsides."

"Well, there was that one witless grandfather."

"Dead, now, and probably for the best. But what of the others? Do you s'pose there's no one in this land with the stomach to stand-to with us? Have they no heroes of their own?"

"Perhaps they're capering nimbly in a lady's chamber, to the lascivious pleasing of a lute!"

Both laughed at this, long and hard, as confident men will do when they think they've got the right of a thing.

A similar scene played out in cities and towns the length of the coast: The Emperor's forces moved in, encountered minimal opposition, and established yet another new base for themselves. The ease with which all of this was accomplished might have pleased His Magnificence, but instead had the opposite effect. As more and more reports came in of his legions' unchecked advance, Mendis became more and more wary. He was not one to obsess over events, and neither was he paranoid, but in his long experience, nothing ever came easily without consequence. The damnable thing was, he couldn't begin to imagine how winning so much territory so quickly could ever prove detrimental to the overall success of his plan. As the forward edge of his forces moved farther and farther inland, all the resources in the now-occupied territory behind them became theirs to use, and the enemy—who and wherever he was—was ceding those resources.

It made no sense.

Finally, Mendis had had enough and summoned his most senior advisors, his most powerful wizard and his most experienced general.

He sat in the dining room of a rustic but nonetheless impressive estate his soldiers had captured not twenty-four hours earlier and drummed his fingers impatiently upon the massive table. Alsig, the wizard, appeared first, as was his wont.

"Magnificence?"

Mendis didn't stand to greet him. "None of that, Alsig, please. We're friends, are we not?"

The wizard nodded. "Ever and always."

To Mendis, his friend looked more like a soldier than a magician. He wore his steel-grey hair close-cropped, and his permanent beard stubble made him look oddly feral. Many were those who would say the man's blue-eyed gaze was cold, but Mendis knew better: Alsig was merely detached, existing, as he did, in multiple realities at once.

Or so men claimed.

"You sent for me?"

"You know I did," Mendis laughed.

"Yes."

The Emperor stretched his hands out to either side, as if to say "Well?"

"You are concerned about the manner in which this enterprise is unfolding," Alsig ventured.

"You know I am," Mendis laughed again. "And I don't know why we waste so much time on such formalities. Why not simply share your thoughts without preamble?"

Alsig cleared his throat, offered a wry grin, and proceeded. "In congress, the other wizards and I have determined that the region we currently occupy has known more than its share of warfare. I believe Newak told you as much. Thus, in some ways, we are now picking over a corpse. Had we come ashore farther south or north, well, we might have had a different experience altogether."

"I see."

"Of course," the wizard went on, "being able to march so far inland without molestation has its benefits, too: our troops are able to acclimate easier, we're able to establish a firm foothold, and we may even learn something of the locals' language and customs before hostilities begin in earnest."

"All very well and good," Mendis replied, "but where is the focus of power in this land? From whence is the greatest threat most likely to come?"

"As always," Alsig said, "that depends upon the type of threat we're discussing. There is disease, for example…"

"Armies, my friend, armies. Wizards, swords, catapults. I'll let you worry about the more…esoteric threats."

"Of course."

A figure appeared at the entrance to the room, Lord Commander Dabis.

"Ah, Creyton!" Mendis exclaimed, "We've been waiting for you."

"I'm sure," the general responded. "I'd have been here sooner if Alsig here had thought to bring me."

"Oh, but I did!" said the wizard. "I simply decided against it!"

The Emperor and his wizard shared a laugh, to Dabis' chagrin. "Amusing, as always, Alsig." The general was all business, all the time, and had little patience for the wizard's notions of humor. "Time and timing are everything in battle, and I should like to have been here sooner, the sooner to return to my soldiers."

Mendis regarded his general, a wiry and self-important but highly competent fellow who seemed to spend his life rushing from crisis to crisis. And thank the gods he did! Mendis couldn't imagine getting anything done without him. "We were just discussing the rather suspicious ease with which our invasion seems to be unfolding."

"Yes, well," said Dabis, "what are we to do if the enemy runs and hides from us? What are we to do if he gifts us with his land as if he had no use for it?"

The Emperor placed his hands face-down on the table, felt the grain of the wood under his fingers. It was a nice, sturdy thing. "Will either of you sit and join me in a meal?"

"Thank you, Magnificence, but no," the wizard said. "I prefer to stand."

Dabis looked from the wizard to the Emperor. "I'm not sitting if *he's* not sitting!"

Mendis laughed yet again. Sometimes, even the wisest of his advisors could be somewhat ridiculous in their eccentricities. "Very well, very well," he relented. "But now, tell me: what's to be done? Surely this Virgin Queen we hear of will muster some forces against us in time!"

"Without doubt," said Alsig.

"And my men will be more than prepared, Magnificence. They shall be *eager* to crush her."

"In the meantime?"

"Continue to expand your holdings," the wizard answered. "Establish forts, manufacture more weapons."

The Emperor looked glumly at the tabletop again. "I certainly hope this Virgin Queen materializes," he said. "It'll be a terribly boring war without an enemy."

Bailis, Fleeing

It was anything but boring to Colonel Bailis. Both the rain and his pursuers had been unrelenting for the past forty-eight hours, and the colonel saw that he'd made a potentially fatal miscalculation. Any army of normal size could ill afford to lose valuable troops chasing phantoms in the hinterlands. But this army, Bailis recalled, was seemingly endless. These troops would never be missed and would like as not chase him until they dropped, because returning to their leaders without the captives—the trophies—they'd been sent for was unthinkable.

Bailis' men would probably have done the same, if promised the right rewards. Now, they ran simply to stay alive. The colonel had dressed up their cause with the trappings of nobility—leading the enemy away from the citizenry, dividing the enemy's main force, wasting the enemy's time and resources and such, but the boys knew the truth of it: they were being pursued by a larger, better-equipped and potentially more skilled party that meant to capture or kill the lot of them. There might even be torture involved.

A blast of lightning overhead momentarily spooked Bailis' mount, forcing the man out of his miserable musings and back into the present. He risked a look backwards over his men and marveled at their fortitude. None was paid enough for this shit; they knew it, and he knew it. Still, they forged onwards, whatever their reasons (and avoiding death was surely foremost among them). Bailis scowled at the sky, which promised no reprieve from its current deluge. And that meant his men would have a devil of a time starting their cookfires later on. If he had one half-competent Shaper with him, they might have at least made do with Campaigner's Fire, but Bailis had sent his only magician off with the other half of his men. He took a moment to pray they were having an easier go of it than he, but he was not hopeful, "For the rain," he had heard, "it raineth every day."

"Stallworth!" he barked over his shoulder.

"Yessir!" the man answered.

"Drop back a ways, first sight of the enemy, you hurry and rejoin the column. I want to know if we're gaining or losing ground."

"Yessir!" said Stallworth.

"And Stallworth!" Bailis added, "Don't let them see you, or you'll only get them moving faster."

But Stallworth didn't respond, because he'd already melted into the rain and the lengthening shadows of evening.

He came back far too soon for Bailis' liking.

"Bollocks," the colonel spat into the rain. "We've got to move faster boys!" he yelled down the column. "Enemy's close and this is no ground for a pitched fight!"

Somehow, some way, they found it within themselves to speed up their slog through the mud. A few men went down, only to be hauled back onto their feet and pushed forward. No one in the company would voluntarily leave anyone else behind, no matter the circumstances. Bailis almost wept with pride, but figured he'd never be able to tell his tears from the rain now drenching his face and beard. *Have to shave the damned thing off. In this weather, it's like wearing a dishrag on my chin.*

Stallworth reappeared. "Gonna run all night?"

Bailis didn't even turn to look at him. "If needs must."

"You familiar with the lakes, then, colonel?"

"Yes, corporal. It's my job to be familiar with 'em, and every other Mahnus-cursed feature of the landscape in Her Majesty's realm."

"You reckon we'll lose 'em in the maze o' waterways before they catch us?"

"That's what I said earlier, isn't it?" the colonel snapped with irritation.

"If we can stay ahead of 'em long enough."

Another blast of lightning revealed the lakes to be closer than Stallworth had expected.

Bailis grinned with grim satisfaction. "We'll manage."

But as the column descended into the lakes' basin, the invaders' silhouettes could clearly be seen back uphill, against the night sky.

"What in the infinite hells are they feedin' those bastards?" Stallworth groused. "They got more stayin' power than a ram in rut."

Bailis laughed, sort of, and urged his mount forward. "Keep pushing, boys! We'll lose them soon enough."

The next lightning strike was so close it nearly caused the colonel's heart to fail. Sitting high on a horse, wrapped in wet steel, he knew the next bolt might go right down his throat. He was about to urge his men into a full-out sprint when something knocked him from his mount and face-first into the mud. He was stunned for the briefest of instants and sputtered and spat to keep the mud out of his mouth. Several hands seized onto his armor and hoisted him back onto his feet.

Stallworth was there, staring into his eyes. "You alright, colonel?"

"What was that?" Bailis asked.

In the next instant, he knew, as a crossbow bolt erupted through the front of Stallworth's right shoulder. The man spun almost completely around and pitched over backwards, making a noise that was halfway between a groan and a scream. Poor bastard's shoulder blade and collar bone were probably shattered, and the bolt might even have ripped through an artery. Over the sounds of Stallworth's suffering, Bailis heard the enemy charge.

At that moment, the heavens opened up with such furor,

such a downpour, that men on both sides of the conflict were washed from their feet and swept downhill towards the lakes. Suddenly, no one was fighting, no one was running; all anyone cared about was remaining upright—an increasingly impossible task. Lightning continued to explode all around the besieged soldiers, and thunder threatened to pound them right into the mud. And then Bailis' worst fears were realized when one of his men was struck by a tremendous bolt from above, which then leapt over to a good ten or twelve other victims. Lightning, it seemed, cared nothing for cause or country, but lashed out with fatal impartiality. Not knowing what else to do, the colonel cowered under his horse, which at least had the courage to stand firm. Rivulets of water ran between the beast's legs; soon, those rivulets formed a stream, and that stream, a river. In no time, the whole slope became a great wall of water, rushing, rushing down towards the rapidly flooding lakes, deciding the companies' conflict before either of them got a chance to swing a sword in anger.

Aoife, Vykers, Aoife's Bower

Inside the Umaena's bower, it was late spring, or perhaps early summer. The air was slightly thicker, heavier than normal, and redolent of lilacs, honeysuckle, heliotrope, flowering plum and other, more exotic blooms no mortal could begin to name. The combined effect of these aromas was intoxicating, and even Vykers was not completely immune to their magics. Indeed, as he lay on a thick bed of the softest foliage, it was all he could do to keep his eyes open whilst Aoife sang to him.

And *why* was she singing to him?

He couldn't remember, or even bother to care overmuch.

What was she singing to him?

He'd no idea and less impulse to ask. It had been a long time, ages really, since he'd felt so relaxed, so at peace with himself.

Languidly, he ran a hand over his face, searching out his absent nose and ears, the way a child will pick at a scab. Yes, still missing. But healing. Vykers peered upwards at the rich purple sky through the maze of vines, branches and flowers overhead, which showed him, if he needed further proof, that he was well into the realm of the fey.

"Is it always like this?" he yawned sleepily.

"It is however we list, but yes, normally I prefer it thus."

Honestly, who spoke like that? As Vykers appraised his companion with a more careful eye, he saw that she'd changed since he saw her last—that, in fact, she'd been continually changing since he saw her first. Now, the colors of the forest bled into her hair and clothing, so that it was difficult to discern where one ended and the other began. She was almost, he thought, a beautiful smudge on the landscape.

"I feel...peculiar," he said at last. "What've you done?"

Her laughter in response was like delicate wind chimes. "Cleaned you up, you brute! Have you some aversion to water and cleansing oils?"

He didn't answer the question. "I feel drunk. Am I drunk?"

"What you feel," said Aoife, "is the life of the greenwood, its power, its essence, its eternal, vibrant growth."

"Feels like drink, to me."

"Would you *care* for a drink?" Aoife asked, her voice a breeze, a rustling of leaves and trickling of a brook.

Vykers saw that the moon had risen. "Sure," said he.

"Cobweb! Mustard Seed! Some nectar for our guest!"

A couple of strange little creatures appeared as if from nowhere and floated in Vykers' direction, proffering a small crystal goblet. The Reaper made a sincere effort to understand what he was seeing, but the faeries' shapes eluded him. Were they toad-like goblins? Goblinesque insects? Hedgehogs with wings? It was impossible to say. Vykers accepted the drink and downed it in one toss, without even bothering to taste it first. But he immediately wished he had. The nectar, as Aoife had called it, was amongst the best, most flavorful things the Reaper had ever sampled, and although it was not alcoholic in nature, it nevertheless spread a warm acceptance throughout his body that seemed to dispel his worries and aches faster than he could call them to mind. A war was coming, for instance, and he didn't much care.

Aoife hovered over him briefly, caressing his brow and

tracing the line of his jaw with her finger.

"You tryin' to seduce me?" Vykers cracked.

"Silly man! With a face like that?"

"You think this is bad, how'd you like to be the Dead 'Un? Now there's a face for you!"

"Oh," said the Umaena, "he's an odd one, all right. And blazing with dark magics."

Vykers sat up. "Is that so? What kind 'o magics?"

"Who's to say?" Aoife replied nonchalantly. "But I'd avoid him if I were you."

"Avoid him? He saved my life."

"Even so."

The Reaper sank back into his bed of leaves and moss, and Aoife resumed her singing. Vykers felt himself drifting off to sleep when he suddenly recalled the Emperor's invasion again. "You know there's a war coming," said he.

"Always."

"Will you be joining in or staying in your forests?"

"I haven't decided."

"Will you be safe here?"

Aoife straddled Vykers' lap and took his chin in her hand. Her green eyes were alive with emerald fire. "I need no rescuing, Tarmun."

"I never said..."

"No one and nothing in the mortal world can ever harm me again. And if there's rescuing to be done, I'll be the one doing it."

It was a staring match, so it seemed, and the Reaper was determined to win it, despite his feelings for the Umaena.

Alas, sleep robbed him of the opportunity.

She was humming, this time, and his head, as far as he could tell, was in her lap. The experience was so pleasant that he was loathe to end it, so he kept his eyes shut and pretended to snore.

"I know you're awake," Aoife said, as she pinched him on the shoulder.

"Can't a man rest a spell without being pestered?" Vykers complained good-humoredly.

"A spell? And just how long do you think you've been sleeping, Tarmun?"

The question alarmed him, and he sat up directly. He looked about, saw little or no change in his surroundings, and said "No idea. How long?"

Aoife smiled at him. "The equivalent of a week."

Vykers leapt to his feet. "A week! A week? How in Mahnus' name…"

"Time is a fluid thing," the Umaena said softly, wrapping her arms about his torso, "like honey. It can be made to run more quickly or slower. Inside my bower, I sometimes choose to stop it altogether."

"You said the equivalent of a week…"

"Yes," said Aoife, resting her head against his belly. "A week in here, but not an hour outside."

Slowly, Vykers sank into a seated position, took the Umaena's hands into his own. They were strange things—increasingly plantlike—but no less beautiful for all that. "But why would you do this?"

"Because of this war you mentioned. You were not ready, not whole," Aoife replied. "But now you are." And she gestured to his face and ears.

The Reaper reached up to his wounds and found them healed. His nose and ears were as they'd always been. "More of your magic?" he asked, not ungently.

"None of mine," she said. "All of your own."

"But…"

It seemed everything he said delighted her, caused her to laugh with sweet merriment. "No, you are neither a Shaper nor an A'Shea. You are…"

"I am…?" Vykers prompted when she trailed off.

"Unique in the world," Aoife answered, a bittersweet look in her eyes. "More than that, I cannot say. Perhaps you'll find your answer with the Sholdorn."

And then the Reaper was alone in a forest glade, the darkness of the night around him almost oppressive.

THREE

Alheria, Lunessfor

If Her Majesty had a surplus of anything, she felt, it was generals. And just now, they were, all of them, panicking.

"You will be silent," the Queen thundered to her assembled officers, "or you will find yourselves outside the gates, spending the rest of your days farming cabbage! Am I understood?"

Her officers dared not even respond in the affirmative.

"I take your silence to mean you agree. Very wise. Cabbage farmers lead considerably more difficult lives than any of you, and I don't imagine you'd last very long at it." Every face that looked back at her was cowed in some way, though one or two also showed signs of resentment or anger. Those bore watching, Her Majesty mused. She took another moment to compose her thoughts, glanced around the war room a final time, and then continued. "*Of course* our invaders have come ashore in numbers! They'd be foolish to do otherwise. *Of course* they have captured our coastal towns and begun their advance toward our major cities. That's no surprise, is it?"

Her generals looked mystified, as if they would say "If all this is so obvious, why aren't we doing something about it?" But they hadn't the courage. So, the Queen spoke for them. "You're wondering why we don't throw ourselves in their path, why we don't mount some sort of resistance." Even if she were not the goddess Alheria, she could have read the confirmation in their faces and posture. "The answer is simple, and I am, quite frankly, dismayed that none of you has voiced it: we are outnumbered and terribly so. There are not enough able-bodied and experienced soldiers on this continent to oppose this force, not by half. What would you have me do? Order your women and children to the front line? They'd be the first to fall, I assure you. And then what would you have left worth fighting *for*?"

Finally, one of her generals found the courage to step forward. "Your logic, Majesty, is impeccable, as always. How…how are we best to serve you then? How shall we be employed to repel these invaders?"

"For now, I would like you to fortify our cities and prepare them for assault and siege." Again, the majority of generals seemed to pout, as if the Queen's plans were beneath them. "It is true that our enemy possesses far greater numbers than we can muster, but we have advantages of our own that he will not be able to counter. Now go, and do as I bid you. When the time comes for further planning and action, you can be sure I will send for you."

Not a one of Her Majesty's generals was happy with this turn of events, but not one of them had a better idea or the spine to carry it out against her wishes. As they shuffled despondently out of the war room, Hoosh approached his mother and stood silently by her side until the last man had gone.

"Well," he said, "that went swimmingly, eh?"

She favored him with a sour expression. "All they know is fighting. I don't blame them. But if we're to draw Mahnus out of hiding, the situation must be made to appear as dire as possible."

"I wish you'd finished him when you finished my brother."

"That battle took more out of me than you'll ever know. Eyatu had grown fearfully powerful, and the Reaper remains as uncontrollable as ever. I needed time to recuperate."

"Speaking of that witless barbarian, where does he fit into your plans for the Emperor?"

"Why Hoosh, my Fool!" Alheria chuckled, "Have you forgotten I've got four of my own?"

The jester regarded his mother with a look of astonishment. "What are you plotting, mother of mine?"

By way of answer, the Queen winked at him and turned away. "You will see in time."

The Fool snapped his fingers in frustration. "How I hate waiting for a good surprise."

Her Majesty moved towards the doorway. "Whoever said it was good?"

Kittins, Yendor & Co., Lunessfor

There were many more soldiers patrolling the city's perimeter than there'd been when Kittins left Lunessfor. News of the invasion had arrived, clearly.

"What do you think?" Rem asked, as he and the rest of the company considered this new development from a half mile's distance.

Kittins reached a hand down and patted his horse on the right side of its neck. "What do I think?" he snorted. "I think there's only two safe places in all the land: the old hag's throne room, or so lost in the middle o' nowhere that no one'll ever find you again. Which do you fancy?"

"Well," Rem drawled. "I've *been* lost in the middle of nowhere. I can't recommend it."

"Then we go in."

Rem saw that his friends and the Red Knight's companions all seemed in agreement. "Just as well," he said. "I've been dying for that bath."

The captain scrunched up his face in disgust. "Again with the bath! What kind o' man are you?"

"The kind who prefers to smell like a man and not a wet dog."

Kittins shook his head. "You got an answer for everything, don't you?"

"Except death," Rem admitted. "Haven't thought up a clever quip for that yet."

"Well," said Kittins, "let me know when you do, and I'll kill you."

Rem changed the subject. "What's the plan once we get inside?"

With a grim rumble of laughter, Kittins responded, "Reckon I'll try to pay Her Majesty a visit."

"Because…"

"Why not? If she kills me, she kills me. If not, she might have something more interesting for me to do than man the walls and wait for the enemy."

"Shouldn't we…I don't know…stick together?"

"What for?" the captain asked irritably. "Aren't you late for a bath?"

"Yes, but after that…I mean, we know each other…we've worked together…"

Kittins cast a stern eye over Rem, Yendor, Spirk and Hjuest's fellows, seemed to reconsider. "Maybe," said he. "You remember that tavern where we plotted to spy on the Great Eight?"

"Aye."

"If I'm still breathin', I'll be there eventually."

The guards at the gate were especially vigilant in interrogating anyone who sought entrance into the city, so it took much, much longer than Rem or anyone else in the company would have imagined to get inside. Kittins disappeared somewhere in the middle of the process, but nobody worried overmuch. The big man could take care of himself and probably had other means of ingress—had to, really, with a face like his.

"Let's see if we can find that tavern," Yendor said a little too enthusiastically.

"Planning to do some drinking, are you?" Rem asked.

"Why in the infinite hells not?"

Rem studied his friend a moment, temporarily at a loss for words.

"What?" Yendor demanded. "Did you think I'd stopped drinkin' forever? We accomplished our mission; ain't I entitled to a little pleasure before the next storm hits?"

Rem turned his attention to Spirk and Ron, but they seemed as flummoxed as he by Yendor's demeanor. "Well," said the actor, "you three go ahead. I promised myself a hot bath, and I mean to have it."

"Ha!" Yendor snorted. "A bath's got nothin' on a good tankard o' Bizzly Brown!" With that, he swiveled away from Rem and began weaving his way through the crowds inside the gate.

Rem clapped his hands on Spirk and Ron's shoulders and said "I'll see you both in a few hours—maybe longer if I find myself in the right company!"

This last comment was much too subtle for Spirk, who could only nod and wave as Rem walked off into the evening. "Fancy one o' them Bizzlers?" Spirk asked his comrade.

"Do I!" Ron beamed. "Been a while since I had a good flagon of ale!"

And it would continue to be a while, because the tavern in question had already begun watering down its drinks in anticipation of an alcohol shortage when and if a siege began. Simultaneous with this threatened shortage, the huge influx of refugees into the city meant more and more customers pushing themselves through the tavern's doors, looking to lose themselves in drink. Thus, supply might dwindle dreadfully, even as demand increased a thousand-fold.

Yendor's lone eye took on a crafty, almost nefarious expression as he began to scheme and plot some means of capitalizing on this impending tragedy.

Weak as the ale was, Spirk was already drunk, but Ron remained sober enough to feel discomforted by the unholy gleam in Yendor's eye. "What are you about, old man?" he inquired.

"Who, me?" Yendor responded. "I'm just wonderin', is all. Just wonderin'."

"About?" There was a dull thump to Ron's left, and he noticed that Spirk had keeled over onto the table top and fallen asleep.

Yendor gazed briefly at the now-unconscious Shaper and then looked back at Ron. "Wonderin', I say, how a man might get his hands on a quantity of drink before all the good stuff's gone. Maybe hide a little stash of it somewheres. Sell a little, too, if the price gets steep enough."

The whole idea seemed extremely shady to Ron, but...he didn't much like the thought of trying to survive a siege with an empty purse, either. Glancing both left and right to ensure that no one was listening in, he said, "What have you got in mind?"

Yendor broke into a wide grin. "Well, our sleepy friend here's a Shaper, ain't he...?"

Long Pete, the North

When he'd been a man—*only* a man—he'd often wondered if he'd been cursed by the gods. But who curses the *gods*? Someone, surely, for Long was worse off than he'd ever been as a man. Now, he wandered the half-frozen countryside, bereft of wife, child, friends, and clothing. Well, the clothing had been his own choice, his own fault, which only seemed to prove that increased intelligence was not amongst his new gifts.

He now knew that he could Jump, and he'd even decided *where* to Jump. The sticking point was, he'd never been there before, never seen it, so he wasn't sure he'd survive the attempt. He snickered at the irony: when he'd been trying to kill himself, he'd been unable. Now that he'd found a reason to live, he was afraid he'd succeed.

And he so wanted to see his child, Esmine, to say goodbye on his own terms.

Overcome by a bout of especially powerful self-pity, he approached a large rock by the side of the road, swept the ice-crusted snow off it, and sat down, with only his coat between his ass and the cold, hard stone. He didn't enjoy the sensation at all, so he commanded the rock to warm up, and—behold!—it did. Long stared into the snowy fields across the road and wondered how to solve his problem. If only he could send someone in his stead, someone who could visit Esmine's location and come back—alive and with proof.

His thoughts drifted to Janks, who scarcely remembered him anymore, and then to Yendor, Rem, Spirk and Ron. No, he'd done them too much harm already. Kittins? He doubted the big man would cooperate and, really, why should he?

Long looked down at his hands and realized he'd somehow grabbed a stick and begun twisting it. In frustration, he snapped it without breaking it entirely and bent the broken halves across each other. He repeated the process over and over until his hands were sore and the thing they held was roughly man-shaped. Now, why had he done *that*? There had to be something higher, more powerful than the gods, and he was to them as this thing he'd made was to him. He pitched it into the bushes in disgust and pulled his coat tighter about himself...

And caught sight of movement off to his right, where, to his amazement, his cast-off poppet had come to life and was even now trundling towards him. As it moved, it seemed to acquire more solidity, more mass, from bits and pieces of leaves and twigs in its path, until it arrived in front of Long, a fully-functional homunculus.

"Will you send me?" it croaked, in the strangest voice ever to grace Long's ears.

"What?" Long asked, instantly embarrassed by his own awkwardness.

"Will you send me to that place?"

Long pulled his feet off the ground, like a ship pulling up anchor, and placed them higher on the rock, out of the homunculus' reach. "What place?"

The thing regarded Long with the utmost earnestness—or so it seemed to the captain. "Your daughter's place."

Now, Long climbed to the top of the rock, well away from his creation. "How did you..." And then he understood. "Ah. O' course. I made you for the purpose, didn't I?"

The homunculus seemed confused. "Did you? I do not know."

And if Long made it, he mused, why should he fear it? He climbed back down into his original position and extended his hand to the thing. Accepting his invitation, the homunculus leapt into Long's palm, and he placed it onto the rock at his side.

"What is your name?" Long asked.

"What *is* my name?" the homunculus repeated.

Once more, Long felt a fool. "Oh, yes, I suppose that's up to me...and I'll call you...'Short Pete."

"Short," the thing creaked.

"Yes."

"Short."

"Now, Short Pete," said Long, "I've never Jumped anyone but myself. Why don't we try something simple?"

Short Pete said nothing, but continued to regard his creator the way a dutiful dog regards its owner.

Long spoke, more to break the silence between them than anything else, "How about we send you across yon meadow?" He pointed in the intended direction and wondered what, if anything, the homunculus could see.

Short Pete nodded.

In a second he was gone. Long couldn't see him, but he sensed the thing's presence anyway. A few minutes later, the homunculus' shape appeared, dark against the melting snow, scurrying towards Long's location. The captain stood to greet his new servant.

"Are you...well?" he asked, unsure if the homunculus had feelings or an awareness of its own health.

"Yes."

Long reached down and lifted Short Pete back onto the rock. "Talkative little feller, though, ain't you?"

"Yes," Short Pete croaked.

"With no sense o' irony. Well, let's try something else." Long pointed to a distant tree. "You see that?"

"I do."

"I'm gonna send you to the top o' that tree and then bring you back. I want you to bring me a piece of it—a pine needle, a cone, something like that."

"I will," Short Pete promised.

And he did, proving that Long could both send and retrieve his servant. But now he had to attempt sending the homunculus to someplace that he, Long, had never seen. "Short Pete," he said, "a tyrant from across the sea has invaded our land. I am going to send you into this man's command pavilion, and I'd like you to fetch a map for me—doesn't matter which map, just anything you can lay your...hands...to. Understand?"

"Yes."

"For this purpose, I will have to leave you there a while."

"Yes."

The creature's matter-of-fact demeanor was almost too much for Long. "You have any worries or concerns about this task?"

"No."

"Very well, then. Off you go!" With that, Short Pete disappeared, and Long was left to his own thoughts for a while, a turn of events he suddenly found most displeasing. Who'd have thought a few minutes with a stick figure could come to mean so much to him? If he could create a little person out of sticks, perhaps he could conjure something even more human...

But that was madness, of course. *If I go about creatin' living things just to make myself happy, who knows where it'll stop?* And then he'd be responsible for them, too. And what if they didn't like him, or they got injured or killed somehow?

No, he had enough guilt about Esmine to last a lifetime... however long that was for a god. He didn't need more souls on his conscience.

When enough time had passed, he summoned the homunculus back into his presence and was delighted to see it had succeeded in its mission. "Did you miss me?" he cracked to his servant.

Short Pete looked taken aback, if such a thing was possible. "Should I?" he asked, his strange voice rising another octave in alarm.

"No, no," said Long, offering a sad smile. "I was joking. But let's see what you've brought me."

Long was expecting a sketch of some village or battlefield, but what he found in his hands left him momentarily speechless. Somehow, the Emperor had come into possession of a detailed map of Lunessfor, including a number of secret entrances to the city of which Long had never before been aware.

"Treachery," he spat.

Mendis and the Imperial Army, High Ceremore

If it was all a ruse, a ploy to goad him into aggressive action, it had succeeded, despite Mendis' best intentions. He simply could not countenance an invasion without war, nor war without bloodshed. He understood full well that he was being manipulated; he expected to give the natives far more than they'd bargained for. And so, upon his arrival outside the next city on his map, Mendis ordered the place burnt to the ground.

Perhaps *that* would get his opponents' attention at last.

"What is this place called?" he asked of the guards.

"High Ceremore, Magnificence," one of them responded.

"High Ceremore? Then let us bring it *low.* Let us leave nothing but rubble and ash. I grow weary of waiting for the natives to find their courage. Perhaps this will inspire them."

"But Magnificence," one of his ubiquitous officers interjected, "won't this enrage the locals, give them more cause to revile us?"

The Emperor turned to regard the fellow with frosty disdain. "You!" he called to a nearby gathering of soldiers. "Get this imbecile out of my presence, and have General Promartis reassign him to one of the other legions—as a *corporal.* Maybe he'll remember his place, then!" It seemed a fair sentence to Mendis when he'd every right to have the man whipped or even killed. No one, after all, should ever question the Emperor's judgment, and especially not in public, and most especially when the proffered insight was self-evident drivel.

It was a cloudy evening and would soon be night. The light of the burning city, Mendis knew from experience, would reflect off the clouds and impart a strange, glowing hue to the proceedings that belied their gravity. For his forces, the night would take on an almost festive atmosphere; for the city's inhabitants...

"Your pardon, Magnificence!" a voice at Mendis' side intruded. A still-gasping messenger had arrived on horseback and run from thence into the Emperor's presence.

"Speak."

"Zertes' detachment has captured one of the native officers."

Mendis smiled. "Excellent news! Now, we are getting somewhere. Where is he being held?"

"In the last estate you stayed in. Shall I send a wizard to take you there, Magnificence?"

The Emperor studied the messenger whilst he considered the question. The other man was dripping with sweat despite the temperature, and his uniform was covered with old mud. "No," said Mendis. "I think I'd like the man brought here, so he can watch this city burn. It may help...clear his thoughts."

The messenger bowed without further comment and raced

off the way he'd come. Soon, the new captive would be brought forward, and the Emperor would at last have his chance to examine the enemy. Experience had taught him to be prepared for disappointment in such matters, as enemies seldom lived up to one's expectations.

Excepting Wykkerian, of course.

Mendis signaled one of his bodyguards. "Water!"

The man removed his own water skin from his belt and held it out to his Emperor. Some rulers there were who would only drink water from gold or crystal goblets, untouched by the grimy hands of working men. Mendis was not one of these. Despite his exalted position, he wanted his soldiers to see him as one of their own, albeit an especially superior one of their own. This paradox might have bothered a lesser man, but Mendis remained stoically unconcerned. He drained half the skin and returned it to its owner.

"My thanks," said he.

"My honor," said the soldier.

There occurred a brief whooshing sound, and a wizard appeared nearby with a stout but bedraggled fellow who could only have been the new captive. With but one wizard to guard him, the man might have attempted to escape. That he did not suggested that he well understood his predicament. Mendis stared at him, and he, unbowed, stared back. The prisoner was no taller than the Emperor, for which the Emperor almost liked him. But the man was much broader of chest, with stout arms and legs, and a full but well-trimmed beard, only slightly the worse for wear after a recent drenching.

"Make him understand me," Mendis instructed his wizard.

"And so he shall." The wizard spoke a few words—muttered them, really—and nodded at his ruler. "He is ready."

"What is your name?" the Emperor demanded of his captive.

"Bailis, sir. I am a colonel in Her Majesty's service."

"Well, *Bailis*, you are addressing the Emperor Mendis Staurachia. Call me 'sir' again, and I'll have your tongue removed."

"There's many a soldier'd thank you for that, Your Majesty."

Mendis almost laughed at the man's pluck, but he wanted

to be certain the fellow understood his new master. "Call me 'Magnificence' when given the chance to address me."

Bailis' face twitched ever-so-slightly as if he might have smirked, but he stopped himself. "Magnificence. Certainly."

"You look cold, colonel. Perhaps you'll enjoy a little fire." The Emperor swept his arm towards the walls of High Ceremore and gazed meaningfully at his prisoner.

"You mean to burn the city?"

"I can see why they made you an officer. Your intuition is excellent."

"You humble me, Magnificence, for I fail to see the purpose behind your plans."

Mendis favored Bailis with an ironic smile. "But it is your plans, your *people's* plans, that are most at issue at the moment. Wine!" the Emperor called out, knowing his command would be satisfied shortly.

"I can see why you'd want to know," Bailis sighed, echoing the Emperor's earlier statement. "I wish I knew them, myself."

"Tsk, tsk, tsk!" Mendis replied. "How disappointing. Do you think I'm to be put off with clichés?" A boy approached with a goblet of wine, and Mendis gestured to the prisoner. "It's a cold night; you're soaked through. Drink up."

Bailis didn't hesitate. If they planned to kill him, there were quicker, easier methods. He drank deeply.

"As I was saying," Mendis said. "Your response leaves something to be desired."

"I meant no disrespect, Magnificence," Bailis answered, "And I thank you for the wine. But if there'd been a plan, I think we'd both have seen it by now."

The Emperor folded his arms across his chest, buried his chin on his chest. "You'd have me believe this Queen you serve is aware of my arrival and has no objections to my encroachments on her territory?"

This time, Mendis was interrupted by the arrival of a captain.

"Everything is ready, Magnificence."

Without breaking eye contact with Bailis, the Emperor said, "Burn it."

The colonel didn't react.

"You are well-trained, colonel," Mendis observed. "And I would not have you think that I'm one of these boorish conquerors who revels in bloodshed—quite the contrary, in fact—but your countrymen must understand that I am here to take possession of your lands and to rule them. There cannot be any doubt of that."

"I have no doubt of your *intentions*, Magnificence," Bailis responded carefully.

Mendis laughed. "Spoken like an experienced politician! I just had one of my generals sent down for a clumsiness you clearly do not possess. But I shall take your bait: who will stop me?"

Bailis looked around for someplace to put his now-empty goblet, when the boy reappeared and offered him a fresh one. "Thank you," he told the boy, who only nodded and went off about his business. "Who will stop you?" the colonel echoed. "It's a question I've been asking myself for some days now. I'd hoped my Queen would have made a better and more immediate showing. There are also a few minor kings about. And then there's a fellow we call 'the Reaper'."

The Emperor's eyes flashed at this and he turned to watch Ceremore burn. "I understand his name is Tarmun Vykers. In my land, we call him Treaman Wykkerian."

"In *your* land?"

"Yes," Mendis said, still watching the flames build. "Were you unaware he'd crossed the sea?"

"There's nothing I'd put past him."

Between the Emperor's wizards and his trebuchets, his forces were having no trouble lobbing or blasting burning materials into Ceremore and, predictably, screams began to arise from inside its walls. Mendis bobbed his head as if he'd seen and heard enough and turned back to Bailis. "And have you ever seen this Reaper?"

"Seen him?" Bailis asked. "I've fought with and against him at different times. Never close up, thank Mahnus, but within arrowshot."

"Have you? He murdered my grandfather...when my

grandfather was a young man. How do you account for that?"

Bailis ran his free hand through his beard, stymied. Unable to answer the question, he changed tack. "Do you mean to let them all die, those inside the city?"

Mendis watched the fire's progress for several seconds and then said, "That is entirely up to them. If they decide to unbar their gate, we shall take them all prisoner. If not…"

Within minutes, the gate was open and streaming with those looking to escape the conflagration inside the walls. Bailis, now on his third glass of wine, barely heard the Emperor say, "I was hoping your people had a bit more backbone. Still, I can hardly object to an easy campaign, can I?"

The colonel felt mildly embarrassed, but kept his thoughts to himself. When wine had loosened the tongue, it was best to clamp the jaws shut.

Vykers, At the Sholdorn

He hadn't walked far when his horse, his unearthly horse, appeared as if from nowhere and nudged him in the ribs with its muzzle.

"*Now* you show up!" Vykers teased. "I coulda used your help back there."

The horse was predictably silent on the matter.

Seeing that it was still saddled and apparently unharmed and unchanged since the last time Vykers had ridden it, he climbed onto its back and said, "Let's pay the Sholdorn a visit, eh?"

It seemed impossible that the horse understood him, and yet it trotted off in a particular direction without hesitation. The Reaper watched the scenery flash by as his mount ran faster and faster, until the world around became nothing more than a greenish-grey blur. Night fell, Vykers felt a brief dash of sleet across his head and shoulders, and still his horse ran. Feeling more than rested from his sojourn with Aoife, Vykers elected to keep going. He'd had enough delay and misadventures: it was time to learn whatever-it-was that the Sholdorn might tell him. In time, his horse began to slow, and the Reaper steeled himself for anything.

He was underwhelmed, at first, with what he found.

The Sholdorn were, on the surface, a very plain and rustic people. They wore mostly unadorned homespun, cropped their hair in utilitarian manner, and were, on the whole, rather terse in conversation. Their guards carried only spears, but Vykers knew them to be exceptionally skilled with those weapons, nonetheless. The last time he'd had dealings with them, the Sholdorn had slighted him in some manner he couldn't quite recollect, and, if he hadn't been preoccupied with other, more-pressing concerns, he'd have annihilated them for the insult.

Now, his horse paced to a stop at the feet of two sentries, both women, who regarded the Reaper dispassionately and waited for him to speak. Already, they annoyed him.

"The Historian of Ahklat recommended I pay your people a visit," was all he could think to say.

"And what is that to us?" one of the women asked.

Vykers thought about asking if they knew who he was, but that struck him as a loser's game. Sighing, he drew a sword from its sheath atop one of his saddlebags. The sentries did not miss the significance of this action.

"You mean to kill us, then, Reaper?" So, they *did* know him.

"Yes," he replied matter-of-factly, as he slid from the saddle.

"Wait," said the second sentry.

"Make it good."

"You say were you advised to visit, but you haven't said why."

It was a fair point. Sometimes, Vykers cut corners in his impatience, and many could not follow the drift of his reasoning. He thought fleetingly of Arune and then chased her from his mind. "I've been told your people might be able to...clear up...a few things, a few questions I have about my past."

The first sentry spoke again, still unbowed and unintimidated. "And so the pursuit of knowledge is your sole purpose in our territory?"

Give 'em their due, Vykers thought, *these women are no cowards.* "Yes," he answered. "For now." He thought maybe that last bit would scotch the deal; instead, the sentries stepped to either side and cleared the path before him. He tossed off a quick salute, remounted his horse, and continued on his journey.

Shortly, he crested a small rise in the road and spied the Sholdorn capital in the distance, a mid-sized city of which he had dim memories, surrounded by a vast wall, of which he had none. He considered returning to the sentries and asking about the wall, but decided against it. He'd find out more about it soon enough.

As he drew nearer his destination, he passed numerous fields, now fallow, that their owners had abandoned to winter's predations. It would not be long, though, before the last of the land's snow and ice were a distant memory, and newly planted seeds began to sprout.

Unless war came and burnt them to ash.

Before he realized it, Vykers arrived at the base of the city's wall, confounded by its surprising lack of a gate. He leaned to one side, examined the ground beneath his horse's hooves: the road was still where it should be, but it stopped at the wall.

"Fuckin' Shapers," he breathed in exasperation. "Hello, the city!" he yelled up at the walls.

"Who calls?" came a distant, lilting voice.

"Tarmun Fucking Vykers!"

And then there was a gate, still closed, but visible.

"The purpose of your visit, Tarmun Vykers?"

"I'm in the market for a new codpiece!" the Reaper shouted back, rapidly losing whatever patience he'd possessed at the start of this dialogue.

"Alas..." the voice atop the wall began.

"Fine!" Vykers cut in. "Fine! I'm lookin' for answers about the past..."

"The past?"

"My past!" The Reaper was just on the verge of losing his temper, when he heard the gates' massive bolt withdrawn and the thunderous rattling of enormous gears and chains. The doors swung to, and, behind them, Vykers saw an equally colossal portcullis rising up out of view. Between the gates and the portcullis were several obvious murder holes, but if any-one stood behind them, he or they were not visible. This was the part that always made the Reaper a little nervous. He could fight anyone on open ground, but concealed enemies shielded by several feet of stone? Suddenly, he wished Arune were still with him. It seemed there were some things Shapers were good for after all. Perhaps sensing his apprehension, Vykers' horse bounded through the gates with a leap so rapid and powerful that it was almost like the few Jumps he'd done with Arune or Pellas. One moment he was outside, wondering how best to defeat the murder holes, the next, he was well inside, facing a large assembly of surprised but unfrightened Sholdorn.

"Afternoon," he said, because he felt the need to say something.

Those gathered seemed to take a moment to compose themselves, then one of the women in front said, "And good afternoon to you, Tarmun Vykers, assuming your intentions are peaceful."

From his vantage point atop his horse, Vykers had a good view of the crowd in front of him, as well as other Sholdorn stationed on the walls or going about their business up and down the streets before him.

Not one of their number was male.

"Where are your menfolk?" Vykers asked.

The woman who'd greeted him replied, "But we have no menfolk. We are Sholdorn."

The Svarren, North Midlands

The Svarren stood upwind of their prey, hidden amongst a vast outcropping of snow-covered boulders. They made not a sound, scarcely breathed, as they watched the first group of humans struggle past. These were not the ones they wanted, not the ones the mistress and her male had ordered the Svarren to attack. But it was terribly tempting. This first group looked bedraggled and all but spent, as if they'd been running for days. Their mouths hung wide, and their eyes were empty, like animals looking for somewhere to die. It was their pursuers the Svarren had been instructed to kill, however, and so, with considerable regret, the savages stood their ground and waited.

They didn't wait long. Just as the last of the humans

disappeared down the far side of the hill, the noise of a larger, healthier band could be heard coming up the near side. The Svarren tensed, eager and erect in their lust for violence. The new group of humans charged into view, most on foot, but several on horseback, all decked out in dark blue armor emblazoned with stars. One of the riders called the whole unit to a stop, whilst he surveyed the horizon from this new elevation.

It was a fatal mistake.

The Svarren shrieked and poured from their hiding places like angry wasps from a suddenly damaged hive. They emerged in numbers their prey had difficulty comprehending or even believing, and they set upon their targets with bestial need. The hunters had become the hunted.

Still, the Emperor's men were well-trained, and not a man of them was a coward. Without needing to be told, they wheeled into position to greet the Svarren attack. They'd never seen or fought an enemy like this before, but that mattered little: steel and discipline could not be beaten. They met the Svarren onslaught head-on, confident in their skill, experience and equipment.

The Svarren were unimpressed. They'd been fighting armored men for centuries—more!—and instinctively attacked the joints and other places not as well covered as the head, chest and limbs. And they outnumbered their foe by a factor of five or six. In no time, the semi-frozen ground became a mire of bloody mud, bile and urine, which steamed in the frigid air, lifting the stench of death into the noses of the combatants with very different results. For the Svarren, it was an intoxicating aroma; for the Emperor's men, it was a nauseating putrescence that made more than a few of them vomit into their faceguards, despite their training. Svarren were shorn of heads and limbs. Many were impaled or disemboweled. And yet these atrocities were repaid in-kind upon the soldiers. Limbs were torn from sockets, throats were ripped out, and eyes were scooped from their sockets like egg yolks from their shells. The gathering darkness was filled with the shouts, screams and shrieks of the enemies, and no one watching from afar could have determined a Svarren howl from a human's death cry. In less time than it takes to eat a good meal, the battle was over, and only three men remained standing. Eager to finish them, a last wave of Svarren pressed forward, only to be held back by one of their fellows, a commander of sorts.

Let them go! He communicated in his guttural language. *And let their masters learn the cost of trespassing on our lands!*

Yes, the others seemed to say, *it is good.* They stepped back and left the terrified survivors to stew in their own sweat and blood. When the Emperor's men stared stupidly back at them, the biggest of the Svarren barked at them, and they ran, stumbling blindly, back down the path they'd arrived on. The Svarren swept into the carnage to eat their fill or scavenge whatever goods they fancied. For some, it was boots or helmets, for others, fleshy souvenirs of their ferocity. Even the bodies of the horses didn't last more than a quarter of an hour.

Her Majesty's men, drawn by the noise of conflict, had snuck back around the front of the hill, where they ambushed the three survivors of the Svarren's assault and dragged them off and far away from the path. Captain Derry decided to keep one of the men for questioning and release the remaining two, the thinking being that they'd return to the Emperor with news of the Svarren, giving him something unexpected to worry about.

Derry pondered his prisoner in silence for several minutes. He and his fellows were slightly shorter than the captain or any of his soldiers, but sturdily built for all that. Derry wondered if all of the invaders were of similar build. Somewhere in his flight, the prisoner had jettisoned most of his armor, but wisely held onto his sword and helmet. He'd suffered a nasty gash on his clean-shaven skin, but his grey eyes were clear and his breathing steady. All in all, the man appeared stoical enough, considering what he'd just been through.

"I don't suppose you speak the Queen's tongue," Derry offered.

The prisoner indicated that he'd heard the question but couldn't understand it.

The captain shook his head in disappointment. "I didn't expect you would. Foolish to ask, really."

"Can 'e draw, captain?" one of Derry's grunts asked.

"Draw?"

"Yeah, you know, like maps and such."

"Excellent thinking, Tibs. O' course, we'll have to find a farmstead or some such where they might have ink and parchment, but it's a start!"

"And if 'e don't cooperate?" Tibs wanted to know.

"Then we make him cooperate," Derry answered. "However we can."

A few of the other soldiers heard this and sniggered amongst themselves, but Derry wasn't having any of it. "None o' that, lads. We may all find ourselves in his position before this is over."

The men's brief levity ceased.

Eoman and his Kinfolk, In the Woods

No one was better at finding giants than other giants. There were specific signs they left in the earth, a certain impact on the branches of trees, and other clues that only another giant would understand. And so Eoman, Beesmarch and the Brothers managed to track down two more of their kin, Whindas and Frest, each of whom claimed to know the whereabouts of still more giants. With every passing league, the King of the Giants' excitement and enthusiasm grew. It had been ages since he'd seen so many of his people together, and the prospect of more was almost delightfully unbearable.

Yet he never forgot the reason for this reunion, nor the likelihood that many of his friends would die in the near future, even if they managed to defeat the invading legions. "Then why do it?" Karrakan might have asked. Eoman wondered if his friend had succeeded in reuniting Mardine with her child and how long it might be before he'd see the shaman again. Of all his friends, Karrakan brought him the most comfort and best counsel.

Eoman slapped branches out of his face as he led his fellows along a river in the northwestern country. It was a wild, mountainous land, full of strange, ancient spirits and crumbling ruins. Most folks avoided it, which made it the perfect place for giants.

"Humph!" Beesmarch grunted, a sure sign he'd something to say.

Eoman gave in. "Yes?"

"The lot of us, wanderin' about together...damned fool strategy."

The other giants remained silent. They knew Beesmarch's temper, and they were curious how this conversation would develop.

"Not if there's killing to be done," Eoman countered.

"We'll find our kin faster if we split up and meet somewhere back in the midlands."

It was true; the King could hardly challenge the wisdom of it. Still, he wanted to maintain as big a force as possible, in the event they ran into Svarren, or one of the Emperor's legions. Eoman expected a fight at any moment, whereas Beesmarch seemed to believe conflict was a ways off yet. "Aye," he said, "'tis true we'd make better time. Then again, I'll feel better-equipped to deal with trouble if there's a goodly pack of us."

"Trouble? Out upon it! What's trouble to a giant?" Beesmarch responded irritably.

They came to a great tree, fallen across the river. Without taking a break from the argument, Eoman gestured that the group should cross with him. "Look, Bees, we all know you're the biggest and maybe the strongest of us, but even a giant like you's no match for an entire army."

Beesmarch muttered and spat, looking for something, anything, to bolster his own argument. "I still say we oughta split up."

"You've been heard."

"You heard me. But did you *listen?*"

Finally, Eoman had had enough. He stopped, mid-bridge, and got right up into the taller giant's face. "Fine!" he yelled. "You want to leave? Leave!"

The other giants, stuck behind Beesmarch, began to retreat slowly off the tree, sensing a blow-up was coming.

Beesmarch, insulted and embarrassed, grew even more belligerent. "Leave? I'm not leavin' our fellows under *your* leadership!"

For Eoman, this was like a slap across the face. "Are you sayin' what I think you're sayin'?"

The five giants on the near shore huddled together, breathlessly, fully aware of what was coming. Beesmarch looked back at them, hoping to see support in their eyes, but their expressions remained neutral.

"You've been bitchin' and moanin' since Karrakan and I stopped by your home, Bees. If you've aught to say, say it now and be done with it. Otherwise, shut your trap!"

"Right, then: I challenge your right of kingship!"

Eoman's eyes grew wide with disbelief. He'd imagined his old friend had entertained such thoughts, but never reckoned he had the courage to voice them.

Without losing a beat, Whindas stepped forward. "Let everyone witness, a challenge has been offered!"

The King chewed on his moustache a moment, seething with fury. "What are the terms?"

Beesmarch considered the question a moment and then said, "First to throw the other from this bridge is King."

Eoman glanced at the river a good ways below. The fall probably wouldn't kill a giant, but the icy surge might. But what could he do? If he hemmed or hawed now, they'd all think him craven. "I accept," he said at last.

"Challenge accepted!" Whindas called out, as if he were speaking to an audience of thousands. "Toss your weapons this way, and wait 'til I yell 'fight'!"

The competitors walked towards their fellows and pitched their weapons onto the riverbank before turning back around and resuming their places mid-river.

Eoman glared up at Beesmarch, angry and disappointed to his core at his friend's betrayal. And now he had to fight him! Over their long friendship, he'd never contemplated such a thing, not once. He studied the larger giant, truly studied him as an adversary for the first time and felt dismay at the daunting task before him—dismay and a profound sadness. He wondered what in all hells was going through his old friend's mind.

For his part, Beesmarch was embarrassed and bewildered: how had they come to such a sorry pass? Eoman must have goaded him into it. He thought back over the last few minutes and couldn't quite see where they'd gone awry. But now everyone was watching him expectantly. He couldn't possibly back out now without losing his very last shred of dignity. His eyes blazed accusation and resentment at his king: *this is your fault!* If Eoman got the message, he said nothing in response.

"Fight!" Whindas yelled.

Although both giants had been expecting it, the call came as a shock anyway, like a rooster crowing an hour before dawn.

Eoman charged directly at Beesmarch, his hands outstretched, as if he would hit the bigger giant in the chest and bull rush him right off the log in one great push. Beesmarch had a longer reach, though, and was able to slap the King's hands away before they made contact. Eoman jumped back and reset his feet. There wasn't enough room on the tree trunk for the combatants to circle each other, so both giants would have to confine themselves to lunges, feints and grappling. Eoman hoped his slightly lower center of gravity would give him some advantage, but Beesmarch's superior reach was a problem the King might not be able to solve. On the other hand, the bigger giant's longer beard offered possibilities, and in their rush to get started, no one had expressly forbidden the pulling of hair or beards...

Beesmarch beat him to it, yanking on Eoman's beard and dragging him towards the brink. The King resisted briefly and then reversed course suddenly, using his momentum to crash into Beesmarch with full force, knocking him over. As he went down, though, he continued to hold onto Eoman's beard, so the smaller giant landed roughly on the log as well.

The fight went on forever. There was plenty of grappling, punching, and stamping of toes. There was enough cursing to fill the quota for a good-sized village. There were eye-pokes, knees to testicles, and, at one point, Eoman even bit Beesmarch on the left cheek. But neither giant made any progress in tossing the other off the log. Finally, Eoman stood, panting heavily and dripping with sweat despite the cool air and dropped his hands to his side. "Bees," he gasped, "this is idiotic. Why are we fighting when there's a world of..."?

Beesmarch hit him on the left side of his head with a massive fist, and Eoman slowly crumpled and then toppled right off the bridge, pin-wheeling down into the raging waters below.

Alheria, In Lunessfor

Alheria sat in a chair in her personal library, her eyes closed and her breathing, deep and slow. Before the Fool could say anything, she stopped him with her voice.

"None of your japes, now."

Hoosh seemed to deflate a bit in disappointment. "But who am I, after all, without them?"

The Queen's eyes remained closed. "I require a few more minutes of silence."

Pouting, the jester found a chair of his own and plunked himself into it, his bells all a-jingle.

"And silence those damned bells!" Her Majesty commanded.

Hoosh waved his fingers and it was done. He closed his own eyes and tried to see whatever it was his mother was fixated on, but, alas, he'd nowhere near her talent. When next he heard Alheria's voice, she was sniping at him.

"Wake up, Fool! Your snores are like to rattle my castle into dust."

The Fool was astounded that he'd fallen asleep and feeling much put out by his mother's accusations.

"Anyway," the Queen went on, "I asked for silence, not clamor."

"Yes, your Majesty," Hoosh answered, somewhat peevishly.

"Yes, your Majesty," the Queen echoed mockingly. "Luckily for you, I was able to complete my search."

Now, the Fool sat up attentively. "And?"

"And...I believe I've the pieces to win this game, yet. The only challenge is in getting them into their proper positions. And that bastard Vykers continues to elude me, even on a horse of my own creation! But I believe I've an answer for that, too."

"Wonderful!" Hoosh exclaimed. "War's won, celebrations to follow!"

Alheria cast him a sour glance. "If I had more time to think on it, I might find your flippancy disrespectful."

"Consider me chastened, mother."

"If you're not now," the Queen warned, "you will be."

Hoosh didn't have long to ponder Her Majesty's comment before a knock came at the open door. The Captain of the Queen's Swords stood there, silently waiting to be acknowledged.

"Yes?" the Queen asked.

"The Dead One has returned, Majesty, and wishes to speak with you."

Alheria smiled cryptically and nodded. "Show him in."

The captain disappeared for a few moments, during which time, Hoosh felt it necessary to weigh in on the topic of the Dead One. "I abhor the fellow. He's entirely too *grave*...if you take my meaning."

The Queen did not laugh. "Taken and dismissed," she said. "If that's the best you can do, I shall need a new Fool soon."

The louder-than-usual footsteps of the returning captain served to alert Her Majesty that he did not want to catch her off-guard. Thus, when he finally stepped into the door frame again with Kittins at his back, the Queen and her Fool were both turned to receive him. Alheria did not rise, but said, "Thank you, as ever, Captain. You may show him in and return to your post."

The captain stood aside and extended an arm into the room, ushering Kittins into Her Majesty's presence. Before Kittins could cast a backwards glance at the man, he was gone.

"So," Kittins said, focusing on the Queen, "you're a god."

"Goddess," said Alheria, "but no one seems to respect feminine titles anymore." She looked up into Kittins' ravaged face and asked, "What is it you want?"

Kittins tried to smile, but it was clearly difficult. "Don't you know?" he taunted, "Bein' a goddess and all?"

"Why must everyone be so impertinent with me?" Alheria demanded. "The erosion of manners in this world will be the end of it."

"I doubt that," Kittins retorted.

Alheria locked eyes with him for a long while, during which time Hoosh feared to breathe too loudly, lest he incur his mother's wrath. Eventually, the Queen said, "Yes, I know what you want. The question is whether you're in any position to negotiate for it."

Kittins adjusted his stance, cracked a kink in his neck. "I think I am."

"Of course. But why? On what basis?"

"Based on the fact I'm still alive. You know I killed your Shaper..."

"He's not dead."

"Crippled, then. You know I did this, and you still let me live. So, I'm guessin' you've got some plans for me."

"You're more astute than I'd given you credit for."

As if to prove her point, Kittins said, "Lotta folks think I'm less perceptive than I am. Gives me something of an advantage."

"Very well," the Queen said, rising to her feet. "You want Tarmun Vykers." Hoosh gasped at this pronouncement, but Kittins showed no sign of surprise. "I think that can be arranged. First, however, I'll need something from you."

"Which is?"

"I'm putting you in charge of the defense of this city against the Emperor's legions."

Hoosh began giggling madly to himself, with his mouth closed to reduce the volume. Alheria reduced it entirely with a wave of her hand, and Hoosh sat immobilized.

"Then...after the war, is what you're thinkin'?" said Kittins.

"Yes."

"But if we lose..."

"Then we'd best make certain we don't lose," Alheria finished, unapologetically.

Kittins scowled at the floor in disgust. "There's always another damned thing to do."

The Queen smiled. "And you're the damned person to do it."

Mendis, High Ceremore

High Ceremore had become Low Ceremore, as low as ashes and rubble, and the Emperor's Legions had acquired thousands and thousands of captives. Mendis decreed that rather than enslavement or execution, the captives should be freed and chased into the surrounding country. This, he said, would increase pressure upon the neighboring cities and towns and they, in turn, would increase the frequency and urgency of their pleas to the land's various rulers for succor. Eventually, they would have to field armies to oppose the Emperor's advance, or he would overrun them. He preferred to do battle in a civilized manner, but he would resort to barbarism if needs must.

Mendis had gotten into the habit of dragging Bailis along with him, day in and day out, on the off chance he had questions about the colonel's homeland. This was odd, from Bailis' perspective, because unless they meant to kill him, he was learning a great deal about the Emperor's forces and his overall strategy. If Bailis could escape...

A messenger arrived and waited to be acknowledged by the Emperor.

"Yes?" Mendis asked.

"One of the men from a forward scouting party has returned. He says the rest of his company have been killed."

The Emperor frowned at this, not in displeasure, but in thought. "Bring him to me."

Bailis understood none of this, of course, but he could read faces and body language well enough. He guessed one of the enemy's Shapers—wizards, they called them—would soon come by to make the Emperor's speech comprehensible. Another round of questions was in the offing.

Minutes later, the messenger reappeared with an extremely bedraggled and nervous-looking soldier. Mendis turned and waved Bailis over. Of course, Bailis went nowhere without the two guards assigned to him, so the three of them walked to the Emperor's side. As the colonel had predicted, a wizard appeared and rendered all speech intelligible to Mendis and Bailis alike.

"Go on," Mendis instructed the soldier.

"We were pursuing the small native force, as you commanded, when we were attacked by...by...monsters..."

"Describe them."

"Freakish, man-like things, they were, all warts and scales

and extra arms and legs—or not enough. Horrible claws and fangs. Horrible, horrible. They ate us."

"Svarren," Bailis interjected.

"Tell me more," Mendis insisted.

"They're just as your soldier says and worse. And they number in the tens of thousands, if not more."

The soldier, upon hearing this, grew frantic and required sedation from the nearby wizard, who calmed him with a series of words that even his earlier spell did not translate.

"Have you no such creatures in your land?" Bailis asked the Emperor.

"We have nightmares of our own, but we've grown accustomed to them. But tell me, Colonel, do these Svarren attack everything equally, or have they some reason to assault my men in particular?"

Bailis was taken aback. "Do you suggest an alliance between the Svarren and my people? Such a thing is unheard of and unthinkable."

"Then they attack anyone and anything they like?"

"Just so."

"Perhaps they could be made to fight for me..."

Bailis had nothing to lose. "I doubt such a thing is possible, Magnificence, but if you were somehow able to achieve that, the results could well be catastrophic. The Svarren are...a wildfire, not to be tamed, nor controlled in any way."

Mendis turned to his wizard. "Take this soldier away. See that he's cared for, and have someone illustrate these creatures for me. I'd like to see for myself what they look like."

"Your will."

Mendis returned his attention to Bailis and peppered him with a hundred questions about the Svarren, their territories, their behaviors, and more. He then discussed the refugees from High Ceremore and where they were most likely to find safe haven. Finally, there was much he wanted to know about the Virgin Queen, and Bailis did his best to inform without giving too much away. After all, he still held out hope of escape and rejoining Her Majesty's forces...where and whatever they were.

At conversation's end, Mendis informed his prisoner that his legions' next target was the high-walled and thoroughly fortified city-state of Nespharia. If the Emperor could capture it, he was confident he could hold it forever.

The Emperor bid a good afternoon to his prisoner and went off about some business that Bailis, being a mere colonel, couldn't begin to guess at. But he did wish he could hate the man. It would have made *being* a prisoner and plotting an escape so much easier. The thing of it was, Mendis was nothing like the tyrant Bailis had been expecting, particularly when compared to the likes of the End-of-All-Things. Oh, he'd destroyed High Ceremore. But he'd allowed its citizens to choose their own fates. Most had chosen to live, and Mendis had let them go. Bailis wasn't sure the Virgin Queen would have done the same in his position. Additionally, the Emperor had crossed the sea—amazing enough in itself—with the largest force the colonel had ever seen. That spoke of leadership, planning and organizational skills that Her Majesty had yet to exhibit, much less demonstrate, in the face of Mendis' threat.

Would it be so terrible, really, if the Emperor prevailed and unified the whole land—the whole world!—under his banner? Such an event would solve a lot of problems: currency would become standardized, communication would center around one official language, and religions…

Bailis suddenly realized he had no idea what the Emperor and his folk believed. Did they also worship Mahnus and Alheria and their host of lesser gods, or did they worship someone, something else altogether? The colonel would have to ask, next time he had the chance to speak with the Emperor. The question was more of a curiosity to Bailis, anyway. As far as he could tell, Mahnus and Alheria hadn't taken a direct interest in the doings of mortals in ages, if ever. A change of gods wasn't the worst thing Bailis' could imagine, and the world might even be better off if his homeland was subsumed by the Empire.

Better than all of this, however, was the sheer number of lives that could be saved if only Bailis' countrymen accepted what seemed increasingly inevitable.

The colonel took in a deep, cleansing breath; the air was sweet, thus far uncorrupted by the stench of battle and the reek of death.

Perhaps Bailis could do something to keep it that way.

Long Pete, On the Road

The Emperor, it seemed, had contingency plans to break any siege against Lunessfor from within, which presented Long Pete with a conundrum: should he intervene on the people's behalf, even though he was apparently at odds with their queen, or should he stand aside and allow war to claim its dead? Mahnus had always been perceived, among other things, as the God of War. But Long hated war. And perhaps that was fitting. A true God of War, after all, should be someone who understood its cost, someone who knew how to contain and control it, someone who kept it on a short leash, not someone who exulted in bloodshed, but someone who strove at all costs to avoid it. In that moment, Long seemed to expand internally, to grow larger and better than he had ever been, outside of fatherhood and marriage, and he became resolved of two things: one, he had to visit his daughter before Mardine got to her, and, two, he needed to keep the Emperor away from Lunessfor.

He was ready, he felt, for the first challenge, having practiced Jumping himself and by sending Short Pete as his proxy. As for the second, well, it wanted further thought. That mad bitch, Alheria, was ensconced in Lunessfor. If only there were some way he could protect her subjects without coming between Her Majesty and the Emperor. How wonderful it would be to watch them kill each other, sparing the world any more of their blood-thirsty machinations.

Long suddenly realized he'd been day-dreaming—and grinning like an idiot, to boot—and quickly pushed thoughts of vengeance aside. His first priority was visiting Esmine. "Short," he called to the homunculus, "I need you to take one more trip."

"Yes, master?"

"And don't call me master anymore. My name's Long Pete."

The little creature's face seemed to light up. "Long Pete? And I am Short Pete!"

"Now you're gettin' it. But just keep it simple 'n call me Long."

"Yes, Long. What is it you wish me to do?"

"Well, first of all, stop talkin' like a courtier. Can you do that?"

It was difficult to read the homunculus' facial expressions, but his body slumped in a manner that suggested disappointment. "I do not know how."

Long thought about it for a spell and said, "Try talkin' more like me."

"Fuck!" said Short.

Long about fell over backwards in surprise. "When did I ever say *that*?" he demanded.

"Earlier today. And several fuckin' times since then."

"I what? I did?"

"Yes, you did. Fuck."

The captain laughed and blushed and regarded his little companion with a mixture of delight and bemusement. "Well... maybe I did. But let's have a little less 'o that cursin'. Just...listen to the other things I say 'n try to adopt my style."

"I will try."

"Good," said Long, "now I wanna send you one more place. It's another place I haven't been, but I think I can still manage it, anyhow."

"What should I do there?"

Long shrugged. "Look around, see what's what."

"What?"

"I mean, take in the details, that sorta thing. Can you do that?"

"I think so."

That was good enough for Long, who bobbed his head in satisfaction, closed his eyes, and began to imagine Esmine's face in as much detail as possible. A few seconds later, there was an abrupt and palpable absence to the captain's left, where Short Pete had been standing, and Long knew he'd succeeded in sending the little fellow along. Nothing to do now but wait.

It was important, Long felt, that Short take his time in scouting Esmine's location, so that Long's own journey thither would be as safe and surprise-free as possible. But every minute seemed like an hour, until he could barely contain his nervous excitement. Eventually, it was all too much for him and he reached out to retrieve his homunculus...

And nothing happened.

Vykers, Amongst the Sholdorn

He'd never say it out loud—he was the Reaper, after all—but finding himself inside a city peopled only by women made him... uneasy. "No men?" he repeated.

"None," the Sholdorn leader confirmed.

"But how do you...I mean, where do these younger girls come from?"

The woman did not answer immediately, allowing Vykers to stew in his discomfort and confusion. After a prodigious pause, she finally said "Surely you know where children come from."

"You know what I'm gettin' at," Vykers snapped irritably. "This can't be the first time you've heard these questions."

The woman, who'd still not introduced herself, gently took hold of the reins for Vykers' horse and began to lead it down the city's main thoroughfare. Not wanting to look like a trophy slave, the Reaper slid out of the saddle and joined his escort on foot.

"We have only one use for men, and that is getting us with children."

"And then what? You kill the poor bastards?"

"Nothing so savage," the woman scoffed. "Most are only too eager for a quick tumble with no further investment."

What could Vykers say to that? It had certainly been true of him.

"We entertain them as long as necessary and then show them the gates."

Vykers glanced around at the growing mob of women following along in his steps and found it easy to imagine why such men wouldn't object to leaving. "A city without men ain't natural."

His guide stopped in her tracks and fixed him with a most

unamused expression. "Not everything that's natural is worthy of one's time or attention. We have no fistfights, no brawls. We've no drunks, no rapists, no murderers. What is it, exactly, that you think the presence of men would do for my people?"

The Reaper sucked at his teeth for a moment, wondering how to parry such an argument, when he finally decided to abandon the whole thing. "Where are we heading, anyway?"

"City Hall. Where did you think? A vast, communal boudoir? I'm sorry to disappoint you."

"Oh," Vykers drawled, "I ain't disappointed. Believe me."

"I'm sure," the woman quipped.

City Hall was an impressive edifice for a city that eschewed all things male or masculine. If Vykers didn't know better, he'd think it had been built in homage to Mahnus, so stout and stately was it. He couldn't imagine Aoife walking its hallways no matter how hard he tried. His giant friends, however, might find it much to their liking.

At length, his guide led him into an antechamber and shooed the rest of Vykers' escort away, closing the door in their faces without so much as a 'By your leave.'

A vast and beautiful stone table dominated most of the room, and the numerous chairs surrounding it took up whatever space was left.

"You are welcome to sit," the woman said.

"Thanks, but I think I'll stand. I've been sittin' too much of late."

The woman rolled her eyes.

"You don't like me," said Vykers.

"I don't care enough to like or dislike you. What discomforts me is your coming here."

There was any number of things the Reaper might have said to that. What he chose was, "You got a name?"

"Of course."

"You gonna tell me, or do I have to torture it outta you?" He was only kidding, but it produced the desired result.

"Ji Nan."

"Ji Nan, huh? Kinda name is that?"

"It is a Sholdorn name. Obviously."

"Right. And what are we doin' here, Ji Nan?"

"You," Ji Nan said with particular stress, "are waiting for the Great Woman."

"Ain't every man?" Vykers asked roguishly.

Ji Nan did not laugh. "Spoken like a man. The Great Woman is our leader, our Lord Mayor and Queen rolled into one. If anyone can answer your questions and get you back on the road, it is she."

"Uh huh." Vykers chose a seat conspicuously near his guide, leaned back, and put his feet up on the table.

"We don't do that, here!" Ji Nan barked.

"Yeah, well maybe you don't, but I do," Vykers responded, after which he farted noisily.

His guide stormed from the room.

In good time, a door on the room's far side opened and two more women came through. The first was quite tall for a woman and rather well-muscled, too. Dark haired and brown-eyed, she locked eyes with Vykers the instant she crossed the threshold, and then stepped aside to allow the smaller, older woman behind her to enter as well.

"Take your feet off the table!" the younger woman shouted at Vykers.

...Which made him disinclined to cooperate. Seeing that refusal might hurt his chances of learning anything from the Great Woman, he thought better of it and slowly acquiesced.

"And stand in the Great Woman's presence."

Vykers was about to lose the last of his patience when the older woman put a hand on her younger companion's shoulder and said, "That won't be necessary, Tarmun Vykers."

The younger woman fumed at the Reaper, but he simply smiled back at her and laced his fingers together behind his head. "I understand you might have something to tell me about my past."

The old woman smiled enigmatically and responded. "Oh, yes. But perhaps we should begin with your granddaughter, here."

Convinced he'd misheard the Great Woman, Vykers just

stared at her until she repeated herself.

"Yes," she said, "Ona, here, is your grandchild."

The young woman stared at Vykers defiantly, as if daring him to deny the claim. He glared back at her. "I don't remember f...I don't recall beddin' any Sholdorn."

The Great Woman smiled patiently. "But that is why you are here, is it not? Because you do not remember who you are?"

Frustrated, confused, Vykers sat back in his chair and drummed his fingers on the table top. "You got anything to drink around here?"

"Of course." The Great Woman whispered something into Ona's ear, and the younger woman balked, before at last relenting and exiting the chamber.

"She's got her grandfather's stubbornness," the Great Woman explained.

"Uh huh," the Reaper agreed. "Whoever he was."

The Great Woman pulled a chair out from the table and sat, adjusting her robes while she spoke. "And how would it serve me or anyone else to lie in this matter? You can see for yourself how much she resembles you—except for that scarring around your ears and nose."

Vykers reached up self-consciously and rubbed at his ears. "Yeah, well, considerin' I didn't have 'em a few days ago, I think I look pretty damn good. Anyway, there can't be ten years between me and this Ona, maybe less than five."

"And you find that meaningful?"

"Means I can't possibly be the girl's grandpa."

"Unless," the Great Woman countered, "you don't age."

In his mind, Vykers thought he could hear an enormous portcullis being raised, its massive chains straining into action, just as he'd heard at the city's gate. "I don't age," was all he could manage before Ona returned with Ji Nan at her side, holding a tray with several mugs and a large earthenware pitcher.

The Great Woman waited until everyone had settled, except for Ona, who preferred to remain standing by her leader's side. "Apparently not."

"And how do you know this?" Vykers demanded.

"What is astounding," the Great Woman replied, "is that it

isn't common knowledge. But you shall see the evidence and judge for yourself."

Vykers wanted to laugh it off, dismiss the woman, his alleged granddaughter, and all of the Sholdorn as utter nonsense, unworthy of his time and attention...but something tickled at the back of his brain and he could not. "Then how old do you think I am?"

The Great Woman and Ji Nan chuckled at this, whilst Ona continued to glare at him. "That," the Sholdorn leader said, "is the amusing part!"

FOUR

Qansip & Driegan, On the Road

Adventure, Qansip decided, was not at all what she'd been led to expect. Adventure was, in fact, a soggy, shitty, and endlessly stupid experience. There was none of the grandeur or excitement she felt she'd been promised. Instead, every hour of every day brought more of the same tedious slog she'd endured since her father had taken her from home—not that she'd walked more than a hundred paces of it herself, of course, but she couldn't imagine how walking the whole distance would have made things any worse.

"Papa!" she called, for the fifteenth time that day, "When are we going to arrive somewhere—*any*where?"

Driegan, tired of hearing his daughter's voice, was half-tempted to let some of the men drag her into the underbrush and have their way with her, if only to shut her up for a few days. Oh, he loved his daughter—or thought he had, when this infernal journey began—but he was nearing the end of his patience with her. He was afraid that if she kept whining, he might sell her to the first peddler who happened along for nothing more than a couple of Peasants. Still, he forced himself to recall that her beauty and her maidenhead might yet fetch him a lordship if he could only bear with her a while longer.

And if Qansip wasn't enough to deal with, the accursed, endless rain of winter's thaw made every aspect of this journey infinitely more difficult than it might otherwise have been. There wasn't a dry boot in the company, nor a dry blanket. The food stores had gotten wet, too, along with anything that passed for tinder. If one of Driegan's men hadn't possessed a marginal talent for shaping, there was a good chance they'd all have died of exposure.

It was becoming increasingly clear they'd have to seek refuge in an inn, someone's home, or even a cave if needs must, until the worst of the deluge had passed. Qansip, of course, would insist on an inn, and Driegan began to wonder if removing her tongue would increase or decrease her value to potential suitors.

Oh, but if there'd been anything—*anything!*—else to occupy his mind, Driegan was reasonably certain he'd have been in a better and more forgiving mood. But the rain continued to come down, without cessation or mercy, as if it bore a grudge against everything under the clouds and wanted only to see it all washed away or forever submerged. Perhaps it betokened the end of the world. Or perhaps it was simply evidence of a lovers' quarrel between Mahnus and Alheria; who could say?

Desperate for anything positive, Driegan stood in his stirrups, spying the path ahead and praying the hoped-for shelter would at last appear. Instead, the land ahead had gone silver in every direction. "Damn!" Driegan spat. They were marching into a Mahnus-cursed flood, and the gods alone knew how wide or deep it might be. Angry, weary, and out of answers, Driegan turned his horse about, faced his men, and said, "There's no going forward, not unless you've got gills."

The men knew better than to show any sign of annoyance at this development, but Qansip lived by different rules and so let out a shriek of frustration as she leapt from her palanquin.

"Do you mean you've marched us all this way for nothing?" she yelled at her father.

"These things happen," Driegan answered coldly, "especially in winter."

"They don't happen to *me!*"

"Now they do," Driegan smirked.

"How are you going to fix this situation?"

Driegan took a deep breath, looked off into the rain to gather his thoughts. "I don't see that we've got any choice but to march back the way we came until other options present themselves."

"Repeat the same misery we've just endured? Are you mad?" Qansip, drenched as a water rat, was anything but handsome now. And her behavior? Gods, her value was dropping by the moment.

A black, unholy feeling suddenly suffused Driegan's being, and he sensed he was about to abandon all parental duties if he couldn't make the girl shut up. "What would you have me do?" he asked in a threatening voice.

"Why," Qansip scoffed, "you might send someone into the water, in attempt to ford it."

It was an idiotic suggestion. Driegan said, "Fine. Get back into your palanquin, and you and your bearers can try."

The mere notion was infuriating to Qansip, but she was too proud to back down from her father's challenge. "Good!" she snapped. "I'll be happy to show you and your men what courage looks like."

Driegan was seconds from striking the girl, when she wheeled away and climbed back into her palanquin. From within, she commanded, "Take us into the nearest water!"

Her bearers looked at one another helplessly and then to their master, but Driegan's expression remained stony and unyielding. Absent other options, the men lifted the palanquin and began to trudge towards the flood.

The rest of the company watched the proceedings with dread. This was one of those lamentable rows that only happen in families, a power struggle over who was right and who would ultimately apologize, everyone knowing all the while that neither side would budge until it was too late, until lasting damage had been done. It was a time-honored if dishonorable tradition, and what happened next was as predictable, as inevitable as nightfall.

As the bearers worked their way into the freezing surge, walking gingerly in order to find the best footing, the two on the far side slipped. Maybe the ones in back had been pressing too hard, or maybe there'd been an unseen drop-off. Whatever the case, all four bearers tumbled into the water, dropping their load as they fought to avoid drowning. To the surprise of those onshore, the palanquin rolled from side to side a little, but eventually settled in amongst the waves and began to sail away on the current. The men in the water bellowed, gasped and begged for rescue—their armor being unconducive to swimming—whilst Qansip shrieked and howled in dismay at her still-gathering plight. Too late, too late, Driegan commanded more men into the water to save the bearers and capture the palanquin, but they managed none of that: the bearers disappeared in the water's depths, and the palanquin rapidly vanished in the rain.

In less time than it takes to change one's stockings, Driegan had lost four porters and his daughter.

Mendis and his Legions, Nespharia

The castle at the heart of Nespharia stood at the end of a long finger of granite, a treacherous causeway, that climbed up from the city below and rose to dizzying heights, beyond the reach of war machines, conventional weapons, or fire. Any army attempting to take the castle would eventually be forced to storm the causeway, leaving itself vulnerable to endless bombardments from above. When the drawbridge was up, a great chasm yawned between the end of the causeway and the castle, and, to make matters worse, there was scant room for an army to assemble should it reach this point.

With a substantial advantage in numbers, the Emperor's forces eventually took the city. The Nespharians fought valiantly and with great courage, but they simply hadn't the resources or experience of the Imperial troops. They slowed the invaders, but could not stop them. The castle, however, was another matter entirely and remained just beyond Mendis' grasp. He could barely look up at it without getting angry.

"I cannot believe and will not accept that we're unable to take it!" he yelled at his closest advisors. "What have our miners got to say?"

A short, stocky fellow in dirt-crusted leathers stepped forward. "That there's the hardest damned rock that ere I've tunneled into. Even with blasting powder or magic, it's slow to cooperate."

"Slow to cooperate, is it?" the Emperor repeated. "Double—no, *triple*—your crews. Keep at it 'round the clock. If nothing else, the clamor will keep those bastards up top from having a good night's sleep."

"Magnificence," the man said, bowing out of the Emperor's presence.

"And what *about* magic?" Mendis demanded of his wizards.

It was Alsig who spoke. "A number of possibilities present themselves. The castle seems warded against hostile Jumping, but we should be able to fly in from above."

"The danger, of course, being that our troops might be seen and thus shot from the sky," Mendis said.

"Just so."

"Unless you've got some means to conceal them."

"To most people, yes. Not to other wizards—and their... *Shapers*...are fiendishly resourceful."

Mendis continued to stare up at the castle. "Can we not fly something else in, like flaming balls of pitch? A plague of insects? Disease-riddled corpses?"

The wizard absentmindedly fiddled with the rings of his left hand. "An immense cloud of poison might work."

"And what is the effect of this poison?"

Alsig seemed confused by the question. "Why, death, Magnificence."

Mendis gave a short grunt of exasperation. "Of course. But on what scale? Does it infallibly kill everyone?

"Ah!" the wizard beamed. "Yes, well, there are many different types of poison that might serve our turn. But perhaps instead of killing them, we could sicken everyone up there, incapacitate them, and then fly in some soldiers when the cloud disperses."

"And then what, imprison the lot?" Mendis asked. "To what purpose?"

Alsig was briefly taken aback by this question, but recovered quickly. "I would never second-guess your decisions, Magnificence. I simply thought if you chose to be merciful, it might weaken this city's last few pockets of resistance."

The Emperor nodded. "Yes, I'd considered that. But I believe I need to make an example of this city, so the next isn't as stubborn.

I showed mercy at High Ceremore; now I prefer to demonstrate my more punitive side. Tell your brothers I want four of our Dread Knights flown up there and dropped inside the walls. They should be largely immune to anything that's shot at them, and I believe the subsequent screams of their victims will cow anyone in the lower city who still thinks to defy me."

It was a large city, and though the Emperor's troops enveloped it, there were still many places to hide. The natives predictably launched sneak attacks from these hidden sanctuaries. Once they understood that the Emperor could be more ruthless than they, their resolve, Mendis hoped, would crumble like the city's defenses.

As per his custom, Mendis and his officers had secured a large, well-situated home as their base of operations. The sun had set and the weather was taking a turn for the worse, so the Emperor decided to spend the rest of the evening indoors. A nice fire and some mulled wine would go a long way towards easing his worries and soothing his homesickness. Yes, he was the most powerful man in the world (though he supposed other men might have believed the same of themselves), but that was small comfort on a wet winter evening when his wife and children were half a world away and beyond communication. He was risking a great deal in this effort to expand his influence, cement his legacy and destroy Wykkerian once and for all. He hoped his sons would be proud; he hoped his ancestors would be proud.

When he entered the house, he stalked straight to the fireplace and plunked himself down in a chair. It wasn't the room's best chair, but at the moment he was too tired to care. Its proximity to the fire was all that really mattered. "Mulled wine!" he called out. He wasn't particular about which of his servants or officers responded to this order, he just wanted it met as quickly and efficiently as possible. Within five minutes, he had his boots off, his feet up, a warm mug of wine between his hands, and his eyes closed. Gradually, he became aware of an uncanny silence pervading the room, so he opened his eyes again to see what the reason was.

An ancient, nearly crook-backed woman stood before him, leaning on a cane.

The Emperor sat up immediately. "How did you..." He looked about and was unnerved to discover that all of his attendants and officers were nowhere to be seen. "You're one of their Shapers, I take it."

The old woman smiled, or anyway he *thought* it was a smile. "You could say that."

This was a dangerous moment, Mendis knew. To be cornered by an enemy wizard or witch without hope of rescue could mean death. "And what do you want?" he demanded, struggling to maintain a confident façade.

"I've come to ask you that very thing. You've invaded my continent and attacked my allies. I don't imagine you've no interest in conquering my country and capital."

Slowly and with studied calm, Mendis took a sip of his wine. "Ah. The Virgin Queen in person."

"The same," Alheria said, nodding ever-so-slightly.

Mendis cleared his throat, sat up straighter still. "May I offer you some mulled wine?"

"Thank you, no," the Queen replied.

Suddenly, the Emperor had a stunning realization. "You speak my language without magic or accent." He thought he saw a sly look cross the old woman's face for an instant, but it was gone before he was certain. "How is that?"

"I would rather you answered my earlier question than dicker over ancient history: what is it you hope to accomplish in these lands?"

Mendis was uncharacteristically torn: he wanted to stand, to use his relative height to his advantage in this conversation, but on the other hand, he was loathe to surrender his position of comfort, which gave him higher status than his uninvited guest. It was also considered polite to stand in the presence of a lady, but, again, she was not entirely welcome. In the end, he chose to remain seated. "That is yet to be determined. I came here looking for someone, your Tarmun Vykers, as I gather he's called. But I find I covet your land and resources as well."

"If you covet your life, you will leave my land and resources alone. As for Vykers, well, I'll let him speak for himself."

"Can you tell me where he's to be found?"

The Queen offered a surprisingly hearty laugh for a woman her age, whatever *that* was. "I am not his keeper, alas. It's all I can do to manage him whenever he's around."

"And yet you've penetrated my wizards' defenses," Mendis countered. "What else have we to say to one another?"

The old woman straightened up and fixed her host with a meaningful stare. "Just this: there is a mad god loose in my land, in the guise of a man named Long Pete. If you happen to run across him, I would recommend you kill him immediately. Burn his body and spread his ashes over as wide an area as possible. I will know if you've succeeded. Do this, and I will bring you the Reaper in chains. Fail to kill this Long Pete, and he will be the wrack and ruin of your empire."

"A god, you say?" Mendis asked, inwardly shaken.

"A mad god," the Queen repeated.

Before the Emperor could ask for clarification, his guest disappeared. In a flash, he leapt to his feet and called out for his attendants, who came running with looks of alarm on their faces. "Send for my wizards!" Mendis shouted. "All of them."

Yendor, Spirk & Co, Southshore District, Lunessfor

They'd been to three shops and had yet to find an Alchemist worthy of the name, according to Spirk's "magic feelings." They were walking along Canal Street, though, when the young Shaper practically jumped out of his shoes.

"There!" he yelped, pointing at an old, condemned fish monger's shop in the front of a larger building.

Yendor and Ron shared skeptical expressions, but Spirk barged right up to the crumbling pile and laid his face against the peeling paint of its exterior.

"In here!" he declared a little too loudly for his companions' comfort. "Fella we're lookin' for is in here."

Ron put his hand to the door handle but found it locked.

"No problem," Spirk said, "I can…"

The door opened, and a raspy voice from within urged, "Come in and be quick about it, then."

"I don't know as I like…" Yendor began, but Spirk had

already crossed the threshold. With a sigh, he patted Ron on the shoulder and followed the younger man inside.

"'S dark in here!" Spirk announced. "I can..."

"Don't!" the raspy voice ordered. "I will adjust the light, if needs must."

Yendor had a secret of his own, though. As he lifted the patch over his missing eye, he was able to see through the blackness, a side-effect or gift from the magic elixir he'd once imbibed. On the far side of the room, a bald man in dark robes was hiding an apparently armless fellow below the counter. He pushed atop the man's head and urged him down, out of sight, before turning his attention to his visitors.

A small circle of light appeared over the bald man's face, managing to capture only his eyes and forehead. "What is it you want?" the man snapped.

"We're lookin' for the best Alchemist in Lunessfor!" Spirk responded jovially.

The light dipped lower on the man's face, revealing a contemptuous scowl. "You're a Shaper, aren't you? Proof, as if any were needed, that your art requires no intelligence."

Spirk frowned himself, and looked about as if someone had broken wind. "I don't understand."

"Of course you don't. And I can't imagine you have anything of interest to say to me."

Yendor had had enough. "Then you ain't half as smart as you think you are." He crossed over to the counter, presented the pot in which the elixir had been, and poured exactly one drop on the counter.

The Alchemist, for that is what Spirk had essentially proclaimed him to be, pursed his lips and said, "There does seem to be..."

Before he could touch it, Yendor covered the drop with his own hand.

"Something unusual there," the Alchemist continued.

Yendor barked out a laugh. "You got no idea."

Spirk and Ron drew up alongside him, looking expectantly into the Alchemist's eyes.

"And what is it you propose?" the man responded irritably.

"I am a busy man, and I don't have time for mindless japes or endless negotiations. If there's something you wish from me, spit it out."

Spirk was about to speak when Yendor gestured for him to hold his tongue. "Just this," the older man told the Alchemist, "You make us...a hundred barrels of this stuff, and we'll let you keep the recipe and whatever you make for yourself."

The Alchemist stared back, unamused. "You imbeciles are wasting my time."

"I didn't mean a hundred all at once; I meant over time. We'll take one, for starters."

"You'll take none. Good day." The Alchemist turned his back, eager to return to whatever business he'd been about when Yendor and his friends entered.

"The Reaper himself loves this stuff, but you can't be bothered, eh?"

At the mention of the Reaper, the Alchemist straightened up and turned slowly back in Yendor's direction. "The Reaper, is it?"

Yendor stuck out his chin and sneered at the other man. "I said so, didn't I?"

"Move your hand," the Alchemist instructed, "and let us see what we've got here."

It was amazing, really, how many little experiments the Alchemist could perform on a single drop of liquid, but after an hour's effort, he finally proclaimed, "I am willing to...negotiate."

"And I gotta piss," Spirk responded.

The Alchemist was momentarily thrown by this comment until Yendor said, "Go outside, then, will ya? We're conductin' business here!"

Once Spirk was safely out of earshot, the Alchemist gazed at Yendor and said, "An idiot Shaper? That's normally an oxymoron, but in this case, just a moron."

"Yeah, well, just don't get in his way!" Ron blurted out, feeling the need to say something in defense of his closest friend.

"I'll try my best," the Alchemist said condescendingly. "Now," he addressed Yendor, "assuming you allow me to work with whatever's left in that pot of yours, I may be able to reproduce its contents within a fortnight."

"Too long," Yendor protested.

"Well," the Alchemist countered with a self-satisfied smirk, "I'm afraid there's no one else in Lunessfor capable of doing this job. Ask around, you'll see." As Yendor was taking too long to mull it over, the Alchemist added, "But I may be able to produce something in a week's time. If I'm lucky."

Yendor placed the pot on the counter. "Then be lucky," he growled. "And don't try anything stupid; I got friends in low places."

"Undoubtedly."

Back outside the shop, Yendor and Ron ran into Spirk, climbing up from the river.

"Did ya piss in the river?"

"I pissed a river in the river."

The next several minutes were tortured with the very lowest brand of humor any trio of men had ever manufactured. If Rem had been with them, he'd have died of shame. Inevitably, though, Yendor got down to business.

"What we need now's a hideout, a place to meet, sleep n' plan without bein' seen or bothered by anyone else. You think you can find such a place?"

"I can try," Spirk replied.

"Do," Yendor commanded. "And maybe we can have a few drinks while we're waitin'."

Aoife, In her Bower

Aoife spent more and more time in a dream-state, an eldritch netherworld from which she could watch, feel and hear everything that occurred anywhere in the actual world, and it occurred to her that she found more to savor in the eruption of a seed, the blossoming of a flower, than she'd ever known in her fellow humans—her *former* fellows, for whatever Aoife had become, she was definitely no longer of their number. She could not help but follow Vykers' escapades, but the rest of humanity held increasingly little interest for her. They were at war again. Again! And it seemed the only thing in which men excelled was destruction. Did it really matter which side won this latest conflict? As long as they left the greenwood out of it, they could tear each other to pieces if they liked.

But there was Vykers, in many ways the very worst of men. How was it possible that she still cared for him, cared anything *about* him? Aoife searched the world's forests, its meadows, its deserts, mountains and jungles. Nowhere could she find the answer to this troubling conundrum. Who or what was Vykers that she should care for him? Could the forest love the wildfire?

Aoife slept, and in that moment, days went by.

She reached out with her thoughts and found her old friend, Toomt'-La, sleeping in his glade. His mind and hers embraced, exchanged what pleasantries and news they could, and disengaged as Aoife's thoughts flew onwards. Where was Vykers, where was her Reaper? What new catastrophes had the willful beast brought about?

Vykers, Amongst the Sholdorn

He'd had enough. "Normally folks who laugh at me end up scoopin' their entrails off the floor."

The Great Woman and her companions eyed him sternly. "Your short-temperedness is legendary, Reaper, but in this case, misplaced. I was not laughing at you, but rather marveling at something I don't fully understand."

"My age."

"Yes."

"Well, out with it then!" Vykers shouted, exasperated. "How old d'you think I am?"

Instead of answering immediately, the Great Woman snapped her fingers in Ji Nan's direction, and the other woman produced a small, ornate box from within her robes. The third woman, Vykers' alleged granddaughter, frowned as if she'd been left out of the joke. Clearly, she knew nothing of the box's contents. The Great Woman received the box and set it carefully on the table in front of her. She then opened it and took out a fragment of stone or pottery about the size of a man's hand. She examined it in silence briefly, and then said, "This is a piece of a fresco or mural." She slid it gently in Vykers direction and waited for his response.

Vykers had to stand and lean well over the table to reach the piece, but he opted not to look at it until he'd returned to his seat. When he finally did, he felt more confused than ever. The fragment featured an excellent likeness of him from the waist-up, beheading an enemy in battle. "So?" he asked the Great Woman.

"You recognize the subject?"

"O' course. But that don't prove anything."

"Would it surprise you to learn that this artifact predates the Great Awakening?"

Surprise him? It was the single-most astonishing thing he'd ever heard. "How do you know that?"

The two older women looked at one another before the Great Woman answered. "We Sholdorn have been collecting artifacts since then. This was one of the first things we found and has been in our possession for more than three thousand years."

Again, Vykers leapt to his feet. "That's bullshit!" he raged. "Three thousand years? D'you take me for an idiot?"

Ji Nan backed away from Vykers' fury, and the younger woman put a hand on her sword, but the Great Woman simply spread her hands out on the table top and waited.

Vykers tossed a chair aside, smashed a second one. "Stupidest. Fuckin'. Lie I've ever heard!"

"Really?" the Great Woman asked calmly. "What do you recall of your parents?"

"Nothin'," Vykers snapped. "I never think about 'em."

"Try."

Just a week or so earlier, Vykers had been willing to believe himself the reincarnation of Mahnus. But to be told he had a god's lifespan without a god's power? That was no gift, it was a prison sentence. Unthinkable. "My memory ain't the best. What of it?"

It was some time before the Great Woman answered. Finally, she asked, "Do you remember Hesh-Tu?"

Vykers winced internally, though his exterior remained stony. He remembered the name…but little else.

"They say," the Great Woman continued, "that she was your all and everything."

The Reaper said nothing.

"Then, do you recall the Daemite King who killed her?"

A deep and gnawing sorrow took Vykers then, and he threw himself back down in his chair, his face in his hands. "Tell me no more," he insisted. "On your life, tell me no more."

Quietly, the Great Woman ushered her companions out of the room and followed them. The sound of the door shutting behind her was barely louder than Vykers' own breathing. He tested the edges of his memory like a child picking at a scab, and he understood there were things he could not remember, but also things he *chose* not to remember. Yes, there had been a Hesh-Tu, just as there'd been a Hobnail. But parents? Brothers and sisters? He could not summon a single name or face no matter how hard he tried. When he opened his eyes again, it was dark in the room and darker outside the windows. Somehow, he'd fallen asleep.

"Woman!" Vykers called.

The door reopened, and a hand appeared, holding a candle. Right behind it was the Great Woman herself. "What have you decided?"

"I'm hungry, for starters. You got any food and drink hereabouts, or do you women live on good thoughts and daisies?"

The Great Woman snickered. "You've recovered your humor, I see."

"If little else."

"I'll send for dinner."

Vykers watched the woman from the darkness on his side of the room. "Are there more pieces o' that mural?"

The Great Woman drew nearer and examined the Reaper in the candlelight. "Didn't the Historian tell you?"

"What now?" Vykers groaned.

"The majority of it is still intact...in the Emperor's palace, across the sea."

Long, At Zillia's Cave

As soon as he forced his way through the invisible wall at the cave's mouth, Long saw a bright flash and felt himself thrown through the air and back out into the snow. *So, that's how it's gonna be!* Long picked himself up and pushed through the barrier again, narrowly avoiding a second blast.

"Who dares enter my home against my will?" a voice shouted.

Long had put up with enough. "Mahnus, the god!" he yelled back. "And if you know what's good for you…"

A third blast bounced him off the invisible wall and set his great coat aflame. "Stop!" Long commanded…and damned if his attacker didn't obey immediately. Nothing further came from the darkness within the cave's mouth, so the captain illuminated the area with a thought, revealing a squat but broadly built giantess of a sort he couldn't remember having seen before. Of course, his thoughts flew to Mardine, but he quickly dismissed them as detrimental to his purpose.

"I'm looking for my daughter," he explained.

But the giantess did not respond. In fact, she didn't so much as blink. Long had frozen her, paralyzed her in mid-gesture. He was about to undo the spell when he realized that it would be easier for him to find and talk with Esmine if the giantess were not in his way.

Forging deeper into the cave, he came upon a number of wolverines, all in attack posture and every bit as immobile as their mistress, if their mistress she was.

"Zillia?" a familiar voice sang out from farther within cave. *Esmine!* The sound of her voice brought emotion welling up in his chest, and he fought back an involuntary sob. How he'd missed her! How he dreaded the conversation to come!

"Auntie Zilly?"

Passages branched off to the left and right, but Long felt the correct direction in his bones. He could sense Esmine's exact location and somehow knew precisely how he'd find her. Rounding a corner, yes, he saw her, sitting on the edge of a bubbling hot spring and idly splashing away with her feet. God though he was, Long could no longer stop the tears from coming as he rushed into his daughter's presence.

"Daddy!" She leapt up and raced into his arms, every bit as overcome as he.

In that moment, Long felt, despite everything, like the luckiest man in the world. And yet he was greedy for more. If only Mardine were there, too. If only she'd accept him—the *new* him—into the family. But he knew his wife: in matters of family, hers was an iron will, much stronger than his. Long held Esmine at arm's length, studying her face, memorizing its smallest detail—the freckles across the bridge of her nose, the missing tooth in her smile, the little scar across her left eyebrow that she'd gotten from a bad fall a couple of years earlier.

"Where have you been, daddy?" she asked, and "Is mama coming, too?"

Long couldn't remember ever hearing his daughter speak so well, but then he hadn't seen her in ages. In his absence, she'd kept growing. "Life goes on," they say, and how right they were! Rather than answer Esmine immediately, Long ran his hand through her hair, wiped a tear from her left cheek with the thumb of his right hand.

"Mama is coming," he smiled sadly. "And soon! That's what I've come to tell you, love."

"And then we'll all be together again!"

For a god, he had a lamentable lack of prescience. "Uh, well…sweetie, I have a little more travelin' to do still…" She didn't like this news, he could see, and he rushed to console her. "But mama will be here!"

"But I want…"

"Hush now, Esmine." He'd never imagined it could be so hard to communicate with his own child. "You and your mother…are all I truly care about in this life. You and your mother *are* my life."

Esmine grabbed onto Long's coat and pulled him close. "Are you in trouble, daddy? I'll protect you…"

And Long understood then that if he didn't leave soon, he'd never leave, come what may. "Sweetie," he said, "is there a…I mean, did you see a…little man hereabouts?"

The sudden change of subject baffled Esmine for a moment, but she finally said "Auntie Zilly put him in a cage. Is he bad?"

Long hugged his daughter, lost himself in the smell of her hair. "No, sweet, he's…he's a friend. Show me where he is?"

Taking his hand, Esmine led her father through a labyrinth of caves, most of which were lit by galaxies of glowing stones in their floors, walls and ceilings. Long wondered how the cave's owner had found the place or if, instead, she'd fashioned it with magic. Whatever the case, it was an impressive and lovely home for his wife and daughter, if it came to that. In a central chamber with a long, low table, Esmine pointed out the cage in question, sitting on a large rock near the far wall.

Short Pete looked up immediately, and Long was shocked by the homunculus' transformation. No longer did he resemble the bundle of sticks from which he'd been made, but his skin had actually begun to look like skin, and his face, like a human face. *Gods*, Long gasped, *he's actually becoming his namesake.*

"Can you get me outta here?" His voice, though high-pitched and squeaky, sounded more like Short Pete's as well.

"Right away," said Long.

"Does he bite?" Esmine wanted to know.

"He'd never bite *you*," her father answered. In seconds, the homunculus was out of his prison, and Long knelt down beside his daughter again. He looked into her eyes, hoping he might forestall her tears. "My beautiful girl, I have to leave you now."

Esmine wept, anyway, as daughters will do when their fathers say goodbye.

"But I know you'll be happy and safe with your mother 'til I see you again," Long concluded.

Esmine clutched onto the folds of his blanket like a ship-wreck victim desperately hanging onto a storm-tossed barrel in an unforgiving sea. "You won't come back!" she cried. "I know it!"

Then, from the mouth of the cave, Mardine's voice: "Esmine! Esmine, sweetie! It's mama!"

Long had seen many things in his time and a number of miracles in recent days, but the speed with which his daughter's expression changed from despair to joy to uncertainty and back to joy was surely amongst the most astounding. Long took a good moment to watch his daughter disappear into the passageway, and then he grabbed Short Pete and Jumped away.

Mendis, in Nespharia

Mendis was not given to fits of rage—it was beneath his dignity as Emperor—but he could nurse a cold fury like no one else in the Empire, and as he sat at last in Nespharia's throne room, he made certain his wizards and his personal guard felt his displeasure. He was still reeling from the Virgin Queen's visit and the ease with which she had sauntered through his previously impenetrable defenses. When he'd demanded answers from his wizards, the most they'd been able to tell him was, "We are examining the issue, Magnificence." *Examining*? Bollocks! If the Queen had been an assassin...

And there was the other thing, the deal she'd offered him: Long Pete for Tarmun Vykers. Between the size of his host and the usually reliable might of his wizards, Mendis had no doubt he could locate this fugitive god. Could his forces kill the fellow, though? And would the Queen actually be able to deliver Wykkerian?

The Emperor's alternative was to continue as he'd been doing and risk another, less benevolent visitation from the Queen. Did he fear her? No one had ever been able to come upon him unawares before; that she had the power to do so was alarming, to say the least.

"Magnificence?" one of the wizards asked.

He'd reached a decision. "We find this god. The search will give us plenty of excuse to ransack the countryside and pillage to our hearts' content. We will be waging a very focused war under the guise of cooperating with the Queen's wishes. It may be possible to serve her needs and our own. And, of course, there's no reason we can't attack her capital once she's given us Wykkerian."

Mendis was rather pleased with himself and decided to put the Queen's visit behind him until his wizards had more to say on the subject. For the nonce, she would leave him alone, as long as he appeared to be upholding his end of their agreement. He had other things on his mind, besides. He wondered, for instance, what it was about this Long Pete god that bothered the Queen more than the Emperor's presence in her land or the threat of Treaman Wykkerian. Mendis had more mundane concerns, as well. The assault on Nespharia had wrought massive damage to the outer walls and burnt much of the lower city's inner core. The natives—those who had survived and chosen to stay—had become a wailing rabble. Should they be enslaved? Chased off? Killed? The Emperor landed on chasing them off, putting more stress on the Queen's resources and those of her allies, making these newly homeless irritants *her* problem rather than his. Mendis wanted to repair and fortify Nespharia, for it was the most pleasant and strategically constructed city he'd visited in this new land, and if he was destined to stay for any length of time, he wanted to be comfortable.

He walked to the nearest window and peered out at the city below. The last of the fires had been extinguished, and the rubble and bodies were already being cleared. Yes, with the magic and manpower at his disposal, Nespharia could be restored—improved, even—within weeks.

He'd show these native bastards what a real city looked like!

Vykers & Ona, On the Road

Vykers burst through the doors and into the street. "My horse!" he bellowed.

A voice at his back yelled, "I'm coming with you."

The Reaper glanced over his shoulder. It was that woman, Ona, his alleged granddaughter. "The hells!" he snarled. Vykers' mount appeared of its own volition, walking around the corner of a building down the street. "You'll never be able to keep up, anyway."

Ona grabbed Vykers' elbow and he stifled the urge to punch her in the face. "I'll ride behind you, on the same horse."

"You won't," the Reaper insisted.

Somehow, the woman got in front of him and said, "And I say I will, damn you!"

Vykers raised a hand in front of Ona's face, extended his claws. "You ride with me, you'll die," he said menacingly.

"I'm gonna die, anyway, you dumb bastard!"

Against his better instincts, the Reaper found himself liking the woman. "That's as may be," said he. "But it'll be a lot sooner and messier in my company."

"So be it," Ona replied. "You're the only kin I've got, and I ain't losing you."

He wanted to laugh in her face, shove her away. Instead, he climbed into his saddle and offered her a hand up. "You're no kin to me, girl," he assured her. "And you'll be glad of it, when I'm done with you."

"Call me 'girl' again, and I'll knock yer fuckin' teeth down yer throat."

Huh. Maybe she *was* kin to him, after all.

The Sholdorn, happy to see Vykers leaving, resupplied him and his companion with enough food and blankets to last weeks. The Reaper didn't plan on being on the road that long.

"Where are we headed?"

"Shit," Vykers complained. "You gonna talk my ears off?"

"Looks like your ears have seen enough grief lately. 'Sides, I'm just asking one question."

"Lunessfor, then, if it makes any difference." He thought she might have more questions, but she surprised him and remained silent.

Despite Vykers' magical mount, the journey to Lunessfor was a long one, and the Reaper needed a day or two to ruminate on his options, so he stopped to make camp. After battle, making and staring into a fire was probably Vykers' favorite activity. It seemed to clear his thoughts somehow, making it easier to plan and prepare for whatever he eventually decided upon. It also gave him time to digest everything he'd learned or been told in the city of the Sholdorn.

He stared through the flames at Ona, pretending he couldn't see past the fire. Why had he allowed her to come along? Could it be that he really believed this nonsense about her being his granddaughter? It was time to put an end to that charade.

"Who was your mother?" he asked abruptly.

Ona answered without looking up from her task, poking

the embers with a stick. "Bindri, Storyteller of the Sholdorn."

The name and title meant nothing to Vykers. "Never heard of her."

"Uh-huh."

"And besides," Vykers added, "you can't be more 'n ten years younger 'n me. I may be a bastard, but fatherin' a child at ten's too much even for me!"

"Yeah," Ona drawled, clearly unimpressed with his argument.

Instantly, Vykers' hackles were up. "What? You touched in the head, girl?"

Ona leapt to her feet. "I thought I told you not to call me that, old man!"

She never saw him coming. The next thing Ona knew, she was lying flat on her back, looking up at the darkened silhouette of the Reaper's head and shoulders as he straddled her waist.

"You try to rape me, and I'll tear your pecker off!"

Vykers slapped her face, hard. "This ain't no game, girl."

Even though he knew it was coming, he was nonetheless surprised when she kneed him in the groin. She was almost as fast as he!

She rolled away into the darkness and came up brandishing her knife.

Vykers flew to his feet and walked towards her, trying to ignore the pain in his balls. "You can't be my granddaughter; you're too fuckin' stupid."

"I would think that's the best proof there is!" she threw back.

"You let me bring you out here, middle o' East Bumblefuck, and there's no one to answer your cries for help? Stupid." He could hear her breathing hard, defiantly.

"Who said I want help?"

Yes, he could kill her. But that wouldn't answer any of his questions. "So, your dam's a storyteller..."

"Was. She's dead."

"Who was your *grand*mother?"

"Chrila."

"Chrila the what?"

"The woman."

"Never heard of her, either. And you know you can't kill me with that knife, right?"

Ona lowered her hand. "I know," she said quietly.

"Then stop pretending you got any say in what's goin' on." Vykers wandered back around to his side of the fire and returned to his seat. "Chrila, huh? And how old are you?"

"Twenty-three," Ona said sullenly, going back to her own side of the fire.

"I think I'd remember if I'd ever poked a Sholdorn woman."

"Unless there's something wrong with your memory," Ona responded. It was said in such an offhand way, but it hit Vykers like a mailed fist. There *was* something wrong with his memory.

He said nothing more for hours, but continued to watch Ona through the flames, and it was true that she resembled him, true that she shared some of his mannerisms and behaviors. "Even if we're kin—and I'm not sayin' we are—I got nothin' for you but a violent death," he said at evening's end. "If any o' that sounds good to you, you're crazier 'n me."

It was raining like all hells in Lunessfor, but it was the kind of city that looked impressive under any circumstances, and Vykers was glad to see it again. He reined his horse to a stop whilst the city was still a child's toy on the horizon and suddenly took a great interest in the creature's mane.

"What is it?" Ona asked, anxious to reach the shelter promised by Lunessfor.

"I don't trust that bitch!"

"The Great Woman?"

Vykers barked out a laugh. "Not that bitch, the other one: The Virgin Hag."

"Why?"

"Long story," said Vykers. "Anyway, I got a job for you…"

It was midday when Ona approached the main gate. She'd never seen, much less been inside Lunessfor, and she was almost overwhelmed at its size and splendor. Even its filth was superlative she thought, as she gazed at a faded bouquet of flowers in the gutter. Vykers had instructed her to tell the guards she was looking to help in the city's defense, but simple plans rarely come off simply.

"You're a big girl, aren't you?" one of the men asked.

Ona bristled at his use of her least-favorite word, but endeavored to focus on getting through the gates. "I'm just here to help."

"I've not heard that accent before," the second man said. "Where you from, then?"

Well, that was a problem. Folks were prejudiced against the Sholdorn, and she didn't really look the part, either. "Down south. Little shithole you never heard of."

The second man guffawed. "I don't doubt it."

"And you say you're here to help?" the first repeated skeptically.

She glared back at him. "I can handle a sword. Besides, the capital's the safest place in a storm, no?"

"Or it might be you're just trying to beat the rush o' refugees."

"Leave off, Narms. She looks more 'n capable o' bashin' in a few invaders' heads. We can use more like her."

And she was in.

The harder part was navigating the city's streets. It took her most of the day to find the neighborhood in which Vykers and his former slaves had last lived. The Reaper wasn't sure if his men occupied the same lodgings, so he instructed Ona to find a prominent street corner and stand and wait. Eventually, he knew, the Red Knight's keen eye and curiosity would bring him out of hiding.

But 'eventually' can be a long wait. The sun went down and a cold drizzle started. Ona couldn't help wondering if this whole thing was a set-up, a test of her determination. Maybe Vykers was leagues and leagues away by now, laughing his ass off at her expense. Still, she waited. By sunrise, she was soaking wet, sore, and miserable. Her brain was in such a fog of fatigue that she barely noticed the man watching her from the opposite corner, a man dressed in red armor.

"Vykers sent me," she rasped.

"Follow me," the man responded, with an accent even more strange than her own.

And was this another test? An ambush, perhaps? Suddenly, Ona was wide awake, seeing everything around herself with a renewed clarity. She followed the man, but made sure she noticed every possible weapon, every possible avenue of escape.

He led her down an alley between ancient buildings and up a rickety flight of stairs at the back of the one on her left. She was almost willing to suffer an ambush if it meant getting out of the Mahnus-cursed wet. The top of the stairs revealed a lone door, at which her guide knocked whilst saying something in a language unfamiliar to Ona. The man—the being—who answered the door could not have been more unexpected if Ona had been under the influence of Wildside Mushrooms. He was quite tall, filled the doorway, and his skin was darker than the darkest wood.

The Ntambi warrior, for his part, regarded Ona with almost as much surprise.

Yendor, Rem & Co, Lunessfor

A freshly cleaned, shaved, massaged and wenched Remuel Wratch sauntered into the Fretful Porpentine like a cat waking from a nap, loosely and languidly. The main room was as crowded and grungy as ever and, in the far corner, Rem's mates were ensconced in their usual chairs.

"Rem!" Spirk cried, as enthusiastic as ever.

Yendor barely lifted his face off the table top, and even Ron was pretty well into his cups.

"You look good," Spirk observed.

"I feel it, too."

"'S the word?" Yendor breathed.

"On my way here, I happened to see Vykers' Red Knight out recruiting. Leastways, it looked like recruiting. The lass he was talking to didn't look the soft and cuddly type."

"What's that to us?"

"I don't know," Rem said. "But it looks like the Reaper might be getting ready to move again."

"So?" Yendor prompted.

"In case we wanted to follow him…" But Rem's statement

met blank expressions from Spirk and Ron, and Yendor could barely keep his eye open.

"We got other plans," Yendor managed at last.

Rem shoved an unconscious man out of a nearby chair, pulled it up to Yendor's table, and squeezed himself in between his fellows. "Do tell."

"We're takin' over the city's ale supplies," Spirk announced proudly.

"Shush, boy!" Yendor barked. "Don't be sharin' that at the top o' your lungs. In fact, don't be sharin' that at all. Let me decide who's in and who's out."

Rem scanned the crowd to see if anyone had heard Spirk's comment, but of course no one revealed anything. "I don't understand," he whispered to Yendor.

"'Simple," the one-eyed man responded. "We're bein' invaded, which means a siege is comin', and when it gets here, we wanna be in charge o' the liquor. That way, we'll always have some, and we'll bring in obscene profits."

Rem had not doubt about the obscene part. "So, this is where you want to spend the war? On your butts, trapped in Lunessfor?"

"Better 'n bein' out front. Trust me, I done both."

This was not what Rem had hoped or expected of his friends, but in Long's absence, it seemed their goals were a good deal less lofty. "What about you?" he asked Spirk.

"We'll we're makin' more o' that magic drink we got underground!"

"Alheria's fiery bush, lad! Am I gonna hafta remove yer tongue?" Yendor barked. "Whisper or say nothin' at all." And with that tremendous effort, Yendor passed out.

Rem watched him for several moments, and then whispered to the young Shaper. "What were you saying about the magic drink?"

Spirk took his turn surveying the room before answering in a most melodramatic whisper. "We found a nalchemiss who can make it for us. And…" he trailed off, embarrassed.

"Yes?"

"I kinda need it. Burnin's been gettin' real bad o' late. I

prob'ly don't go a single candle without hurtin'.'"

The actor put a gentle hand on his friend's shoulder. "I'm sorry to hear that. It must be...it must be a difficult burden to bear."

"Yeah," Spirk confessed. "And I don't like bears, neither."

"Uh, yes," said Rem. "But what do cornering the ale market and magic elixir have to do with one another?"

Spirk staggered to his feet, swayed once or twice, and then took Rem by the hand. The Shaper looked around furtively and then said, "Come out back, 'n I'll show ya."

Long, In the Woods

The instant he Jumped away, Long thought better of it. Why not stay and have it out with Mardine? He might win! He might convince her. They could all live in that cave forever, safe from the madness of the outside world. Or not. Alheria herself had killed him once, so she said. If that was true, what was to keep her from trying again? Unless and until he had an answer for that, Long couldn't return to Esmine's cave. It was too great a risk.

There was also the issue of the map Short Pete had stolen, a map that detailed secret ways in and out of Lunessfor. Long wouldn't object to anyone killing Her Majesty—turnabout is fair play, after all—but he did have friends in the city, or so he supposed, and he didn't believe everyone deserved to die for Alheria's treachery.

Short Pete, still in Long's grasp, shouted up at his master. "Getting a little tight down here!"

At which pronouncement, the captain dropped him immediately. "Sorry, I was just thinking..."

"There's your first mistake."

"I need to get a message to Yendor and the lads, but I can't chance a visit to Lunessfor."

"So, bring 'em here," Short said, matter-of-factly.

"Short, you're a genius!"

"Took you long enough to figure that out," the homunculus complained.

But Long was no longer focused on him. Instead, he'd closed his eyes and was mumbling, "Come to me, come to me, come to me," over and over.

There was a now-familiar whooshing sound, and suddenly Spirk and Rem stood before him, looking utterly mystified.

"Long!" Spirk yelled in glee, as he wrapped his old friend in a powerful hug.

"Spirk!" Long reciprocated. "Good to see you!"

"Get off me!" Short screamed, from beneath Rem's foot, causing the actor to leapt sideways in alarm.

"What in the infinite hells?" Rem cried.

"It's Short Pete!" said Spirk. "And *really* short, now. Where'd he come from?"

Everyone looked down at Short, and from thence to Long. Finally, Long said "I made him, right? But that's not why I brought you here."

"Yeah," Spirk interjected, "how did you..."

"Never mind. I need you to take this map to Yendor..."

Rem shook his head. "He's back to his old habits, I'm afraid."

"Is he? Kittins, then! Find Kittins, and give him this map. Tell him I stole it from the Emperor's army."

"I stole it!" Short objected.

"But I..." Rem began, before Long sent his friends away again.

"Thank Mahnus!" Short sighed. "I thought those two would talk my ears off."

"Yes," Long grumbled, "thank Mahnus."

Qansip, Adrift

She felt like a captive on a dragon's back, forced to ride along wherever the great beast, the river, chose to travel. Its terrible breath was damp and frigid, leaching into her very bones; its voice was alternately hypnotic and thunderous, making sleep a dangerous risk when watchfulness was her best hope of survival. Should she leap from this dragon's back? No, she thought, the fall would kill her, for she had never learned how to swim. Swimming, as everyone knew, was for the common folk, those who worked with their hands, sweating and grunting like animals. And Qansip was not an animal. Thus, she cowered in the least-flooded corner of her palanquin, hoping against hope that her unlikely vessel would survive long enough to deliver her from her captor's clutches.

The relentless rain was not favorable to such fantasies, however, and it was all Qansip could do to avoid adding her own tears to the deluge. What in Alheria's name had she done to deserve such a fate? And what could she do to appease the goddess? Did anyone, anywhere still pray to the gods? As she didn't know how to start, she decided against it altogether. Anyway, her teeth were chattering from the damp and cold.

Inadvertently, she thought of her father. While theirs had never been a storybook relationship, she'd always believed her father loved her. Surely, he would find a way to follow and rescue her from her plight. Then again, it was his fault she was in such peril in the first place. It would serve him right if she drowned...or was captured by river pirates—if there was such a thing. She frightened herself just thinking about it.

She pushed her curtains aside, hoping to find herself closer to one bank or the other, and noted instead that the river had widened considerably. Eventually, there had to be other boats on the water—ships, even. Someone would find her before she froze or starved to death. Perhaps the storm was keeping everyone ashore?

She woke up hours later, amazed that she'd even fallen asleep, and saw that night had come. It didn't seem possible and it certainly wasn't fair, but things kept getting worse and worse. In her misery, she huddled back under her blankets and returned to fitful sleep.

Driegan, On the Road

He wasn't much of a father; he knew that. Most of the time, he didn't care. But to think that he might have lost Qansip because of his own stubbornness and short temper was almost more than he could bear. At the very least, a man should be able to control his baser emotions, particularly when they got in the way of family...and profit. Well, the solution was simple—to conceive if not execute: he had to find his daughter, whatever the cost.

He'd no need to notify his men, of course, because they followed him wherever he went; that was their job. Most of them, he figured, had already concluded that Driegan would spare no effort to find his daughter, which was just as well, and if they attributed all this to a father's love, so much the better. In the mud and misery of life on the road, sympathy often inspired more loyalty than mere money ever could. His men might abandon him at the first 'better offer' to come along, but if they believed him to be a loving and heart-sore patriarch, their father essentially, well, they were likely to stay a good deal longer and put up with a lot more grief. At least Driegan hoped that was the case. He was carrying a small fortune in gold and jewels about his person, but it needed to last for months, potentially.

He reined his horse—the only horse in his company—to a stop and studied the sky. It didn't look like the rain would ever cease, just as the months of snow before it had seemed endless and particularly brutal. What in Mahnus' name was going on in the heavens, anyway? If every season was to be its worst in ages, men might be best served to hole up in caves, away from the snow, rain and sun.

The men had begun to sit, and Driegan couldn't allow them to get too comfortable whilst there were still hours of daylight left in which to search for his daughter.

"No rest for the wicked," he joked. "Onward!"

Nobody laughed.

Beesmarch & Co., the Forest

They couldn't find Eoman, though they searched for two days and nights, wading into the icy water up and down both river banks and calling their king's name until they'd all lost their voices.

Beesmarch was distraught. He hadn't meant to kill his old friend. Hells, he didn't even want Eoman's crown. And he

certainly didn't want it said that he'd cheated to get it, that he'd
thrown that last punch when Eoman was suing for peace. What
could he say to the others, though? What would it matter, if they
failed to find Eoman alive?

The morning of the third day, the giants were gathered
'round an enormous fire, and Beesmarch noticed them all looking at him in silence.

"What?" he snapped.

"You're the king, now. What's next? Where do we go from
here?" One of the three Brothers asked.

Beesmarch tugged at the unruly hairs of his left eyebrow—
a habit in which he only indulged when nervous. There didn't
seem any point in arguing that Eoman was still alive; he'd have
returned if he had been.

"What was it you wanted to do instead of finding our kin?"
Another of the Brothers prompted.

"There was no 'instead of'," Beesmarch explained. "And now
that there's one less of us, it don't make as much sense. Anyway,"
he rumbled, "it seems meet we honor Eoman's last wishes."

"Oh, *now* you want to honor his wishes…" Whindas quipped
angrily.

Bees moved to strike him for the insult, but the Brothers
stepped between them. "This quest was about *bolsterin'* our
numbers, not whittling 'em down! No more blows between us!"
One brother said.

Bees and Whindas stood down and retreated to opposite
sides of the fire.

"Original plan, then: we search for more of our folk,"
Beesmarch mumbled, weary of it all.

Breaking camp and resuming the search for other giants
was one of the most difficult things Beesmarch had done in ages,
but his fellows called him king now and expected him to act the
part. Eoman had dreamed of reuniting giantkind and chasing
the invaders from the land. Beesmarch could think of nothing
better or more worthy at the moment.

But every stride, every mile, every league they traveled,
he imagined his companions staring knives at his back, wishing him ill for what he'd done. And he couldn't apologize. Not

enough anyway, and if not enough, why start? Why make himself look a mewling imbecile? He'd challenged Eoman fairly, the king had accepted his challenge, and fate had chosen its champion. Wherefore should he apologize?

Because Eoman had been his friend.

And it's one thing to take a friend's authority, but quite another to take his life.

Still, Beesmarch was too stubborn, too prideful to give voice to the hurt he felt or lament the hurt he'd caused. Grimacing at these thoughts, he hitched his pack higher upon his shoulders and quickened his pace.

The rest of the day was interminable, so bedeviled by regrets and second thoughts was the new king. Should he make everyone turn around, dedicate one last day to the search for Eoman? Should they leave someone behind, in case his old friend somehow turned up? Should Beesmarch be the one to stay behind? Could he abdicate his title and responsibilities, just chuck the whole lot whilst waiting for a miracle?

No; Bees was many things, but never a coward. He looked back at his companions; they were grieving, but not giving up. They continued to tread in his footsteps and would do, he didn't doubt, until a new king came along.

Late afternoon, they came across giant signs, little symbols etched into trees about twelve feet off the ground. If Eoman had still been leading the group, he'd have recognized the marks and could even have named the giant who'd made them. Beesmarch, alas, could not. Some king of the giants. But he *was* able to determine the etchings were relatively recent, so that their author might still be in the area. The news couldn't undo the damage, the loss they'd all experienced in the past two days, but the prospect of meeting another of their kind was heartening, nonetheless.

With a renewed sense of purpose, the giants pushed onward into the early evening when a horrible din arose from the far side of a distant hill. Beesmarch had his suspicions, and a glance at his mates told him they shared his thoughts. Without a word, they raced towards the hill, while the clamor behind it grew louder and more terrible.

A giant was bellowing in pain and rage.

Beesmarch abandoned any attempts at stealth or caution and barreled right up to the hill's crest. Before his companions reached his side, the new king let loose with a roar of his own and disappeared down the far slope. Whindas reached the hill-top next and froze in his tracks a moment, stunned by what he was seeing.

Not far from the hill's base, a group of some fifteen-to-twenty human soldiers was struggling with an unfamiliar giant they'd somehow managed to rope and chain. Whenever it seemed the prisoner might break free, one of the soldiers whipped him savagely across the face, neck and shoulders. As soon as Beesmarch made his presence known, however, the sol-diers dropped their chains and began to fall back. When they caught sight of Whindas and the Brothers, their careful retreat became a full-out sprint.

But giants have longer legs.

Beesmarch raced right past the new giant, now struggling to free himself from his bonds, and went after the humans like a hunting dog after a hare. Whindas stopped to help, but the Brothers joined their king in the chase. A couple of soldiers turned around and foolishly attempted to hold the king off with their swords, but Beesmarch bashed his way right through them and grabbed each man by his head, squeezing both like overripe plums. The juice they spewed was nowhere near as sweet-smelling or pleasant, but it made Bees smile all the same.

Seeing this horror, the other soldiers redoubled their efforts to race away, screaming and howling all the while, as if they might summon more of their comrades to help.

They giants didn't care. The humans could bring their entire invasion force as far as Bees was concerned. "Too many and not enough," was the giants' motto in combat: too many to defeat, but not enough to fulfill the giants' battle lust.

When Beesmarch and the Brothers had slaughtered the last man they could find, they returned to the once-captive giant and introduced themselves. The new giant was of average height for his kind, with a flat nose, a low brow, and a few missing teeth.

"My name's Fendrick" the stranger said when they

approached. "And I'm much obliged for your help. Not that I couldn't have handled the little shits myself, but…"

It turned out that Fendrick had a wife and child nearby, and he'd been out foraging for game when the soldiers surprised him.

"Now, I s'pose we'll have to head south or east," he mused aloud.

"Or fight," said Beesmarch.

It was as if Fendrick hadn't noticed the other giants, for he said "I can't fight 'em all by myself…" And then his voice trailed off. "Say," he murmured, "never seen so many of us in one place before."

"That's because we're rounding up all our kin and rousting these same little shits from our land—*all* our land," Whindas interjected.

"What," Fendrick asked in an awed hush, "killing humans?"

"If needs must," Beesmarch replied. He could see by the glint in Fendrick's eyes that the idea appealed to him—and why not? Giants had long ago reached an uneasy truce, a sort of unspoken agreement with the native humans, that killing each other was unacceptable, except in the protection of one's family. But every giant harbored a secret desire to test himself against mankind's best. Svarren, Oursine and other races offered a good physical challenge, but none possessed mankind's combination of ingenuity, determination, and arrogance.

"I'm in," Fendrick announced, after thinking on the matter a whole minute. "Just let me make sure my good wife and boy are safe."

"How old's your boy?" Whindas asked.

Fendrick shook his head, "Not old enough."

It was getting dark fast, and Beesmarch didn't want to stand around discussing such matters while the invaders were still lurking about. "Let's find your family, then," he said. "And get them away from here."

FIVE

Mendis, in Nespharia

Mendis was sparring with one of his swordmasters in a broad outdoor plaza when messengers delivered the doubly bad news of Svarren and giant attacks. He immediately tossed his practice sword to one of his nearby servants and headed for Nespharia's main keep. "Find Colonel Bailis and have him meet me in the war room. And send a wizard or two along with him."

The Emperor wasn't unduly concerned: he'd encountered creatures of all kinds in expanding his empire back home; he was mostly interested in learning about the locations, numbers and strengths of the native, non-human species. He also wanted to understand whether these latest attacks were the coincidental actions of creatures defending their territories, or whether they were somehow allied to the Virgin Queen's interests. Yes, they'd made a deal. That didn't mean he trusted her. In Mendis' experience, the most treacherous of people were those with whom one had agreements. As long as he *expected* betrayal, he felt, he could never be betrayed.

Upon arriving in the war room, the Emperor demanded a fresh shirt of the first servant he encountered. "This one's sweated through. And bring me a pitcher of cold water with fruit in it!" He tossed the shirt to the servant and crossed to a chair by the room's only fireplace. In seconds, he had his boots off and his feet warming comfortably by the flames. By the time Bailis arrived, Mendis had donned his new shirt, quenched his thirst and determined what he wished to say to his captive advisor.

"Colonel!" the Emperor said cheerfully without rising from his seat. "You're looking hale."

"Yes," Bailis blushed. "I'm afraid I'm being fed a little too well by your cooks and getting too little exercise in the bargain." Mendis laughed heartily at this, and Bailis continued. "But I'm beginning to learn your language, so perhaps one day your wizards won't be necessary."

The Emperor offered a sly smile. "Not for translation, perhaps, but they do other things for me, as well."

"Without doubt," Bailis conceded.

Around the room, one of Mendis' ubiquitous servants was lighting wall sconces and candles in order to stave off the gathering gloom. The colonel stepped into a new pool of light so that the Emperor could see him more easily—out of courtesy, of course, but also, Bailis hoped, as a means of making himself appear more trustworthy, as if to demonstrate that he had nothing to hide.

"We continue to have interesting encounters with creatures of your land," Mendis said casually.

Bailis wasn't surprised. "Oh?"

"More of your freakish, misshapen savages, as I gather."

"Ah," said Bailis. "Svarren."

The Emperor tested the strange word again on his tongue, "Svarren," and then washed it down with a sip of water. "I've been meaning to ask, are these Svarren thinking creatures, or beasts?"

"They can reason, have language of a sort, I'm told. Certainly they're ferocious, but we've never found them to be a match for good military strategy, discipline and a bit of magic."

Mendis considered these words a moment before continuing. "And you're certain they are not allied with any of your local powers? With your Queen, for instance?"

Now, it was Bailis' turn to pause and weigh the import of what he'd just been asked. The wrong answer might commit him to one side or the other well before he was ready. "I hardly think them any different from wolves, Magnificence."

"Even wolves can be used in battle."

"You're right, of course."

"Tell me, again, everything you know of them."

For the next half hour, Bailis told the Emperor everything he knew and had ever heard of the Svarren, after which effort, Mendis still had questions.

"Why has your Virgin Queen never attempted to eradicate these creatures, then?"

"I wouldn't presume to guess..."

"Indulge me," the Emperor said forcefully but not without charm. "What do you *imagine* is the reason?"

Bailis looked about the room, caught one of the wizard's eyes, and returned his gaze to the Emperor. "It might be that she is preoccupied with running and consolidating her kingdom. Or perhaps the Svarren serve some purpose..."

The Emperor leaned back, stretched his arms over his head luxuriantly. "They provide a distraction, a diversion, a scapegoat, even." He looked over at his captive and added, "I see these thoughts disturb you, but then you've never ruled. Your Queen is up to something, Colonel. I'd pay good coin to know what it is."

Was that a bribe? Bailis kept his mouth shut, and the Emperor changed subjects.

"Elsewhere, my men have run afoul of giants, and before you ask, no, my Empire has no giants, either. We've plenty of other beasties, both fantastical and fell, but no giants, alas. Come," Mendis gestured. "Sit. I'll send for our supper, and you'll tell me all about these giants."

Again, Bailis told the Emperor all he knew, and again Mendis probed for any possible military threat or advantage giant folk might present. Bailis had never seen more than a few in his life, and two of them had been female. He couldn't see how even a handful of giants working in unison could pose much of a threat to either side in this conflict.

"But let us suppose," said the Emperor, "that every force in your land ends up working together by happenstance or intent to expel my legions. Do you think them capable?"

"The Svarren, the Oursine, the giants, the wolves and Mahnus-knows-whatever-else?"

Mendis nodded.

"It seems beyond unlikely, but I imagine that if it happened, it would go hard for your armies. I've seen..." Bailis was thinking of the faeries and other fey folk who joined in the battle against the End-of-All-Things. For some reason, he decided not to share this information.

"What?" Mendis asked, leaning forward.

"I was going to say I've seen nothing to suggest such a thing is possible," the colonel lied, "but then I've never seen the like of your armies, either."

The Emperor stared at him skeptically for several seconds and then seemed to lose interest. "Thank you for your time," he said dismissively. "You may return to your quarters."

That the Emperor was a canny and dangerous man, Bailis was convinced. He was as different from the End-of-All-Things as a man is from a boy. Mendis might not have possessed the End's arcane power, but his military might and acumen were unequaled in the colonel's estimation.

Omeyo & His Svarren, Northern Midlands

Omeyo had traveled both far and wide in his career, but he'd never seen such uniforms, nor heard such a language. Invaders, then.

They had not lasted long against Omeyo's Svarren, but they'd made an impression upon him just the same. He could tell they were well-trained, well-supplied men of purpose and discipline. In a toe-to-toe battle on an open plain, Omeyo knew his Svarren would eventually be overwhelmed and crushed. The obvious answer, then, was never to engage the invaders on their terms, but only upon his own. In the woods, in the swamps, in the dark, the Svarren would hold the advantage. It was vitally important, too, that he and his pack never attack the invaders' main force, but ever and always its exploratory scouting parties and supply lines.

At the same time, the land teemed with those who fled the invaders, and the culling of the humans' numbers, the feeding, would never be better for the Long Teeth. Was it possible to both fight the invaders *and* slaughter the refugees? Somehow, Omeyo suspected that such greed would only visit disaster upon his new people.

Fortunately, the Woman was of the same mind: *deal with the threat first and then tend to the harvest.*

Omeyo watched a distant line of soldiers moving up the defile below him and ordered his own fighters to duck out of sight. The men looked like ants down below and, in a strange way, behaved like them, too. Omeyo and his Svarren had wiped out an entire platoon, and yet the invaders simply sent more troops out into the wilderness, clearing the path, perhaps, for greater and evermore frequent expeditions by the invaders' main force. Omeyo's pack had little difficulty with an enemy platoon. This larger company, though, promised a much greater challenge. It probably even had Shapers, against whose magics Omeyo had no answer. If the Woman had been present…but no, she'd stayed with the main body of her people.

The general sank onto his haunches, a practice he'd never done much in his life until he'd joined these Svarren, and turned his back to the defile, thinking. It was earlier in the day than Omeyo would have liked, but at least the clouds were providing some shadows. The first task was to identify the enemy's Shapers and eliminate as many as possible before they could respond. He gestured silently to the brightest of his fighters and the creature bounded noiselessly to his side.

"Shapers," he whispered, pointing first to his own eyes and then below.

The beast, whom Omeyo had taken to calling "Sage," blinked in understanding and crept into position for a better view of the approaching company. Several heartbeats later, he returned to Omeyo's side and held up two elongated and gnarled fingers. He then patted himself atop his head repeatedly, making a soft slapping sound.

Ah. Two with no helmets.

Good, Omeyo nodded. *Good.* He then turned back to the defile himself and verified what Sage had observed. Yes, the two without helmets were the most likely candidates. Now came the dangerous part. The general caught Sage's eye again and summoned him back to his side. He picked up a fist sized stone and pointed to the other Svarren, crouching nearby, and then back to the Shapers. There were thirty-some Svarren. If they all focused fire on one of the two Shapers, they might at least cripple the man. Hells, they might even kill him if they were lucky. Sage scuttled over to his fellows and communicated Omeyo's plan. Whatever happened, the general anticipated those below would come boiling out of the defile's uphill end, looking for blood. If Omeyo's pack could lead them back to the main Svarren host...

His Svarren gathered their stones—many taking two or three—lined up along the lip of the defile and, on Omeyo's signal, hurled them at the two men without helmets. So much for focusing fire. Still, to Omeyo's surprise, the Svarren were excellent shots. They must have had much more experience than humans using rocks as weapons. One of the Shapers went down immediately, whilst the other struggled with the dual tasks of protecting himself and returning fire. The Svarren let out hoots and whoops of savage glee and had to be pulled from the brink by their human leader.

"They come!" Omeyo yelled. "Back to our people!"

He hadn't taken enough time to actually witness the soldiers' reaction, but he didn't need to. They were under attack and meant to retaliate. His pack, of course, wanted to stay and fight. In their blood lust, no opponent was too great. Omeyo pushed and pulled on his nearest fighters, but it was Sage, again, who got them moving.

"Back to the others!" Omeyo reiterated.

At last, they cooperated and scampered off in the proper direction. Omeyo was hard-pressed to match their pace, but as he knew they didn't dare return to the Woman without him, he wasn't overly concerned about being abandoned. Behind him, the invaders snarled and cursed.

The chase was on.

Kittins, Spirk & Ron, Lunessfor

Kittins was taking inventory in the royal armory when Spirk and Ron appeared out of nowhere and knocked a pile of breastplates off a table, causing such a terrible racket that even the normally stoic Dead One was momentarily agitated.

"What in Mahnus' name are you two idiots doing here?" he barked.

Spirk stumbled backwards in alarm at Kittins' tone and crashed into a great pile of spears against the wall, sending them tumbling helter-skelter across the floor. Just as he bent down to retrieve one or two, Kittins' great hand swooped into view and jerked him away from the mess, depositing him in a clear space on the floor some ten feet from where he'd been.

"Stay!" the big man ordered.

"Yessir," Spirk and Ron said in unison.

"Now," Kittins rumbled, "did you two just pop in to ruin my day, or is there some extra special hell you've cooked up for me?"

As he worked his way over to Spirk, Ron said, "We was told to bring you somethin'."

Kittins crossed his arms over his chest. "What?"

"This map, here," said Spirk. He held it out to the captain as if Kittins might eat him if he got too close.

The captain whipped it out of the Shaper's hand and crossed to a spot where the light was somewhat better. He unrolled the map and stared at it for several long minutes. "Where'd you get this?" he said at last.

"Mahnus—Long Pete gave it to us," Spirk replied.

Kittins sneered at the mention of Long's name, but kept his eyes on the map. "And where'd he get it?"

"From the invaders' camp, so he said," Ron offered.

Now Kittins looked over at his former companions, his hideous face a mask of intensity and suspicion. "The enemy camp, is it? And why'd he ask you to bring it to me?"

"'Cause o' all o' them secret passages it shows and such," said Ron.

"He's afraid for Lunessfor," Spirk added.

"Is he?" Kittins asked, his voice sharp with skepticism. "Then why didn't he deliver this himself, him bein' a god and all?"

"On account of Alheria!" Spirk said.

Kittins looked back down at the map and seemed to forget all about Spirk and Ron. After several minutes of this, the Shaper took ahold of his friend's hand and Jumped away. When they were gone, Kittins crossed to the armory door and called into the hallway. "Lieutenant, have somebody bring me some writing materials!"

The unseen lieutenant replied in the affirmative and jogged off down the corridor, leaving Kittins alone. Once again, he studied the map. It detailed all the obvious ways in and out of the capital city, but featured an astounding number of secret entrances as well. Of course, the whole thing could be a work of fiction, the product of an overactive imagination. But if it was not, if it was genuine...All Kittins had to do was seek out one of its hidden passageways to determine the truth of it. If the map was accurate, he had a much bigger problem on his hands than he'd bargained for. And there was something else to consider: how had this map fallen into the enemy's hands? Unless the Emperor was a fool—a proposition Kittins sincerely doubted— he'd made copies, just as the captain planned to do.

Lieutenant Torle returned, carrying a roll of vellum, several quills and an inkwell. "Will there be anything else, sir?"

"No," said Kittins brusquely. He'd no interest in chit chat or satisfying the other man's curiosity. If his men hated him, so much the better.

Torle saluted, did an about-face and left the room.

Kittins got down to work. Ironically, he was able to use the table top recently cleared by Spirk and Ron. He was no artist and the light was not ideal, but an hour's labor produced a map almost equal to the original. After letting it dry, Kittins rolled up the copy and stashed it inside his doublet. The original, he'd take to...

Or would he? Alheria would already know everything the map contained, wouldn't she? Of greater interest was how it had fallen into the Emperor's possession and what Her Majesty planned to do about it.

The captain decided to sit on the original map for the time being, but verify its authenticity through a little exploration. Scanning the map, he found an alleged tunnel leading from his favorite district, South Shore, directly into the castle.

He cracked an unholy grin in anticipation.

Vykers & Co, On the Road

Vykers was practicing his knife-throwing when Ona returned with the Red Knight and the Reaper's other former slaves.

"I taught it chust came natural to you," Hjuest called out as he spied Vykers.

"I'm throwing left-handed," Vykers retorted.

"Why?" Hjuest asked, sliding out of the saddle.

"In case I get my right arm hacked off."

The Red Knight laughed heartily at this. "So," he said, "vee go beck on de road!"

"We do. You all supplied?"

Hjuest thumped a hand on his bulging saddlebags. "Vee are."

"Good," Vykers said. "Let's mount up and go." Without waiting for a reply, he kicked dirt over his meager fire and fairly leapt into his own saddle, a feat at which the Red Knight could only whistle in admiration.

Hjuest and the others fell back into the routine as if they'd been born to it, and Ona envied them. If she had been expecting Vykers' thanks, she was sorely disappointed. He was used to giving orders, not asking permission. It seemed the Red Knight would ride at Vykers' side, with the large, dark warrior directly behind him. Ona would have to mix in with the other, somehow-less-important members of the crew. In many ways, she reflected, this made it easier for her to study her grandfather without him glaring back at her. The man was a living impossibility.

At the group's front, Vykers was excited to be back in motion again. The idea that there might be a puzzle detailing his life to be found in the Emperor's far-off court both tantalized and vexed him. He wanted his answers immediately. Also, traveling to the Emperor's court might cause him to miss the bulk of the coming war. But it might present opportunities, as well.

They rode through the day and into the late afternoon, Vykers always taking care to ensure his horse didn't outpace the others' mounts, a mix of natural and supernatural ponies. Along the way, they caught sight of refugees more than once and even a few herds of deer and elk charging deeper into the wilderness. Once, they saw a detachment of enemy troops in the distance and the Reaper couldn't resist moving closer to investigate.

"But master," Hjuest began, "dey outnumber us ten-to-one. Is dis vise?"

"You don't have to come along," Vykers shrugged.

Of course he did! The Reaper would lose all respect for him and his brothers if they remained behind whilst he confronted the Emperor's men. With a sigh that was more physical than vocal, Hjuest spurred his horse to follow, and the rest of the group did the same.

The invaders' outriders spotted them almost instantly and doubled back to alert the rest of their company. In no time, the invaders had pulled into a tight, defensive formation, despite their superior numbers.

Vykers pulled up just beyond what he judged to be bow-range. It was a distance he'd observed countless times, and he knew it almost by instinct. Someone yelled something unintelligible at him, whereupon Hjuest translated.

"'E says you must stop and dismount."

The Reaper didn't like being told what to do, so he climbed all the way up and stood on his saddle, making a much greater target of himself but also improving his view of the enemy's force. "Tell them to fuck off," he commanded.

"Are you sure?" Hjuest asked. A look from Vykers confirmed the command, and the Red Knight winced as he translated.

The Emperor's men burst into laughter. When their merriment died down, there was more unintelligible shouting.

"Vat is your name?" Hjuest said after a pause.

"That's all?" Vykers asked. "Sounded like he said a lot more 'n that."

Again, Hjuest winced. "Vell, he said 'Vat is your name, stupid vun?'"

Vykers turned briefly to the back of the group, fixed eyes

with Ona. "You wanted to come along," he told her. Then, to Hjuest, he said "I am called 'The Reaper'."

The enemy's response was instantaneous. They broke into a charge.

"Ha!" said Vykers, in obvious delight.

Shit! Thought Ona. *What have I done to myself?*

Vykers jumped down into his saddle and the rest of his group made ready for combat.

Ona sat motionless in disbelief. *We're all going to die!*

"I'd draw my sword if I were you!" Vykers chuckled back at her. How in Alheria's name could he laugh at a time like this?

At the front of the enemy's company, scores of foot soldiers raced toward Vykers' position, while the two ends of their line made as if to wrap around the Reaper's crew. The enemy's mounted knights rode just behind the line, waiting to jump in wherever needed. The two sides' positions were such that the sun was setting behind the invaders, casting their bodies into stark silhouettes, while Vykers' gang blazed with reds and oranges, the one side shadow, the other, fire.

Vykers drove his horse forward, and it closed the gap faster than the mortal eye could track. One moment, he'd been yards away, the next, he was in their midst, whirling like a bladed tornado. His victims didn't even have time to scream. Confusion ruled. The rest of the invaders staggered and stumbled to a stop, unable to comprehend what was happening, but unwilling to retreat.

The Red Knight and his companions came galloping forward, hollering and making as much noise as they could. Well behind them, Ona followed half-heartedly. She feared no one in single combat, but this pandemonium was beyond madness. A sword or an axe might come from anywhere. Yet, she could hardly remain aloof, lest the others accuse her of cowardice—assuming any of them survived. Well, there were worse ways to die than in the Reaper's company.

For Vykers' part, he was in a sort of battle-mad ecstasy. Never before had he raced into a fight on such a magnificent beast. It was every bit as fast, as instinctive as he, and its movements accelerated his own to the point of rendering his attacks almost invisible. The Reaper felt such power, such invulnerability. Was this how the gods felt? His mind flashed on Long Pete, and he laughed. No, the gods were foolish, conniving creatures; he was Death.

Around him, blood showered and spurted. The air was thick with the heady aroma of it, mingled with sweat, with urine, with the odor of brain fluid, with shit. There was also the discordant music of clashing arms—steel on steel, on flesh, with gasps, grunts and curses aplenty. Here and there a death scream pierced the air, but none of them came from Vykers or his company.

The invaders had overestimated their chances and underestimated their value as fertilizer.

In time, the enemy's force broke into smaller, more mobile groups and attempted to flee. The Reaper, however, was not feeling merciful. At his example and urging, his men chased and cut down as many of the invaders as possible. One or two might have gotten away, but no one seemed overly concerned about it. Indeed, Ona was elated to count herself still among the living.

As darkness fell, Vykers dismounted and began cutting the heads off the dead. "Can you write?" he yelled over to an exhausted Hjuest.

"Vat?" the Red Knight asked, confused by the non-sequitur.

"Can you write in these bastards' language?"

Hjuest glanced at the other men for affirmation that he was in fact hearing his master correctly. They all returned his look of confusion. "Yes," he told the Reaper.

"Good," said Vykers. "I want you to spell out 'Reaper' with these heads."

"Won't they just get dragged off by animals?" Ona asked.

"No," Vykers replied, "'cause you're gonna stake 'em down for me."

"But..."

"Do it."

She understood his thinking: it was a warning, an unmistakable warning to the larger enemy that Vykers was not fucking around. He meant to kill all of them if he could. But his orders to Ona were also a warning, of sorts, that his will was not to be challenged. As she began searching for sticks to sharpen into stakes, she wondered for the hundredth time what she'd gotten herself into.

Long & Short, Midlands

Long sat on a sodden mound of dirt in the middle of an equally sodden meadow, chasing his thoughts around the inside of his skull like a crippled child playing at Blind Man's Bluff.

"You might not mind the cold and wet," Short complained, "but I ain't a god, and it's chappin' my ass but good!"

Long waved a hand disinterestedly and the patch of ground between himself and his homunculus caught fire and grew into a cozy, self-maintaining blaze.

"Ah," said Short, "that's better." After a prolonged silence, he added, "Regular chatterbox, ain'tcha?"

"What?" Long asked, as if waking from a dream.

"I say, you're a regular chatterbox today."

The captain shrugged apologetically. "I was just thinkin'."

"Now don't start that nonsense!" the homunculus warned. "Nothin' good ever comes of it."

Long turned his full attention to his companion. "You really *are* Short Pete, aren't you?"

"Guess so."

"Alheria's teats, but I got a way o' messin' things up," Long lamented.

"Aye."

Long winced, "Thanks."

Another extended silence blossomed between the pair, until Long had a sudden idea. "Say, Short...you've been dead, right?"

"Dead as yer prick and twice as cold."

"Thanks," Long said again. "What I mean to ask is, what's it like? Was it a feeling? A place? Or just a whole lot o' nothin'?"

The homunculus sat by the fire, his legs splayed wide like a rag doll's. "Oh, it's a place alright. Leastways, it was for me."

Long felt his heart beating faster and wondered why it was so. "And?"

"I hope you've given me immortality too, Long Mahnus, 'cause I never wanna go back. Terrible place, with bodies and pieces o' bodies lying all around, not an inch o' soil between 'em, moaning and wailin' like the huswives after a battle. It was darkish, but I couldn't see the sky 'cause my face was in some bloke's armpit, and it's hard to move with all o' them other bodies atop o' you."

"But it *is* a place?"

"I just said so, didn't I?"

"Could you hear anything else, besides the moanin'?"

Short Pete considered a moment. "Rumblin'. Sometimes there were this low hum. Think I mighta heard vultures, too. Why you askin'?"

"I dunno," Long sighed.

Short let him stew for a good while, before he interrupted the silence a third time. "So, what's the plan, Cap'n?"

Long laughed. "Plan? You think too highly o' me if you think I've got a plan."

"Maybe that's why I'm here, then, Long. To help you make one. What are you thinkin'?"

The captain stretched out, 'til his posture mimicked that of his diminutive friend. "One, there's a war settin' in, and I got friends I wanna protect. Two, assumin' I ain't lost my mind, Alheria killed me before I was born..." Long laughed again, and the sound indeed had a tinge of madness in it. "And I need to find out why. Three, I'm guessin' she still wants me dead, which means four, I gotta get her first. Five, I miss my family. Six..."

"Hold it! That's enough fer now. Seems to me them first few can all be answered with one simple step."

"Which is?"

"We gotta go back to Lunessfor."

"Well, dammit it all, Short! I just gave our map away!"

The homunculus shot Long a reproachful look. "You don't really need a map, do ya?"

"No," Long allowed. "I s'pose not."

"I s'pose not," Short echoed.

"But surely Her Majesty will..."

"What? She never noticed you there before!"

"Alright, alright! We'll go!" Long griped. "I'm just not sure where we should…"

"Just pick a nice, quiet spot."

"Okay. But you asked for it…"

Qansip, Adrift

The rain had stopped at last, but the river remained a great, bloated beast, uninterested in Qansip's concerns or survival. She hated it and cursed it a thousand times an hour, but the river remained unmoved by her rancor and unresponsive to her threats.

And she was as cold as she'd ever been—not corpse cold, mind, but nearly so—and as wet and as hungry and as sleep deprived.

The palanquin listed unexpectedly to Qansip's right and seemed for an instant as if it might dump her into the water. When the sideways slope of its deck finally fixed at an angle without getting better or worse, Qansip realized her unlikely vessel had gotten caught on something—an old tree stump, perhaps, or the wreckage of another craft. Once it became clear that the palanquin would never come free of its own accord, Qansip slid on her belly to the very edge to investigate the problem, whereupon an enormous pale creature leapt up at her…

Only, it was not a creature, but a giant arm or, more accurately, a *giant's* arm, with a grasping hand the size of a dog. Qansip rolled onto her back and kicked herself as far from the hand as she could while still remaining onboard. The hand reached right across the deck and returned to the water on the palanquin's far side, bringing the vessel's back into a horizontal position, if a bit deeper in the water than normal. On the end of the arm, a blast of spray announced the arrival of the giant's head above water. Without opening his eyes, the huge being coughed and choked and gasped for air. After an eternity of this behavior, his breathing grew calm and he cracked his eyelids, revealing bloodshot and weary eyes. Almost off-handedly, he gazed at his surroundings until his eyes happened upon Qansip.

"Hello," said he, in the deepest voice the girl had ever heard.

Suddenly, she became aware that parts of her arms and legs weren't entirely covered, so she pulled her wet blankets more fully around herself. "Good...good afternoon," she ventured.

"You look drenched," said the giant.

"Nowhere near as much as you!" Qansip retorted.

"No, you're right about that." After a moment's consideration, the giant continued. "You fancy gettin' out of this river?"

"Why?" Qansip snapped. "So you can eat me?"

"Eat you?" the giant asked, taken aback. "Scrawny little thing like you?"

"Scrawny?" Qansip squeaked in outrage. "I'll have you know..."

The giant ignored her and began dragging the whole palanquin towards the near shore, but Qansip could hardly protest since getting to shore had been her dearest wish for days. As long as the giant didn't eat her. Her savior grew taller as he moved into the shallows. Qansip wondered if she could make a run for it as soon as the palanquin ran aground. She was just on the brink of action when the giant let go and collapsed facedown onto the muddy embankment, his sides heaving like a great bellows, his breath roaring like waves of the sea. Qansip watched from her bundle of blankets, trying to decide whether to wait until the giant fell asleep—as it seemed he might—or bolt immediately, while his back was turned. While she was struggling to decide, his breathing slowed and became nearly inaudible. Perhaps he had fallen asleep after all.

With all the caution of a mouse sneaking up on a fox, Qansip climbed out of the palanquin and tip-toed over to the giant, inching closer and closer to his head. She just had to be sure that he—His huge hand whipped off the ground and seized her in its grip. She yelped in surprise and terror, but before she was able to work up a good scream, the giant shoved her into the cavern between his shoulder and the damp soil beneath.

"Must...stay...warm..." he rumbled.

But she hadn't heard real rumbling until he began to snore.

She'd been afraid her captor would roll over on her in his sleep, but he did not. And she did warm up, lying next to him. In fact, it was the warmest and, eventually, driest she'd been in ages. She was still worried he'd eat her when he awoke, though, and she fretted for hours about how she might defend herself when that time came. Thus, she was mortified when she opened her eyes sometime later and night had fallen. She could hardly believe that she'd been asleep as well and now understood that her next chance at escape wouldn't happen until sunrise, at least. What was she to do? What was she to…

When she opened her eyes again, it was late morning under cloudy skies, and the giant had moved off downriver a ways. Her chance had come at last! With her heart pounding in her throat, Qansip leapt to her feet and dashed upriver as fast as her little legs would carry her. She ran unmolested until the river rounded a bend, where she stopped, amazed that she'd gotten so far without being recaptured. Daring a look backwards, she saw that the giant wasn't after her. Relief quickly turned to indignation. How could the great oaf ignore her so easily? Couldn't he see she was no mere peasant girl? Anger swelled in her majestic bosom, and she stalked rapidly back within sight of the giant.

"Hey!" she yelled. "Giant!"

He looked up without hurry from whatever it was he'd been doing, saw her, and returned his attention to his task. That was simply too much for Qansip.

"Hey, you big idiot!" she yelled again, "I'm talking to you."

The giant actually dared to pretend she wasn't addressing him! Furious, Qansip searched for and found a small stone on the ground nearby. She picked it up, hefted it once, and hurled it in the giant's direction. Luckily for her, it fell well short of its intended target, because even the effort angered the giant. He surged to his feet, reaching his full height for the first time since Qansip had met him, and the young woman almost fainted from the size of him. Now, he did move towards her, and she turned to run in earnest. One moment she was sprinting over the damp grass, the next, she was dangling by one arm, ten or more feet off the ground. The giant was going to eat her this time, she was certain. Out of the corner of her eye, she saw he face draw near, so she quickly clamped her eyes shut, that she might not witness her own doom.

"What is your name, girl?" the giant's voice thundered.

"M-m-my name is Q-Q-Qansip," she replied. "I'm n-n-named after a p-p-princess!"

"They must have piss poor manners in *that* kingdom," the giant observed. "My name's Eoman, and I'm a real king...or was. You want to talk to me, use my name."

Qansip said nothing, but nodded feebly until Eoman put her back down.

"Now, why don't you make yourself useful and gather some firewood, while I keep tryin' to get this fire goin'?"

Ah! So *that* was what he'd been doing. Now she thought on it, fire seemed like a good idea, an excellent idea. As long as he didn't use it to roast her alive.

She was not enamored of manual labor, was Qansip, but her distaste for the cold and damp was even worse, so she set about her chore with a zeal her father would never have recognized. Thinking of him, Qansip wondered whether he was still angry with her, whether he'd been searching for her, and whether he was even still living. She felt an unfamiliar pang of...sorrow? Shame? She had never been a particularly introspective creature, and examining her feelings and actions now was not pleasant for her. Fortunately, her arms were now full of firewood, and she was able to return to the giant—to Eoman—with something to show for her efforts.

Eoman said nothing when she dumped her wood next to him. He might at least have thanked her. But he *had* managed to get a small fire going, and she decided to let his ingratitude pass. In time, the small fire had grown into a healthy blaze. Qansip, no longer shivering and damp, announced that she was hungry.

"So?" asked Eoman.

"I thought you might want to get us some food," Qansip explained.

"Us? I'm nobody's lackey, girl—least of all, yours. Besides, I'm still drying out."

Qansip was not used to being spoken to in such a manner by anyone but her father, but she didn't see how she could possibly bully the giant into doing her bidding. Frustrated, she lapsed into sullen silence.

The day progressed, and Eoman seemed thoroughly content to remain by the fire, running his fingers through his beard and tossing an occasional stick onto the embers. When he ran out of firewood, he rose and stretched.

"We need more wood," said he. "Maybe there's something edible around here, too."

"You will come back, though?" Qansip asked, trying to keep the worry out of her voice.

"Probably," Eoman smirked. "We'll see what we see." With that, he strode off into the bushes and trees that lined this side of the river.

When they'd first met, Qansip had been afraid the giant would eat her. Now, she was afraid of facing the wilderness without him. Above all, she hoped he'd be back before sunset. In her palanquin on the river, she'd had no fear of wolves or Svarren, but on shore, they posed all too real a threat.

Perhaps she should be kinder to the giant.

Mendis, In Nespharia

The latest report described an attack upon one of his forward companies by a small band of warriors, led by a demon on a nearly invisible horse. The Emperor's men had been routed, and a subsequent visit to the site revealed a gruesome message from the Reaper. Mendis was paradoxically elated. Wykkerian had revealed himself at last! If he could capture the man himself, Mendis would no longer be bound by his agreement with the Queen and would, therefore, be free to assault her capital... assuming his wizards could keep her at bay. Anyway, he'd no idea how or where to find this Long Pete fellow and was even less certain how to kill him. Indeed, for all he knew, Long Pete might be his best, most natural ally.

Things were going well on other fronts, as well. Messengers from the Tsundi and B'Shar reported little resistance to their efforts at conquering the north and south respectively. It seemed Mendis' wizards had been correct that this new land was beyond war-weary and its people possessed little stomach for further conflict. Had Wykkerian cowed the whole continent? Such was his reputation, certainly. And it didn't much matter to Mendis. The point was that imperial casualties were low, morale was good, and only the Queen's strange magics seemed to pose any concern. And Mendis' wizards were hard at work deciphering those, as well.

Feeling downright buoyant, the Emperor signaled to his guard that he was ready to hear the petition of the locals who'd dared to remain and made the long climb from the lower city to see him. Now, he would show these people how an Emperor ruled.

He sat in Nespharia's throne as comfortably as if he'd been there all his life, and he knew he looked the same. He'd been born to rule. Thus, when the small contingent of angry natives entered his presence, they swallowed their hurt and their pride on the instant and fell to their knees. Mendis was most pleased.

His wizards had enspelled this throne room such that anything spoken in any language was immediately made sensible to anyone present. This made Mendis' job much easier.

"You wished to speak with me?" he called out in his most benevolent voice.

The startled townspeople regarded each other in confusion and then shoved their spokesman forward. He was a solid man of medium height, brown hair, brown eyes and an especially bulbous nose. He looked like someone accustomed to hard work and honest treatment; he looked reasonable.

Mendis felt he could work with him. "What can I do for you?" he prompted.

"Well," the man began, "we're, uh...we're grateful you didn't kill all of us after takin' our city, your Highness..."

One of the wizards cut in, "We address the Emperor as 'Magnificence'."

"Your Magnificence..." the man amended.

Mendis nodded in acknowledgment. "Go on..."

"But now we got no means to live and no means to *make* a living."

Mendis smiled, all understanding. "What is your name, friend?"

"Garret, Magnificence."

"Garret. A fine name! I can certainly see why you feel as you do, Garret, but it's possible you misunderstand my motives: I am not here to destroy you, but to build you and your people up. This is why, as you noted, I did not kill your fellow citizens. Instead, I intend to welcome you into my empire, an empire that spans two continents and thousands of years! No longer will you be victim to the petty squabbles of city-states and minor kingdoms. When I have completed my conquest of this land, you will have one ruler, one military, one currency, one faith, one legal system and more. You will know fairness and justice, security and dignity."

Garret looked to his comrades who seemed unanimously awe-stricken by the Emperor's statement.

"But I will do more for you, my newfound friend: I will eradicate the Svarren and bring your giant folk to heel. I will make the oceans safe for everyone to travel and, in doing so, I will open up new avenues of trade and exploration."

Garret was dumbfounded. "I...we...this sounds wonderful, your...Magnificence."

"And so it shall be," Mendis beamed. "But in the short term, you'll be wanting work, food and shelter, no? Say the word, and I'll assign you to my force rebuilding your city. You'll have everything you need."

The natives huddled briefly and Garret reemerged from their number with a great, goofy smile upon his face. "We accept your offer, Magnificence. How can we not?"

"Excellent!" Mendis cried as he stood and spread his arms wide. He looked over to his guards and added, "See that these men are well placed and cared for, and death to the man who mistreats them in any way."

"Your will, Magnificence," one of the guards responded.

"And bring me colonel Bailis," Mendis tossed in on a whim. He was in such a good mood; it was almost intoxicating. While someone went to fetch the colonel, the Emperor crossed the room and sat at a table he often used for private meals. There, he found an ever-full decanter of red wine and a plate of cheese. The locals had a peculiar cheese that seemed to get tastier the more it deteriorated. It didn't look much like something one ought to put in one's mouth, and yet it was frightfully delicious. Mendis helped himself to a glass of wine and a generous slice of the cheese whilst he waited for Bailis' arrival, surprised at how well that wine and cheese complimented one another. He was still pondering this when the colonel and his guards arrived.

"How would you like to work for me, Colonel?" the Emperor asked as soon as Bailis came through the door.

"I'm speechless, Magnificence."

"Which only increases your value!" Mendis joked. "I've got plenty of long-winded advisors and staff as it is. But let me come to the point: I'll have need of men of percipience and judgment if I'm to win over the natives and successfully assimilate them into my growing empire. I would like, for starters, to put you in charge of those citizens who still remain in this city. You'll continue its reconstruction and ensure that all voices are heard and sides are well-served and content."

"You humble me, Magnificence," Bailis responded, "to think me worthy of such an enormous task."

"And yet I do. And you shall be well compensated. I'll name you 'Lord Bailis, Governor of Nespharia' and give you this city as your domain when my troops and I leave for the west."

"Outside of Her Majesty—whose motivations few can guess and none dare question—we've known nothing but tyrants and lunatics in this land. I believe...I do believe if anyone can unite us, it is you, Magnificence."

"Then you accept my offer?"

Bailis got down on one knee and lowered his head. "I do."

Mendis rested a hand on the colonel's shoulder. "Then rise, Lord Bailis of the Staurachian Empire. We've much to accomplish."

The Alchemist, Yendor & Co., Lunessfor

Although the Alchemist was doing his best to hide it, Yendor could tell he was drunk. Of course Yendor could tell! Yendor'd spent the better part of his life drunk and he knew every sign and symptom. And there was no question of why the man was pickled, either. He'd succeeded in replicating the magical elixir and had either been celebrating the accomplishment or simply sampling the wares for safety's sake and gotten carried away. All this Yendor understood the moment he and his friends stepped through the Alchemist's door; all this was confirmed the moment the Alchemist spoke.

"Victory!" the man sang out, in a far jollier mood than Yendor, Spirk and Ron had ever seen him.

"You're drunk!" said Ron, somewhat diminishing Yendor's observational prowess.

"'S what if I am? Am I not the greatest Alchemist in the world?" He held up a rare glass goblet, half-full of pale gold liquid. "But here's my proof! Let this celestial liquor speak on my behalf."

"'E's layin' it on with a trowel, isn't 'e?" Yendor muttered to Ron out the corner of his mouth.

"It smells right to me!" Spirk offered.

The Alchemist stooped behind his counter, belched loudly, and lifted a small keg into the light. "I made you a touch more than I agreed to, in thanks for bringing this my way."

"You like it, then?" Yendor asked, stupidly.

"Like it? Friend, you could rule the world with this—what are you planning to do with it, by that way?"

Suddenly, Yendor became cagey again. "That's private-like."

"Is it?" the Alchemist giggled. It was a high, tittering sound that seemed quite ludicrous coming from so pale and dour a fellow. "As you like, then. I'll have more for you next time."

Yendor gestured for Ron to accept and carry the cask, not trusting Spirk with the job, and nodded to the Alchemist. "Yes. See you then."

"Yes!" the Alchemist giggled some more.

Back outside, Yendor quickly herded his friends into an alley. "Did you find a secret place, like I asked you?" he demanded of Spirk.

"'Course I did!"

"Well, what are we waiting for? Can you do your magic trick, now?" he asked the Shaper.

Spirk smiled, and suddenly Yendor's ears were flapping.

"Not *that* trick, you whoreson zed!" In a trice, his ears stopped wiggling. "Take us to our new hideout!"

Comprehension slowly crept across Spirk's visage until, at last, he gestured for his friends to draw closer. He wrapped them all in an awkward hug and instantly everything grew dark.

The air was cooler and smelled slightly musty.

"You can let go of me now," Rem suggested. "And maybe magic-up some light for us."

"Not yet," said Yendor. "I wanna try something." Lifting the eye patch off his dead eye, he discovered it was still able to see in the dark. "We're in a storage room 'o some sort. Lots 'o old chairs 'n tables 'n portraits 'n whatnot."

"How can you tell?" Ron wanted to know.

"Never you mind, my lad. Old Yendor's gotta have a few secrets, don't he?" To Spirk he said, "Alright, go ahead and light something up for us." Apparently, he was still learning the value of specificity where giving instructions to Spirk was concerned, because no sooner had his words left his lips than he, himself, began glowing like a harvest moon. "What in Mahnus' name...?"

"Sorry," a now-visible Spirk shrugged sheepishly. "I couldn't think o' nothin' else."

"Might be there's some torch-making materials amongst all this other stuff," said Rem. "We're going to need a better source of light..."

"What d'you mean, 'better'?" Yendor bristled.

The men bantered and bickered for a while more, while they cleared a table, surrounded it with a number of mismatched chairs, and placed a glowing vase at its center.

"Looks kinda homey!" Spirk announced with great satisfaction.

Although Yendor was loath to part with his cask, he was unable to carry it a moment longer and so lovingly set it down on the table. "Anybody see any cups or bottles anywhere? We need to uncork this sweetheart and have a taste of her quality!"

"I thought we had other plans for this batch," Rem reminded his companion.

"And so we do!" Yendor agreed. "But we can't unleash it on an unsuspectin' public 'til we know it's safe! And besides, there's more 'n enough here to go around."

Rem could see from the looks on his friends' faces that he'd be alone if he chose to abstain. With a sigh of resignation, he pulled a flask from inside his vest. There was still a bit of brandy in it, but it may as well have been horse piss compared to what was coming. Without a word, Rem uncorked the flask and poured its contents onto the floor. "We can use this," said he.

And use it they did. Over and over.

Untold hours later, they awakened to find they'd built strange sculptures from the room's furniture, painted childish images on the walls with dust and spit, and, most inexplicably of all, changed clothes with each other. Despite these oddities, to a man they felt better than they had in ages.

"Ah," said Rem, "this is grand stuff, this elixir! What shall we call it?"

Yendor, who'd begun disrobing in preparation for a return to own clothing, replied, "It does need a name, doesn't it? How about 'Plotz' Potable'?"

"Remuel Wratch's Restorative?"

"Can't be," said Yendor. "You're dead, remember?"

Ron, in endeavoring to get out of Yendor's trousers, instead tripped and fell onto his side. Nevertheless, he offered, "Nessno's Magical Drink?"

"Not very catchy, that," Rem answered. "Rem's Remedy?"

"Nah," said Yendor.

Spirk, who'd pulled his shirt over his face, mumbled, "Long Pete's Happy Stuff?"

"Long's Old Peculiar!" Rem shouted enthusiastically.

In the end, they voted on it, and Long's Old Peculiar won out, with Yendor being the only no vote. It wasn't that he didn't think Long worthy, but Yendor'd been the one to save enough of the liquor to have it reproduced and he damn well wanted some credit. Still, he consoled himself with the knowledge that more beverages were in the offing, and he'd certainly be able to name one of those after himself.

Once everyone had managed to reclaim and restore his own clothing, the group got down to business.

"What's the next step in this plan of yours?" Rem asked Yendor.

"Well, first we gotta spruce this place up a bit. Then we gotta make sure nobody can get in here but us. After that, we hafta rob the city's biggest brewery."

Apparently, Ron and Spirk were already aware of Yendor's plans, but Rem remained confused. "A brewery? Why don't we rob a bank? They're certain to have more coin on hand..."

"'Cause it ain't coin we're after, Rem. We're lookin' to steal the brewery's ale."

Driegan & his Escort, Midlands

In his exhaustion, Driegan didn't see or hear the enemy's scouts approaching until they were within hailing distancing of one another, and, by then, it was too late to run away, and he and his men certainly didn't have the energy to give chase. As Driegan watched the scouts wheel about on their mounts and gallop off, he knew his only hope of remaining free was through negotiation. He sat on his own horse, dejected but not defeated. There was a way out of every predicament.

He figured if he offered the invaders some of his treasure, though, they'd take it all. If he tried to hide it amongst his men, the enemy would find it. Thus, there was only one thing to do: forsaking his chests of coin, Driegan located his three largest gems and swallowed them. They went down painfully, even with large gulps of wine to ease their passage, but the effort brought Driegan a certain peace of mind all the same. He would always have something to bargain with.

In the meantime, he instructed his men to march, double time, in the direction opposite the scouts' retreat. No sense in making his capture easy for the enemy, after all. And perchance he'd think of something, some useful stratagem while he awaited their return.

Or not. Too soon, he heard the thundering of cavalry at his back. Quickly, he slid from his saddle and summoned one of his men to his side.

"Take my cloak and climb into my saddle," he commanded.

The soldier, not nearly as stupid as Driegan suspected, said "Nah, nah. I ain't takin' your place just for shits and giggles. You'll have to pay me."

"Right," Driegan said, and stabbed him in the gut with his dagger. Hastily, Driegan dressed the still-dying man in his cloak, jammed a couple of rings on his fingers and then kicked him in the face 'til he died. The other men were so shocked by this action than none found the strength to speak. "Good," Driegan snarled at them. "And if you know what's best for you, you'll keep your mouths shut."

When the enemy force arrived, everything suggested Driegan's company had pulled their leader from his horse and killed him for getting them caught. The enemy commander barked out a series of harsh, unrecognizable words, and his fellows began to surround Driegan's men, who, despite the language difference, knew enough to stand still and offer no resistance. In the middle of the pack, Driegan kept his eyes down and feigned absolute submission. He believed he and his men would be taken captive and marched back to wherever-it-was these invaders had chosen to station themselves. It was possible they would execute him eventually, but not, he hoped, before they attempted to question him. At that point, he would bargain with them. He possessed gems, after all, and probably useful information, as well.

No, Driegan Deda was a long way from finished.

Kittins, Beneath Lunessfor

The passageway was not especially well-hidden, but it did require a great deal of strength to access it. Fortunately, Kittins had more than enough for the task. He stretched his great arms and placed a hand on either side of the false fireplace and pulled.

He wasn't sure which way it was meant to move, and, at first, it didn't budge. Eventually, though, he felt it give in his direction, and he persevered until it came free of the wall. Behind it, as he'd suspected, a dusty and fully cobwebbed passage led off into darkness. The smell of the Aumbre wafted out of the hole, suggesting the way forward was damp at the very least and perhaps even submerged. Well, Kittins had drowned before, if it came to that. He knew what to expect.

On the fireplace's far side, the captain once again grabbed ahold and dragged until the entrance was sealed behind him. Then, he paused to take stock and let the darkness envelop him. He heard no telltale dripping, no lapping of waves and was almost disappointed. Using his flint and steel, he struck sparks to the torch he'd brought along and, satisfied with the flame this produced, walked farther into the tunnel. He doubted anyone had come or gone this way in ages, but he reckoned he'd know better soon enough.

He'd chosen this particular passage because it seemed to connect to others barely hinted at on his map. If there were more, who knew where they might lead? And who knew who had built them? In the past, Kittins had not been a particularly curious man. In recent years, however, he'd learned the error of his ways, as astounding revelations piled up faster than he could count them, and all of them, all of them, intimating a larger and more elaborate design then he'd previously been aware of.

In some ways, this mystery and his growing desire to try Vykers in combat were all he had left. He understood, as he'd told Rem, that the opportunity to have a family of his own had passed him by; he understood that service to and promotion with Her Majesty was fool's gold, a meaningless exercise in self-abuse, under an unknowable being who cared little or nothing for his own needs and desires. Oh, he would kill her, if he could. If only he knew how to begin…

The passageway descended slowly at first and then got steeper as Kittins moved along. Still, there was no dripping or other signs of moisture. Yet the Aumbre's aroma persisted, like a bad thought that would not be banished. The possibility that there were hundreds of thousands of tons of water coursing overhead bothered the captain not at all. When death finally came for him, it would be a sword through the back, a barrage of arrows, or some other, equally martial act.

Down he traveled, and down and down some more. He'd no way to gauge the passage of time in these lightless depths, no hourglasses, no candles, no bells. But his gut told him he'd been descending for over an hour. To his surprise, he suddenly arrived at an old steel door, crusted with rust at its edges and locked with an equally rusty lock and chain. Kittins hated the thought of having traveled so far, only to reach a dead-end. He lashed out at the door with his right foot, but though the object of his scorn boomed in the darkness, it remained otherwise unchanged by the blow. So be it. Kittins found a dry patch on the floor on which to place is torch, and then he backed away from the door a good twenty paces. Like an enraged bull, he charged the door, turning his left shoulder into it at the last second, and blasted the thing right off its hinges and into the hallway beyond. Kittins stumbled a few steps farther and fell to his knees, wincing in pain.

"Bastard," he groaned.

His shoulder crunched and crackled a little as he rolled it forward and back, but seemed to remain in working order despite the impact. The door, however, was finished.

After a brief respite, during which the captain retrieved his dwindling torch—another problem he'd have to deal with sooner or later—Kittins passed through the now-open doorway and continued on his journey, ruminating on the door's purpose and what might lie beyond it. Gradually, he became aware of a high whining noise, almost above the range of human hearing. The farther he walked, the more intense the sound became, until it was actually painful to his ears. And then, unexpectedly, the passageway ended, and Kittins found himself staring at a stone wall, not much different from those to his left and right.

The whine continued.

Kittins drew his sword and banged its pommel against the wall directly in front of him, resulting in a dull knocking sound. He tried the walls on either side, and his sword rang, but the stones beneath it made little sound. So, the passageway was meant to continue but someone had sealed it off and made it look like a dead-end. Not very clever, really, as Kittins thought about it. Who guards a dead-end with a steel door? What was beyond this false wall, though? Even as he pondered the question, the whining increased in volume and urgency, to a point where it almost seemed like a cry for help.

But Kittins was nobody's savior.

Still, he was curious. Again, he glanced at his torch and estimated that even if he left now, he'd lose his light well before he returned to the surface. And what was a little darkness to him? The more pressing question was how he might break through the wall. Unlike the door before it, the wall did not look or feel like anything that could simply be kicked in or demolished without tools. He had his sword and long knives, of course, but they seemed hardly suited to the task. Nothing for it then, but a long climb back to the surface to fetch a hammer and chisels.

The whining and wailing beyond the wall continued.

Vykers & Co., the Forest

The Reaper was behaving very strangely, from Hjuest's perspective. They'd ridden hard for a particular forest, and, when it came time to make camp, he'd instructed them to build their fire on a bed of stones, using only deadwood for fuel. He was adamant that nothing be carved or cut from living trees or bushes. It was all very odd, if easy enough to accomplish. Then, when night fell, Vykers said he needed to wander off alone for a spell. The rest of the men turned their heads almost in unison to stare at the Red Knight, but what could he tell them? He'd no idea what the Reaper was up to.

Just before he vanished from sight, Vykers called back, "And keep your hands off the girl!"

The object of his comment was clearly insulted by it, but she was safe. She didn't look the kind of wench one tangled with, anyway. As if she could read the Red Knight's mind, Ona scowled in his direction and made a very overt display of placing her hand on the hilt of her sword.

"I am no fool," Hjuest chuckled, trying to make light of the situation.

"All men are fools," Ona retorted.

"I have heard dat before," he grinned.

"I am sure you have."

Hjuest gave up. The woman wanted a fight—or something—and he wasn't disposed to cooperate, especially with Vykers' words still ringing in his ears.

There was no one in the world like Tarmun Vykers. Perhaps there'd once been others, but he was alone, now, unequaled and beyond definition. Even the gods existed in numbers, or so she had always been taught. Vykers, though, remained inexplicably singular. She could feel the Reaper's footsteps on the surface of this same world just as a spider feels a fly in its web, only this fly was much too dangerous for any spider's liking, and she would sooner have killed herself than him, the last and only of his kind. And what kind was that, exactly? Even her greatest trees had no memory of others like him. For all her newfound senses, Vykers was the one mystery that remained beyond her understanding.

He drew near, and she revealed herself to him, materializing from the forest shadows. "Are you lost, Reaper?" she teased.

If she'd caught him off-guard, he gave no sign of it. "When aren't I?" he grinned. "Seems I always end up where I'm meant to be anyway. Don't it, though?"

Aoife smiled. "It does. But will we agree on *why* you're meant to be here?"

"Oh," said Vykers, "I reckon there's a couple 'o reasons."

"I'm sure," the Umaena replied with a hint of light-hearted sarcasm.

She offered her hand, he took it, and without any apparent travel, they were once again within her bower, where the full moon reigned and a million stars blazed down from above. On this occasion, they were quick to bed, tearing at one another's clothing with an abandon born of insatiable need too long denied. Vykers found that Aoife had changed; there were faint, eldritch tracings on her skin, like the whorls on a leaf or in the bark of an ancient tree. Her hair smelled of flowers, of grass, of endless summers and snowfall. Her irises had become twin whirlpools of nature's colors and changed from cornflower to indigo to emerald and more at a mesmerizing rate. It was like watching an endless succession of sunsets, and the Reaper was hard put to break eye contact. Had she enspelled him? He could not have cared less.

Vykers had changed, too, and he hadn't. The grievous injuries Aoife knew he'd suffered throughout their acquaintance had all faded without leaving the faintest of scars behind. It was impossible, of course, but then they were both impossible. They were, in paradox, a matched pair of anomalies. Nevertheless, their goals were antithetical, as the Umaena had often observed. What was it, then, that united them?

Aoife's need pushed these thoughts aside. Her body wanted what it wanted, and to embrace Vykers, to take him inside, was to embrace a massive, cresting wave, a tornado, a wildfire. His raw, elemental hunger consumed her.

Afterwards, basking in the heat and heady scent of his body, she toyed briefly with the notion of combining their power, their objectives, but as her pulse and breathing slowed and the forest again intruded upon her consciousness, she understood that such a thing could never, *would* never be. Indeed, she wondered if the day might not come when they'd be enemies, the one forced to kill the other as Alheria had allegedly killed Mahnus.

Vykers snored lightly, ingloriously, in her ear, and she nudged him with an elbow to roll onto his side. Her attention returned to the Greenwood.

"I didn't just drop by for a little slap-and-tickle," Vykers admitted as she awoke.

Romance was not amongst his talents.

"I'd have been disappointed if you had," said Aoife.

The Reaper looked out into the night, gathered his thoughts. "I need your help."

The Umaena about fell out of her bower and onto the forest floor, below. "The Reaper needs someone?" Aoife joked. "Where are the scribes to record this historic event?"

This time, it was Vykers who took Aoife's hand, gave it a gentle tug. "I've gotta get myself and my men across the sea again. Fast."

Ah. He wanted to use the Here/There.

"And the return trip?"

For a moment, Vykers looked confused. "This is something I gotta do...a step at a time."

Aoife could guess. With the Emperor and seemingly every male inhabitant of his distant land currently invading, it left the door to the proverbial henhouse unattended. Vykers could steal inside and then..."Are you plotting murder?"

"What?" he asked, with more of the same confusion. Then, "No; it's something to do with me, it's personal."

Personal? They'd just been as intimate as two people could be, and yet his heart remained impenetrable. "Yes," Aoife said, "I'll help you."

He seemed relieved, kissed her and said, "I s'pose I should go fetch the men..."

Aoife glanced into the night. "Or I could have them brought hither."

Vykers could well imagine what that might entail and how well it'd be received by his little company. "Best I do it," said he. "Don't wanna spook the boys."

The Umaena wasn't convinced, but unwilling to say so. "As you say."

The Reaper was back down on the forest floor, already facing the direction of his camp. There was little that escaped his mistress' attention in the forest.

When he strode back into the firelight of camp, it was as if he'd been gone just long enough to relieve himself. His men—and Ona—were just where he'd left them.

"Forget someting?" Hjuest asked.

Vykers shook his head. "I need you all to pack up and follow me."

The Red Knight was about to object on his fellows' behalf. What was the point in making camp, only to move it so soon? But he kept his mouth shut. His master was not to be second-guessed.

Mendis, In Nespharia

Mendis was down in the lower city, watching his troops drill in the yard and spying on Lord Bailis' efforts to assimilate the locals when an officer approached.

"Magnificence," the man said, bowing ever-so-slightly.

"Any news of Wykkerian's whereabouts?"

"Alas, no, Magnificence. But we've captured more prisoners."

The Emperor sighed. He was fed up with 'more prisoners.' So far, only Bailis had been of any value. "And?"

"It was thought you might wish to question them."

"No," Mendis replied irritably. "Have Bailis and one of the wizards question them. And tell my staff to bring me no more news that isn't!"

"Isn't, Magnificence?"

"*News!*" Mendis clarified. "News that is neither new nor of interest. What is my staff for if not to handle such mundanities?"

The man bowed again, said a quick "Your word, your will," and scampered back to wherever he'd been. Mendis ground his teeth at the fellow's 'message.' The worst of it was, he had a meeting soon with that very staff and knowing them as he did, he could already hear what each of them would say. Dabis would argue for an assault on the Queen's capital. Promartis would suggest moving the Emperor's base to warmer climes. A third would insist that capturing Wykkerian first was all that mattered. And then the wizards would set to babbling or pontificating, as their moods dictated.

Some men believed that strength, intellect or charisma were a ruler's greatest assets. Mendis knew patience to be most important, patience with his own forces and patience with the enemy. Through his studies and through personal experience, Mendis knew that too many kings and emperors had been goaded—by their supporters, their enemies, sometimes even themselves—into actions that led to downfalls that might have been prevented with a touch more patience. Often, such rulers recognized the foolhardy nature of their actions, but hadn't the will to resist pursuing them, anyway. When the end finally came, it was always to the bitter fulfillment of their expectations.

Mendis would not be such a fool. If capturing Wykkerian and conquering this land took him an unprecedented twenty years, he would consider the time well spent, despite the long absence from his court and family. He had been born and trained to rule the world, to unite its disparate peoples under the banner of the Staurachian Empire. He would do no less.

The meeting unfolded precisely as the Emperor had predicted, up until he slammed his pewter mug on the table top and demanded his advisors' attention.

"Enough!" he commanded and said nothing more until the room became silent. He looked around the table and met the eyes of each of his generals and wizards. "I have said—and more than once—that we shall cut this continent in half, that we shall serve as the anvil upon which the twin hammers of the B'Shar and Tsundi shall break the wills of the native peoples. But I have also said we shall accept and welcome any native man or woman who seeks to join our empire. Let our allies play the villains; we'll play the saviors and endear ourselves and our empire to these rustics. They'll come, as I believe Lord Bailis has, to view us as the better choice, the wiser choice for their allegiance than this haggard Virgin Queen they speak of. And yes, in time we'll march upon her capital—not to make war, however, but to seduce her subjects into joining our cause." The Emperor looked at every face around the table a second time, ensuring that everyone had both heard and understood his message. "Good," Mendis concluded. "You have my leave to go—except for Lord Commander Dabis and High Wizard Alsig."

The Emperor's advisors filed out of his presence, some making small talk, others lost in thought. In less than two minutes, only Mendis and his closest advisors remained. Even the Emperor's bodyguard had departed, knowing there was little danger to their lord with Alsig at his side.

Mendis crossed the room, found a decanter of wine on a nearby shelf, and poured himself a cup. "No more questions or talk of strategy until and unless I say differently," he said to his Lord Commander. "This open debate amongst my counsel smacks of doubt—or worse. Do you mark me, Dabis?"

"Well, Magnificence."

"Excellent," Mendis smiled, though whether he was referring to his wine or Dabis' statement, the Lord Commander could not tell. "Now leave me to speak with Alsig."

Dabis showed Mendis the crown of his head, and then silently left the room.

"And for what shall I be scolded?" the wizard asked, without effort to mask his gentle sarcasm.

"Your tone, for starters. Beyond that, you know why I'm unhappy. Or you should."

"Well, as I've said, we're working on the problem."

"Work better," Mendis answered. "I don't want that *woman*—for want of a better word—surprising us again. We'll never be entirely free to pursue our plans as long as she can pop in on me whenever she likes."

"Consider me chastened."

"You don't sound it. But you will if she murders me in my sleep...unless of course you fancy the throne yourself."

This time, the wizard did appear chastened. "Never, Magnificence. My family has served yours for generations, and I have no other ambition than to continue doing so."

The Emperor seemed satisfied, for he changed the subject. "And what other news have you?"

Now, the wizard puffed himself up like a rooster, happy at the chance to show off what he'd learned. "This continent is smaller than our own by a fifth to a quarter. It is difficult to be more precise without more study. At any rate, this land extends farther north than ours, but ours reaches much farther south. There are, as you might expect, numerous languages and dialects, but, on the whole, the natives believe in versions of the same gods. There are several different types of currency, but Her Majesty is attempting to standardize that; she's just not managing as quickly and efficiently as we would. We are still learning of the land's sentient races, as you know, and the study of its birds, beasts and fishes may take years to accomplish. But of greatest interest, as you've noted, are these Svarren, these giants and a few other hostiles."

"Do they—individually or collectively—pose any threat to our cause?"

"Your legions have never been defeated."

It was an evasive answer, which told Mendis that his wizards were not yet comfortable enough in their research to make guarantees. "Very well," the Emperor said, subdued. "We'll talk more of this anon." The wizard was about to depart when Mendis spoke again. "Have you and your brothers finished with my map?"

"Your map...?" Alsig echoed.

"Yes, the map of Lunessfor's secret ways. Have you finished with it?"

"Pardon, Magnificence, but I—*we*—don't have it. I assumed you'd..."

"I haven't seen it since I turned it over to you," Mendis exclaimed. "Find it. Bring it back to me." This last was not shouted, but said carefully, slowly, so that the wizard could not mistake his master's message.

"I shall."

The Emperor turned away, clearly done with his wizard for the evening.

SIX

The Fool was no fool. What though his mother, Her Majesty, had been reasonably good to him, he was well aware that he did not figure into her final plans. The rules were such that only one could prevail, and he couldn't imagine her allowing him that honor in her stead. What was to become of him, then? Was he meant to stand by like one of his mother's hounds, all loyalty and no brains, until the moment she needed him no more?

It was true that he had no greater ambition than the life he currently enjoyed, eating the finest meals, drinking the finest wines, and occasionally diddling the finest courtesans. He enjoyed a good book and adored a good nap. But the time would come—was in fact approaching—when he would lose all of those things and very likely get nothing in return.

There had to be an alternative, a better way, if a man could find it. And so he'd begun experimenting. He had placed, for example, a long-forgotten map from his mother's library into the invaders' hands. He was certain the Queen wouldn't miss it, having more urgent concerns of late, and though he couldn't be sure the enemy would make use of it, he felt better having taken some action on his own behalf.

But was there anything more he could do? His thoughts drifted to that hideous oaf, the Dead One, and he wondered if the brute might be prodded into making Her Majesty's life more difficult. Hoosh propped himself up on his elbow in bed and pondered the possibilities…

Amongst which was Tarmun Vykers—always Alheria's

pawn, never her master. The Fool was convinced Vykers would relish the chance to put the Queen in her place. The only trouble there, of course, was that Vykers hated him. Did he hate him, however, as much as he hated Alheria? And what could Hoosh offer the Reaper to earn his trust?

Oh, it was going to be a wonderful evening of plots and intrigues, an occasion that demanded the most playful, the most garish of the Fool's outfits.

Eoman & Qansip, Ashore

The young woman, little more than a girl, really, sat down with an elaborate sigh.

Eoman ignored her and stared into the fire. He would not be rushed into any decisions or actions by the strange little creature, no matter how much she wished it.

"Are we going to just sit here forever?" she asked.

He'd known her but a very short while, and already he hated the sound of her voice. "We? You're free to leave whenever you like."

"Don't be stupid!" she scoffed. "You rescued me from the river, and now you're responsible for seeing me to safety."

"Oh, is *that* how it works? Might as well toss you back in the water, if you're goin' to be that much trouble."

The girl pouted. "Well, *are* you planning to sit here forever, then?"

"I might do," Eoman admitted. "Haven't decided."

To his relief, the girl, Qansip, fell into a sullen but welcome silence. Eoman needed to get rid of her somehow and the sooner the better. Her constant yammering made it difficult to concentrate, and the giant needed to sort through his thoughts and feelings before he could determine his next course of action.

He'd lost his title. His *crown!* He could barely remember his life before old Yerls had passed it on to him. He'd worn it for so long, he'd learned to take it for granted, the way a person takes his body for granted. Oh, but he felt its loss now. *I am no longer King!* He lamented. *Beesmarch is. Beesmarch!* All hells, he'd probably disbanded the group by now and gone back to his tree. So much for uniting giantkind.

But if he hadn't...where might they be found? And where was Eoman now, for that matter? Downriver, certainly. But how far? He struggled to recall the lay of the land. Few had traveled it as much as he, and yet its details eluded him, causing him to wonder if he hadn't perhaps hit his head on a rock or three on his trip downriver.

The girl sighed theatrically.

Eoman pretended not to hear.

The thing was, if he somehow managed to return to his friends, how would he ever reconcile himself to life as Beesmarch's subject? Eoman didn't know how to bow to anyone, much less that surly bastard Beesmarch. Then, too, there was the question of how he'd be viewed and received by the others. He feared to see either pity or contempt in their eyes, and the gods forbid they should laugh at him. If only Karrakan had been present—

Karrakan! He, too, had traveled south, in order to escort Mardine to Zillia's cave. Of all his friends, Karrakan was closest, in every sense of the word. Also, he'd no idea that Beesmarch had taken Eoman's crown. If Eoman could reach him, they could journey back to the rest of the group together, and—

The girl.

Eoman leapt to his feet. "I've got to go," he said without making eye contact.

"Good!" said Qansip. "And I'm going with you."

Now he looked at her. "No."

"And who's going to stop me?"

Eoman was momentarily flabbergasted by the girl's moxie. "Are you mad?" he demanded. "I could grab your arms and tear you in half without a thought."

"But not before raping me first, I'm sure."

The girl had a talent for turning his brain inside-out. "What? Why in Mahnus' name would I want to do that?"

"Don't deny it," Qansip snapped. "I've seen you look at me."

"But I haven't!" Eoman protested. "I've made a point *not* to look at you!"

"Which only proves how badly you want to!"

The giant wanted to roar in frustration, but refused to give Qansip the satisfaction. Instead, he began grabbing the ends of burning logs and tossing them into the river, in preparation for departure. Then, he stomped on the embers beneath, making sure to extinguish all trace of fire. "In the first place," he rumbled at last, "we're different species, and I'd sooner have sex with a goat. In the second, such a thing would kill you, either by crushing or..." He couldn't finish the thought.

"Or what?" Qansip smirked. "Are you truly so huge?"

She was touched, was what she was. There was no other explanation for it. He shot out a hand and wrapped his great fingers around her throat. "I will snap your neck, little thing, if you don't shut up at once!"

Qansip's eyes grew round with fear, and she seemed to stop breathing.

Convinced he'd made his point, Eoman let her go. "Now, I'll let you come with me on the condition that you keep quiet. You talk, I leave you. Understood?"

The girl nodded, on the verge of tears. No one, not even her father, had ever talked to her in such a manner, or offered such a believable threat to her safety.

"The bad news is, we have to cross the river. I'll wade in 'til it's up to my shoulders, and you climb on at that point. It's a big river, but I've swum worse. Grab whatever you need from your...carrier-thing." Eoman then looked up at the sky; there was still enough day left to make progress.

Without further delay, he walked into the river and waited. Qansip let out a brief squeak as she stepped into the frigid current and immediately checked to make sure she hadn't angered the giant. He turned away from her and grinned. So, the girl could learn. He still had no idea what he was going to do with her, but at least he'd gotten her to stop yapping at him. He felt a small tug as she grabbed ahold of his clothing and dragged herself up onto his upper back. She inhaled sharply as he sank into the water and began swimming, but again made no further sound.

The water was icy and the current strong and treacherous,

but Eoman would not have taken the risk if he couldn't handle it. The swim took maybe a half hour, and the effort deposited the giant and his passenger quite a ways downriver from where they'd been. Eoman emerged from the water tired, but not exhausted and began rifling through his various pouches and pockets for flint and steel. They needed a fire to dry themselves before any more travel was possible. Again Eoman surveyed the skies. The gods willing, there'd be no more rain for some time. He'd had enough wet to last 'til the mid-summer solstice.

Yendor & Co, Lunessfor

The brewery had been protected by several guards, but its owners had never considered magical wards, and so it had been fairly easy for Spirk and friends to Jump into the warehouse and Jump back out with as many barrels and casks of ale as they chose to steal. And the best part was, they didn't even have to lift the things. Spirk simply touched them, and the group and its new ale reappeared in the hide out. Of course, this trick probably wouldn't work next time they tried it; the brew masters would surely acquire magical protections after suffering such losses. For now though, everyone was immensely pleased with the plan's success, and no one more than Yendor.

The men worked rapidly to settle all of the barrels and casks that could be lowered onto their sides, and Yendor set to removing the stoppers from their bung holes with a heavy wooden mallet. Soon enough, they'd breached every barrel and cask; it was time for the next step in the plan. With a large, specially made funnel, Yendor poured a liberal dose of Long's Old Peculiar into each hole, recorked it, and pounded the stopper in place with such zeal that he doubted anyone would ever remove it again. When he sealed the final cask—one of the smaller ones—he bade Ron shake it up a bit before Yendor knocked the stopper free a second time, which was every bit as difficult as he'd hoped.

"Let's have a taste, eh boys?" He sang out. "Might as well see what our wares are worth!"

Rem, who'd gone along with this nonsense mostly out of

boredom, offered to take the first draught, and he found the newly altered ale completely agreed with him. "Yendor, old man, you might have hit upon something here!"

Yendor, who of course drank second, couldn't help but agree. "Oh," he smiled, "we'll make our fortunes with this stuff, lads!"

When the cask was half-empty and the four thieves blissfully drunk, Rem made some offhand comment about skent, and Yendor stopped in his tracks as if frozen.

"Skent," said he. "I wonder what'd happen if we added a pint or two to the rest o' this cask."

"You'll ruin the flavor, that's sure," Ron offered.

"Stopper that hole, boys!" Yendor commanded. "I need to get my hands on some skent, and then we'll see what we see."

But Spirk and Rem had already fallen asleep on two of the room's dusty couches, and Ron was rapidly fading.

"Never mind," said Yendor. "I'll do it meself. Seems I'm the only one can handle his liquor, anyway." So saying, he sealed the cask and plunked himself down in a moldering, overstuffed chair and immediately joined his mates in sleep, there being nothing else to do. No one could enter or leave the hideout without Spirk's help, and it would be some time before the young Shaper was in any condition to work magic.

Hours later, the men were awakened one at a time, either by full bladders or empty stomachs, but feeling positively buoyant, nonetheless. After a brief discussion, the group decided to Jump out of the hideout on separate errands: Spirk and Ron, to find and purchase a few days' food, Rem, to gain whatever information he could about events in the city, and Yendor to locate some skent, a quest for which he was uniquely qualified.

Everyone reunited outside The Fretful Porpentine (there being no point in going inside and drawing undue attention to themselves) and then set off to find a dark alley from which to Jump back to their hideout. That task accomplished, they tucked into as fine a meal as they'd had in some time.

Around a mouthful of food, Yendor asked, "What 'ave you learned, Rem?"

Lounging on his now-customary couch, the actor replied, "City's starting to lock down. Folks have to prove they're subjects of the Queen in order to get through the gates. But she'll have to get stricter still if she doesn't want to be overrun by refugees."

"What about goods comin' in?"

"Oh, food, drink and weapons get waved right on in. They're stocking the larders for a siege, I think."

Yendor watched Spirk and Ron munch merrily on their supper for a moment. "Well," he said, "it won't much matter how much ale they import, if our drink works like I think it will."

"Speaking of which," Rem interjected, "what's the point of adding skent to an already perfect beverage? Skent's the most foul-tasting swill imaginable."

"Oh, aye," said Yendor, "but it's got one highly useful quality: it's addictive, which the other two ingredients ain't—least not as much. So, folks'll try our brew, fall in love with it, and come to need it. And we four'll become stinkin' rich!"

To Yendor's surprise, it was Ron who voiced reservations. "I dunno," said he. "I don't like the idea o' gettin' folks hooked on anything. Me da was a wildside mushrooms man. Killed him, too."

"This is different," Yendor protested. "You ever have one bad moment with our magic elixir?"

Ron allowed as he hadn't. "Still, it's the skent worries me."

"Son," said Yendor, "I'll wager I've drunk more skent than any man alive…"

"Alive' bein' the key word."

"Yes, and I'm still here, ain't I?"

It was not a debate Ron could win. Not with Yendor, and Rem and Spirk seemed disinclined to participate. Thus, Ron stood by whilst Yendor poured a measured quantity of skent into the group's sampling cask. After sloshing the whole thing around a bit, Yendor asked, "Who'll be the first to try?"

"Might as well be me," Rem replied cynically. "My lot can't get much worse."

There followed a strange, dreamlike period in which the men sang, sniffed one another's footwear, rubbed cheese in Spirk's hair, howled like dogs, painted their chests and faces with soot, and generally behaved like lunatics. When the effects of the beverage wore off, one and all were delighted to discover there was no hangover or any other negative consequence apart from the memory of their foolish behavior. There were things they could not explain, to be sure, such as how Spirk's tights had become stuffed with squashed grapes, or why Yendor's beard was filled with tiny frogs, and no one could say how or why the imprint of bare buttocks had ended up in the dust of the ceiling, but on the whole everyone was pleased with the experience.

"Boys!" Yendor beamed, "I believe we got ourselves a winner!"

"Aye," Rem chuckled. "Now, we must to market!"

Long & Short, Lunessfor

"I'da thought you'd have chosen an inn or a flophouse," Short complained. "But this?"

Long looked around the cell—or would have, if not for the complete absence of light—and answered, "It crossed my mind, but this is the place I remember best. Or most. Certainly spent enough time here."

"Oh" said Short. "I expect you deserved it, then."

The captain laughed. "You sound more 'n more like yourself with every passing day."

Short said nothing for a spell, and then, "Where's this cell located, anyway?"

"House Thornton."

"What in all hells? What good's that to us?"

"Well," Long replied, "I don't imagine Her Majesty'll think to look for us here."

Short sighed, producing a sound more worthy of an angry squirrel than a man. But then, he wasn't entirely a man. "You figure we'll just walk out of here, do ya?"

"More or less, aye."

"And then?"

"I hadn't gotten that far."

"Not much of a god, are you?"

Long shook his head, though Short couldn't see it. "Not much. But come along anyway. Let's see what happens."

What choice did the little homunculus have? When Long stood, he did likewise. Long opened the door, and Short followed him through it into a dark, dank corridor.

"Can't we just Jump somewheres else?"

"I kind o' want to see who's about."

"Madness," Short muttered.

"Probably."

Sure enough, they rounded a corner and surprised a guard who'd been nodding off at his post. The man let out a quick yelp and, as he inhaled to begin hollering in earnest, Long panicked. He wanted some sort of spell to keep the guard quiet, but, unable to think of anything under such pressure, he yanked the enraged axe handle from the belt of his great coat and reached out to knock the fellow unconscious. The axe handle, however, had other ideas. What should have been a simple, easy swing became an increasingly furious flurry of blows. Long tried to drop the handle, but it wouldn't let go. The guard got out a final scream that was quickly cut short by the handle, now pulping his skull. Long recoiled in horror, but still could not rid himself of the handle, nor stop its vicious motion. He became faintly aware of Short begging and pleading with him to stop his assault, and yet he could not. Bones crunched, muscle and skin became jelly, and still Long swung the handle. Tears burst from his eyes and flew down his cheeks—tears of shame, sorrow and regret at first, and then tears of anger. He was a god!

And when he remembered that, the axe handle fell from his grasp and clattered onto the stone floor.

"Mahnus' balls, Long!" Short breathed. "What in the infinite hells possessed you to do *that*?"

Long Pete looked down at his little friend, mortified and mystified in equal measure. His legs seemed to lose their strength and he tumbled, shoulder-first, into the near wall, where he collapsed in grief. He put the back of his hand to his mouth, stifling a sob. It was only then that he noticed he was spattered in blood. "It's…it's that handle," he moaned. "Who would make such a thing?" But he knew. He knew. "I have to get rid of it," he told Short. He bent down to retrieve the hated thing and held out his other hand to the homunculus. "Come."

Short shrieked. They landed, for want of a better word, in a grey, shimmering void, with nothing below or above them, and nothing in any other direction either. The homunculus clung to Long's coat like a possum to its mother's back, for fear of falling into infinity. "Where are we?" he shouted in a high-pitched squeal of terror.

"I don't rightly know. All I thought was *'away'.*"

"Well, take us *away* from here!" Short implored.

There was a brief, disorienting swirl of motion and color, and a forest sprung up around them. In the distance, a group of men were saddling horses and packing their gear. In their midst stood none other than the Reaper.

"Have you lost your mind?" the homunculus asked Long. "He's the very man should never get ahold of that handle."

"My brain says you're right. My gut says otherwise."

"That's what you get with a tiny brain and a big belly."

Vykers, of course, had noticed the captain's sudden appearance and started walking toward him. Short scurried behind his friend's coat and attempted to stay out of sight.

"So, you're still alive," the Reaper remarked. "Dressed like an idiot and covered in blood, but alive. Might be you're more 'n human, after all."

"More," Long agreed. "And less."

"Right. There something you wanted?"

Long held up the axe handle so Vykers could see it.

"If that's s'posed to mean something, friend, I've not idea what it is."

"This handle's enchanted—not by me, and not in a good way. I'm thinkin' it should only be wielded by someone whose ferocity matches its own."

"I didn't used to believe in magic weapons, but...pass it over. We'll see what we see."

Long handed the thing to Vykers, careful to maintain the distance between the Reaper and himself, and stepped back, awaiting the other man's assessment. It didn't take long. Almost as soon as the wood of it hit Vykers' palm, his mouth stretched into a disconcerting grin.

"Oh, aye," said he. "'Tis a rare thing, this. And an angry."

"So I gathered," Long responded.

Vykers took a few experimental swings with it, appeared to grow almost giddy. "But why give it to me?"

"It feels like something oughta belong to you."

The Reaper laughed long and hard at this, but it was not a happy sound, unless the hissing of snakes, the howling of wolves, or the roaring of charging bears is happy.

Long Jumped again, only to come to rest in the jakes of The Fretful Porpentine.

Short gagged at the odor. "You've really no gift for this at all, have ya?"

Omeyo & His Svarren, Following the Legions

The Svarren continued to gather and mass. Omeyo wasn't quite sure how they managed it, but he was glad of it nonetheless. It was clear to him and his mate that the invaders intended to conquer and subjugate the continent, and that meant eradicating the Svarren, eventually. And so, once again, it was kill or be killed. He wondered, fleetingly, if there'd ever come a time when his survival didn't depend upon preemptive murder. He wondered, too, if it was even in his woman's nature to simply abide. He'd never expected to see old age, but the closer he got, the more he fancied it. If only a man could get there with his wits intact…

Svarren scouts reported to the Woman that the invaders were slowly advancing westward, in an endless column a mile wide. Omeyo could hardly credit such information, but then he'd seen stranger things. Much stranger. Where were these newcomers headed, though? The most obvious targets were located to the north and south of their line. Did they think to separate and isolate allies? Perhaps they overestimated the locals. Whatever the case, they were headed west, and Omeyo felt there must be a way to exploit their decision. If, for example, the Svarren attacked the head of the column, the invaders would grind the Long Teeth into oblivion. If the Svarren attacked somewhere near the middle of this great column, both sides could wrap around and flank Omeyo's fighters, effectively

surrounding them. But if Omeyo and his Svarren attacked from
the rear...what, then? He might slow the invaders' progress, but
he doubted his Svarren could ever break the enemy's will. After
considering these options, Omeyo concluded that the best tactic
would be a series of hit-and-run attacks all along the column, on
both sides, at irregular intervals. This unpredictability would
set the invaders' nerves on edge and possibly cause their leaders
to reveal their ultimate goals. The only difficulty was in getting
the general's Svarren on either side of the column. Ultimately,
he'd have to dispatch a small army of his very fastest fighters to
outrun the invaders and cross well in front of their column. The
two armies of Svarren would have to work independently, but
it was something they'd done for ages, and Omeyo supposed
he'd have to trust to their experience in such matters. The secret
to great leadership, he felt, was in identifying and utilizing the
unique skills of one's troops, staff or workers.

Omeyo would let his fighters do what they did best.

Alheria & Mendis, Nespharia

This time, she tapped him on the shoulder as he bathed, causing him to jump and splash like a cat in a well. Almost, he
screamed, but silently thanked the several gods he hadn't. It
was Her Majesty, damn her. Of course it was!

"I am not accustomed to being surprised in my bath," he
said in as calm a voice as he could muster. "At least not by
women of your age."

"Your bath," the Queen replied, "your *privacy*, is of no interest to me."

"Clearly," said Mendis, looking around to confirm that, yes,
she'd again managed to immobilize his guards. "Nevertheless,
the fact remains that I am an Emperor and entitled to some
measure of respect."

"Entitled, invader?" Alheria retorted. "We shall see. I've
come for news of your efforts in locating and destroying Long
Pete."

Seeing his options were limited, Mendis lay back in
the bath and continued his soak. "I take it you've captured

Wykkerian—Vykers—then and are simply awaiting confirmation of my success..."

Alheria said nothing.

"Or you haven't, and you're hoping I'll do your dirty work
in blind faith that you'll uphold your end of the bargain. Then,
once I've accomplished my task, you'll ignore me."

"I could ignore you now, little man," the Queen said icily.
"Your machinations are of little interest to me. But I won't have
it said that I don't keep my promises..." With a rather dra-
matic wave of her arm, a large, heavily muscled man in chains
appeared at the foot of Mendis' bath.

As the Emperor stared at the brute, he could see the man
had been beaten, gagged and very probably sedated in some
way. Mendis stood, oblivious to his own nudity and the chill
of the room's draft on his wet skin. Yes, the prisoner looked
very much like the Wykkerian of legend, the man depicted
in murals, tapestries, books and sacred scrolls. Suddenly, The
Emperor stepped closer; he felt the same thrill he might experience examining a sleeping cave bear. Here, within reach of
his hand, was the most infamous villain in the history of the
Empire, and Mendis could kill him with a simple flick of a knife.
On the other hand, Wykkerian might snap out of his stupor at
any moment. Mendis realized he ought to have been terrified
but was not. He marveled at his own courage under such unfa-
vorable circumstances.

"This looks to be the man," he said finally.

"I can unfetter him, if you doubt it."

Mendis turned to Her Majesty, stepped out of the bath, and
retrieved a nearby bolt of cloth in which to wrap himself. "Have
you drugged him?"

"Drugged him, enspelled him, and beaten him twelve ways
from Lons Day." Alheria waved her arm again and the prisoner
disappeared. "And so he'll remain, until you've killed Long
Pete and offered acceptable proof of it." Mendis was about to
respond when she continued, "And give my compliments to
your magicians—wizards—they're tricky little monsters."

"Not tricky enough, it would seem," Mendis sighed.

The Queen vanished with a laugh that seemed to linger

long after her departure.

Mendis dressed himself and set about finding his staff who, once encountered, emerged from their collective stupor as if they'd never been affected. The Emperor considered another conference with his wizards, but what was the point, really, since their magic offered no impediment to the Queen's visitations? The same was true of his officers and knights. What good were their swords and bows against the Queen's magics?

There was good news, to be sure, in the capture of Wykkerian, and Mendis would like to have exulted in it...but first he had to satisfy a foe in the Queen who might turn out to be worse than the Reaper, if such a thing was even possible.

The Emperor was not much of a drinker, but he wanted something now—a great deal of something.

"A bottle of brandy!" he shouted as he walked into his usual meeting room. Without hesitation, one of his servants rushed forward holding the requested beverage. Whatever else one might say of his servants, they were well-trained. Mendis eschewed the accompanying goblet and headed for a window overlooking the lower city. He'd come to appreciate the view, but he knew the time was fast approaching when he'd have to accompany his legions west. He was not and never would be the sort of leader who led from behind. And as for the hunt for Long Pete, well, he'd have to put some serious effort into it. If the Queen was powerful enough to catch and subdue Wykkerian, who could say what she might do to the Emperor?

But if she was so powerful, why didn't she just catch this Long Pete herself? Without question, Her Majesty was not being entirely forthcoming.

And suppose Mendis simply pretended to look for Long Pete for months and months? It wasn't as if the Queen would suddenly release Wykkerian, was it?

In the middle of a good gulp of brandy, the Emperor laughed and subsequently fell into a coughing fit that shocked his staff. He waved them off and returned to the notion he'd found so amusing: he might never discover Long Pete's whereabouts, but he now knew Wykkerian's. It might prove easier to steal him from the Queen's castle than chasing down the other man.

If only he could locate that missing map…

Alternatively, Lord Bailis might know some means of sneaking into the capital. Would he help, though, if Mendis explained his goals? Doubtful. Of course, he could command compliance, but he was just building trust with the fellow. Bullying him into betraying his former ruler didn't seem a good way to maintain that effort. And he couldn't lie to Bailis for the same reason.

Perhaps he could manipulate the Reaper, then? He'd been taken captive, after all, and poorly used. Surely the Reaper would harbor nothing but resentment—outright hatred—for Her Majesty. If Mendis' operatives managed to free Wykkerian, he might just destroy Lunessfor from the inside-out. And in that hurly-burly, it would not be difficult to, say, hamstring the distracted Reaper and bring him to justice.

The Queen, for her part, would be watching Mendis' legions marching westward—away from her kingdom—and his smaller detachments frantically searching for Long Pete. Let her think she'd cowed the Emperor; let her think him anxiously struggling to fulfill his end of the bargain she'd forced upon him. Her overconfidence would be her undoing.

Alheria & Hoosh, Lunessfor

"But I thought you had a different plan for your boys, as you call them," Hoosh protested.

"I asked them, and this one volunteered," Alheria replied. "They're very obedient, very…*loyal*, and anyway I've still got the other three at my disposal if worst comes to worst."

The Fool didn't like it when the Queen didn't confide in him prior to making major decisions; it only underscored how little she valued his judgment. And if she was this tight-lipped about her dealings with the Emperor, why would she ever reveal her plans for Hoosh?

All he could do was play along. "And how did the Emperor take all this?"

Her Majesty actually laughed. "Oh, he works very hard at maintaining his dignity, his sense of control. He's a much better joust in that regard than Eyatu ever was."

"And the real Vykers?"

"As slippery as ever. I thought at the very least I could locate his horse or companions, but I've had no luck." The Queen fell silent, then, and returned her attentions to the scroll she'd been reading when the Fool walked in. This was how Her Majesty dismissed her subjects; one moment they were part of her conversation, and the next, invisible and inaudible.

Hoosh Bindy did not like it. He'd never given her cause to doubt him before, had in fact been amongst her most devoted. And for what? She'd killed Eyatu and the others. How long did he have left himself?

He mumbled a few words of fealty and bowed out of his mother's presence.

He hoped the Emperor was making good use of the map Hoosh had given him, but hope was not surety. Thus, he needed other pieces in play, as the Queen might say. If she couldn't find Vykers, Hoosh didn't figure to have much more luck. But there was still the Dead One, who'd shown open rancor and contempt for Her Majesty on more than one occasion. Possibilities existed there, the Fool's only qualm being that the Dead One scared the shit out of him.

Hoosh stumbled into his chambers, which were decorated—*festooned*, he often proclaimed—with puppets of every sort, shape and size. How ironic it would be if he himself turned out to be the greatest puppet in the kingdom. He flung himself down on his enormous, overstuffed bed and looked up at the ceiling, lost in thought.

Long Pete might be an option, after all, mightn't he? Having just come into his gifts, he might not relish an immediate departure, buying the Fool more time to…well, just more time. The tricky part would be trying to meet with him without Alheria finding out. What Hoosh needed was a way to distract her, a diversion of sorts. The options were endless, but his patience was not. Still, he'd seen how well his mother had exploited Eyatu's impatience, and the Fool would not make the same mistakes.

A bookseller, Lunessfor

Lib Flemic, the bookseller, would have made an excellent Fool, if not for the fact that there was even less demand for Fools than for booksellers, and unless that Hoosh Bindy character passed unexpectedly, Flemic's vocation did not seem likely to change. Still, with his garish attire, the ludicrous tuft of hair at the front of his otherwise balding head, his sparkling blue eyes, and his continuous chortle, he seemed more suited to foolery than intellectual endeavors. Bookseller he was, though, and, as such, he was determined to offer his clients the best books and friendliest service in the land.

Alas, not all of his clients appreciated his efforts. The Alchemist, D'Marei, for example, had little use for extraneous levity from those he considered underlings.

"Right on time!" Flemic greeted the Alchemist. "Just after sunset."

"Of course. And you continue to dress like a clown."

"Nonsense!" the bookseller chortled. "Nothing wrong with a bit of color!"

The Alchemist brushed past Flemic and worked his way into the stacks and shelves of books behind the counter, just as if he owned the place.

"What can I do for you?" the bookseller asked.

"Apart from murdering your tailor?"

Flemic chortled.

"Nothing," said the Alchemist, "that I cannot do better for myself."

Undeterred by his customer's manner, Flemic followed the man around his shop, never straying more than three feet from his side and chortling all the while.

"That really is quite annoying."

"What's that?" the bookseller asked, chortling.

"That laugh of yours—some sort of nervous tic, is it?"

"Nothing of the kind!" Flemic declared. "I'm just trying to be companionable."

"Stop trying. It's having the opposite effect."

"Oh," Flemic chortled, "I rather think that has more to do with you than me."

The Alchemist looked up from the tome he'd been examining. "Is that so? Shall I give you something to laugh about then?"

Right on cue, the bookseller chortled. "A jest, you mean? I adore a good jest."

Suddenly, there was dust in his face, and he found himself unable to move. The Alchemist's pale face loomed into view, like a rising moon. He passed a large, stoppered vile in front of Flemic's eyes and said "Then I am certain you'll adore this." With a loud pop, he removed the stopper. Next, he gently tilted the bookseller's head back. "If you resist swallowing this, you may well drown, and you don't want to be buried in *those* clothes."

Flemic wanted to chortle, but wasn't able to manage it. The fluid trickled and then tumbled down his throat…and then it was over. With a second dusting from the Alchemist, Flemic regained control of his body and remarked, "That wasn't liquor, was it? Because I've never had liquor. I try to keep myself pure… I…" His voice tapered into silence. And he started chortling.

More than usual.

"Why," said he, "that stuff's delightful. *Delightful!*"

"Yes," said the Alchemist, watching him with a raptor's interest. "Isn't it just?"

Flemic's chortling evolved and grew well beyond its normal boundaries until it encompassed giggling, cackling, tittering and even a smattering of guffaws that sounded as if they'd been made by a donkey in rut. "I am seized with the sudden urge to sing!" the bookseller exclaimed as he raced for the door. "You'll be alright if I leave for a bit, won't you?"

How he got all that out between gales of laughter was a mystery to the Alchemist…but not one he cared about overmuch. "I'll be fine, I'm sure."

The bookseller commenced with the promised—or threatened—singing, but his client heard mercifully little of it before Flemic danced through the shop door and out into the street. The Alchemist experienced a brief moment of levity as he imagined the other man being beaten into submission and then unconsciousness by neighbors fed up with his antics. It probably wouldn't occur, of course, but even an Alchemist could dream. In any case, he'd achieved what he'd wished to achieve in visiting.

Vykers & Co, In the Forest

Vykers' team was nervous, even if he was not. As he led them deeper into the forest, the bushes and trees seemed to grow wilder and more menacing. The insects, birds and squirrels looked on with a palpable air of displeasure and judgment. Hjuest did not fear them, except in their roles as footmen to the larger, more dangerous denizens of the fey typically associated with Vykers'...*companion*, call her.

The whole group, excepting Ona, had been through the Here/There with Aoife before, but every time they encountered the strange woman, she seemed less and less human and more...*other.*

At last, Vykers raised a hand, bringing the company to a stop in a small clearing. "We'll wait here," he said. "Shouldn't be long."

And he was right. Aoife appeared immediately, sprouting from the ground between the horses and rapidly attaining her full height. Any other horses—any *normal* horses—would have been startled by the Umaena's abrupt and bizarre arrival; these horses simply regarded her with expressions of placid amusement. Their riders, however, we not so composed, and several flinched or gasped as if struck.

Aoife spun in a slow circle, measuring everyone in the group and then, without taking her eyes off Ona, said, "And who is this?" in a voice clearly directed at Vykers.

"Kin, or so I'm told." Vykers was happy to see his reply had instantly blunted any potential jealousy from Aoife, if only for the sheer audacious implausibility of it.

Her head snapped in his direction. "What?" Normally guarded, she made no effort to hide her confusion this time.

The Reaper shrugged.

In the meantime, Ona had gotten down from her saddle and assumed a defensive stance, as if she thought the other woman might attempt to strike her.

Aoife scoffed at this. "Believe me, girl, if I wanted to hurt you, I'd have done it already."

"Uh-huh."

Well, she certainly *sounded* like Vykers. Aoife crossed to the man in question and whispered, "We'll speak more of this later...For now," she said aloud, "I shall take you all back across the sea. Home." This last word had a visible impact on the Red Knight and the two or three of his companions who'd learned its meaning in the Queen's tongue. Good. Aoife was doing this as a favor to Vykers, but whether it turned out to be a favor for his men was up to them. Home, Aoife had once learned, could be a place of horrors as well as comfort.

Without stepping nearer or grasping anyone's hand, the Umaena stamped her feet and the entire party sank—plunged— into the ground. Whatever cries of surprise or terror they might have offered were lost to their violent passage through soil, bedrock and worse. They tumbled, whirled and spun head-over-heels; their mounts did likewise, but with far less complaint. It was a wonder, a miracle that no one was hurt in the course of their journey, and when they at last emerged in a field of long grass, they were all as exhausted as if they'd just fought a mighty battle. Even Vykers fell to his knees and commenced to stretch out on his back, his chest heaving, his mouth twisted in a scowl of displeasure.

"Gods, woman," he groaned. "If you meant to teach me a lesson, I'm afraid I missed it."

"Just this," Aoife smiled, "power always has a cost."

The Reaper sat up. "You're telling *me* this?"

"Not telling, exactly. Reminding is more like it."

Vykers looked around at his men, all more bedraggled than he, all more humbled. And then there was Ona, stoic and... angry?...as ever. "Well," said he, "the place smells right, anyhow. Wouldn't you say, Hjuest?"

The Red Knight rose on shaky legs. "Aye. It smells right."

Scanning the area, Vykers spied a goodly clump of bushes not one hundred paces distant. "Let's make camp over there," he declared. "Plenty of kindling and cover from passing troops. You're all too beaten up to travel any more today, anyhow."

Though she had been planning to return to her own grove, Aoife accompanied the Reaper and his team to their destination, hoping to have a final word about the girl in private. As soon as they drew near, however, great bolts of lightning shot from the bushes and struck Aoife squarely in the chest. She should have been thrown backwards and died at the very least. Instead, she stood her ground and her eyes grew a blazing red. Vykers' men, their horses, even Ona hit the ground and lay there, hoping any new bolts would miss them. Only Aoife and Vykers stayed on their feet, defiant.

"Endu-Ro!" Aoife screamed. "Show yourself, coward!"

The satyr leapt from the undergrowth and sneered in Aoife's direction. "I warned you, did I not?" he roared. "I..." Suddenly, he faltered, his confidence shaken. "You are...it cannot be..."

Aoife howled at him in a voice composed of several voices, the voice of a mob. "I am," she boomed. "I am now your goddess, and you will obey me or perish in agony."

The satyr began to tremble, though whether from rage or fear, Vykers could not tell. "But how? How can this be?" he asked plaintively.

"I was chosen; you were not," Aoife thundered. "I was chosen; you were not." Over and over she said it as she moved ever closer to the object of her fury. "Bow to me, Endu-Ro, or die."

"Bow to a human?" he shrieked, causing the other humans present to shrink away from his wrath.

Only Vykers stood his ground, surprised and intrigued to see Aoife behave so imperiously in an instance that did not involve her brother. He'd believed only the End could inspire such anger in the woman; now, he understood for good and all that she was changing. She'd become as confident, as powerful as he, and perhaps more so.

He wanted her as he'd never wanted anything else in his life...that he remembered.

He looked over at Endu-Ro just in time to see him explode in a shower of gore. Pale green tendrils spontaneously erupted from the soil to take possession of the satyr's remains, and from those clumps of activity, great thorny bushes emerged.

"You were expecting a protracted battle?" Aoife asked

Vykers, who watched the whole encounter with his mouth hanging open. "I don't have time for such nonsense."

Ona and the rest of the team had been spattered with and by Endu-Ro and busied themselves in cleaning him off their faces, armor and horses. But it was evident they now regarded Aoife differently as well.

"What was that bit about you being a goddess?" Vykers asked bluntly.

The Umaena smiled and wrapped her arms about herself as if the question pleased her immensely. A second later, her demeanor changed and a fierce look took hold in her eyes. "It's true."

"Then the Queen, Alheria..."

"Not my Queen, not my goddess, not my concern."

Vykers looked for something, anything in her face that might suggest she was joking, but he found no such evidence. "As you said, we'll talk later. In private."

Aoife quirked an eyebrow at him and smiled seductively. "Oh, *now* you'd talk?"

This time, Vykers was not surprised when she vanished. If she was changing, he was still becoming more attuned to her emotions and rhythms. With a sigh, he turned to find his squad staring at him expectantly.

"Hjuest," said he, "point us towards the Emperor's city. We'll head out first thing tomorrow."

Kittins, Beneath Lunessfor

It was a day before Kittins was able to return to the wall and pursue the source of the whining behind it. This time, he'd come prepared and carried a massive hammer with which to smash through said wall. As he drew near, the now-familiar whining and wailing commenced and grew in strength. What in Mahnus' name could be making such a noise? He couldn't wait to find out. With a quick series of massive blows, he reduced the wall to rubble and stepped through into the darkness beyond...

The thing that lay on the floor nearby and stared in his direction with sightless eyes could only be described as an abomination. Having been called one himself on numerous occasions, he discovered he fell well short of the mark set by this...*creature.*

It might once have been human. But if that were so, it would not still be alive. It was white all over—a sickly, glistening white. Whatever hair it originally possessed was gone, long gone by the look of it. Its eyes, ears, nose, and teeth had been removed. Its legs were fused together, and its arms were little more than flipper-like appendages. An iron collar about its neck and another around its waist were connected by a large, rusty chain that held the thing in place in the center of the chamber. All in all, it looked more like a deformed seal than a man, which thought gave the captain pause: what in all hells was he looking at?

The thing stopped its shrieking when Kittins stepped into its presence and swung its head to-and-fro, as if seeking him out.

"Kill me," it croaked at last, with a wet, mushy diction. "Kill me, I beg."

Kittins scanned the room, looking for anything that might lend the scene more sense—a door, a straw mattress, an old dish of food, a torch. Nothing presented itself. The creature had been walled in, as unlikely as that seemed.

"Who or what are you?" Kittins demanded.

"A dead thing, lacking only a death."

Kittins chuckled at the irony. "Some say the same o' me."

The thing did not share in his levity. "Kill me, kill me, kill me."

"Not yet," Kittins replied. "Got some questions, first."

The creature mumbled and gibbered its disappointment.

"Who are you?"

"Am? No one. Was? Alheria's."

"Alheria's? Alheria's what?"

"Bastard. Her bastard."

Kittins considered this a while, and then continued, "And why are you here?"

"Arrogance? Punishment? Insurance? Kill me. Kill me now!"

"Silence!" the big man countered. "Or I'll leave you as you are."

The creature stopped vocalizing on the instant.

"What do you mean by 'arrogance, punishment, insurance'?"

"Only one can."

"Only one can what?" Kittins had half a mind to kick the horrid thing in the face for being so damnably obtuse.

"Ascend, ascend. Only one can."

Nothing frightened Kittins, but he felt the goosebumps rise on his forearms nonetheless, so uncanny were the circumstances. Briefly, he debated whether he truly wanted to hear what was coming; ultimately, he could not resist.

"And what does 'ascend' mean?"

The thing heaved and doubled over, as if it wanted to vomit, but nothing came up. This was followed by a volley of noise that was either sobbing or giggling, if not both.

"What does 'ascend' mean?" Kittins repeated into the darkness.

"Mother is a goddess," the thing slurred. "But not yet an Overgod."

Kittins grimaced. Every answer brought a dozen more questions. How long could he converse with this abomination before he lost his own mind? Through clenched teeth, he asked, "What's an Overgod?"

"Not mother!" the creature cackled. "Mahnus forefend! Not mother!"

The captain ran out of patience. "What in the fuck is a fuckin' Overgod? Tell me now, or I mend this wall and leave you here forever!"

"Fuck?" the thing echoed. "Fuck *you!*"

Kittins smashed its head in with his hammer, and kept swinging until the thing at his feet was little more than bloody mush. The captain stepped back into the main passageway, leaned his back against a wall, and stayed there, breathing deeply, for some time.

A memory came to him then, of killing the Queen's Shaper, Cindor. Kittins and Rem had stabbed the man repeatedly and taken his head clean off...and yet, Kittins understood, the Shaper survived. Mightn't this be possible for the thing he'd just killed, as well?

He didn't think so. Someone—Alheria, perchance?—had maimed it, and it had never recovered. All the same, it had survived enough isolation, starvation and other such cruelties to drive anyone mad.

But what in the endless hells was an Overgod?

Yendor & Co, Lunessfor

"And 'ow do I know this here ain't stolen?" the barkeep challenged Yendor as he thumped on the small cask the other man carried.

Yendor broke into a broad smile. "By samplin', o' course! You've never had nor tasted the like o' this before!"

"Ha! I've never drunk from the jakes, neither, but that in itself don't recommend 'em!"

"Put your hands on a tankard, and my drink'll speak for itself!"

The barkeep scoffed. "Mighty claims, mighty claims! But I ain't lived this long by swallowing every cup o' swill put in front 'o me. Let's try it on the barflies!"

Yendor, being a devout drunkard himself, instantly recognized a suitable subject for the purpose sitting not two stools away. "Say there!" he called to a disheveled heap in a man's tunic and hose. "Care for a drink on the house?"

The heap smiled, slicked his thinning hair back with a spit-moistened palm and said, "Those be magic words, m' friend! Pour us a goodly goblet, and we shall partake."

Magic words? The whole moment was magic, as far as Yendor was concerned. This other bloke was like a long-lost brother, a bosom companion of the highest order, and the old souse, Yendor, took great pleasure in the bestowing of his gift upon his new friend. He watched with a raptor's focus as the man took a great quaff of Long's Old Peculiar. The barkeep, too, seemed more than professionally interested. To their mutual delight, the barfly's face lit up like moonrise, and an expression of absolute wonderment spread rapidly across his face. "What magic is this?"

The barkeep pushed his own mug into Yendor's face and

demanded his promised sample. "Anyone can buy a sot's gratitude with free spirits," he remarked. "But a man born to the
tavern trade? Gimme a measure of your ale and we'll see what
we see."

What he saw—or more accurately envisioned—was profit,
more profit than he'd known in years. "It's not bad," said he.
"You got any larger quantities than them little tastin' casks?"

"O' course!" Yendor beamed. "But, er, maybe it's wiser to
spread the wealth around, share with a few other businesses…"

The barkeep knew where this was going, knew he was being
crudely manipulated, but the allure of the vendor's strange ale
was such that he could not resist. "Nah, nah! Let's not be rash,
now. I'm prepared to offer you enough coin for an exclusive
contract."

Yendor ran his fingers through his beard, tapped his fingers
against his lips in a parody of calculation. "Deal!" he said at last,
though he'd no intention of abiding by it.

The barkeep shook Yendor's hand and asked, "When can I
have my first barrel?"

"I'll have my Shaper bring it by this afternoon."

"Oh," said the barkeep, suddenly impressed. "You've a
Shaper, have you?"

"And who don't?" asked Yendor, suddenly impressive.

True to his word, the first barrel arrived more or less on time
and the barkeep was only too happy to pay for it.

And pay for it he would.

Back in the gang's hideout, Spirk demanded another mug of
Long's Old Peculiar in exchange for having completed his deliv-
ery. Naturally, his companions teased him about it, suggesting
maybe he was developing a dependence upon the stuff—and
if anyone would know, it was Yendor. But the uncomfortable
fact was, it was the only remedy Spirk had found for the ever-
increasing burning that was, of late, driving him to distraction.
How in Mahnus' name had Pellas endured the sensation as
long as he had?

And then Spirk remembered: Pellas—D'Kem—had possessed an elixir of his own, hadn't he? It couldn't have been

anywhere near as lovely as the stuff Spirk was currently enjoying, because he couldn't recall ever seeing the old Shaper smile after drinking from his flask, whereas Spirk giggled and floated about the room, figuratively and literally.

"That's enough o' that now, son," Yendor said. "You're startin' to make the actor look like a shy little milkmaid by comparison!"

"Former actor," Rem interjected, after which he let loose with a lengthy and forlorn sigh.

'No reason you can't go back to it."

"Apart from bein' dead, you mean."

"So make up a new identity. Ain't that what you actors do?"

"If only it were that easy," Rem lamented.

"Well, we gotta do something!" This, from Ron.

Yendor sat up, suddenly feeling under attack. "But we *are* doin' something, lads: we're workin' on gettin' rich!"

Spirk floated gently down into a seat at the older man's side. "But what's to-do while we's a-waitin'?"

"Aye," said Rem. "We've been running and fighting and scheming so long, sitting still seems rather a bore."

"There's always the war..." Ron offered.

"Ah, yes," said Yendor. "The war."

Long & Short, Lunessfor

Long had managed to make his great coat look like a full set of clothing. Short's size, however, was too difficult to explain with simple magics, so Long disguised him as a stool. Thus protected from scrutiny, both men witnessed Yendor's entire transaction with the barkeep from a distance of not more than ten paces.

"Can you get off me now?" Short groused. "Your ass is killin' me!"

Long stood, but made no further response to Short's commentary. "What is that old reprobate up to, I wonder?" He muttered to himself.

"Who, your one-eyed friend? No idea."

"Nor me," said Long, "But I mean to find out."

"Think I'll wait here," Short replied.

Long barely heard him, so intent was he on the cask the barkeep was even now mounting on a shelf behind the counter. "Got some fresh ale, have you?" Long asked, pointing his nose at the cask.

"I might. This one costs a bit more for a taste, though." He looked Long up and down. "Might be too dear for you."

"That so?" said Long. "I believe I've got the coin," whereupon he reached into his pocket and came out with an illusory Hero, replete with the burnished image of one Tarmun Vykers.

The barkeep actually blushed as he snatched it away from Long's hand. "Well," he coughed, "it ain't *that* dear, but I'm happy to pour you a pint *now*, friend."

"Do so!" Long commanded good-naturedly, "And I shall let you know what I think of your newest spirit."

To say that he was amazed, upon tasting, is an understatement. He was flabbergasted. And he knew, with one mouthful, what his old friend had done.

But how? And why? And what might happen if Yendor's brew caught on? The whole city would…

"I'd like to buy the lot," Long proclaimed.

"No sir," the barkeep grinned back at him. "Not for Her Majesty's crown! This here ale's gonna make me rich!"

"How much coin would you need to stop selling it?"

The barkeep sniggered at the idea.

Long realized he now had the power to force the issue, but if the other man was so bent on having his way, he'd own the consequences, too. "Can't blame a fellow for tryin'," he said, as he took another swig of his ale and headed back towards Short…

Who was suffering mightily under the weight of an enormous brute with even worse hygiene than Long.

"I believe," said Long, "that you're sittin' on my stool."

"Fuck off!" the brute belched, whereupon, with a mere wave of his hand, Long rendered the man stark naked. In a trice, the brute's attitude changed from belligerence to confusion and confusion to panic. He let out a curiously high-pitched wail of dismay and bolted for the door, to the thunderous heckling and laughter of the other patrons.

Soon, the tumult died down and Short grumbled, "Serves

the bastard right. Nearly snapped me in half, he did! Never make me into a stool again!"

"You'd rather a chamber pot?"

"What's that, god humor?"

Long shrugged, "Must be," and sat down on his friend to stifle further commentary. The thing of it was, he had greater concerns than whatever Yendor was up to. Much greater. But it was hard to concentrate on Alheria or even the coming war with Yendor running about Lunessfor doing Mahnus-knew-what. *Ha!* Mahnus had no idea, and that was the problem.

He focused again on the ale in his hand. There was magic elixir in it, and no mistake. But there was also a trace of skent, as well. Yendor meant his drink to become addictive. It was as short-sighted a plan as he'd ever seen from his former companion; sure, it would make his old pals wealthy, but who knew what it'd do to the rest of the city?

And then it dawned on Long: a little pandemonium might keep Her Majesty occupied long enough to...what? Catch her unattended? Confront her? He doubted he possessed the strength yet to overwhelm her. Still, a war outside her walls and chaos within them would make it much easier for Long to move about and buy the time he needed to determine his next steps.

Beneath him, Short muttered something about noxious odors.

Eoman & Qansip, In the Wilds

Eoman had resolved himself to carrying the girl for the rest of their time together, however long that might be. It was just easier than slowing his pace to match hers, and besides, he hadn't the patience for it. This Qansip walked through the countryside as if she were at the head of a parade. And Eoman had never much cared for parades. They were human spectacles of vanity.

The important thing was reaching Karrakan before the shaman wandered off to parts unknown, and Eoman would not be diverted or distracted from this effort. He and his passenger had recently come out into open hill country, though, and caution was needful. It was true that, being a giant, he could spy things farther away than most humans, but it was also true that he was easier spied, as well. That being the case, he skirted the tops of hills instead of cresting them. No point in making himself a target, after all.

Not that Qansip's constant babble was helping in that regard. She simply would not be quiet, even though he'd warned her many a time and oft that her chattering might act like a beacon to potential enemies. And worse than the threat they posed was the utterly insipid nature of her monologue—a lengthy series of 'I' statements punctuated rather infrequently by the occasional, perhaps even accidental, question about him or giantkind in general. After hearing her talk for hours, he felt he knew everything there was to know about her...and nothing at all. How could anyone in any culture ever become so self-absorbed? Finally, he'd had enough and he set her down.

"You have got to shut it," he insisted. "Or I'll leave you here. Your endless prattle is driving me mad, and I need my wits about me."

Qansip fumed. Again, he had dared to rebuke and threaten her. "Why is it always about you and your needs?" she spat back at him.

His mouth fell open in disbelief. "Me and *my* needs? The gods themselves couldn't get a word in edgewise when you're talkin'!" Qansip shrieked in fury at this remark, and Eoman quickly put a huge hand over her mouth. "Damn fool girl!" said he. "You'll bring the Svarren down on us, sure as I'm standin' here." The girl bit him, but he scarcely felt it. "If you don't like my terms, you're free to go," he told her before releasing his grip.

She kicked and punched at him before pulling away. "Fine!" she said. "I don't need help from a great, smelly beast like you!" With that, she swiveled her head to and fro, seeking out the most favorable path away from her tormentor and stomped off in a huff.

Eoman would not be manipulated. He did not watch her go, did not even react to her going. Instead, he continued in the direction he'd been traveling, as if she'd never existed. Several minutes passed, and she came squeaking after him.

"Long Teeth! Long Teeth!"

He looked in the direction from which she'd come and pushed her behind him. "As I said." He waited, but nothing appeared. He didn't smell them, either. Qansip clung to his leg and looked up at him in sufficient terror to convince him she'd seen something, but...

Reluctantly, he climbed the nearest hill, with Qansip right behind. From the top, he could see that, yes, there were Svarren in the distance, moving from right to left across his field of vision. Some of the creatures paused to stare at him, but none raised any alarm or expressed any further interest in him.

Odd.

"Aye," Eoman said softly. "Svarren they be, but strangely uninterested in us." Remaining where he stood, he rotated slowly 'til he'd come full circle. Nothing in any direction but the now-fading Long Teeth. "Let's get on with it," he told Qansip and lifted her back onto his shoulders.

As he resumed walking, he made a mental list of every explanation he could think of for the Svarren's apparent indifference. They were already chasing prey, for example. Or were prey themselves, desperate to escape pursuit. Given the creatures' languid pace, neither of those possibilities seemed particularly compelling. They might have been going to meet up with others of their kind, or they might have been scouting ahead of a larger party. But why didn't they whoop and shriek upon sighting him? It made no sense. The Svarren's appearance, however, did have the effect of temporarily silencing the human girl, so it wasn't all bad.

Like the rest of Starling Company, Amath was anxious to get on with the real fighting. This endless marching seemed of little purpose to him, even if it did open new territory and expand the Empire's holdings in this strange land. Amath was not an explorer and wanted only to do what he'd been trained to do: fight.

When the call went out for a water break, he looked about for a place to sit and noticed a large stone atop a nearby hillock. That'd do. The weather was mild and the sky overcast, but marching in armor was still an exhausting, sweaty job, and all Amath wanted was a few minutes' rest. By himself. He slogged up the hillock and plunked himself down on the stone, not caring in the least whether he dented or scratched his armor; the Emperor's smiths would always make more. Amath uncorked his canteen and raised it to his lips…and that's when he saw the giant in the distance. He dropped the canteen and sprang to his feet, charging pell-mell down the hill towards his commanders.

"Begging your pardon, Sergeant, but there's a giant to the southwest!" he proclaimed to the nearest officer. "You can see it from that stone, yonder."

The Sergeant, a tall, wiry fellow whose name Amath had forgotten in his excitement, asked no questions but made straight for the spot Amath had indicated. The sergeant's body language suggested that, yes, there was indeed a giant approaching, and Amath knew for a certainty that his water break was over.

Eoman smelled them before he saw them, which either meant they weren't bright enough to approach him from downwind, or, more likely, that they were surrounding him. The way his luck had been running lately, he suspected the latter, and, damn it all, he'd lost his axe when he'd accepted Beesmarch's challenge.

"We've got a problem, girl," he rumbled.

"My name is Qansip."

"We're bein' surrounded. By enemy troops, I imagine."

"Put me down, then!" she demanded. "I don't want to be seen being carried like a child."

But you are a child, Eoman wanted to tell her. "As you wish," he said. He set her down and took a goodly step away from her, so as to create the suggestion that they were traveling companions and nothing more, which was, of course, the truth. Would these soldiers believe it, though? Eoman was pessimistic about his chances.

The order had been passed through the ranks to subdue and capture the giant rather than kill him outright, because the

Emperor might see some value in questioning or studying the creature. At the very least, it would make a fascinating addition to his menagerie.

Despite his company's numeric superiority, Amath was nervous. He'd never seen—much less fought—a giant before, and he'd no idea what to expect of the monster. As the circle of his fellows drew tighter and tighter around their prey, Amath spied a young woman standing well away from the giant.

She raised a hand and said something loudly, and though Amath comprehended not a word of it, he understood the giant's facial expressions well enough. The great thing looked shocked, stunned and angry at the woman's comments, whatever they'd been.

The circle tightened still more, and Colonel Trieps barked at the giant and woman to stay where they were. Amath could see the giant's eyes darting back and forth, searching for weakness amongst the Emperor's troops, or perhaps some avenue of escape. Amath expected the giant to grab the woman and threaten to kill her if he was not allowed to depart, but he did nothing of the kind.

Trieps, brave fellow that he was, urged his horse to within ten paces of the giant and shouted, "Let the woman go, monster!"

It was obvious the giant did not speak the Emperor's tongue, but he understood the colonel nonetheless. He stepped slowly away from her and held his hands out in front of himself, palms-up, as if to say "I have no weapons."

Trieps dispatched two of his men to escort the woman into the safety of his presence. As she drew nearer, Amath was smitten. He'd never seen a fairer wench in all his life, despite her filthy, rumpled clothing and tangled hair. He could see, too, that the other men shared his assessment.

Eoman watched Qansip melt into the body of the surrounding troops with a mixture of disbelief and self-reproach. He'd always known her to be a vain, self-serving thing. But to hear her denounce him after all he'd done for her?

Still, he didn't have time to dwell upon the wretch. His immediate concern was his own safety. The men surrounding him didn't seem inclined to let him walk away. He held out his hands.

"See? Empty."

Spears and truncheons appeared amongst the soldiers, and here and there a crossbow. Eoman thought they meant to kill him...until he saw the chains.

"No," said he, "you'll have to kill me. I'm no man's prisoner."

A contingent of soldiers pushed in behind Eoman's back, presumably going for his legs, so the giant spun to frighten them off, but of course other soldiers pushed in from the direction he had been facing.

A spear stuck him in the left calf.

The giant roared, much like a bear or great cat, and flailed at the front line of soldiers. It seemed to Amath that their target was more interested in keeping them all at bay than in fighting, but the colonel had called for his capture and captured he would be. Several of Amath's comrades peppered the giant's legs with crossbow bolts. Amath felt a hard shove in the back, and he stumbled free of the line and well within reach of the now-angry giant.

Amath looked up into his adversary's enormous face and felt more fear than he'd ever known in his life. Feebly, he extended his mace.

The giant, meaning perhaps to rip the mace from his grip, reached down and grabbed Amath's hand instead. With a powerful jerk, he tore the soldier's whole arm from its shoulder, leaving Amath to stagger backwards in shock and dismay. He looked around plaintively at his fellow soldiers. Would someone please help? Would anyone please tell him this was all a bad joke? Why...

Blood geysered from his shoulder, in such a hurry, such an awful hurry...

Amath fell face-first into the grass.

Now he'd done it. He'd inadvertently killed one of the bastards and they'd make him pay for it tenfold, as humans always did. The spears came out and went in, into Eoman's hips, into his legs, until he could no longer stand on his weakened, bloody feet. Slowly, he sank to his knees as the invaders crushed in around him and beat him into submission with maces, clubs and sword hilts. If only he still had his axe...

Eoman wasn't out long, but long enough. His captors had him well and thoroughly chained, and it looked like they were prepared to drag him if he wasn't in the mood to walk. They tugged on his chains and shouted at him, and he rose reluctantly to his feet. He hurt all over, felt like he'd been thrown down a mountainside. He took a moment to study his chains. They'd been intended for oxen, he imagined, but were more than strong enough to hold him.

For now.

And where was little Qansip? Right where he figured she'd be, astride a horse, stationed beside what looked to be the group's commanding officer.

Would she put in a good word for her giant savior? She'd yet to look back in his direction, and he suspected the answer was no.

SEVEN

Vykers & Co, In the Emperor's Lands

Once again, Vykers was struck by how much warmer and somehow heavier the air seemed compared to that back home. Always, he could feel it moving across his skin, like a lover's caress, promising mysterious pleasures and urging him to contentment. But contentment was not Vykers' way.

He and his band had ridden for two days, encountered no one, and seen little of note. The Reaper was bored. He knew why, of course: everyone from *this* side of the sea was over on the other side, sacking his homeland. Briefly, he felt envious—the greatest conflict in a lifetime, and he was not involved. Not yet, anyway. Defender or liberator, it was all one to him, so long as he was victorious in the end.

Behind him, Vykers' heard his men's whispered conversations in a hodge-podge of different languages. Hjuest could sort it all out, but to Vykers it was flat gibberish. The only person who wasn't speaking, didn't ever speak, was Ona, which, from the Reaper's experience, probably meant she had the most to say. He wouldn't give her the satisfaction. She'd chosen to follow him, against his wishes or advice, she could damn well suffer the consequences.

Still...how in Mahnus' name could she possibly be his granddaughter? Endless hells, his head hurt just thinking about it. He supposed he'd have his answers—and they, their reckoning—sooner or later.

Vykers scanned the horizon. It looked like there was a small forest to the northwest, maybe a good place to make camp or even to summon Aoife, if needs must. He didn't think she'd come, but he surely enjoyed thinking about it.

A line of trees and shrubs crossing the group's path indicated the presence of a river. "We'll follow that," Vykers announced. "'S gotta lead to a town eventually."

"And vhy do ve vant a town?" Hjuest inquired. "Isn't it dangerous to let too many people see us?"

The Reaper looked askance at his Second. "I'm gonna forget you questioning me for now. I want to find a town so I can assess just how bare the Emperor's left his cupboard. Understand?"

Chastened, Hjuest shrugged. "Ya, ya. I see."

They rode straight for the trees, where they confirmed the presence of a river.

Vykers leaned his head upriver. "This way."

It wasn't long before the group saw little docks here and there and even the occasional rowboat. What they did not see was people.

"So far, it's looking like dey are all gone," Hjuest allowed.

The Reaper said nothing.

In time, they came to a small village. The first building—and the one of most interest—was an inn, nestled beneath the boughs of a gigantic tree. Vykers slid from his saddle. "Secure the horses," he said over his shoulder, not caring who did the task, but confident it would be done.

As he approached the door, Vykers saw that the steps and front door were well-maintained. He reckoned the women were in charge now. He passed under the Inn's sign without reading it—'W'-something—gripped the door handle, and pushed inside...

Where he was surprised to see a lone man behind the bar, cleaning bottles with a cloth. The barkeep looked up at him and said, "Leave your weapons outside, if you please."

"I don't please," Vykers responded. "But I don't need 'em, either." He popped his head back outside and told his crew to leave their weapons on their mounts. It was then that he realized he'd understood the man inside and had even answered in the same tongue. Rather than let confusion consume him, he shook his head at the impossibility of it all and went back inside. This time, the barkeep had both hands on the bar and a neutral expression on his handsome face. His long, red hair was swept back behind his neck, tied or secured by something the Reaper hadn't seen yet.

"Welcome to my inn," the barkeep-now-owner said. "I hope your intentions are honest."

Vykers wasn't especially cold, so he eschewed the black stone fireplace for a table near a window. "What we intend and what happens ain't always one and the same."

The innkeeper cracked a wry smile. "True enough. Something to drink?"

The Reaper nodded, aware that his men and Ona were watching his every move, scrutinizing his every word. "How is it you ain't accompanied your Emperor across the sea?"

"He's not my Emperor," the other man said easily. "And I don't share his ambitions." The innkeeper then went about placing empty mugs in front of all Vykers' crew, and then came back around with several pitchers of ale that he obtained from a room somewhere in back.

In his absence, Vykers noted a sword on the wall and a lute resting on the far end of the bar. "Those yours?" he indicated with his eyes as the innkeeper filled his mug.

"Yes," the man said, without elaboration.

"You any good with it?"

"Which, the sword or the lute?"

"The lute. I can already see you can handle a sword."

"Can you?" the innkeeper demurred. "I favor the lute nowadays. Would you care for a song?"

"No," said Vykers, matter-of-factly.

The innkeeper paused for a moment, bewildered, and then said, "I see. Well, to each his own. What brings you to town?"

Vykers tasted his ale. "Good stuff, this."

"Glad you like it. I'm afraid I can't offer you a meal. I don't get many groups any more, and I'm not prepared. I've got a bit of cold meat and cheese."

"This'll do," the Reaper responded. "Don't wanna put you out."

"And, uh, the reason for your visit?"

"Just a little mid-day break on our travels."

"To?"

"What's a man like you doing behind a bar in the middle 'o nowhere?" Vykers asked abruptly. "Runnin' from something, are you?" Around him, his fellows put down their mugs and stopped their chatter, nervous that something was about to transpire.

"You've a keen eye, stranger. I guess you could say I'm running from trouble, if you like, which is why I've been so nosy about *your* intentions."

"Put your mind at ease, then," Vykers said. "You've got nothin' I want. 'Cept maybe a couple more gallons o' this brew." His gang exhaled audibly and fell into laughter. Even Ona seemed to brighten up. Hells, thought Vykers, she's probably sweet on this red-haired, lute-playin' devil. And then he thought maybe he could fob her off on him. "You in need of a serving wench?" he asked the innkeeper.

Instantly, Ona was on her feet and out the door, slamming it behind her with authority.

The innkeeper dealt with the awkward silence that followed by refilling Vykers' mug and working his way around the rest of his fellows. When everyone had enjoyed his fill, the Reaper stood and gestured at the door, wordlessly commanding the men outside. He had no local currency, but he placed a gold Royal on his table to offset that inconvenience.

When he was back outside and had retrieved his weapons, the innkeeper emerged, holding the Royal out, and said, "Whatever this coin is, it's far more gold than you owe me."

"Toss it here, then," said Vykers.

The innkeeper tossed the Royal as instructed, whereupon he saw a brief flash of movement, heard a metallic clinking sound and looked down to see the coin cut cleanly in half, lying in the dust of the road. When he looked back up, the Reaper was grinning at him and sliding his sword back into its scabbard. "You take half, and I'll take half."

It had been a worthwhile stop. Vykers had learned that a

significant portion of the local population had traveled across the sea, enough to empty at least one village and rob an otherwise thriving inn of its customers. He'd learned, too, that not everyone shared the Emperor's goals. And all of this was good, because it suggested he'd meet less resistance than he'd expected and, in fact, that he might even find allies.

Hjuest rode to his left. Vykers glanced over at him and smirked to himself. The Red Knight had a thousand questions and was struggling to work them out on his own—out of fear of taxing the Reaper's patience, perhaps, or simple stubborn pride. It made no difference. There was value in such a struggle, whatever the reasons for it.

Vykers reflected on his own questions, took stock of what he knew and what he suspected. In some ways, it was like having a broken bone beneath the skin. There was clearly something amiss, and he had a general idea of what and where, but the specifics eluded him. For example, he'd become painfully aware of the fact that there was something wrong with his memory. He'd listened to other folks—traveling companions, mostly—recount endless tales of their daily lives, from the present to their earliest days.

Vykers could not remember his parents.

He'd heard many a song about his exploits over the years, but could not recall the details—save one. He'd once had a great love before Aoife. And the woman's name had been...

Infinite hells! If he hadn't felt so strong, so limitless, he might've suspected that he'd caught some horrible disease. Why could he not remember his own life? He turned in his saddle, pretending to search the group's backtrail, and stole a look at Ona. His granddaughter? He'd once scoffed at the idea of magic swords—he remembered that much. And he'd been proven wrong. So, the girl could be kin. She did have a certain "Don't fuck with me" air about her. She was large for a woman, lithe and well-muscled. If Vykers had living grandchildren, he supposed they'd look much like Ona. He drummed his fingers on the horn of his saddle. Sometime, when things calmed down a bit, he'd have to ask the girl more about her mother and grandmother.

Enough of that. Vykers turned his thoughts to the Emperor's Palace. He reckoned Aoife might have dropped his gang closer, but he wanted some time to get familiar and comfortable with the Emperor's realm before he went charging into the palace. A wise man scouts the territory before assaulting the throne. Somebody'd told him that once. Hells, he might've said it himself.

He and his team continued to travel northeast on the road they'd discovered in the last town. And it was an impressive road—wide, free of weeds, level and well-maintained. Better than anything he'd walked in Her Majesty's kingdom. Of course, with such a large number of the Emperor's subjects now overseas, the roads were likely to fall into disuse and deteriorate somewhat. The hidden costs of conquest.

The Reaper closed his eyes and allowed himself to be lulled into a mild trance by the movements of his horse's gait. He smelled the beast, of course, along with the sweat of his fellows, and the grasses alongside the road. Funny, he was untold miles from home and yet so much was familiar to him.

His men—and Ona—were probably hoping to find another village and inn in which to bed down for the evening. Not Vykers. Give him a patch of grass near a blazing fire beneath a wide open sky, and he was as content as he could ever be...outside of battle. The absence of a village bothered him not at all. Thus, they would again sleep outdoors. Anyway, it was through campfire chatter that Vykers learned the most about his men and their disparate languages and talents. He still hadn't bothered to learn all their names—and why would he? Their inevitable deaths would only be that much harder to stomach—but he'd learned much about them as men. As for Ona, well, she remained sullen and aloof. He supposed it was time to have that talk.

He caught her eye and waved her over to him, patting an empty spot on the ground on his left. He thought for a moment that she might decline, but he was pleasantly surprised when she got up and joined him. Before she could say a word, Vykers shooed the men to his right and her left with a wave of his hand.

His smile told them it wasn't personal, but he wanted to speak to the girl in private. In truth, it couldn't *be* more personal, but they didn't need to know that.

"What?" she said finally.

"You tell me. You learned what you came to learn?"

"I don't know what that is, except that you're a bastard."

Vykers' sudden burst of raucous laughter sent a brief ripple of alarm through the others, but when it was evident no anger or violence were forthcoming, everyone relaxed. Ona, however, was not amused.

"See what I mean?"

"A man don't survive in battle by makin' friends with the enemy."

"Not everything's a battle."

"Isn't it?" Vykers challenged the girl. When she struggled to respond, he went on. "Tell me more o' your grandmother, then."

Ona looked down at her hands and inspected her finger-nails. She'd bitten them all to the quick, Vykers saw. "Nana was small and delicate," Ona said in a far-away voice. "Even in her age, she had the air of a little girl. Toward the end, she'd walk around, barefoot, in a white shift, clutching a handful of flowers, offering one or all to everyone she met."

"And her name?"

"Deshira."

"Huh," said Vykers. The name meant nothing to him. "She have a nickname?"

"Besides Nana? No."

Vykers frowned. *This is pointless!*

"But Deshira was her Sholdorn name. Before that, she was YntOnia."

That name echoed in the Reaper's skull. *That* name he'd heard before, somewhere. He probed. "That where 'Ona' comes from?"

Ona's visage lit up for an instant and then returned to its normal state. "I never thought of that."

"And this Entonia," Vykers continued, "was born where?"

"YntOnia."

"'S what I said. Where was she born?"

"On the northwest coast, somewhere. I can't remember the name of the village."

"Fishin' folk, then."

"Yes."

They fell into silence and sat that way, side-by-side, until Ona eventually stumbled off to her bedroll. Vykers watched her go and could not deny a certain familiarity to her movements.

Mendis, Eoman & Qansip, Amongst the Legions

Even on the march, Mendis' wizards were able to ferry prisoners into his presence for his assessment. Frankly, the Emperor such saw occasions as welcome departures from his otherwise dull routine. Eating the world at twenty miles a day was glorious, tedious work. He wouldn't have minded a few more battles, but inspecting new prisoners was almost as interesting.

He'd recently interviewed a small band of mercenaries who were only too happy to join his cause for the promise of clean cots, coin and stability. One man in particular, one Driegan, had been particularly eager to sign up, seemed intelligent enough, and though Mendis trusted the fellow not at all, he felt his newest convert might serve in the short term as a go-between of sorts in his dealings with the locals. It was a job Bailis did brilliantly, but one man alone could not do everything that needed doing. Thus, the Emperor had sent this Driegan off to the language tutors, those who would teach him the Emperor's tongue in the shortest time possible. If Driegan proved worthy, Mendis would happily employ him. If not, the fellow's corpse would serve as excellent warning to any who would betray His Magnificence.

Today, though, his wizards—and by extension, his troops— had done him most excellent service in bringing him an actual giant and a rather fetching young maiden. Although Bailis could have translated for him, Mendis preferred to speak directly to his newest prisoners and so instructed his wizards to enspell them for understanding.

He felt a moment of indecision as he pondered which of the two to interrogate first, but finally decided the girl would be most impressed in seeing how well he handled the giant—a task made easier, certainly, by the score of heavily armed troops manning the giant's chains, in addition to the handful of wizards standing nearby. The Emperor gazed into the giant's eyes and understood that his prisoner would kill him in a heartbeat if given the chance. Mendis approached him, nonetheless.

"What is your name?" Mendis asked loudly, as if the giant were hard of hearing.

"Bugger off," the giant responded, eliciting gasps of shock from his handlers.

"A funny name, that. Were you named after a favorite pastime, or is that merely a popular greeting wherever you appear?"

The crowd of troops, advisors and wizards laughed merrily at the Emperor's jest, though the giant wasn't anywhere near as amused.

"Well, Bugger Off, as you may have surmised, my legions and I are taking over your land. You can either cooperate, or..."

"Bugger off."

"Yes," said Mendis, "We've established that. What is not so clear to me, however, is whether you're fully cognizant of the predicament in which you've found yourself."

The giant sneered. "In my experience, big words are the coward's substitute for action."

"That's as may be," Mendis allowed, "but I'm happy to know you've got at least a few of your own." When the giant said nothing in response, the Emperor continued. "I have several questions for you, as you might imagine. Now, as I started to say earlier, you can cooperate and possibly earn your freedom, or I can extract what I need from you by magic, torture, or both. I prefer not to be so heavy-handed, but I will have what I'm after."

"And the girl?"

Mendis cast a glance in her direction and saw she was following the proceedings with interest. "And what is your interest in her?"

"I notice she's not in chains."

"Well, I think we can handle her. How did you come to be traveling together?"

"I saved her life."

Mendis spread his hands wide. "That's between you and her. It has no bearing here."

The giant offered a mighty frown and stared down at his feet.

A light breeze kicked up, giving Mendis an involuntary shiver that he hoped his prisoner hadn't seen. "If you won't give me your name..."

"Eoman."

"Ah! Very good. *Eoman*, then. Eoman, how many of your folk, how many *giants* are there in this land?"

"Hundreds of thousands."

Now it was Mendis who frowned. "A lie, clearly, by which I conclude there are not enough for your liking, and so I doubt thousands. Hundreds, I might accept."

Damn the man! He was too clever by half. "I am hungry," was all that came out of Eoman's mouth.

"I imagine so. Must take a lot to fill a belly that large," Mendis replied. He then turned to his advisors and said, "Let's have some food for my colossal friend, here!" The Emperor said nothing further until a great spit of still-sizzling meat arrived in the hands of two guards. "I'll deliver it," he said, much to his retinue's consternation. The nearby wizards readied themselves for anything, but Mendis was able to hand it off to the giant without incident. Or thanks.

Eoman tore into it, burnt lips and tongue be damned, and stared at his captor from under his bushy brows the while. When he'd finished, he tossed the bare spit aside, careless of where it might land. "And to drink?"

"Oh, yes!" the Emperor feigned embarrassment. "How could I forget? Somebody bring our guest our best vintage!"

Once again, it was only a matter of a few minutes before a cask of wine was produced and placed just within Eoman's reach. The giant tasted it carefully, deemed it acceptable (and free of poison), and took several prodigious gulps. "Human kings," he muttered to himself. "They have all the best stuff."

"I am not a king," Mendis corrected, "but an Emperor."

"Yeah," said Eoman caustically, "and I'm not a king, either. Anymore. You know the difference between a king and a commoner?"

"A king has an army at his back."

"The better to stick him full o' knives."

Mendis offered a small, tight smile at this and brushed the comment aside. "You could be free, you understand, if you're willing to tell us a bit more about your people, their disposition, and their relationship, if any, to this Virgin Queen."

"Why are you here?" Gulp, gulp.

"Several reasons, really. I mean to expand my empire, of course, and I certainly enjoy exploring new territory. But I am also looking for a man you natives call Tarmun Vykers."

Eoman drained the cask and put it down with a satisfying thump. "And I hope you find him," he smiled cryptically, wiping a purple stain from his beard.

His interrogation of the giant hadn't gone as planned, but neither had it been a complete disaster. He no longer believed the land's giants could muster the numbers to threaten his own forces; Eoman's comment about Wykkerian suggested his quarry was still alive, and, finally, there seemed to be no love lost between the giant and his former traveling companion.

As for the girl, well, she was dirty and disheveled, but there was something about her that piqued Mendis' curiosity. Not that he had *much*, mind, but enough to prod him into a decision. Again, he turned to his staff. "See the girl gets a good bath and a clean change of clothing—whatever we've got that's remotely serviceable."

Yes, he would interview her, too, once she'd had the chance to refresh herself. Perhaps he'd even summon her to dine with him in his personal tent. Just a meal and a nice chat. He'd often found that a pretty face did wonders for the digestion, and there was no harm in conversation.

Having made up his mind, he thought no further about it until dinner.

It was clear the girl thought highly of herself and, in fairness, her outward appearance was evidence enough why she might. The Emperor liked to think of himself as a man of ideas and action, though, and not mere superficial impressions. He would judge her as much or more by her mind, by her character, as he would by her beauty. And, anyway, his immediate task was to sound her for information.

With that in mind, he once again requested that one of his wizards be stationed within earshot, so that his dinner guest's language was easier to understand and his own easier to communicate. The wizard in place, Mendis thought himself prepared to entertain the young woman.

But he was mistaken.

When she arrived, fresh from her bath and attired in a surprisingly beautiful and well-fitting dress, he inhaled in shock and nearly forgot to exhale again. Here was the most beautiful creature he'd ever laid eyes on.

Not that this was relevant in any way, he told himself. She was, despite her beauty, just another prisoner to be interrogated.

Then why had he invited her to dinner?

Surely, he was just observing decorum, demonstrating his magnanimity and regal nature. After all, there was more to the job than simple butchery. There was diplomacy, for instance. There was also reconnaissance. In short, he had a number of perfectly valid reasons for inviting the young woman to his table.

He doubted his lady wife would agree, however.

Well, he'd done nothing wrong. And, anyway, he was the Emperor.

He stood up from his seat, helped the young woman into hers, and then returned to his own. "I am the Emperor, Mendis Staurachia. And what may I call you?"

His guest's eyebrows shot up and her mouth formed into the most perfect little 'o.'

"Yes," Mendis smiled. "With my wizards' help, you and I can understand one another...or at least we can *communicate*, as you saw earlier today." He chuckled at his joke, but noticed that she did not. So much for understanding.

"I am Qansip Deda, only child of Lord Deda of Eastcliff. I am sure he will be willing to pay most handsomely for my return."

Mendis gazed at Qansip. Most handsome, indeed. "Of

course," he said. "Before we discuss such details, however, there are things I would ask you. Wine?"

"Yes," said she.

He noticed she didn't say please or thank you. Even his children said those words. He poured her a glass anyway and watched her as she took her first sip. She was a rare thing, that was certain. Her hair was the color of honey and, under her fine brows, her deep brown eyes possessed seemingly endless depth. The skin of her face was flawless and fairly begged to be touched, whilst her lips were so luscious that Mendis was nearly entranced by them. Her neck? Gods, perfection! It plunged down past her lovely collarbones to...to...

"And how did you end up in that giant's company?" the Emperor asked, desperate for something besides his guest's bosom to occupy his thoughts.

Qansip fixed him with a flirtatious and challenging gaze. "Running from you and your soldiers."

"And yet it seems I've caught you anyhow."

The girl smiled and quickly glanced away. What an exquisite courtesan she would make...for some lord or other.

Mendis picked up a carving knife and rested its blade against a small roast one of his servants had just delivered. "And how is your appetite?" he inquired.

"Bottomless," Qansip replied.

Beesmarch & His Kinfolk, In the Wilds

Their party had grown to fourteen, and Beesmarch, as much as he fancied himself the antisocial hermit, was in better spirits than he'd been in years. If only, he thought, if only Eoman could have been there with him. This dampened his mood considerably, but there was naught to be done. He could not change the past, only shape the future. So, fourteen they were. They might have been sixteen, but Beesmarch refused to let a young giant couple join in his quest. Their task, Beesmarch insisted, was to produce children, and as many as possible. In case of the worst, their family would safeguard giantkind against extinction.

It was an odd way of looking at things, but, as King,

Beesmarch found himself thinking all kinds of new and unexpected thoughts. Such was the burden of rule. Such was the burden his old friend Eoman had born for ages without complaint. Bees thought of an old quote, "Uneasy lies the head that wears the crown," and thought more highly of his late friend than he ever had during Eoman's life.

Well, onward.

Bees was not sure how many more giants he and his followers could round up, nor was he entirely certain what they'd do once everyone they could find had assembled. But he knew they'd be battling the invaders. His challenge was in trying to anticipate where, when and how that might occur. He would, of necessity, consider the views of every one of his subjects. Hopefully, one or more of them would have valuable ideas on the topic. At the moment, their king had none.

Vacillating between euphoria at seeing so many of his kind and regret at the loss of Eoman, Beesmarch found he could hardly concentrate, hardly make a coherent decision by himself. He also harbored some fear of the browbeating he'd receive from Karrakan when the shaman finally caught up with the group and learned what had transpired. Karrakan might even challenge him for the crown, and then what would Beesmarch do? He could hardly afford another conflict. Losing would seem a terrible rebuke, and winning might well result in more tragedy. But what if he offered it freely? Would that make things right, or inspire the contempt of his fellows?

Sod leadership!

The new king was dragged from his introspection by a high, shrieking squeal he recognized as Svarren in origin. Instantly, all of his kin were silent, straining to glean as much from the sound as possible—the direction from whence it had come, the distance, whether it was a cry of rage or pain, from a male or female, along with any other noises that might clarify the potential threat.

"I hear swords," one of the giants said.

"Which way?" Beesmarch inquired.

"This," said another giant who'd essentially taken on the role of scout since he'd joined the party. Without waiting for

Beesmarch's say-so, the scout ducked low and pushed quietly through the bushes, mace in hand.

The other giants looked briefly to Beesmarch for reassurance, but the best he could manage was a curt nod, then off they went, in the scout's footprints.

Fortunately, they were downwind of the invisible combatants. Giants can be surprisingly stealthy in the wild, despite their size, but they can also be rather fragrant. With the wind in their faces, it was much easier to sneak up on the Svarren and their foes…who turned out to be some of the very invaders the giants had planned to destroy. The whole of Beesmarch's force crouched in the high, brown grass, squinting into the breeze and marveling at the spectacle before them.

Not two hundred paces distant, a large squad of soldiers was engaged by a much bigger force of Svarren. The soldiers, caught in the open, pulled into a tight circle, where they would stand and survive, or be overwhelmed and die. Beesmarch was impressed by their discipline and courage, but could muster no sympathy for their plight. Truth be told, he wasn't sure whom to root for. He wanted the invaders gone and the Svarren dead. He and his friends could either wait until the fray was finished and attack the victors…or they could join in on one side or the other, tipping the scales whichever way they chose.

"What do we do?" the scout whispered to his king.

In his peripheral vision, Beesmarch could see the rest of the giants watching him, waiting to hear the answer to that question. He turned to them. "What do you fancy? We'll be on the winning side, whatever we do. I'm thinkin' we reveal ourselves and negotiate with whoever's left standing when they're done."

"So…no killing Svarren nor humans?"

"I dinna say that…But I do think we need at least one human captive for questioning and such."

"And maybe a Svarra, too," one of the other giants offered.

"Let's stand, then," Beesmarch said. "See how they like a bunch o' giants at their backs."

All fourteen stood, and, indeed, it wasn't long before the Svarren and their foes took notice and stumbled to an awkward suspension of hostilities.

Native humans might have called out to the giants for aid; the poor souls in the eye of the Svarren hurricane simply stared at the giants and awaited their judgment. One of the Svarren detached himself from his people, however, and began walking towards Beesmarch's position. To Bees' astonishment, the Svarra was no Svarra, but a man.

"Who are you, then?" Beesmarch demanded when the man was close enough.

"My name's Omeyo."

If the giants had been expecting enlightenment, the man's name offered none.

Bees gestured towards the combatants in the field. "What's happening here?"

Omeyo looked at him as if he were an idiot. "It's a fight, isn't it?"

Lippy little bastard. "Humph!" said Beesmarch. "I can bloody well see that, Tiny. But what's a human doin' fighting with Long Teeth?"

"We're on the same side: killing invaders." When that didn't produce a response, Omeyo said, "What side are *you* on? Will you help us eradicate these marauders, or do you mean to attack my Svarren?"

Over the man's shoulder, Bees watched the strangest stalemate he'd ever witnessed, as both sides continued to twitch and snarl at each other, but nevertheless await his decision. "We'll help you kill them soldiers. But, mark me, leave one or two alive, and get away from here as fast as you may once the fightin's done. I won't promise your safety if you tarry."

Omeyo rubbed the back of his head, pursed his lips and said, "Agreed. We'll spare two, drag off some dead for eating, and leave you and yours alone."

The scout cut in, "You mean to eat the flesh of your own kind?"

Omeyo winked at him. "I might do. What's that to you?" So saying, he spun 'round and headed back to his Svarren. With a whoop, they resumed their attack.

"Let's finish this!" Beesmarch told his companions. With a great, ear-splitting roar, he raised his cudgel and stormed into the open, with the rest of the giants hot on his heels. The Svarren peeled away from the giants' side of the circle and allowed Beesmarch and his brothers room to attack. The invaders, brave though they were, experienced though they were, had no answers for this sudden development, and the battle was soon over. For thirty or forty breaths, the giants and Svarren stood panting, sizing each other up and contemplating their chances if they turned on each other. As promised, two soldiers, battered and broken, remained alive in the center of the carnage. Before the Svarren could change their minds, Beesmarch strode forward and swept both into the air and out of the Svarren's reach, dangling a soldier off the ground in each massive mitt.

"Ye can go now," he told Omeyo and his Long Teeth.

The man nodded, grunted something to the creatures on his left and right, and began his withdrawal.

Beesmarch spoke to the men still suspended in his grip, as he watched the Svarren drag several corpses away. "Be thankful it's me holding ya!" said he. They didn't speak his language, of course, but they seemed to understand anyway.

When the last Svarren had disappeared, Beesmarch dropped his captives and cursed. "Little bastards get heavy after a time," he complained. "Ye wouldn't think it ta see 'em, though, would ye?" He looked over at his comrades, who awaited further instructions. "Let's get away from all this blood and find someplace to make camp, see how fast these little shits can learn our tongue."

Kittins, the Streets of Lunessfor

Kittins stared down at the naked dead man and felt nothing, in spite of the fact the man's extremities had been eaten by the very swine he'd been attempting to...what, exactly? Kittins didn't care. This wasn't a murder, wasn't a suicide—who kills himself by pig, anyway?—and yet the captain wasn't remotely curious.

Until he caught a glimpse of the Alchemist, watching through the gathering crowd. He pretended he hadn't seen him and told the nearby constable, "It's nothing to do with me or Her Majesty. Don't even look like a crime, really. Just some idiot drunkard come to bad end."

The constable, a warty-face fellow with perpetually sad eyes, said, "And that lunatic smile on his face?"

Kittins shrugged. "Wildside mushrooms? Spiritual nonsense? Who knows. Who cares. There's a shit storm comin', and this here's nothin' by comparison." Before the other man could say more, Kittins walked off in the direction of the Alchemist. Behind him, the constable bent down and studied the corpse up close.

The crowd melted away from Kittins, allowing him easy access to the Alchemist. He thought perhaps the man might bolt, but instead he stood his ground and watched Kittins approach.

"Strange to see you out-o'-doors in the light o' day," the captain said by way of greeting. "'Specially since you're s'posed to be dead."

"And you," the Alchemist replied. "Though it is nearing sundown."

"I'm gonna assume your appearance here ain't coincidence. Who was the fellow?"

The Alchemist didn't deny it. "A bookseller."

"'S too bad. I've grown to like books." This seemed to surprise the Alchemist, who studied Kittins with renewed interest. Kittins offered a sly if hideous grin in return and said, "How's a bookseller end up half-eaten in a pig-sty?"

"Drug problem?" the Alchemist suggested.

"Drug problem," Kittins repeated. "That your professional opinion?"

"Yes," said the other man. "I believe he ingested too much of whatever-it-was he was taking, went mad, and, well, you can see the results for yourself." The Alchemist moved as if the conversation was over, but Kittins grabbed him by the arm.

"This drug," he said, "ain't gonna be a problem for Lunessfor, is it?"

"Not from me," the Alchemist said, offended. "I cannot, however, guarantee that others won't misuse it." He looked down at Kittins hand, still locked onto his arm, and dissipated in a cloud of grey dust.

So, he'd been the one responsible for the bookseller's death. He'd as much as admitted it. And what did one death matter, in the grand scheme of things? The real concern was widespread use of whatever the Alchemist had given the man. Her Majesty had tasked Kittins with securing the city from external threats, but if it was already crumbling from within, Lunessfor might be doomed anyway.

A light, misting drizzle began to fall. Kittins looked up into the darkening sky and decided he'd best continue his subterranean explorations. He needed to prevent the enemy from sneaking into the city, yes, but he was now also interested in finding a suitably secret escape route in the increasingly likely event things went south.

He felt better underground, somehow. More relaxed, more himself. That merited further examination, Kittins thought, but he wasn't the thinker he'd once wished himself to be. Things had a way of turning out differently than one planned or imagined. He'd once believed he could save up enough coin in the army to buy himself a farm or perhaps some sort of little shop, find himself a wife and have a son or three. He let loose a brief snort of contempt. What a fool he'd been. Well, he was still in Her Majesty's army, more or less, and though he could probably demand the gold needed to buy himself a farm, he knew now that his fate, his doom, would allow no fantasies.

He'd brought an oil-soaked torch with him, and the flint and steel to spark it, but the more time he spent underground, the more comfortable he felt in darkness. Besides, he knew the main tunnels well enough. He might light his torch when he got to one of the unexplored branches and then again, he might not. There was something weirdly thrilling about wandering blind into the unknown.

After some time, he came to one of those new branches and headed down it, curious to learn what he could hear, smell or feel that could not be seen. He walked cautiously, with a surprisingly light step for someone so large and muscular. He had one hand extended in front of his chest and the other planted firmly on the hilt of his sword—not out of fear, mind, but pragmatism. Anything that got in his way had to die.

There were, naturally, a couple of occasions in which he

smacked his forehead or shoulder on a stony protrusion, but he healed quickly and had a high tolerance for pain. The inconvenience of such moments was not enough, yet, to induce him to spark his torch, and he had even less desire to do so after he heard the first footsteps behind him.

Yes, several someones were shuffling his way, attempting silence with middling success. He heard them, but then he'd been listening for such sounds. Now, he wanted someplace to hide. He placed both hands on the wall and quickened his pace, searching, feeling for anything, any crevice that might serve. The sounds behind him grew louder, and he thought he detected a glow back there. Just in time, he found a series of waist-high boulders on his left, between himself and the tunnel wall. There would be room behind them to lie down and, if he remained silent, those approaching would never see him. He felt his way around the boulders and found he could even crouch without being seen, if he pressed himself flat against the stones.

Soon, he could smell torches and hear breathing, in addition to the continued shuffling of feet. They were good, these strangers. No chatter, no telltale clinking of armor or weapons. As they drew near his position, Kittins held his breath entirely. He couldn't hide his body odor—nor could they—but perhaps they'd have too much on their minds to notice. The seconds crept by like minutes. Kittins filled the time by trying to divine as much as he could about the strangers by the few sounds they did make.

There were five of them, for instance. They were dressed in leather armor. He smelled both the oil on their leathers and on their swords. Two different oils, for different purposes. Their odor and the weight of their footfalls told him they were men. Once they'd passed, he risked a peek at them and saw that he'd been wrong in one respect: there were six of them. He noted, too, that their leathers had been dyed or painted black. That made sense. Two of them carried torches, and the rest were empty-handed, their weapons being sheathed to reduce the chances of banging them on the tunnel walls.

Kittins emerged from his hiding place and followed their

light. He let them get far enough ahead that he could see only the flickering glow of their torches, and by this method, he kept up with them without being seen himself. It was more challenging than he might have expected, though. When they stopped, for example, he had to stop as well and immediately. If they slowed their pace for whatever reason, he had to adjust. A couple of times, he heard brief, whispered exchanges between them, but he was unable to make out individual words.

Inevitably, time became a factor. Lunessfor was a large city, but a man could walk across it in less than an hour if he took the right roads at the right time of day. It was, after all, situated on an island in the middle of a river. Thus, Kittins reckoned those he was trailing would emerge into the city or castle if he allowed them to continue much longer.

The spontaneous sound of weapons clashing and strange, inhuman yelling pushed all previous concerns aside and now Kittins worried about what might be coming his way. Accordingly, he drew his own sword and stalked forward into the now-erratic torchlight in hopes of getting a better view of whatever was going on. What he saw confounded him.

Five of the six men were still on their feet, but one was down. Around and between the men, an angry horde of little men swarmed, shouted and shrieked. They could only have been goblins.

There'd been a time before the first battle with the End-of-All-Things when Kittins would have sworn such things were the stuff of children's fairytales. Now he knew better. And, more often than not, these fairytale creatures were much worse than advertised. The captain stood back in the shadows, watching and wrestling with the question of whether or not he should intervene and upon whose side.

Without really knowing why, he raised his sword and waded into the fracas.

Vykers & Co, On the Road

They came upon the smoking remains of a village, and Vykers immediately dismounted, had to get down on his hands and knees and examine the wreckage for clues as to the attackers' strength and numbers. What he found—or didn't find—was bewildering.

"No feets," said the big Ntambi warrior—the first words Vykers had heard from him in ages.

"Yes," the Reaper agreed. "Where are the enemy's footprints?"

Several of his companions joined him on the ground. Only Hjuest and Ona remained mounted. Someone had to maintain a higher vantage point, after all.

Vykers stood, turned in a slow circle. It was a beautiful day in...wherever-it-was...except for the charred and smoking cottages. A light breeze blew the smoke away from Vykers' crew.

"Where are the dead?" he wondered aloud.

"All the dead," Ona offered. "I don't see so much as a dead cat."

The Reaper walked farther into the village and came upon a well whose stones had somehow been partially melted and turned to sludge. Vykers stayed clear of it. Across the road, he spied some deep depressions in the grass in front of a ruined shop. He went over and stared at them, but could make little sense of it.

Down the road a bit, he entered the bones of a blacksmith's. It looked almost normal, except that the roof and two of the walls were gone. Tools and weapons were scattered across the straw-covered floor, but the forge still burned, albeit at a much cooler temperature than normal. The mystery engaged Vykers more than the tragedy. He was about to leave when he saw the axe head. It was lying amongst some shovel and rake heads on the far side of the shop. He picked it up and considered its heft and the sharpness of its edge.

"I can fit that for you." Ona had followed him.

He turned, surprised. "Can you?"

"I've done my share of smithing."

He tossed her the axe head—a nice, soft, underhand throw, to ensure she caught it without incident. Why had he taken such care? He didn't want to think about it. "Haft's back on my horse. I'll go 'n fetch it."

Along the way, he continued his scrutiny of the buildings. High up on an external wall, a large, round bloodstain suggested a head had been smashed against the stones. How did a head get up there, and where was the body?

When he got back to his horse, he told his men, "We'll camp here. I wanna know what happened to this place, so we don't run afoul of it ourselves."

If any of them were anxious about the Reaper's pokey pace, none were inclined to challenge him. And, really, they were his men, each and every one. He'd won them in combat, set them free, and returned to give them new purpose. Was there any better job for a fighter than traveling with the best of their kind? If Vykers had commanded them to walk on their hands to the Emperor's palace, they'd have done it or died trying. Now, all he asked of them was a nice, roaring fire, some water—if any might be found—and any food that might have been left behind by who or whatever had attacked.

Later in the evening, Ona returned with Vykers' new axe.

"It's done."

Vykers took it from her without getting up from his place by the fire and tested its weight and balance.

"It's a nasty thing, that," said Ona.

"Oh?" asked Vykers in feigned innocence. "How d'you mean?"

"I can't say. It's got all the right qualities. But it *feels* wrong."

Vykers ran his fingers over the spot where the haft ran through the loop of the axe head. Ona had secured it with good, iron nails without cracking the handle in the slightest. The whole weapon seemed to hum or throb in the Reaper's hand. "I like it," he pronounced.

It was as much thanks or praise as Ona would get, and she took it gratefully. She only hoped she was wrong about the axe.

"What do you men suppose destroyed this village?" Vykers inquired of the group.

One by one, his men offered thoughts and theories, either in some broken version of Her Majesty's tongue, or through Hjuest's efforts as translator. They considered the smashed buildings, the strange depressions in the ground, the foul, stinking puddles of dissolved objects, and the complete absence of bodies. Their conclusion: whatever had attacked the village—and they were all in agreement that it was not an army—was unlike anything any of them had ever encountered. On the one hand, Vykers found this bothersome, because it was easier to plan for and fight something they understood. On the other hand, if none of his men had any knowledge of this thing or things, that could mean it was fairly uncommon, rare even. In other words, the land wasn't rife with these things, which was welcome news. The Reaper had crossed the sea for several reasons, but fighting the local wildlife wasn't one of them.

The group might've slept indoors—there were one or two structures remaining that would have served—but Vykers again refused to consider it. It was nice getting away from the dreary weather back home, and the Reaper was not alone in his desire to bask in the comparative warmth of his new surroundings, and brigands or monsters be damned!

A great shudder roused him from sleep. The ground was shaking—not like an earthquake, but at regular intervals. Vykers noted the fire was fading, so he quickly tossed more wood on the flames and nudged the men closest to him with the toe of his boot. One of those men turned out to be Ona, who got up without speaking, realized what was wrong and quietly drew her sword.

"Dere is someting out dere," Hjuest whispered once he'd risen.

Vykers glared back at him, and looked over at Ona, who rolled her eyes: *no shit.* Vykers couldn't help chuckling softly to himself.

Tense seconds turned into minutes before Vykers judged the threat had subsided, if not passed altogether. "You got any animals over here that're big enough to make the ground rumble?"

"By demselves?" Hjuest clarified. "No. In a herd, sure, ya."

"This was no herd."

"Ya. I know."

The sober expression on Hjuest's face was all Vykers needed to tell him this *something* in the darkness was a problem of unknown dimensions, in every sense of the word. He let loose a sigh that was more like a growl.

It was always some damned thing.

Driegan, In Mendis' Camp

Driegan was in excruciating pain. He thought he'd been clever in swallowing his gems and thought so still, even though they'd bound up his insides and made him barely able to move. He couldn't understand it; he'd accidentally swallowed cherry pits before and never had any difficulty. Maybe it was due to the gems' larger size or sharply angled facets? Gods, if he could just get them out, he'd never be so foolish again.

He needed an A'Shea. Did the invaders have such people, though? He hadn't seen one and became increasingly worried with every passing hour. He feared he'd have to confess what he'd done, and the enemy would cut him open to retrieve his treasure rather than help in any way. But if he did not tell anyone, he feared he might die from the pressure and painful cramping.

For a while, he'd held out hope that things would work themselves out naturally. Now, he could barely walk, and a cold and constant sweat betrayed his discomfort. What to do, what to do? He couldn't concentrate.

He and his former servants and guards shared a crude pen under the watchful eyes of a dozen or more soldiers. The allowance for the prisoners' needs was a rain barrel and a pit toilet in the pen's far corner. Once, Lord Driegan would have sneered at such primitive accommodations. Now, he only prayed he could use the toilet, audience be damned.

He received no sympathy from his fellow prisoners. They'd seen what he'd done to their comrade when the invaders approached. None of them believed he wouldn't resort to similar treachery again if the opportunity to spare or elevate himself arose. He wasn't at all sure *they* wouldn't betray him if they got the chance, either. So, how could he control them? He'd no more coin with which to buy their loyalty, and, in his current condition, physical intimidation was out of the question.

As he stood in a half-crouch, pondering the issue, a man in an odd-looking doublet and hose walked up to the pen and pointed at him. "You, come," he said.

"Me?" Driegan grunted stupidly, surprised at the man's abruptness.

"Was I not clear?" the man said imperiously. "Come over here, now."

Driegan gritted his teeth and limped over to the stranger.

The man grimaced and said, "Are you ill?" When Driegan didn't reply, the stranger placed a cool hand on Driegan's forehead, moved it to his chest and, finally, to his lower abdomen. A wicked smile came to his lips then, and he spoke a few words in a language Driegan did not understand. Suddenly, his pain grew so intense that he thought himself moments from death. There was a terrible, sharp movement in his lower gut, followed by a short but severe sensation of tautness and, lastly, a warm wet gush behind which his cramps seemed all but gone.

When he looked down, Driegan saw the shapes of his gems in a pool of blood in the stranger's palm, as well as a great wash of blood down his lower belly, down his groin, down his legs.

His eyes rolled up in his head and he tottered over onto his back.

He woke up on a military cot, disoriented and afraid. A chubby-faced man with a bad haircut and a robe of coarse material attended him.

"What?" Driegan blurted. "What...?"

"Rest yourself. Your wound is healing even now."

Driegan craned his neck and looked down at his stomach.

"As I said," the chubby-faced man assured him.

Another voice, behind him, startled the patient. "Ah, the purse-bellied native awakes!" The stranger who'd injured him sidled into view.

"How is it you speak my language?" Driegan asked.

The stranger offered a patronizing grin. "I don't. You've merely been made to understand ours." He gestured to Driegan's chubby-faced nurse.

"And is this man an A'Shea?"

"That term is new to me, but if you mean to ask if he's a healer, then yes."

"I've never encountered a male healer..." Driegan said, trying to forestall any further talk of his gems.

"So, *Lord* Deda," the stranger smirked, "what are you doing wandering the country with a Prince's ransom in jewels in your gut? My friend Meerish here tells me they might have killed you if I hadn't interceded."

"And I imagine getting them back is out of the question?" Driegan said.

"Really," the stranger replied. "I should think I'm due something for saving your life."

"That would be quite a reward, though..."

"More valuable than your life?"

Driegan had no answer for that. He was too weak to argue anymore and, besides, his interrogator had every advantage. "Are you a Shaper then?"

"I am a wizard. Frankly, the title 'Shaper' seems a bit pretentious."

"And your name?"

The other man straightened. "I can see you're accustomed to asking the questions," he said. "But you'll have to lose that habit. You belong to the Emperor now, and he'll brook no questions from the likes of you."

Driegan was at a loss for words—a rarity, certainly, but one he suspected would become more and more common.

"Yes," the wizard continued. "I know all about you. Your countrymen were eager—eager, I say—to inform against you, and you have rather a loose tongue when under sedation."

It seemed he was trapped, then. "What are the Emperor's plans for me?"

The wizard laughed. "Presumptuous, aren't you? What does a god care for a fly?"

Then why not just kill me and be done with it? Driegan wanted to retort. But of course he was afraid the Emperor and his servants might feel inspired to do that very thing. Resigned, he laid his head back down and let out a long, slow breath.

"For the time being," the wizard said, "you belong to me. I'll allow you a few more hours of rest, and then you'll begin learning the Emperor's language."

Ron, Spirk & the Gang, the Hideout

Ron was becoming worried about Spirk. Since they'd all created Long's Old Peculiar, the young Shaper spent more and more of his day drunk. Having by now passed a great deal of time in Yendor's company, Ron was not anxious to see his friend follow in the older man's footsteps. Or stumbles. Sure, Ron had tried reasoning with Spirk, but Spirk always found some silly way to redirect the conversation or distract him. People thought Spirk an imbecile, but he could be quite cunning when it served him.

Talking to Spirk hadn't changed anything, so Ron resorted to stealing the Shaper's mug and hiding it...which is futile, really, when dealing with a Shaper. Instead of bothering to look for it, Spirk simply summoned it back into his hand and refilled it.

Ron looked to Rem and Yendor for assistance, but they were occupied with concocting more of their brew for sale and distribution. The Fretful Porpentine alone was ordering it almost faster than Yendor and crew could keep up. Oh, their personal stash was in good shape, but they'd need to pay the Alchemist a visit again, and soon. Anyway, the two older men were of no help in weaning Spirk off their product.

Desperate, Ron decided to piss in Spirk's drink whenever his friend wasn't looking. If he could just make the flavor disgusting enough, he reasoned, Spirk would have to swear off it. And so, as the Shaper snoozed away on a dusty old fainting couch, Ron snuck behind a tower of moldering furniture with Spirk's mug and added his own very special contribution to its contents.

Which is when a large portion of the wall exploded inward, followed by three men who appeared to have been in a bad fight. The subsequent appearance of Captain Kittins in the hole in the wall seemed to explain everything. The men fell onto the floor and struggled in vain to right themselves. Kittins looked about, noticed his old comrades in various states of surprise and said,

"What in Mahnus' name's going on here?"

"We might ask you the same," Rem answered.

Pretending to come in for a closer look, Ron furtively returned Spirk's mug to its former location and pretended a great interest in Kittins' arrival—not a terribly difficult thing, under the circumstances—whilst really keeping a close eye on his friend, who'd been startled awake by all the commotion.

"What is this place?" Kittins demanded.

"No place in particular," Yendor replied.

"You want me to take your other eye?"

Yendor was not happy. "There's no need for threats, old man."

"It's our hideout," Rem cut in, "or was. But it's good to see you and your...friends?"

Kittins went over and kicked the one who was closest to standing. "No friends o' mine. I found 'em trying to sneak into the castle. My guess is they're part of the invadin' force. We all ran afoul of some Mahnus-cursed goblins, and..."

"Boblins?" Spirk squeaked, bolting into an upright position.

"Goblins, boy. Goblins. Seems there's a lot more to this city than any of us ever knew." In the silence that followed, Kittins continued to search the room—old habits and all that—and finally came back to his former associates. "What are *you* doin' in here, anyway?"

"Makin' the most wonderful exclicker!" Spirk declared. Before Ron could react, Spirk grabbed his mug and staggered forward to offer Kittins a taste.

The big man took it and knocked it back, thirsty from all the fighting he'd done. He then made an ugly face—uglier than usual—and declared, "This stuff tastes like piss!"

Ron inched slowly backwards, hoping to lose himself in the shadows.

"It most certainly does not!" Yendor countered. "Maybe the lad's mug's at fault. Try this!" So saying, he offered Kittins a taste from his own mug.

This time, the captain sniffed before tasting and, having done so, decided to bolt the rest in one go. "Much better. That first mug musta been the boy's chamber pot!"

Everyone had a good laugh at that and most especially Ron, who was relieved to know he was not going to die any time soon.

"But about these men..." Rem ventured.

"When I'm done drinkin'," Kittins insisted, as he held forth Yendor's mug for a refill. How many fights have been preceded by those same words? Can anyone count so high? This time, however, those words were followed by Long's Old Peculiar, an ale without precedent or parallel, and whatever fight had been in Kittins when he arrived was quickly quenched. Soon, the big man, like everyone else who'd ever tried the stuff, was feeling better than fine. He became more talkative than the rest of the crew had ever known him and told a variety of jokes, none of which were particularly funny. Spirk loved them, but then Spirk was pickled with the same ale.

"How many Bemites does it take to start a fire?" Kittens called out brightly.

Rem rolled his eyes. "I imagine you'll tell us, whether we ask or..."

"None!" said Kittens. "They ain't got the sticks!"

While Spirk howled at this, the other three men exchanged looks of confusion and disbelief.

"Is this how *we* look when we're in our cups?" Rem wondered.

"Ah, what's wrong with it?" Yendor asked. "Let 'im have his fun. Truth to tell, I'm surprised to learn the man knows how to smile."

Now the captain sauntered around the room, singing an old sea chanty or some such. His diction was so slurred, no one could make out the lyrics, but they all smiled back at him indulgently.

Right before he passed out, Kittins commanded his comrades to take care of his prisoners, who hadn't dared rise since they'd arrived.

"Spirk!" Yendor called over. "Spell these three so's they won't try anything."

The Shaper rose obediently from his couch, fell back, rose again and negotiated his way over to the still-prostrate prisoners. One was unconscious, one seemed in great pain, and the third watched Spirk nervously.

"Kittens for Kittins!" Spirk giggled and waved his arms theatrically. To everyone's alarm, the soldiers had been replaced by great, snarling forest cats. Spirk shrieked, waved his arms again, and the men returned to their usual forms.

"Just put 'em to sleep, lad!" Yendor coached.

That, Spirk accomplished with ease, to everyone's relief and his own most of all.

"Wonder how the captain found us?" Rem asked.

"'S a good question. Sadly, we'll have to wait 'til he wakes to find out. Meantime, Spirk, you'd best shape that wall, Shaper. Put it back together. Make it better, even, than it was before." Yendor directed. It was a gloomy, dusty, cobwebby place, but it was their own, and Yendor would allow no one else to enter if he could help it. Besides, he had inventory to protect.

Kittins woke sometime later, to find Yendor and Rem gone and the two younger men asleep and snuggled up against each other—not in the manner of lovers, but of small children who'd drifted off whilst at play. He kicked them awake.

"What in the endless hells?" Ron complained. "What'd you do that for?"

"You sealed up the wall! How do I get outta here?" Kittins demanded.

"Spirk takes you."

"And these others?"

"Them, too."

Spirk again began waving his arms, when Kittins stopped him. "Not now, boy. When I'm done with these men, here." He pulled his long knife, walked over to the still-snoring invaders, and kicked one, just as he had Ron and Spirk. "Wake up, fucker." He'd chosen the less beaten of the three, but the man remained sleeping. Kittins kicked him harder.

"It's a magic sleep!" Spirk protested.

Kittins growled and turned in his direction. "Is it? Well, wake 'em the fuck up!"

Spirk did as commanded, because, after all, the captain had

been *his* captain once upon a time. Kittins crouched down next to the closest man and slid the end of his dagger ever-so-gently up the man's nostril.

"Shaper," he called over his shoulder. "Can you make 'im understand me?"

"I dunno," said Spirk, "Never tried."

"Try."

For several minutes, Kittins repeated the phrase, "Do you understand me?" over and over whilst Spirk tried everything he could think of, until finally the man on Kittins' dagger point said, "Yes."

It was at first, as interrogations go, fairly mundane. There were no great surprises, no questions left unanswered. Kittins didn't even need to resort to torture. The men were agents of the invading Emperor, who had been gifted with a map by someone on the inside. That much, Kittins had already deduced. The men didn't know the identity of the traitor, also no surprise. It had to have been someone in the Queen's inner circle, or perhaps the ruler of one of the city's Great Eight. And what had these men been planning to do inside the castle? This was the shocker: they were planning to locate and kidnap the Reaper. To the best of Kittins' knowledge, the Reaper wasn't in Lunessfor. Unless…the invaders were referring to one of the strange, magical Vykers look-alikes who made up the Queen's honor guard. The captain could see now that he'd been foolish to let that curiosity go so long unexamined. But there had been and even now was so much else that needed investigation. How could one man, alone, possibly…

"I might need you lot's help," Kittins rumbled at Spirk and Ron.

"I been helpin'!" Spirk protested.

"I mean outside o' here. Longer term. The world's goin' to shit, and you're all holed up in here…doin' what, exactly?"

Spirk explained, as best he could, with numerous corrections from Ron. At the end, Kittins said, "That's your big plan? Steal some ale, mix it with magic piss and make yourselves rich? 'Scuse me!" he scoffed. "I was under the impression you lot cared about this miserable hellhole of a city."

Spirk started to weep. "What can I do?"

"You can start by magicking these bastards out into the wilds somewhere."

The Shaper looked up, hopefully. "You ain't gonna kill 'em?"

Kittins held his dagger still, though he gave it a slight twist. "I'd like to, but they might come in useful down the road if they remember I spared 'em."

Soon, Spirk had pulled himself together, the men had been whisked away, and Kittins was enjoying another, if much smaller serving of Long's Old Peculiar.

"How'd you find this place?" Ron asked him out of the blue.

"We were stumbling around in the dark. I was herding 'em, really. And we saw some light shining through the cracks in your wall, heard some voices."

"Well, Spirk's fixed that. Wall's better than ever."

"Good," said Kittins. "We may have to live here, when all's said 'n done."

Mendis, With His Legions

It was a cool night and yet Mendis lay sweating in his bed, in the darkness of his tent. He could not get the girl out of his mind. He'd tried concentrating on his own lovely, faithful and dedicated wife. He thought, too, of his children, his sons...and his daughters. How could he look any of them in the eyes again if he...

No! He would not allow that thought to continue. He had his faults, perhaps, but weakness had never been one of them. From an early age, he'd possessed willpower, self-discipline. Over the years, he'd been able to withstand loss, hunger, physical pain, lack of sleep and more. Many of his trials had been intentionally self-inflicted, as tests of his resolve. He had never wavered, never faltered before. Nor would he now.

He decided to focus on the progress of his invasion. His legions were making excellent time in crossing the continent and had managed to capture a number of larger towns and cities. Hostiles who fled north or south in order to regroup were met and crushed by the Tsundi or B'Shar, exactly as Mendis had predicted. Captives were offered citizenship in the Empire—after service to its Emperor, according to their talents. Lastly, refugees flooded and overwhelmed the still-unconquered cities, again, just as Mendis had promised.

Not that there weren't challenges and difficulties. The land's Svarren still swooped in out of the darkness from time to time, savaged the column's flanks, and disappeared like ghosts. It was like being attacked by a flock of starlings, both in terms of the damage they did and the difficulty in catching them. The giants, too, remained elusive, a threat more imagined than seen, save the one captive. And they hadn't gotten much information out of him. Qansip claimed—

Mendis thought of the flawless skin of her neck, how delicate it appeared, how beautifully colored. He wanted to plant his lips there, work his way up to her exquisite jawline, or down to her—

He sat up in bed, pushed through his bed curtains, and summoned the wizard who stood in attendance in the far corner of his tent.

"Yes, Magnificence?"

"A sleeping draught, if you please."

Such manners this Emperor had. The wizard smiled back at him and said, "It is my pleasure," and produced a vial from somewhere inside his doublet.

"How much do I drink?"

"All, Magnificence."

Mendis was unconcerned about poisoning. He'd been enspelled against almost every contingency, except for those things he did to himself by choice. He took the stopper from the vial and downed its contents in one swallow. The taste was horrid, of course, but who drank such potions for their flavor? He dismissed the wizard and walked back to bed.

It wasn't long before he fell into a deep and uneventful sleep.

The next day, he decided to distance himself from the native girl. Eventually, perhaps, he'd even have her sent off to one of the cities they'd conquered. He couldn't help the occasional surreptitious glance in her direction, just to make sure she was bearing up and all. But by and large, his mind was on his campaign and its next target. As the day wore on, he caught himself looking for Qansip too often and reprimanded himself for doing so. She was just a girl, after all, and the first one he'd met in this land. Surely, she was not as exceptional as he'd imagined. Perhaps all women her age were as fetching. And, then again, perhaps Mendis was just homesick and missing his wife.

Only, it wasn't his wife he was picturing naked.

He spurred his horse and rode farther ahead in the column. Maybe one of his officers would have an interesting tale to tell.

In his bed, Mendis lay awake and listened to the rain on his tent. It was a hard, relentless rain, but the tent was well-oiled and not a drop reached the Emperor. But the sound, loud though it was, could not lull him to sleep nor distract him from his thoughts of Qansip. For the second night in a row, he requested a sleeping draught. The wizard, a different man from the previous night, obliged without hesitation. Again, Mendis drank it off and returned to his bed to sleep.

In the morning, Qansip's face was the first thing that came to the Emperor's mind. As he sat on the edge of his bed and stared at his bare, knobby knees, he wondered if he hadn't been poisoned after all, for Qansip was like a poison in his mind and in his blood. He could dismiss the greatest atrocities with nary a backward glance, but flush Qansip from his mind? Not so far.

He considered whether sending the girl away would be enough. Perhaps he should have her disfigured? Killed?

No; he was not a tyrant. The problem was his, not the girl's. Still, he had to rule and to do that well, he needed to keep his wits about him. He would send her away. Now he'd decided, he couldn't imagine why he hadn't done it already.

Perhaps because he hadn't wanted to.

Somehow, over the course of the day, he failed once again to banish the girl from his presence. He returned to his mage for a third night running. The first man who'd supplied him with a sleeping draft was back on duty and frowned ever-so-slightly when Mendis ordered another draft.

"Speak!" Mendis told the man. "I would know your mind."

"Speak, Magnificence? But there is nothing in particular on my mind."

"Do you think me a fool? You're worried I'm becoming dependent upon your potions, aren't you?" Mendis demanded.

"Nothing could be further from the truth!"

The wizard remained silent. One does not interrupt the Emperor in his anger.

"Give me what I've asked for, and let me worry about whether it's a problem or not," Mendis concluded.

"Of course, Magnificence," the wizard replied.

This time, Mendis waited until he'd passed through his curtains to drink the draught. For some reason, he felt self-conscious, drinking the stuff in front of the wizard—which struck him as preposterous. He was the Emperor. If he declared that skunk spray was perfume, then so it was and so it would be and none would dare to contradict him.

He slept again without dreams and awakened feeling as though he'd been cheated. He felt his thoughts wandering towards Qansip, and he forced himself to think of breakfast instead. Breakfast and exercise, he decided, would do wonders for him.

It had been some time since he'd walked with and amongst his foot soldiers. That seemed just the thing. After a nice meal of sausages, local eggs and potatoes, Mendis strapped on the rest of his armor and sought out one of his legions. There was discipline within the ranks, but also comradery, and the occasional joke—so long as it was only occasional—was more than welcome. The Emperor reveled, too, in the looks on the men's faces as he worked his way amongst them. He knew his presence bolstered their spirits, and theirs did the same for him.

The day was approaching lovely. What clouds remained in the sky were of the pillowy white variety, and the almost-warm breeze brought with it the scent of new growth, of grasses, of leaves. There was even a hint of spice that intrigued the Emperor, and he determined to learn more when the opportunity presented itself. The exercise was invigorating, too. It was so good to stretch the legs and work up a healthy sweat. Everything seemed so pleasant, in fact, that Mendis was considering spending the whole day with his foot soldiers…

Until he heard Qansip's laughter bubbling up out of nowhere. He felt a brief twinge of panic, followed by anger. Not twenty paces away, the girl sat behind one of his officers as they rode by on the man's horse. Mendis immediately stepped out of the ranks and called to one of his other officers, who answered without hesitation.

"Magnificence?"

"Follow that officer. Tell him his Emperor commands him to take the girl to the back of the column. Tell him that if I see him again today, I'll have him flogged." The obedient officer was hard-pressed to conceal his surprise, but Mendis let it go; he just wanted Qansip out of sight and, he hoped, out of mind.

The incident had ruined his mood, though. He stood and watched the men he'd been marching with pull away as they continued on their path. He waited. Finally, his usual retinue approached, including his closest advisors, his horse, and his manservant. He raised his hand and waved to the lot, and the manservant dutifully led his horse in his direction.

For the rest of the day, Mendis rode and brooded in silence.

Following a fourth night of sleeping draughts, the Emperor decided to confront his problem head-on. He asked for Qansip to be sent to his tent, to join him for breakfast. As ever, a wizard stood nearby to ensure both parties understood one another. Mendis wanted to get this over with, but seeing her again, up close, temporarily weakened his resolve.

"You are well, I trust?" Whatever his plans, it was important his subordinates treated his guests with honor and respect.

"I am." She offered no thanks, but he didn't notice. He did see all the little things such women do to entice men: brushing her hair back out of her eyes, touching her lips, making eye contact and then blushingly looking away. He saw all those little things, and yet he wanted her. "And you?" she asked.

"Well," said he. Why was she asking? Surely, she had no real interest in him, an invader. "I am quite well," he assured her. "As, I hope, everyone is under my rule. Mine, you will find, is a well-run and rather benevolent empire." He expected a reaction to that, a look of skepticism, a snort, even an argument. Something. She touched her hair, licked her lips, and looked away.

"Where is the officer I rode with yesterday?" she inquired.

Mendis lifted a goblet of wine to his own lips, drank, and replied, "He has been reassigned."

"But he was merely showing me your troops," she pouted.

"That is *my* prerogative," he answered. Because he didn't want to appear petty or jealous, he added, "But I can show them to you as well as anyone, if you're truly interested."

"Oh, I would love that!" she sparkled.

Had Mendis but known it, this was his last chance, his last opportunity to save himself. Alas, he did not.

EIGHT

Long & Short, The Fretful Porpentine

Long discovered he was able to make himself appear as anyone else he could imagine and had spent the past several days experimenting with his newest ability. He made similar experiments with Short, but, try as he might, he was not able to increase the homunculus' size; thus, Short's options were limited to things like chickens, cats, and tiny dogs. Unfortunately for him, cats and dogs didn't tend to walk on their hind legs, so he spent most of his time as a chicken. To make matters worse, he made an especially ugly one.

"You got a mean streak. You know that, Long?"

"What? Why do you say that?"

"You brought me back to live out my days like this? I'da never done that to you!"

"Coulda been worse. I coulda made you a potted plant."

For all his new-found facility with disguises, Long hadn't managed to wander far beyond the Fretful Porpentine. There were, he told himself, several perfectly valid reasons for this. For one thing, he was curious to see the impact of Yendor's ale on the community firsthand. For another, well, he was stalling. He hated to admit that about himself, but he still hadn't come up with a plan that allowed him to confront Her Majesty and survive.

That started to change the moment Hoosh Bindy walked through the inn's doors.

The man had a visible aura. No one else seemed to notice it, not even Short, but it was as clear as sunshine to Long. Slowly, Hoosh became aware of Long, as well.

It was difficult to get near the Fool, because everyone seemed to know him and, knowing him, expect some entertainment. Long made eye contact with the fellow just enough to establish that a meeting was necessary. The other man didn't seem to disagree. First, however, he had to discharge his duties as Fool.

The barkeep plied him with Yendor's ale, and the Fool fairly exploded with exuberance and musical flatulence. Apparently, that was the preferred type of humor for the patrons of the Fretful Porpentine, for the room burst with a raucous jollity that Long had never before noted there. Even Short, in his chicken guise, found reason to laugh, though it sounded to most folks like clucking.

In the middle of this merriment, Yendor himself appeared with Rem in tow, to deliver another, larger barrel of his product, which they brought into the inn on a wheelbarrow. Long hid in the shadows and watched, though he needn't have gone to such effort. Yendor would never have recognized his friend's current face. The transaction completed, Long watched his former companions' departure with a wistful sadness that was only disrupted by the arrival of the Fool at his side.

"We should talk."

"Aye."

"In the pantry?"

"An excellent suggestion," Long agreed.

Hoosh showed the way as if he were employed in the place, and whenever any of the clientele attempted to interrupt or halt his passage, he sprinkled them with dust from a pouch at his waist, and they completely forgot what they'd been after.

"Nice trick, that," Long observed.

"You flatter me," said Hoosh. "I can't even imagine what you're capable of. Ah, here we are!"

The pantry was a small room, lined with food-laden shelves from floor to ceiling. As he was turning to close the door behind them, Hoosh stopped. "This your chicken?" he inquired.

"He's mine, yes."

Hoosh shrugged. To each his own.

Once the door was closed and secure, the Fool spun a tale that shook Long Pete to his core. He wanted to laugh derisively in Hoosh Bindy's face, to call him a liar or worse. He wanted to kill the man for the news he'd delivered. Yet, when the Fool had finally finished, Long had a hard time finding his voice.

"No questions?" Hoosh prompted.

"None," said Long. The whole thing made a sort of horrible sense that seemed to put all of his struggles over the past few years into a new and ghastly light. Some truths could not be escaped: his best and happiest days were now behind him, and all that remained was growing torment and eventual oblivion. He knew now why some went mad and was tempted to embrace insanity, himself, to give in to its seductive whisperings rather than suffer a single minute more. But there was one last bit of good he could do for the world. He would not be remembered for it—or anything else, for that matter—but he'd perish knowing he'd done it. He hoped that knowledge would be enough to drive him through the dark days ahead.

"What will you do?" Hoosh asked at last.

"Kill the Queen, I reckon."

"And how will you do that?"

"Damned if I know. But I'm guessin' the Reaper'll play his part."

"And me?"

Long took a lengthy pause, stared at the Fool without blinking. "I imagine I'll have to let you win."

Bindy's face was a mixture of relief and dread. "But that means..."

The captain hung his head, saddened and bone-weary. "Yes. I'm well aware."

He'd discovered he could sleep in the owner's bed during business hours without interruption—partially because the door was locked (no impediment to a god) and partially because the owner and his immediate family were always so busy. The arrival of Yendor's brew had turned an already popular inn into a boisterous madhouse, in which money changed hands faster than whores spread the clap.

And so Long lay in bed, grappling with a future he'd never foreseen and certainly didn't want. His choices had been reduced to horrendous or nightmarish. Either way, he'd experience more suffering and death than he'd ever imagined possible, and he'd been in some fucking dire situations.

He rolled onto his side and regarded the homunculus. .

Short Pete looked back at him. "So?"

Such a tiny word, yet so full fraught with import.

Long rolled the opposite way, from which vantage point he was able to watch the sun set. "I dunno." And, really, how *could* he know? If he finished, he'd be, in his estimation, simply fobbing the whole mess onto someone else the next time 'round. Alternatively, he could arrange things so that the Fool was last, but then the whole damned cycle would begin all over again, and he'd have abdicated all power to change things. *Could* they be changed, though? If, say, he, Alheria and the Fool banded together, could they somehow rewrite the rules together?

From everything he'd seen and experienced, it didn't look as if Her Majesty was open to doing anything differently than she already had. After all, she was in the strongest position, despite the Emperor's invasion. Indeed, if Long had learned anything, it was that Alheria would use this same invasion to serve her own ends. Whether the Emperor won or lost, the outcome would favor the Queen.

Long wondered if the Emperor understood that. And then he wondered if informing the fellow of Alheria's plans would make any difference. Men were awfully stubborn when it came to war.

Of course, there was always the Reaper's option. But the mere thought of it left Long torn. How ironic, Long mused, that they'd all spent so much time and energy over the past few years fighting a lunatic who called himself the End-of-All-Things, when it had been Vykers and only Vykers all along who possessed such power. Left to his own devices, the Reaper would eventually, inevitably clean the slate, put an end to the posturing, the games, and the suffering of innocents. Yet it was the fear of what comes after that end—the undiscovered country, from whose bourn no traveler returns—that gave Long pause. What if whatever came next was worse?

Long considered all the possibilities and found none

remotely palatable. The only tiny blessing he could identify was that he had some say in the final outcome.

He wanted a nice mug or ten of Yendor's brew, but was feeling too dispirited to rise from his borrowed bed. "Say, Short," he began, "you s'pose you could fetch me a nice pitcher of that special ale they got downstairs?"

The little homunculus grumbled but rolled off the mattress onto the floor. "You gotta open the fuckin' door!" said he.

And with a thought, Long did.

Vykers & Co, On the Road

His men were full of theories about who or what it was that had rampaged across the countryside, but there was no consensus amongst them, and considering that they were more or less natives to this land, their ignorance was not reassuring. There was, too, the randomness of these attacks, for while many farmsteads, villages and towns had been obliterated, others seemingly along the same path had not.

Vykers rode into one of these miraculously unscathed hamlets and, through Hjuest, confronted the first people he encountered, who were busy, as it happened, planting great stakes in the ground as a defensive measure.

His first question was a stupid one, but Vykers could think of nothing better. "What are you folk doing there?" he yelled from the back of his horse.

Hjuest translated. Vykers waited. The locals responded. Slowly, weirdly, Vykers came to feel he understood their words without Hjuest's translation.

But that wasn't possible. Leastways, it had never been before.

Several minutes of heated discussion revealed that these villagers had learned of the fate of their neighboring settlements, but none present had personally witnessed anything. No one could tell Vykers who or what the enemy was. And why did he care, anyway? The locals wanted to know. He was obviously a foreigner. What business had he with any of this?

He might have said as he often had in the past, "Because I'm the Reaper, and I make it my business." But he looked at these poor, doomed rustics—the very dregs the Emperor had left behind—and understood he'd be doing them no favors by making promises, real or implicit. If he discovered the perpetrator or perpetrators of these attacks and it was in his interest to act, then he would. Oh, he was powerfully curious, no question. He would have loved to ask Arune what she knew or sensed. If Arune weren't dead. He felt a momentary twinge, a hitch in his breathing, and he moved on. His primary goal was and remained reaching the Emperor's throne room, there to see the mural detailing his history.

Belatedly, the villagers asked if Vykers' crew had any news or might be of service in their cause. *Oh, fuck it,* Vykers thought, and climbed from his saddle. He instructed most of his team to help the locals in crafting and planting their stakes and fortifying their defenses. He had Hjuest ask one of their number to lead him on a tour of the town's periphery. Ona, of course, wanted to come along, but Vykers wouldn't have it. It didn't look good, didn't feel right to have her trailing after him everywhere he went. Besides, he didn't need the distraction.

By midday, the Reaper had the whole, meager population of the village at work digging trenches, pitfalls, erecting thorny hedge-barriers, setting fire traps and anything else he could think of. He placed the town's entire supply of bows and arrows on the roof of its tallest structure. Two men, he set to work cutting a hole in said roof with axes, so that it might be accessed from inside, without exposing the would-be bowmen any more than necessary.

Still, how does one prepare for an attack that may never come, from an enemy one knows nothing about? The questioned both thrilled and perturbed him.

Near sunset, Vykers acknowledged the obvious, that he and his crew would be staying for the night. The villagers seemed glad of his presence; they wouldn't be, come morning, when he and his packed up and left.

For the time being, everyone seemed content, and the village even acquired something of a festive atmosphere. The locals, who normally spent nights indoors, set up a large bonfire in the village square. They hung a spitted pig over the flames, someone broke out a small cask of wine, and a fiddler appeared, as if from nowhere. There was cheese to be had and fresh bread, too. If the Emperor had depleted his lands of manpower, he'd still left plenty behind worth savoring. Soon, there was singing and dancing and the execution of countless pranks. Vykers was pleased to see his men—and Ona—enjoying themselves for once. He had not been a kind or gracious leader, and though he did not see himself changing, he was glad for the crew's chance at merriment.

Of course, Vykers neither danced nor sang. But he watched, and that was enough. The local folk were not handsome—perhaps their best and brightest had joined the Emperor's cause—but they were as real, as genuine as the soil beneath his feet. Good stuff, good folk, good food, good wine. The celebration petered out as the night wore on, as the combined effects of too much food, wine, dancing and laughter took their toll. Vykers alone remained awake and alert.

So he was the first to sense danger.

A short, sharp tremor rattled the ground and was over so quickly that the Reaper nearly thought he'd imagined it. Except the night all around him had become eerily quiet. Beyond the firelight, a vast something seemed to take flight, only to come crashing down nearby with a force that shook Vykers' being with even greater violence than the first tremor.

Everyone woke up; some of the villagers even screamed.

Vykers and his men found their weapons and formed a large circle around the fire, with their backs to the flames, leaving enough room for the townsfolk behind them. In a second's time, he inspected his crew and knew them to be ready for whatever was coming. The townsfolk, however, were on the verge of panic. The Reaper barked at them in words they could not have understood, but they understood his tone. They quieted, held their breath and waited.

A horrible growling wail sounded—a noise worse than the death screams of cattle and the raging shrieks of raptors combined. It was polytonal and multi-voiced, and yet it clearly came from one thing, one entity, one furious, mad being whose existence seemed the essence of torment. Some, near Vykers, answered with screams of their own, lesser cries of pain or fear. He didn't understand their reactions. Anything that made a noise like that was alive and could be killed.

Something mountainous rumbled into view at the firelight's edge. It blocked out the moon and stars and, for the villagers, seemed to block out hope as well. Many of them bolted for their homes, no longer confident in the martial prowess of their guests. Buildings wouldn't save them, though, Vykers knew. Steel would.

And then, Vykers heard something he wasn't expecting, something he could never have anticipated: the thing called to him.

"Reeeaaapeeerrr..."

He felt the eyes of everyone in his company upon him.

The thing slid, slithered, crept closer, without shaking the ground as it surely had earlier, but not entirely without noise, either.

"Reeeaaapeeerrr..."

A huge and unspeakably misshapen face loomed into view, largest on a body of such faces.

"Frog?" Vykers asked, more to himself than the creature before him.

"Reeeaaapeeerr!" the thing screamed back, dragging more of itself into the firelight.

Vykers heard the soft but sudden gasps of shock from his crew, heard their feet nervously stepping ever-so-slightly backwards, smelled the stink of their fear. As he looked up at the Frog, he couldn't blame them.

The boy, as boy he should have been by the calendar, was now larger than any creature the Reaper had ever seen, larger than the leviathan that had once attacked his ship, larger even than some castles he'd visited. Clouds of vile pestilence seemed to emanate from his form, making him—it—seem all the more gigantic. And his size was only part of his terrible aspect, for, like the chimeras that had inspired him, the boy was an impossible amalgamation of other creatures, other monsters. Without question, he had continued the all-devouring ways he'd begun when Vykers saw him last. Now, the multiple eyes in the Frog's multiple faces shone with malevolence, reflecting the flames of the dwindling bonfire.

Vykers felt the sword in his grip and wished he'd grabbed his new axe instead. He tried to calculate his chances of getting to his gear before the Frog attacked and decided that even if he made it, his crew might not.

He dropped his sword, eliciting another round of gasps from his fellows.

"Frog, I came back for you," he lied.

"Frog?" the monster echoed. A different mouth opened and launched a tongue at one of the men. There was a loud thwack, and, in the next instant, that man's hindquarters were dangling from that mouth.

"Frog!" Vykers roared in fury. He'd no idea what to do, how to attack something so vast. He'd hoped that some part of the boy was still...the boy. "Get back!" he yelled at his crew. He expected another tongue any moment. Or maybe a spiked arm or scaly tentacle might lash out at him.

But it's never the thing you're expecting that kills you.

Beesmarch & His Kinfolk, In the Wilds

Beesmarch was busy torturing the prisoner when Karrakan unexpectedly reappeared, angry as a nest of hornets at the bigger giant's behavior.

"Hold!" he yelled from the trees as Beesmarch bore down on the invader's chest with a massive foot.

The other giants looked an odd combination of elated to see the shaman and ashamed to be caught displeasing him.

"Hello to you, too," Beesmarch said sourly.

"What are you doing to that man?"

"Torturin' him. What's it look like?"

"Why are you torturing him?"

Beesmarch rolled his eyes. "To get information, what else?"

"Does he speak our tongue?" Karrakan challenged. When he got no answer, he continued, "Do you speak his? No? Then it's just fer spite, is it?"

Everyone looked down, away, or anywhere but at Beesmarch or Karrakan.

"If you mean to kill him, kill him and be done with it," the shaman scolded. "Our king would never countenance such behavior..."

"Well now, that's the thing, you see," one of the others interrupted. "*Bees is* our king now."

"What?" Karrakan shouted back, shocked.

"Bees is king."

"How? Where's Eoman?"

"Bees..." one of the Brothers began.

"I can speak fer meself!" Beesmarch cut in. "I challenged 'im, he lost, I'm king."

"Well, you sucker-punched him when he'd stopped fightin'..." another of the giants said.

"Sucker-punched? Hmph!" Beesmarch roared. "He got winded, I saw an openin'. A real king don't stop fightin' 'til he's won!"

Karrakan let the bickering continue while he tried to make sense of what he'd just heard. His friend had been king for as long as the shaman could remember, and that was a long time indeed. And now the grumpy old bastard Beesmarch was king? "Where's Eoman?" he demanded of a sudden.

"Dead," said Whindas. "We think."

"Dead?" Karrakan slammed his staff into the ground and a swarm of blood-red will-o'-wisps came spewing out the top, zipping and flittering about each of the other giants, who, for all their size, seemed terrified of the little mites. "Explain!"

Beesmarch complied; he could do little else. When he'd finished, Karrakan said, "I will find him, or I will find his body. That is the least service we owe him. Make camp, and let me concentrate."

"But I am king," Beesmarch responded, halfheartedly.

"You'll do as I say, Bees, or I'll plague you with biting flies for the rest of your days."

"Humph," said Beesmarch. But he let his prisoner go and instructed to others to start a fire and forage for food. If anyone could determine if Eoman yet lived, it was the shaman, and Bees was more than willing to let him try.

The shaman sent out his apparently inexhaustible army of will-o'-wisps in search of Eoman. Many flew off in every direction at speeds no raptor could match; others simply winked out as if suddenly extinguished. Karrakan knew better. Will-o'-wisps were of the fey and traveled byways beyond mortal ken. They would find the former king, Karrakan had no doubt.

What to do with Beesmarch, though? The shaman was so furious at the bigger giant, he was tempted to lay down a challenge himself. Much better to have Eoman restored to his proper position. And yet, the other giants had followed Bees and done his bidding without contention. What a mess!

The following day, all of the giants save Beesmarch and the Karrakan decided to bathe themselves in a nearby lake. They invited their king, but he declined, partly to watch over the shaman, who was still engaged in his strange castings, and partly because he hated water. At last, Karrakan seemed to return to the present. The king had been hoping for good news, but preparing himself for the worst as well. The look on Karrakan's face, however, was not enlightening.

"What news?" Beesmarch asked, endeavoring to keep his emotions in check.

"He lives," Karrakan said flatly. "A captive of the invaders' armies."

The bigger giant nodded, thrust out his chin. "Then I will rescue him."

"You're an idiot," the shaman replied dismissively. "One giant—even a score of us—against tens of thousands?"

Rebuked though he was, Beesmarch would not give up. "It may be we have allies you're unware of…"

"What, have you made friends with the Svarren?" Karrakan scoffed.

"Well, as a matter o' fact…"

Mendis & Qansip, In Camp

Finally, Mendis had not needed a sleeping draught; he'd had Qansip—still had her, in fact. Even in sleep, and perhaps especially then, she was a paragon of feminine beauty. Her hair formed a golden nimbus about her head as she slept. Her skin was without wrinkle or blemish. Her lips—gods, her lips!

The Emperor struggled with what he'd done. Certainly other rulers, other *Emperors* even, had had their mistresses, their concubines. And that was fine for other men. But Mendis had always prided himself on his honor, his virtue. Now? He rested a hand on Qansip's naked back, felt the warm smoothness of her skin and himself responding to it. Surely no one would begrudge the Emperor this one dalliance, being so far and so long from home, waging such an ambitious campaign on the Empire's behalf...And, too, it was not as if he were a tyrant. He sighed. He'd been arguing with himself for hours now to no avail, no purpose; it was time to live with his decision and make no apologies for it. He was, he believed, the most powerful, most important man in the world. Why should he not enjoy the rewards that naturally belonged to one of his position?

He rose and requested a bath. His many servants and attendants worked hard to maintain neutral expressions at all times in his presence, but most especially this morning. The Emperor feigned disinterest in their thoughts and opinions with regard to his newest companion, but he scanned their faces, each and every one, for any sign of judgment or censure. He would not have Qansip made to feel badly merely because he fancied her, nor again would he apologize for doing so.

After his bath, he ordered breakfast for two and challenged his staff and his wizards to come up with fresh and fashionable clothing for his mistress. She must have, he insisted, clothing as lovely as she—a tall order, to be sure, in a camp fixing to break up and return to the march, but the Emperor was not to be denied. More, he demanded such attire be found with all haste, that Qansip might be ready to ride with him on his daily inspection of the troops.

Fortunately, Mendis' wizards came through with a series of beautiful dresses and gowns that his tailors, shorthanded though they were, were able to adapt and adjust to suit the girl. Mendis did not ask the provenance of the dresses. He didn't care. All that mattered to him in the present was making Qansip happy and seeing her at her best.

She rode behind him on his stallion, wrapping her arms around his waist, and he felt a flush of pride that she should do so. She was his! She wanted him and he, her. He sensed an awkwardness from his staff and everyone he passed. Of course. They were uncertain how to feel or behave around Qansip. But the Emperor held his head high and smiled broadly, thereby letting them know that *he* felt no so such awkwardness. In time, he knew, his troops would grow accustomed to seeing Qansip by his side and think nothing of it.

It was not possible, in one day, to show his consort the entirety of his forces, stretching as they did from his current location to the eastern shore. But Mendis was able to offer some notable highlights. He was very proud of his lancers, for instance, and his longbowmen put on an archery exhibition that thrilled the young woman. It was his Dread Knights, however, that impressed her most, as he'd expected. Even on horseback, the solid steel monsters were taller than she, and they marched without tiring. Naturally, Qansip was full of questions.

"How do they march?" she demanded playfully. "Is there someone inside them?"

The Emperor laughed at her childlike wonder. "No, sweet. They weigh far too much for that. It's magic, of course."

"Is it?" she thrilled. "And is this all of them, or are there more?"

"All?" Mendis echoed in surprise. "Any one of these could conquer a kingdom, and I have eleven!"

For a moment, Qansip seemed confused. "Eleven? Why not make another and have an even dozen?"

A shadow passed fleetingly over Mendis' face. "I had a dozen, but one of them...suffered an accident."

"Truly? Tell me more!"

"There's no story, there," Mendis answered dismissively. "The point is, with the ones I've got, I can conquer the world."

Qansip was unrelenting. "But why not make another and even them out? Why not make an *army*?"

Although he enjoyed the girl's youthful enthusiasm, her focus on the number of Dread Knights had become irksome, so he quickly changed the subject. He talked about the overall number of his troops. He spoke at length about his wizards. Then, he moved on to the magnificent castles of his homeland, the beautiful beaches and bounteous orchards. Secretly, he could not wait for the end of the day's march, when he could retire to bed with his prize, his treasure, once again. More and more, he wanted her more and more. He'd made his true conquest between the sheets, and nothing else mattered quite so much anymore. Everything he said, everything he did was simply a bid to pass the time until nightfall, until he could be with her entirely once again.

But even in bed, it seemed, Qansip's curiosity would not abate, much to Mendis' chagrin.

"You say one of your Dread Knights could conquer a kingdom," she whispered, trailing an idle finger across his naked chest.

"Yes," he confessed.

"I'd like to see that."

There it was, and how could he say no without seeming weak or foolish? "And so you shall."

"Tomorrow?" she squealed in excitement.

"As soon as the opportunity presents itself." It was a good answer, he thought. One that allowed him plenty of leeway in the event there were no suitable targets within the next day's march. He only hoped Qansip was done with the subject for the time being.

Both his wizards and his scouts reported a mid-sized city to the southwest of the column's position. The Emperor, his consort, a wizard and one of the Dread Knights could be there by midday—faster, if the wizard transported them all. Mendis wanted this task, this chore over with and opted for magical assistance in traveling thence. The Dread Knight would perform its task, Qansip would be satisfied, and Mendis could resume focusing on the larger issues at play. As much as he craved constant congress with the girl, he never forgot Her Majesty was out there, somewhere, working on plans of her own.

Dread Knights were keyed to respond only to certain people, but always to the Emperor. Once Mendis gave the command, the thing set off towards the walled city at a brisk pace. Even a half mile away, Mendis, Qansip and their wizard could hear the growing alarm from the city's guards, atop the wall. They shouted orders and fired warning shots with their longbows, but the Dread Knight moved inexorably forward. Mendis heard the chains on the city's drawbridge engage and subsequently saw the bridge begin to rise. The Dread Knight continued, undeterred.

"But how will he get across that moat and over the walls?" Qansip inquired.

"Normally, those are problems he'd figure out on his own, but as I don't want to spend all day here, I think we'll fly him over." He nodded to the wizard, who returned the gesture and promptly faded from view. Mendis redirected his consort's attention by gently turning her chin back to the city, where the Dread Knight was slowly rising into the air. This provoked a great volley of arrows and stones, but none seemed to bother their target in the slightest.

The cries of alarm from atop the city's walls grew louder and more urgent, and flocks of soldiers could be seen rushing to reinforce the regular guards. Soon, a hundred men or more watched their mysterious enemy pass right overhead and begin its descent into the city proper.

Qansip heard a woman scream, and she smiled, only to frown a few seconds later. Mendis assumed she'd had a change of heart, but he was mistaken. "But how are we to witness this conquest from out here?" Qansip demanded.

Mendis chuckled. "You won't want to see what's coming, believe me. The Dread Knight will fight until he's killed everyone in that city, or they've fled. Neither their weapons nor their magics will be of any use."

"It that so?" Qansip trilled. "He sounds like a real Tarmun Vykers!"

The Emperor's mood darkened almost instantaneously at this comment, but he managed to keep his frustration out of his face. "Yes, yes…" he said flatly. "But now, would you like to return to my legions, or would you prefer to stay here for a light lunch?"

"Oh, I'd love to stay! I'm just dying to know whether the locals will choose to fight or flee!"

"Stay it is, then!" Mendis proclaimed with flaccid mirth. He unfolded the blanket he'd carried upon his arm and spread it out on the grass. As soon as the wizard returned, Mendis would request a selection of meats, cheeses and fruits from camp. He enjoyed demonstrating the privileges and powers of his office, from the mundane, like lunch, to the extraordinary, like employing the Dread Knight to destroy yonder city.

If the Emperor had any qualms about sacking a city as entertainment for his mistress, he stifled them quickly and well with thoughts of how she'd reward him for his indulgence. He had a moment of clarity, in which he understood there was little he wouldn't do to earn her amorous attentions, but then he told himself that the ruination of these people could easily be folded into his larger military strategy. He wanted to be a fair, a just ruler. But he also needed to demonstrate his might from time-to-time, lest the natives lose respect for his authority.

It was all rather silly, as far as Qansip was concerned. Everyone in the Emperor's service seemed bent on treating him as if he were some sort of god; to her, he was a short, adorable little man who took himself far too seriously. His stern facial expressions and grave pronouncements only made her want to laugh. Oh, but he was wealthy and showered her with gifts that beggared anything her father had ever given her. Fleetingly, she wondered if Driegan was still alive, but, because there was no profit in it, she quickly returned to her fantasies involving the Emperor. She'd allowed him to bed her, not because she loved him, but because it was past time she gave vent to her passions, and also because she knew how badly he wanted her. She was flattered at first—he might come to rule the whole world one day, and *she* was the sole object of his desires. It wasn't long, however, before she realized that his passion for her was far greater than hers for him; indeed, she could hardly say she loved him and didn't suppose she ever would. She could make use of his need, though. She suspected that marriage was out of the question, but perhaps he would grant her a realm of her own to rule. Really, there was no telling how far the Emperor was willing to go, and Qansip was certainly eager to find out.

While he blathered on about making a statement to her fellow natives, she listened instead to the crashes, the explosions, and the screams coming from the beleaguered city. It truly was impressive how much damage and terror one Dread Knight could inflict. The drawbridge came down again, so that frantic citizens could escape the carnage. Soon, they began gathering in a field a few hundred paces from the main gate, shocked to discover they weren't being pursued beyond the city's walls. One of their number noticed the Emperor and his companion watching them from a distance and made sure that all of his fellows saw them as well.

"I hope my wizard is on his way," Mendis said, more to himself than to Qansip.

The mob began moving in his direction. He guessed it would take them five minutes, at least, to reach him, but he was in no mood to find out. Worse, he did not want to lose face with Qansip. The prospect of having to turn tail and run was unacceptable. The closer the mob got, though, the more likely this seemed.

"What shall we do?" Qansip inquired, making no effort to hide her excitement.

Luckily, the wizard chose that moment to return from the city's interior.

"Take us back to our forces," Mendis commanded. "And let us know when the Dread Knight has completed his work."

The wizard nodded and did as instructed.

Alheria, Lunessfor

The Emperor had too many soldiers, too many resources. Inevitably, he would conquer the land and probably even succeed in winning the people over to his way of doing things, for whatever difference that made. That was her thanks for saving them all from Eyatu. Some might argue that Eyatu's predations had been her fault; Alheria did not agree. Is any mother responsible for the actions of her adult children? Granted, Eyatu was a god, but she held that the principle was the same. In any event, the peasantry would all flock to Mendis. And Lunessfor would come under siege...which was just as she'd planned, for it was that siege, she believed, that would finally draw Mahnus out of hiding and allow her to kill him—again and with finality.

Yes, it was all rather distasteful, but she couldn't very well change things for the better if she didn't ascend, and she couldn't ascend unless she was the last. There were some rules by which even she had to abide.

She felt herself scowling, would've been surprised if the expression wasn't permanently etched into this particular face, and then Alheria looked out from her gazebo into her garden. Well, it was all her garden, in truth. But this little one, this immediate garden, brought her more comfort than all the conversations, all the books, all the sweetmeats, all the wine in the world. And yet, she would have to part with it eventually in order to achieve the ultimate more.

Alheria closed her eyes. She felt every one of her countless days. How had the others managed it, the ones before? She doubted any had faced the challenges she had. Ah, but enough self-pity. The Queen focused her thoughts on her remaining bastards, located each, and set to planning their separate dooms.

Every so often, her thoughts wandered to her roses, which bloomed irrespective of climate, season or weather. She shook her head in wry amusement. She cared more for those roses than she did for her own offspring. But then her children were far, far thornier and much less lovely to gaze upon. The swamp witch Croonbasket, for example, had never shown any affection or duty towards her mother, and her actions involving the Dead One had been both insolent and dangerous. Luckily, Alheria had a gift for making the best of other people's mistakes, and Kittins would play his role in ensuring it was the Queen and not Vykers who triumphed. But Croonbasket had to die, and soon. The only reason she continued to breathe was that Alheria was having second thoughts about the wisdom of keeping Hoosh around for her confrontation with Mahnus. She wasn't sure he could be trusted, and maybe, the goddess thought, she should just get the Fool out of the way once and for all. She certainly didn't believe that he was or would be content to come so close to victory and still lose.

So: Croonbasket next, or Hoosh?

A bumblebee buzzed past—the first of the season—and it was everything Alheria could do to avoid perceiving it in some metaphorical sense. Sometimes, things were simply what they appeared to be, and even though the Poet had once written "There's a special providence in the fall of a sparrow," a bumblebee was often only a bumblebee.

Ona, Hjuest & Co, the Ruined Village

The survivors sat on their asses in the dirt or dew-dampened grass, unable to make sense of what had transpired. They barely moved, even to quench their thirsts or empty their bladders. No one spoke, as there was nothing to be said. They passed an entire day in this manner.

The next, they stood around the body in a broken circle, still struck dumb by the impossibility of the night's events, struck dumb, too, by their outcome. The Reaper was dead. His purplish-red cadaver, little more than a skeleton swaddled in coagulate gore, lay in a pool of the same sludge the crew had seen elsewhere. Only now, to their infinite sorrow, they understood its significance.

The monster Vykers had named "Frog" had sprayed him with acid—vomited it forth, really—in an area too wide to escape with a simple dive or somersault. The legendary warrior could dodge swords, spears and arrows it seemed, by not geysers of acid.

Hjuest looked up from the corpse and assessed the damage the Frog had done to the town. Many buildings he'd smashed or burned and many townsfolk he'd devoured, but he'd left most of the Reaper's team untouched. To bear witness, the Red Knight supposed. And then the colossal monstrosity had bounded off into the darkness with a series of ground-shaking leaps. Or perhaps they'd been steps. Or short flights. The Frog's true shape defied understanding, even by those who'd seen it up close.

And Hjuest didn't care, anyway. Tarmun Vykers was dead. Hjuest's mentor and *tor*mentor, his hero, and his curse was dead. Hjuest had no idea how to proceed. "Vat do vee do vid... vid him?" he asked Ona.

She knew why: the Red Knight considered her next-of-kin. She hoped this deference ended with this one question; she'd no interest in leading this group of men—or anyone—anywhere, for any purpose. She could not replace her grandfather and would not try. "Burn him?" was all she said. The big Ntambi warrior muttered something about making a pyre, which surprised Ona, because she'd underestimated his grasp of her language.

Somewhere, a woman sobbed in despair. Someone else cried out feebly in pain or for help, even a full day after the attack. Ona had no hope for them, with the Frog roaming the countryside. Without the Emperor's legions and Shapers to protect them, the locals were doomed.

In time, the pyre was ready—a great heap of a thing just beyond the town's outermost buildings—and Hjuest asked for volunteers to help him lift and deposit Vykers' remains on top. A few of the men stepped forward, but only one other was needed, so wasted was the body. Ona insisted that she be that other.

She'd seen a mummified body once in her youth, something the Sholdorn had found in a cave near their capital. The body of Vykers was similar, except for the bloody coloring. He looked like nothing so much as a skeleton wrapped in leather and then drenched in red, brown and purple waxes. For the first time, she really saw his claws and canines. How could this thing ever have been her grandfather?

His body creaked and gurgled as Hjuest and she hefted it first to waist level and then up and onto the pyre.

A soft, prolonged groan came from its mouth.

Ona leapt backwards in fear.

"It is only gases," Hjuest assured her. "It happens all de time."

Yes, of course. Ona knew that.

The body groaned again, louder.

This time, Ona approached the body. "That doesn't sound like gas to me." She reached out and put a hand on Vykers' left arm. She felt a faint trembling and gasped in shock. "I think," she panted, "I think he's alive."

At this pronouncement, Hjuest and the other men surged forward and examined the Reaper more closely. From their angle, they could not fully see his face, but, like Ona, they touched his arms or legs.

The body groaned.

"Gods!" the Red Knight cried. "How horrible."

"Light the pyre," the Ntambi commanded.

It was unthinkable. "He's alive!" Ona protested.

"We cannot help him. He only suffer," the warrior countered.

The body groaned.

The Ntambi warrior approached with a branch from the town's dwindling bonfire. Ona and Hjuest seemed paralyzed with uncertainty, so the warrior moved the flames closer to the pyre, whereupon the flames extinguished. The Ntambi seemed frustrated for a moment, until the various twigs, branches and logs that made up the pyre began moving. In seconds, they transformed into bark-and-leaf colored arms, large and small, that embraced the Reaper even as they held the Ntambi warrior at bay. He, not being a fool, stepped away from the pyre with all haste.

"Do not touch him!" warned a voice from the within the pyre. "On pain of death, I charge you stay away!"

"I know dat voice," Hjuest whispered to Ona.

Part of the pyre shifted, shaping itself into the form of a woman, standing over Vykers' body. Green vines and creepers sprouted and wove their way up the woman's legs and torso. Soon, a recognizable face developed, even as moss, grasses and tiny leaves continued to fill in the details.

"Stand back!" Aoife commanded. "Tarmun is alive and will continue to be, if I have anything to say about it."

Within the cage of arms at the woman's back, a greenish-gold light began to pulsate with the rhythm of a heartbeat. But whose, Ona wondered, the Reaper's or the woman's? As the men in Vykers' crew seemed too stunned to speak, Ona stepped into the void. "Even if you're right, what sort of life can he have from this day forward?"

Aoife scoffed at the question. "That is not for you or anyone save Tarmun to determine."

"And will you be the one to nurse him back to consciousness?"

The Umaena stood strong. "You know I will."

"And us?" Hjuest inquired.

"Stay, go. I care not."

Hjuest glanced at his fellows, considered their mood, and answered. "Vee stay."

Whereas Vykers' men had spent the previous day or so wondering how it was possible he'd been killed, they now struggled even more to understand how he hadn't. It was the kind of conundrum that drove men mad. Fortunately, Ona was a woman and, thus, far more practical.

"Let's don't waste our time sitting around, waiting for the Reaper to wake up. There are folks here who need attention. There are homes that need some rebuilding. There's food that has to be fetched, and firewood, too."

Even the Umaena smiled at this.

He heard a horrible belching sound, followed by a pain so thorough, so pure, it was unlike anything else he'd ever experienced. He was on fire, and then he was numb, and then he was on fire, and then numb again. He lost his sight, his hearing, his sense of smell, and finally all sense whatsoever. He drifted in a lightless, colorless space, barely able to string two thoughts together. He became aware of his own heartbeat, though he knew not what it was. He felt himself breathing, understood there was effort involved, continued anyway, without knowing why. He became aware of a word, a single word: reaper. It echoed almost continually until he finally grasped its meaning. *He* was the Reaper.

He slept.

There were sounds. Buzzing, droning, incoherent mumblings. He responded. Soon, he felt jostled, and an unpleasant creakiness came upon him. He wished to go back to sleep...but the noises wouldn't let up. They were talking. Who they were and what they were talking about eluded him. He yelled, or thought he did. He felt a brief pressure on his arm, then heard more buzzing. The pressure disappeared, but left behind a dull ache. More pressure, more aching. The noise around him grew in volume. He was about to scream when everything fell silent, mercifully silent.

A soft, warm sensation washed through him, and he returned to sleep.

Everything hurt. He'd been aware of a general pain throughout his body, but it was building, building, ever so slowly, getting worse with every breath. He imagined it would continue to grow until it consumed him, or he died. Somehow, this did not frighten him.

He recalled being in pain, in agony, before. Once, he'd had a spear thrust through his back. Another time, he'd been peppered with arrows. On one occasion, he'd been poisoned, and had vomited and shit blood for days and days. There was a time, too, long forgotten but suddenly remembered, when he'd had burning oil poured all over him from above. He also remembered having been partially flayed, before escaping his tormentor. He'd been smashed in the left side of his face with a mace, once as well. When he thought about it, what hadn't he experienced? He'd been crushed, drowned, burnt, ripped apart, sliced open...why had he forgotten all of this? And was it his current pain that jogged these memories free now?

He was the Reaper. He'd fought in countless battles and wars and been mortally wounded a thousand times.

And yet he had no scars and no memories.

The pain was so horrible, all he could do was scream himself into unconsciousness. He'd barely the strength to twitch his extremities, but he could scream. Another man might have begged for an end to this misery, for death. The Reaper simply didn't know how—how to beg, how to quit, how to die. That, and he wanted revenge. He wanted to inflict this same pain and worse upon who-or-whatever it was that had injured him.

He screamed and screamed until it was the only sound he could ever remember making or hearing. A cool hand landed gently on his chest, and his pain abated to some degree. It was not gone, but it was tolerable, bearable.

This time, sleep was a choice, and that was progress.

He was Tarmun Vykers, the Reaper. He'd been drenched in a vile substance that ate away at his flesh, his muscles. He'd been carrion...but now he was recovering. He'd like to have laughed at that, but hadn't the energy. He was still battling the pain with every heartbeat, and it seemed that each time he thought he understood it and its limits, some new catastrophe befell him and showed him yet more of its quality. Vykers' thoughts drifted to the End-of-All-Things, Eyatu, who'd turned out to be the god of winter. Was there a god of pain? Or was it instead a free-acting force, like sunshine or darkness? Whether divine or natural in origin, Vykers felt like its conduit, for all that he'd suffered, for all that he'd delivered.

The hand was back, accompanied by a familiar, soothing voice. The Reaper awoke—or thought he did. Maybe he continued dreaming. It was some time before he realized that he could not open his eyes because he had none to open. He dimly remembered the fear he'd once felt at the prospect of losing his hands and feet. They had grown back, though, and he held the same hope for his eyes. Already, his hearing had improved.

He was the Reaper, and he was alive. If he concentrated, he could pick individual words out of the sing-song noise surrounding him. He even believed he smelled smoke, the first odor of any kind he'd noticed in some time.

Someone lifted his head; he grew dizzy. A cool, sweet fluid came into his mouth and ran down his throat. Gods, he was thirsty! The drink disappeared long before he'd had his fill, and he wanted to complain, to insist he could handle more. His head returned to its previous position.

He slept.

Eoman, In Chains on the March

Once, he'd been a king, roaming the land to his heart's content; now, he was a slave, measuring the same land in miserable chain-bound half-strides. The Emperor's magicians had done their part to render him docile (though he was more resistant to their arts than they knew), and his every day was an endless march of drudgery and shame. At least the invading soldiers did not mock him—their leader wouldn't allow it. Still, it was fair to say they did not treat him kindly or with any sort of respect. They feared him, yes, but not nearly as much as they might have if he'd been free, which occurrence he dreamt of daily. Oh, wouldn't he love to smash their little iron heads together? To toss them fully-armored upon a fire and watch them squirm and pop like crabs?

It *was* a dream, though, for theirs was the largest army he'd ever seen. Striking out at his handlers would be suicide, and he hadn't quite fallen so low just yet. He expected that the invaders would encounter resistance eventually. In his experience, the native humans had never been the sort to surrender or appease anyone. He'd seen their queen in action, and he'd fought along-side Tarmun Vykers. When the native response inevitably came, he could either aid its progress from within the invaders' forces, or he could perhaps use the distraction to escape. Time, he felt, was his greatest ally, and patience his greatest asset.

There was still, however, the matter of the human girl, Qansip. After all he'd done for her, she'd abandoned him to his fate without making the slightest effort on his behalf, whereas she was clearly doing quite well for herself, as evidenced by her parading around with the invaders' leader as if she'd gotten a new toy. Did the man even realize his predicament? Eoman thought not. And it served the bastard right. Sooner or later, the girl would drive him mad, force him to do something he'd regret almost immediately. Eoman grinned when he thought of the damage she might do.

It was his first grin in ages. When he wasn't slogging along in the invaders' column, he was pulling their wagons out of potholes, clearing the road ahead of obstacles, or hauling fire-wood for the army's myriad campfires. They whipped him if he showed the slightest hesitation in performing these tasks, or the magicians cursed him with biting flies and the ague. None of these punishments was especially vexing; but Eoman wanted his tormentors to think they were, lest they devise more brutal means of motivating him. And so he put on a mummer's show of flinching when whipped, or grimacing when plagued with phantom pinches and cramps. These foreign bastards had no idea how much pain a giant could handle, and Eoman preferred to keep it that way. He was fascinated, though, with the question of how much pain *they* could tolerate.

New grass sprouted to either side of the army's self-made road, and Eoman's thoughts drifted off to the many things he enjoyed most about spring—the emergence of hibernating plants and animals, the birth of young animals, the blooming of flowers and the fresh growth of leaves, the streams and rivers swollen with sweet, delicious snowmelt, the warm patches of grass in sun-drenched meadows or sun-dappled woods. There were places he liked to be at certain times of the year, but he wouldn't see them this time around. Not unless something changed and quickly. As he looked about himself, the giant was struck by the contrast in the beauty of his surroundings and the ugliness of his lot. Life had a nasty sense of humor.

He looked up from the fresh mud beneath his feet and noticed one of the invaders' officers staring at him, a short, broad-chested fellow with an iron grey beard. Rather than look away, the man made a subtle but clear gesture with his hands, the native military's sign for "Wait." Eoman checked the man's face again to be sure he'd seen correctly and was rewarded with a small nod. Why was a member of the invaders' army using hand signals from the native army? Was he a spy? Had the Virgin Queen infiltrated the invaders' force? And what did "Wait" mean? Was something supposed to happen? How was he meant to react? Unable to stop and question the fellow, Eoman furrowed his brows in thought and continued pushing himself forward. Wait, indeed.

Bailis, In Mendis' Camp

Bailis was conflicted. He'd voluntarily abdicated all responsibilities to Her Majesty because he'd believed in and been inspired by the Emperor and his vision. Bailis worried now, though, that he'd done so on too brief an acquaintance. The Emperor's recent...*dalliance*, call it...with the local girl was cause for concern. Bailis had seen it too often before, which was one of the myriad reasons he'd never accepted the often-proffered promotion to General, himself: it was hard to lead when the men were either envious or contemptuous of you. Also, the distraction didn't help. Bailis wanted the Emperor focused on the mission and not the miss.

He didn't like seeing the giant in chains, either. Of course he'd been prepared to see men captured or killed, and he still dreamt of eradicating the Svarren. But he wasn't anywhere near as comfortable with the thought of enslaving or murdering the giants—especially after he'd gotten to know Long's wife, Mardine.

And then there was the fact Bailis had essentially committed treason in joining the Emperor's side. The thought ate away at the colonel, like a worm in the heart of an apple. He was a traitor. He'd betrayed his own people, his own soldiers, his homeland. And yet, he still wanted to believe in the Emperor, still wanted to believe in a more efficient and equitable government that did more for the common man. He frowned and scratched his beard. Yes, he'd sworn fealty to the Emperor, but perhaps it was still possible to serve Her Majesty, as well. There had to be all manner of little actions he could take to ensure the safety and well-being of his countrymen without incurring the Emperor's wrath.

He would think on it.

He would think, too, of ways to loosen this Qansip's grip on the Emperor.

Mendis' Sentries, Western Midlands

Pulling picket duty in the middle of the night was pulling the shortest of short straws. It mattered little that the men had the world's greatest army at their backs, especially when that army was asleep and hundreds of strides distant. The enemy's arrows or spears could fly out of the darkness much faster than reinforcements would ever arrive from camp, meaning that if hostiles were watching, death was almost a certainty. Someone had to stand guard, however; someone had to listen and watch. Someone had to warn the rest.

Most men were not fond of picket duty. Uthen loved it. He loved being out on the edge of the Emperor's force, encountering the new land by himself (there were always men to his left and right, but they were removed enough that Uthen would pretend he was alone). He enjoyed the odd sounds and unfamiliar aromas of the Emperor's new land. He thrilled at the idea that he might be the first Imperial soldier to lay eyes on a new animal. The strange sounds that made picket duty so unnerving to others made it all the more thrilling to him.

But he was no love-smitten schoolboy. He'd been fully informed of the dangers that lurked just beyond his field of vision. He'd heard all about the Svarren, the Oursine, the giants and other such creatures. He was not anxious to meet them, but he believed he could spot them before they saw him, thus allowing him to alert the rest of the troops before an attack arrived.

He was only partly correct.

It was a dark, moonless night, but that alone posed no difficulty for Uthen. He liked the dark and savored the challenge of listening for threats that could not be seen. On this occasion, the night obliged him. A single, upward-inflected squeal gradually built to a chorus of shrieks, guttural croaks and eerie cooing sounds. Uthen noted that the men on his left and right heard all of this, too, and one of them set off to warn the army...whereupon the noises stopped. When additional troops arrived, armed for immediate conflict, they heard not the slightest squeak from the blackness beyond the pickets.

After the additional troops had returned to camp, the chorus of cries resumed. This time, Uthen took charge. "Run and fetch a wizard this time," he chuckled sardonically. "If our hosts want to play, we'll play." It came out braver than he felt. There was too much noise to have come from a mere handful of…whatever they were. If they should choose to charge before the wizard arrived…

They did not. In fact, they again fell silent when the wizard trudged into view. He was a short, squat, black-haired fellow named Ademus, and, like many of his kind, had little patience for fools or foolery. "What news?" he demanded.

"The locals are baiting us," Uthen answered. "Making their presence known only when we guards are alone, but disappearing when anyone else arrives. I thought you might lob some fire at 'em."

Ademus smirked. "Of course you did. First, let's see what's out there, shall we?" He turned towards the night and extended his hands before himself. Uthen caught a brief flash of movement, and the wizard went down, bleeding profusely from a head wound. One of the other guards began furiously firing arrows in the direction from which the blow had come, whilst another of the guards yelled for aid at the top of his lungs. Uthen ducked down and rushed to the wizard's side. He grabbed the man by his feet and hurriedly dragged him towards camp. During this frantic retreat, he spotted a primitive but nasty-looking spear lying bloodied in the grass. He assumed its thrower had been aiming for the center of Ademus' head and missed, but it made little difference. Uthen doubted the wizard would survive the blow or the rough journey back to safety.

Then it occurred to him that this had been the enemy's plan all along, to goad him and his mates into exposing one of the Emperor's wizards. Could they kill enough wizards to make a difference, though? Uthen didn't want to find out.

They came in the heart of the night; they came just before dawn. They descended, shrieking, upon the Emperor's troops; they attacked in deathly silence. They came in sporadic waves; they attacked en masse. They chose a single point of focus; they attacked everywhere at once. It was, the troops understood, a strategy designed to set their nerves on edge and make sleep all but impossible. But knowing all that did little to minimize its effectiveness. The Imperial wizards were hard-put to neutralize the Svarren, who seemed to boast some immunity to their arcane attacks. Sword, spear and arrow were effective, but only if the defenders were awake and facing the proper direction when attacked.

In a quick meeting with his senior staff, Mendis did not seem overly concerned. "They're trying to force us to stand and fight them," he announced, "which is utterly idiotic. We would annihilate them in a pitched battle."

"May I ask, Magnificence, why we don't honor their wishes in this regard?" General Promartis inquired as gently as possible.

"Because I won't have them or anything else in this land thinking we can be manipulated. And, anyway, their efforts to engage us make me wonder why they don't want us continuing our march westward. Are they trying to buy time for some special purpose? Or is there something they don't want us to see?"

"We've found nothing of particular interest in the lands ahead," Alsig replied.

"No," Mendis mused. "It doesn't much seem like an attempt to stop us from moving forward—more an attempt to slow us down, to distract us." He turned to his wizards. "Double the time you spend scanning the countryside. And double your manpower. I want to know what they're hiding from us, and I don't want to lose one wizard more." To his officers, he said, "Leave some veterans of these attacks on the outer flanks, but rotate the rest of the men inwards. Let's put some fresh troops, some fresh eyes out there."

"Yes, Magnificence," his staff responded.

Mendis rolled his shoulders, working some stiffness out of his neck. He hadn't slept much or well the previous night, but not for the usual reasons. Qansip kept him rather busy while he was awake, and once he'd fallen asleep, she had an awful habit of monopolizing the bed and its blankets. He'd be hard-pressed to banish her from his bed and expect the same affectionate attention she currently lavished upon him whenever they were alone. He ruled the largest empire the world had ever seen, and yet he could not rule his mistress. On the contrary, he was beginning to fear she ruled him. What could she ask that he dared refuse? He caught a brief whiff of her perfume on his collar and suddenly could not wait for the day's march to end.

Driegan Deda first sighted his daughter as she rode past him on a horse, alongside a man he now knew to be the Emperor. On another occasion, whilst he was dining with his language tutor, he spied her accompanying the fellow into his pavilion. She never came out again while Driegan watched. Most recently, he'd looked on in bitter frustration as Qansip was paraded around the morning muster as if she were a prize-winning pony. On every occasion, she'd been wearing a different gown. On every occasion, the Emperor seemed more and more enamored of her.

Driegan sucked at his teeth and spat into the grass. There had to be some way he could profit from this turn of events, some way he could recoup what was his by right of fatherhood. He wanted his freedom, for starters. And if the Emperor was bedding his daughter, spoiling her marriage value, Driegan wanted coin, land, a position in the new order of things. How to get it, though, especially when he could not get near Qansip? His tutor was as immune to entreaty as iron to weeping. The bastard simply would not let Driegan out of his sight. Even the army's pit toilets were subject to patrol. Why this should be, Driegan could not imagine, but it served as the perfect example of the Emperor's security: nothing was left to chance, nothing was overlooked, everything was accounted for.

Still, it galled Driegan that his daughter should have more freedom, more status than he. After all he'd done for her, all he'd given her…Well, he would find a way. He always had.

It was, ironically, in the pit toilets that the idea finally came to him: he would be honest, direct. It was, for Driegan, a novel approach. He would tell his tutor that the girl was his daughter. His tutor, being a master skeptic, would drag him in front of the girl for confirmation, and she would acknowledge him. But it had to be done at the right time; he had to catch the girl and the Emperor in the proper mood. He recalled how he'd always hated being interrupted in the middle of business; he would not make the same mistake himself.

The People of Lunessfor, Lunessfor

Public sex acts were rampant, as were all the other normally frowned-upon activities. There was, for example, a naked piggyback race involving a score of contestants, right in the middle of Broad Street. One street over, a small crowd was engaged in a literal pissing match to determine who had the best aim and who the greatest reach. Of course, there was a farting contest! How could there not be? One fellow even amazed the crowd by playing the crumhorn through flatulence alone. Over on Fleet Street, a vendor was selling sausages shaped like penises—an item as popular with men as with women. Not all merriment was profane, however. There were hordes of folks with painted faces and bodies, mismatched clothing, silly hats and more. There were jugglers, acrobats and fire breathers. And, perhaps most surprising, those with deformities finally felt comfortable displaying themselves in public. In short, the whole of Lunessfor had erupted into a carnival atmosphere, from the wealthiest neighborhoods to the lowest of hovels. And the best of it was, benevolence reigned. There was not a bitter thought nor a word spoken in anger the length and breadth of the city.

And it was all because of Long's Old Peculiar.

If it pleased the multitudes, it did not have the same effect on Her Majesty. Once again, she dragged Kittins into her library to question him.

"You asked me to prepare the city's defenses," the big man protested, "and that's what I've done."

"Do you think the city's current atmosphere conducive to a solid defense?" Alheria snapped.

Kittins had had enough. "What's it to do with me? Where's your Lord Mayor? Where's the Constable?"

The Queen let out a long, exasperated exhalation. "Do not play the fool with me. I've one too many as it is," she scolded. "We cannot afford to be caught with our pants down—literally or figuratively—when the enemy comes a-calling. An alert citizenry is a prepared citizenry." As Kittins said nothing to interrupt her monologue, she continued. "I want you to quash this festival—or whatever it is—and ban any further celebrations until and unless the enemy is defeated."

"Just to be clear: the people are happier than they've been in ages, and you want me to put an end to that."

Alheria fixed Kittins with a look so cold it might have frozen fire. "If you don't do it, I will. I can promise you that you won't like my solution."

"If I'm to assume all the duties of the city's other offices and officers, I would at least like to know why I am so...fortunate."

This time, Her Majesty smiled. "Because you are a thing of darkness, captain. *My* thing of darkness. The Lord Mayor, the Constable and all the others are credulous simpletons, without either the brains or the backbone to do what must be done. Their faces are the happy facades of honesty and competence. Your face? A nightmare. And, as you well know, the real work gets done in the shadows, where they all fear to go."

It had been a strange and unsettling speech, and, for a goddess, she was awfully sneaky. Kittins could think of no other word for it. Instead of revealing herself to the world and simply willing things to be as she wished them, the Queen insisted on scheming and skulking. What was she up to? What in Mahnus' name...

Ah. Mahnus. Perhaps there were things she didn't want her former mate to see or become aware of. They had, as everyone knew, once been lovers. In fleeting conversations with the Reaper and his men, Kittins had come to understand that Alheria, Her Majesty, had confessed to killing Mahnus. But then she'd claimed he'd been—what?—reborn in the person of Long Pete. Kittins shook his head. It was like the plot of one of Rem's plays. Kittins wouldn't have paid two Shims to see such nonsense...and now he was living it.

And Rem, Yendor and the others weren't going to like this news, this directive from Her Majesty, but Kittins had to enforce it. Eventually. Alheria couldn't rightly expect him to impose his will on the entire city in a mere few hours, could she? No, he reckoned, this could take two or three days. By which time, Kittins hoped, he and the boys would have devised an alternate plan for their ale. Kittins might even have the beginnings of an idea, himself.

"What??" Yendor was apoplectic. "Things've never been better 'round here!"

"She's a god. Or goddess. Anyway, you don't like it, you go argue with her."

"Damn it all!" said Yendor, throwing his mug onto the floor in disgust. "Who knew the gods were such bullies?"

"Anyone payin' attention," Kittins snorted.

Yendor kicked at the fragments of his mug. "And I went 'n busted my Mahnus-cursed drinkin' mug, too."

"Might be I got somethin' even better in mind."

It wasn't like Kittins to get involved with the gang, but there was no doubting his say-so when he offered an idea.

"What've you got in mind?" Rem inquired.

"This ale o' yours is bloody addictive, isn't it? Makes work all but impossible, right?"

The gang stared at Kittins, waiting for the proverbial other shoe to drop.

"So, what happens if we put this stuff in the hands of the enemy?"

There followed an extended silence in the gang's hideout as each of the men thought the question through to its logical end. Spirk, predictably, never made it that far.

"What?" said he.

"What?" Kittins echoed. "Come up to street level and take a gander at yer fellow citizens. It's a city-wide orgy up there." After seeing Spirk's panicked reaction, he amended his statement, "On second thought, just trust me. The whole town's gone mad. 'Magine if the enemy starts drinkin' this stuff?"

"It could end the invasion!" Rem proclaimed.

"Could do," Kittins agreed. "Or at least blunt their progress 'til we come up with somethin' better."

"I like it!" said Yendor.

"Glad to hear it," Kittins replied. "'Cause you're doin' the bulk o' the work!"

NINE

Vykers, The Ruined Village

Vykers' nerve endings were on fire as his body rebuilt itself. He experienced periods of peace, of calm, but each was inevitably followed by longer stretches of unbearable agony, when he felt as if he were being burned alive, again. He couldn't have said what was worse, the pain, or the lulls during which he did nothing but anticipate its return. Yet his awareness, deliberate thought, returned to him little by little, hour by hour, until he could almost will himself awake. Almost. A familiar presence and its familiar magic kept him under, like a parent holding a stubborn child in the bath. He wanted to get up, to rise, but it—*she*—would not let him.

If not for his vague and fleeting memories, he would not have known other states were possible, would not have believed there was anything other than pain and darkness. Thus, he fought to latch onto those elusive memories whenever they appeared, struggled to decipher their meaning, as if, in doing so, he might find deliverance.

Gradually, external sounds intruded upon his dreams and memories, and Vykers was bewildered, until it occurred to him that he was hearing voices. Who was speaking or what was said, he'd no way of knowing, but it brought him some small measure of comfort to hear that there were others nearby in addition to the one who made him sleep. More, the realization that his hearing was improving suggested he might regain his other senses, as well, and the opportunity to focus on something besides his tormented dreams gave the Reaper hope.

The familiar woman lifted his head. He could tell she was trying to do so gently, but there was no gentle in his world; there was only pain. A cool, sweet something trickled into his mouth and down his throat. Soon, to his surprise, a pleasant sensation filled his belly. He groaned for more, and the woman granted his request.

He drifted into unconsciousness.

It was impossible to get close enough to the Reaper to gauge his progress. The thorny nest Aoife had created for him kept everyone well away, and it frustrated Ona no end. She had to settle for brief glimpses of Vykers' body, and what little she saw baffled her. He'd been burned almost to the bone, but now he was a slender, pinkish-white thing that looked more like a victim of prolonged starvation than incineration. How, though? How was this possible? Was the Reaper's mistress truly so powerful that she could effectively reanimate and heal the dead?

Every so often, other members of Vykers' crew would suspend their efforts to rebuild the town and drop by to monitor his recovery. The Red Knight, in particular, made a habit of it.

"Have you reconsidered your plans?" Ona asked him on one such visit.

"Have you?" he responded, not by way of challenge, but out of genuine interest.

"No."

"Den here vee stay."

"And if he never improves beyond this?"

"But I sink he vill. Look how far he's come!"

They fell into conversation about their homelands, their old lives, the things they missed most about their pasts. Ona did not trust most of Vykers' men, knew, in fact, that one or two of them might even attempt to violate her if the Reaper passed, because they were men, they were killers, bastards and thieves at heart. Oh, serving Vykers had ennobled them to some degree, giving them purpose beyond fighting and pillaging, but they'd been born and bred to battle and everything that it entailed. Hjuest was different. Loyalty was everything to him, it seemed, and he would never betray the Reaper's orders or wishes, even if his master died.

Ona respected Hjuest. He was not the handsomest fellow she'd ever seen, and he was a good head shorter than she, but if she were forced to choose a companion amongst the crew, she could do a damned sight worse than the Red Knight. If the Reaper didn't recover, she saw potential in a friendship with Hjuest.

Ngoro was as committed to staying as the rest of the group, but he missed his home. He'd been awarded to Vykers as a slave and had resigned himself to being so as long as the Reaper lived. The notions of freedom or of returning home had never occurred to him; now that they had, he found them torturous. He missed his people. He missed the climate, plants and animals of his home. He missed the foods and the women. He even missed the music of his mother tongue.

He needed something else to occupy his mind.

He watched Hjuest's interactions with Vykers' girl—his granddaughter, if Ngoro understood correctly—and wondered what she was playing at. She'd managed to keep everyone else at arm's length, but Hjuest she spoke with freely. She didn't appear sweet on the man, but Ngoro didn't count himself an expert on women. For his part, Hjuest seemed cordial enough, if not exactly warm. It was a mystery for which Ngoro was thankful. Without it, he'd have nothing to do but rebuild the town or stare at the Reaper's body.

And how had the Reaper survived his wounds? Was it the green woman's doing?

He was not a god. Of that much, Aoife was certain. She could not, with equal confidence, call him a man, though. But if he was not a god or a man, what was he? Who or what was this creature with whom she'd become so inextricably entwined? She had often noted that he and she were opposites—he, destruction, and she creation—and though it seemed the one could not exist without the other, did that explain her feelings for him?

He screamed. At least, she thought it was a scream. His throat and lungs were in such a tender state that little sound came out. It was more like an anguished hiss. Aoife could not imagine the pain he'd endured or had yet to endure. She could not fathom the mind or minds that had created him to inflict and receive such suffering.

The gods of men were insane. Vykers was proof of that. She felt no jealousy at being excluded from their number. The gods to whom *she* was beholden, the ones who'd raised her to their level, were older, far older, and had other priorities entirely. Perhaps they were even at odds with the gods of men.

Vykers coughed. His stomach rumbled audibly. Aoife fed him.

Mendis, In Camp

The attack came at four in the morning, by Mendis' reckoning—an hour or so before the bulk of the army awakened. This was not unexpected, though the method of it was. Darting in and out of his wizards' range, the Svarren threw, shot and launched flaming pitch beyond the pickets on both sides of the column, so that, in short order, the Imperial army was trapped between two walls of fire. Whilst the soldiers and wizards fought to suppress this fire, the Svarren attacked with huge numbers farther down the line, to the east. With their focus thus divided, Mendis' troops were unprepared for the giants' assault on the opposite side, up the line to the west. The Svarren shrieked and bellowed, but the giants were all business. They stormed noiselessly out of the dark, smashed through the Imperials' defenses, and plunged to the very center of camp, where one of their kin had been held captive. Will-o'-wisps flooded the air, like a million dandelion seeds on the breeze, confounding the soldiers' vision and making it nigh impossible to count the giants' numbers or determine the direction of their retreat.

Long minutes of battle later, it became clear that the Svarren were using some magic of their own to counter the wizards' attempts to douse the flames, so that Mendis was forced to tap into the army's water supplies to aid in the fight. Scores of fifty-gallon barrels were hauled near the fire lines and smashed open with axes. Meanwhile, the Imperial archers peppered the scrub beyond the flames with thousands of arrows, until the sun rose at last, and it became evident that the enemy had fled.

It was not all bad for the Empire: there were plenty of dead Svarren on the column sides of the fire lines, creatures who'd given their lives to advance the flames. And there had been casualties beyond the fire as well, though they'd apparently been dragged away by their fellows, leaving only their blood behind. Mendis' forces, on the other hand, had suffered few casualties from the Svarren. It was the giants who'd done the most damage, killing or wounding almost a hundred men before vanishing into the countryside. It was not the number that mattered, though. What were a mere hundred lives to an army of hundreds of thousands? No, what wounded morale (and Mendis' pride) the most was the fact that the enemy's plan had actually worked. It seemed they'd carried out the whole exercise in order to free the captive giant, and they'd succeeded. It was an embarrassment, a rank repudiation of everything the Empire's discipline stood for.

And then there was the loss of water to consider. An army the size of Mendis' required its own traveling city for support, its blacksmiths, bakers, surgeons and the like. Fully one-fourth of his host's number was made up of support personnel, who required nearly as much food and water as his troops.

Mendis sent out word that the column would stay encamped at its current location for another day. He then demanded to see his staff in his tent forthwith.

"We have been led to believe," he began once everyone had assembled, "that this land's Svarren and its giants did not and would never work together. Clearly, things have changed. I think it prudent, therefore, to assume that everyone and everything we encounter will be part of some effort against us. Henceforth, you are to kill any non-humans you encounter on sight. Whatever intelligence they might offer is undoubtedly of less significance than the threat they and theirs pose to us. As for humans, we will ask them to choose immediately between loyalty to us and our cause or death. We will have no more interrogations, no more reclamation projects. The natives will either join us or die. The choice cannot be made any simpler."

Mendis paused to study his advisors for understanding. Seeing no signs of confusion or discontent, he went on. "Additionally, I will offer a bounty on the heads of Svarren, giants, humans or anything else that reasonably presents a threat to us during our scouting missions—I'll leave it to the Exchequer to work out the details. But I want those heads to line our road from coast to coast. Accordingly, I want to double the number of scouting parties and quadruple the size of each group. We cannot have hostiles lurking in the undergrowth on either side of our path. Today's attack suggests they think us missionaries or some such, here to bask in the beauty of the countryside and perhaps even pick Forget-Me-Nots if the mood arises."

This last got a nice smattering of laughter, and then the Emperor continued. "If the locals are probing us for weakness, they will be sorely disappointed in what they find. You may all return to your posts, except for my wizard friends."

This was not happy news for the wizards, but they steeled themselves for the Emperor's anger.

"Magnificence?" their leader inquired of the Emperor.

Mendis glared at the man. "We have been together a long time," he said. "We've dealt with every sort of hell the world could throw at us."

"That is true."

"You and your fellows have typically been the most competent and often most fearsome example of Imperial power...how or why have you all become so inept of late? Is it to do with this land? Is there something in the air or water that I can't smell or taste? What keeps you from barring Her Majesty from our camp? How is it these savages seem so little affected by your magics?"

Alsig was a long time in answering, stalling to the point of insolence. "Magnificence," he said at last, "it has been like trying to start a fire with rain-drenched wood. It often feels as if there is a spell upon the land entire, some vast, overarching magic that blunts our abilities."

Mendis considered this response for an equally long time. "Find an answer. The success of our campaign depends upon it." The old wizard nodded in affirmation, but Mendis could see there was something else on his mind, something with which he wasn't comfortable, but that he felt needed to be addressed. The Emperor had no trouble guessing. "For a wizard, old friend, your expressions are awfully transparent. You're concerned about my...companion."

Alsig's eyebrows shot up in surprise as he reappraised his Emperor. "Have you ever been tested for talent?" he asked. "You've struck the very marrow of my worries."

The Emperor laughed loudly. "Come now, I'd have to be a stump, a stone, to be unaware of the impact the girl's presence has had upon my inner circle. You all think such a dalliance beneath me. Perhaps you feel for my lady wife. But am I not the Emperor? Am I not entitled to some small measure of comfort, of pleasure, whilst I manage and expand our empire? When have I ever denied any of you your little...diversions?"

It was as defensive a lecture as the wizard could ever remember from his Emperor, which only served to worry him more. But because Mendis was no fool, there was nothing Alsig could do to the girl without incurring the Emperor's wrath. Then the other man surprised him.

"Still," said Mendis, "I'll grant you that things might go a bit more smoothly around here if she were relocated—say, to Nespharia. Bailis is governor and our expert on local peoples and their customs. I'm sure he can make Qansip more than comfortable, and I'll still be able to visit her as I list."

He had the air of a man who knows he's shared a good idea, and the wizard couldn't help but agree. More, he thought it possible that the Emperor might lose interest in the girl, even forget about her if she was not on his arm everywhere he went. Her distance also made more extreme measures possible, if needs must. After all, he'd a duty to serve the Emperor, but a no-less important duty to serve the Empire, as well.

"I'll chat with Qansip about all of this over dinner," Mendis continued. "And then you can whisk her away to Nespharia in the morning."

Qansip maintained an admirably placid expression as Mendis

informed her of his decision, but inwardly she seethed. It wasn't that she cared overmuch for the Emperor, though she liked him well enough. It was more that she feared losing the position and influence she'd worked so hard to win. She'd sacrificed her maidenhead, for instance, and felt that for that she deserved at least the fortune, trappings and respect of an Emperor's wife. She had never deceived herself into thinking that he'd take her with him when he returned to his palace, and, in fact, she was rather relieved he would not. For all his wealth and power, he was not the kind of man she'd imagined for herself. He was too serious, too busy (for want of a better word), and, lastly, too short. No, she wanted a man like the legendary Reaper, a big, muscular brute who took what he wanted and damn the consequences.

As she listened to Mendis drone on about Nespharia and how she could help rebuild it and boost the morale of its people, she began to see possibilities in the Emperor's plan. Without Mendis breathing down her neck, she might effectively act as the city's ruler. Oh, Mendis had said something about a Governor Bailis, but this didn't worry Qansip. Bailis was a man, after all, and could be manipulated, just as she'd manipulated the Emperor. In time, she might supplant this Bailis as ruler of Nespharia, and who could say? Perhaps Mendis might even make her the city's Queen.

A part of Qansip recognized such thoughts as girlish fantasy, but another part reminded her of how far she'd come, how much she'd accomplished. Who knew what the next few months or years might hold in store for her?

She forced herself to concentrate on Mendis once more, in the hopes that more information might clarify her options.

Unfortunately, her father chose that moment to reappear, like an illness she thought she'd long since beaten. Suddenly, he was at her side, fawning over her and the Emperor alike.

"Great Magnificence," he oozed. "Forgive my intrusion, but I see you've met my daughter, whom I've not seen myself in weeks."

Mendis looked momentarily stunned, as if he'd been struck. He glanced about his tent for any of his staff, wondering how this native fellow had gotten so close. It was yet another egregious mistake from his security team, and he was fast tiring of it. He was about to summon the guards when he saw Qansip watching him, gauging his response to the stranger's violation of protocol. He decided a demonstration of self-confidence was his best course of action.

"Her father, you say?"

Driegan nodded eagerly and rubbed his hand up and down Qansip's shoulder, which of course made her cringe.

"Father," she said flatly, making no effort to disguise her displeasure at his timing.

This too, Mendis noticed. "If I am remembered of it, you were assigned to learn our language and then help in instructing your countrymen..." He let this hang in the air a moment and then went on. "How comes it that you're standing here, interrupting my meal?"

"A fair question, sire," Driegan replied obsequiously. "An excellent question. But, as I say, I haven't seen my daughter in some time—thought she had died, in fact."

With as much patience as he could summon, Mendis put down his cutlery and offered Qansip's father nothing but a steely-eyed glare.

"But perhaps," Driegan added, "I can chat with her later, now that I know she's in good hands." He didn't wait for further response, but quickly retreated into the cloud of support personnel.

Mendis thought Qansip might apologize on her father's behalf, but he was rapidly learning that she never apologized for anything, ever. It was, he felt, a serious flaw in her character, but perhaps in this instance she was too embarrassed by her father's unexpected appearance. He took a sip of wine and considered his companion. Merely looking at her evoked passions in him he could ill afford at the moment, and her father's presence only made things worse. "And what shall I do with your father, then?" he asked Qansip.

"Send him away," said she. "And keep me here."

The Emperor tried a different approach. "My love, the road is no place for someone of your quality, your beauty. You may as well ask doves to travel amongst the oxen, or a butterfly to light amongst the black flies at the knacker's. Nespharia, though, can accommodate your every need, indulge your every whim. In the city, you'll live in comfort, in luxury, as you deserve."

What could the girl say to that? His speech had mirrored her private thoughts, though she doubted he knew the extent of her ambitions and appetites. As for her father, "Then keep my father here. I'm no longer a child, to be badgered and bullied at every turn."

As far as Mendis was concerned, the matter was settled.

Long & Short, The Fretful Porpentine, Lunessfor

"I'm a damned fool," Long muttered, as he sat on the edge of the bed in yet another room that wasn't his.

"You've just now figured this out?" Short responded.

Long gazed wearily at the simulacrum of his old friend. "Sorry, forgot you were there."

"Did you, now?" he asked. "But I'm always here!"

Long stood, distractedly, and paced the floor of the room he hadn't rented.

"Well, what is it, then?"

Again, Long looked down at Short. "It's this city. It's like an onion. Layer upon layer of magical protections."

"And?"

"It could take me weeks to get through all of 'em—if I'm able to get through any—and into Alheria's throne room."

Short yawned and stretched his little arms out to either side. "So? How's that make you a fool?"

"I just never noticed it before."

The homunculus crossed over to the bed and scrambled up to the spot where Long had been sitting. From there, he trundled across the blanket to the pillow, where he proceeded to make himself comfortable.

"What are you doing?" Long demanded.

"Taking a nap. What's it look like?"

The captain shrugged. Although he'd made Short—this

version of him, anyway—he wasn't close to understanding him. He would have thought the little homunculus incapable of sleep, or at the very least disinterested in it. But Short went to it with a zeal that would have made housecats envious.

Alone with his thoughts, Long began to panic. He could not hide in borrowed rooms forever. Eventually, he would have to act, to confront and kill Alheria. A more daunting task, he could not have imagined. The arcane protections she'd placed about herself, the layers of the onion, had most likely been designed and constructed with him in mind. Unless the full gamut of Mahnus' abilities returned to him quickly, it was unlikely he could penetrate Her Majesty's defenses before she found and struck at him first. The Fool, Hoosh Bindy, had offered to help, but Long didn't think the man could offer much more than a momentary distraction. How was Long even to get near Alheria?

He thought back to the few occasions he'd been within a stone's throw of her. Then, she hadn't recognized him. All hells, he hadn't recognized himself. So perhaps her defenses were of broader purpose than he'd supposed. Perhaps they simply repelled those who meant Alheria harm.

Suddenly, Long got the beginnings of an idea. An evil, despicable idea. For a while, he couldn't breathe, just thinking about it. Of course, he now knew he no longer needed to breathe, but old habits die harder than old harridans, by which he meant Alheria. If he did this thing he'd envisioned, if he actually carried it through to fruition, he would surely be the most loathsome creature in existence.

He threw up his hands in surrender. He was doomed, anyway. What difference, really, did it make if he went out a hero or a pariah? A happy ending was not in his stars.

Eoman, Beesmarch & Their Kinfolk, Western Midlands

Eoman was overcome with emotion, unable to separate his relief and gratitude at having been freed from his continuing anger towards Beesmarch and even the others who'd tolerated the bigger giant's belligerence. The former king was overjoyed to see Karrakan again, but felt a lingering humiliation at having lost his crown.

It was all he could do to thank his rescuers. "I am in your debt," he said softly, almost as if he was afraid to hear those words, himself.

The others smiled, patted him on the back, embraced him, but it was all very awkward. Only Karrakan stayed by his side, and Beesmarch stood well away from everyone else. Thus, it was the shaman, as always, who began the healing.

"Seems to me you two need a few moments alone," he suggested at a volume everyone else could hear. "The rest of us will find a suitable spot for camp nearby."

Eoman and Beesmarch either could not or would not look one another in the eyes, but they both watched the rest of the group shuffle off into the trees. Finally, Beesmarch said, "Damn it all, Eoman, it was a mistake! Alright? I let my temper get in the way and made a right mess o' things."

"And nearly killed me in the bargain."

"Yes, well..." Bees trailed off. "You ain't dead, so..."

"So?" Eoman prompted.

"So...that's good, right?"

"Oh, forget you hit me when I wasn't looking?" Eoman bristled. "Forget I took a long fall into an icy river? Forget I almost froze, before almost starving to death? Forget I was captured by..."

"I am sorry!" Beesmarch yelled in aggravation. "Couldn't be sorrier. And on top o' all that, I hate being king."

Eoman laughed, but it was a mirthless, defeated kind of sound. "And I loved it." Before the other giant could interrupt, he quickly added, "But what's done is done. Yours is the honor now, and yours the burden."

"But I don't want it," Beesmarch protested.

"No more o' that!" Eoman admonished him. "Such mewling is unworthy of our king, and you *are* our king now, Bees. I will help you, serve you, advise you in any way I can. But you'll have to do your part; you'll have to do justice to the title and lead our people."

It was an inspiring little speech, Bees thought. The kind

a king might give, but that he could not. He felt destined to fail, and he couldn't escape the notion that Eoman was thereby punishing him.

"Let's find the others and see what sort o' meal we can come up with!" Eoman said. "I haven't had a full belly in the longest time."

The group spent hours hunting and foraging; it takes a lot to feed so many giants. Fortunately, they were all experienced hunters and, with the seasons changing, there was more game about than any of them had seen in ages. By moonrise, they were all ensconced around a roaring fire, lustily stuffing themselves with fowl, with rabbit, with deer, and even with trout. They also produced a few rarities from their various pouches and knapsacks, as giants will on special occasions, and so there was hard cheese, thick, grainy crackers, a leather of dried preserves, some honeycomb, and more. To Eoman, it was the greatest feast he could ever recall, and despite the giants' equally giant appetites, it took more than an hour for everyone to finish, at which point belts were loosened, buttons undone, boots kicked off and tossed aside, and a thick fog of contentment descended upon the group.

There was, naturally, a great deal of discussion about the Svarren, the invaders, and what should be done next. It should have been riveting stuff for Eoman, but he was too busy basking in the company of his friends and fellows to care overmuch about the long view. And besides, Beesmarch was king now, and Beesmarch could handle it.

Gradually, Eoman found himself on his back, his head resting on someone's kit. Karrakan's will-o'-wisps were buzzing and fluttering about him, about some task Eoman couldn't begin to comprehend, though he did feel more relaxed, more at peace than he'd been in recent memory. Like as not, the little creatures were tending to the giant's many hurts, physical and emotional, for in no time, Eoman drifted off to sleep.

He awoke with the sunrise, to find his companions already—or still—debating their next course of action. One of the Brothers stepped forward to declare that, the previous day's action aside, no Svarren could ever be trusted. This giant had an elaborate plan to deceive their new allies and, when the invaders attacked, abandon the Long Teeth to their fate. Another of the Brothers denounced this plan as dishonorable, whereupon the first brother asked when Svarren had ever demonstrated honor of any kind. In short order, all three brothers fell to bickering, and Beesmarch was forced to step in and restore order. Did anyone else have any ideas or suggestions?

Eoman sat up and began picking bits of bark and charcoal from his hair and beard.

"Eoman?" the new king said, with an obvious edge in his voice. "You gonna stay silent forever or have you got anything to add?"

"Me?" the former king replied, all innocence.

"Yes!" Beesmarch confirmed. "You see any other Eomans 'round here?"

It wasn't especially witty, but the comment broke the tension nonetheless. Even Eoman laughed.

"Well," said he, "we can always make war with the Svarren later...if any of us survives these invaders. I've never seen an army so large, well-trained and well-supplied. Even if we found every last one of our kin, we'd never be a match for these humans, toe-to-toe. So, I'm thinkin' we can't face 'em toe-to-toe. Not even with the Svarren on our side."

"Humph!" Beesmarch responded. "What then?"

Eoman scratched the top of his head and then examined his fingernails thoughtfully. "We go after their supply-lines. We starve 'em out, or make 'em die of thirst. Army that size needs regular meals 'n water. We take that away from them..."

An explosion of boisterous laughter and conversation followed as the group of giants collectively warmed to the idea. Eoman sat back and enjoyed the moment. He might not be king anymore, but he damned sure knew how to lead. He caught Karrakan looking at him, and the shaman winked in approval.

It had been good to be king. It was great to be Eoman.

Omeyo & the Woman, Western Midlands

Omeyo and the Woman were in agreement with the giants: their first priority was hectoring the invaders (out of their land entirely, if possible); they could then resume their more-traditional hostilities afterwards, if they so desired. If anyone survived.

The plan was to weaken the invaders' supply lines, to limit their resources and otherwise make every westward step a chore. The giants had volunteered for the task of reducing the enemy's access to fresh water, so the Svarren would tackle two other parts of the job: chasing game animals out of the area, and assaulting the army's production centers, the first of which was Nespharia. The Svarren horde was more than large enough to handle both tasks, but the general and the Woman wanted the bulk of their force to hit the city. His scouts had informed Omeyo that the place was still rebuilding from the invaders' attack, so there might yet be weaknesses to exploit. If his fighters could cause enough damage, enough chaos, the enemy might be tempted to turn back. There was no telling how such a move would impact the invaders' morale; there was no way to calculate the resultant loss of new resources.

Omeyo was pleased. He would not allow himself to dream that he might actually conquer the city and then possess it, but he felt better about his situation than he had in some time. And he liked his Svarren's chances against the invaders garrisoned at Nespharia.

Kittins, Yendor & Co, Western Midlands

They'd purchased two enormous wagons and four oxen to pull each. The price was steep, but the boys had money to burn and, they believed, a noble cause inspiring their actions. It would not be a long journey, thanks to Spirk's magics, but they hoped and expected to make several trips, depending on the success of the first. Of course, with Long's Old Peculiar, success was a foregone conclusion.

Kittins had chosen Rem to ride along in his wagon, whilst relegating Yendor, Ron and Spirk to the second wagon. Over their time together in the icy north, Kittins had learned how to get along with Rem. He didn't think any amount of time or proximity would make the old drunk or the idiot Shaper easier to endure, and Ron was just the odd man out. But it was fine. Each team had its load of barrels to protect during the relatively short drive to the enemy column, at which point, they all expected to be relieved of their cargo.

The Dead One felt almost lighthearted with anticipation. He was back in the wilds again, the weather was cooperating, and there might even be some fighting in the near future. Even if there was not, it was wonderful getting out of Lunessfor for a day or two and away from Her Majesty's scrutiny. And, as much as Kittins liked to pretend otherwise, he enjoyed the occasional company of his former companions. They'd known him back when, after all. Before he'd become a monster.

He listened as Rem told tales of his life before the End-of-All-Things, and though Kittins had heard many of them before, there were always new details and embellishments that made the listening more enjoyable. When he'd first met the former actor, he'd had nothing but contempt for the man. Rem had seemed a pretentious wastrel and fop. Now, Kittins knew Rem to be brave, clever, and loyal. He was a good man to have around, to break up the monotony of any journey, and was, in many ways, as level-headed a fellow as Kittins had ever encountered. Yes, if the question were raised, he supposed he would have called Rem a friend, and the captain had precious few of those.

About an hour into their trek, a great herd of elk came thundering past the wagons, seemingly careless of their presence. At first, Kittins was baffled, but the sight of so much meat racing by sent him scrambling for a bow. Fortunately, Ron was of the same mind and had already shot a large buck three or four times before Kittins found a bow of his own. The herd disappeared into the surrounding tall grass and bushes, and the wounded buck slowly toppled onto its side.

"Looks like your aim's improved," the captain told the young man.

Ron blushed, as expected. "Well, I been workin' on it."

"Keep at it," Kittins said gruffly. No sense in coddling the kid.

There followed some discussion about the herd's sudden appearance, but no one had any viable theories, and the group's attention eventually turned to dressing and cutting up the buck.

"Let's not," said Kittins. "Better to leave 'im whole until we mean to cook 'im."

As it sounded like sage advice and nobody dared contradict the big man, they all tossed the carcass onto Yendor's wagon and resumed their journey. Late in the afternoon, they spied the invaders' column in the distance.

"Gods!" Yendor remarked. "Makes the End's horde look like a child's parade."

Kittins grunted in agreement.

"We should run into their scouts any time, now," said Rem.

Kittins grunted a second time.

"You gonna do the talkin' when the time comes?" Yendor wanted to know.

"No. Rem should do it. He's the best story-teller," Kittins replied, to everyone's surprise.

They didn't have long to wait. But a few minutes later, a small scouting party pushed its way through the underbrush and into the wagons' path. They weren't enough men to seize the wagons by force, but everyone understood that they could summon infinite reinforcements. One of the scouts turned to his fellows and did just that. Immediately, a lone rider turned tail and rode off in the direction of the invading force.

"So far, so good," Yendor said quietly.

"Famous last words," Kittins answered grimly. The captain then passed the time, watching the sun sink towards the horizon. Before it set, a much larger party showed up, complete with Shapers—or whatever passed for them in the invaders' army.

Soon, Kittins and company were able to understand and converse with the new arrivals.

"What is your cargo and where are you heading?" One of the Shaper-types demanded.

Kittins eyed Rem, who came in right on cue. "We're hauling

a load of ale to Mescond, up north a piece."

"Not anymore, you're not," the Shaper said. "The Emperor's Legions will buy your ale."

Because it wouldn't do to give in so easily, Rem protested. "But what of our regular customers? What of our contract?"

"They can look elsewhere for their ale. You'll find the Emperor's offer is more than generous, especially if your ale is any good."

Rem was about to agree when the Shaper continued. "And we'll take that buck, there."

"And what are you offering for him?"

"Nothing. All game in this region belongs to the Emperor."

Kittins lost his temper. "The fuck it does!" said he, jumping to his feet.

The invaders clutched their weapons and prepared for hostilities.

So much for the plan.

"Now, now!" Rem boomed. "No need for anyone to get hurt." His voice thundered across the area as if he were still performing with his company. "Take the buck, we'll manage."

"What in the infinite hells?" Kittins growled at him under his breath.

"You're the one put me in charge, here," Rem returned. "Let's see this through."

Slowly and radiating resentment, Kittins sank back onto his bench. He could see that everyone in the invaders' party was staring at his face, or what was left of it. Good. He hoped it gave them nightmares.

The last rays of sunlight were just fading when the wagons and their escort reached the army proper, which had finally come to a stop and set about making camp. Or camps. The invaders' Shaper called for one of the cooks to come forward and sample Long's Old Peculiar, to verify that it was, in fact, worth purchasing. When the cook responded with an enthusiastic yes, another man came forward with a small box full of Imperial coins.

Rem was about to complain, when Yendor nudged him. "It's gold, and a lot of it. Anyway, the money's not our main concern."

Rem nodded. The less said around the invaders, the better.

"Have you more of this stuff?" the Shaper asked. "The cook would very much like us to buy all you've got."

"More?" said Yendor. "Oh, aye, we've got more."

"Good," the other man replied. "You know where to find us."

They rode back in silence a good while, but once they'd gotten clear of the invaders' scouting parties, Yendor, Rem and company had a good, long laugh. If the bastards wanted more, it was more they'd get.

Vykers & Aoife, The Ruined Village

"Do you know me?"

Vykers' voice crackled and clicked oddly as he spoke. "Aoife."

"Yes," she said, her voice a caress. "And do you know what it was that attacked you?"

The Reaper was silent for some time. "The Frog."

"Or Tadpole, yes."

So, he understood. She had warned both of them, early on, when there'd still been a chance for the boy. And now the boy—or rather the thing that he'd become—had to be killed. Aoife said nothing more about it. She knew Vykers would come to the same conclusions. For all the pain he'd endured, it seemed there was always more to be suffered.

He became aware of his fingers and flexed them slowly. Which hurt, of course. He laughed. What didn't, anymore? He had... ten. Ten fingers. He flexed his toes. All there, all hurting. He struggled to lift a forearm, and it was like trying to lift the moon off the horizon. He broke out in a trembling sweat, just attempting it, but he managed it.

"Gently, easy," Aoife murmured.

He wondered if being born was so painful.

"Thirsty," he croaked, and she obliged him with cold, clear water. "Hungry," he said, and she fed him a flavorful gruel that sent a pleasant warmth throughout his body.

He was alive. He'd been bathed in, blasted with fire, and he'd survived. Add how and why to the ever-growing heap of questions he'd been compiling of late. Being roasted alive put things in perspective, though, and he was content to find answers as they came.

"My men?"

"Still here," Aoife answered.

"Good."

He slept.

He wanted to sit up. She urged against it, but no one could argue with Vykers when he had his mind set on a thing. It was a slow, agonizing process, and by the time he'd achieved his goal, the Reaper was drenched in sweat.

"What is that stench?" he demanded.

"Your sense of smell is returning," Aoife replied. "Good, good."

"Bad, bad. Is that me?"

Her silence was answer enough.

He forgot all about his odor, however, when he saw his legs. They looked like the bony legs of a child—smooth, pink, hairless skin with no muscle whatsoever. Vykers looked down at his chest and then studied his arms. They were equally undeveloped.

"I can't fight the Frog like this!" he protested.

"And yet you're strong enough to complain."

If he had in fact been a child, he might have sulked or pouted. "I need a bath and some solid food, some meat."

Aoife sighed. It was nice to have Vykers back, even if he was still recovering.

When he emerged from the cocoon Aoife had built for his rehabilitation, his men all gasped with one voice. "Fuck are you all lookin' at?" he groused. "Let's get some meat on the fire, so's I can get some meat on these bones!"

His team leapt to their feet, only too eager to do his bidding. For days—weeks?—they'd held deathwatch, hoping for the impossible, preparing for the worst. All at once, things were looking much, much better, even if Vykers was just a shadow of his former self.

"Do I look that bad?" he asked Ona.

She made a face. "It's hard to say."

And it was true. He'd gone from looking like a blood-drenched skeleton to an emaciated old man with the skin of a newborn. Creepy was the first word that came to Ona's mind. His recovery thus far, though, was nothing less than miraculous, and it didn't seem so far-fetched that he might regain his old mass and strength. She watched him hobble over towards the fire and sit on some stones nearby. Only then did she realize he was naked. Rather than call attention to that fact, she retrieved one of her own blankets and offered it to him.

"Thanks," he said.

Ona was so shocked to hear gratitude from the Reaper that she almost fell over.

Vykers had been eating and drinking almost without cessation since he'd rejoined his crew by the fire, and it was difficult to imagine where he was putting it all. Ona became convinced that if she stared at him long enough, she could actually see him filling out.

He wanted to know how long he'd been out, as he put it. He wanted to know what they'd been doing all that time, and whether they'd seen any further signs of the monster that had sacked the town and reduced him to a wasted cadaver.

But it had failed to kill him, and that mistake would seal its fate.

'You're not planning to go after him anytime soon, I hope," Ona cautioned.

"Soon enough."

There was no point in arguing with the Reaper, even in his weakened state. He wanted revenge, Ona guessed, and damned was the man or woman who stood in his way. Oh, she couldn't begin to imagine how the frail creature before her would accomplish the task, but, unlike the Frog, she would never underestimate him.

Eventually, Vykers exhausted himself with food, drink

and talk and fell asleep where he sat. The big Ntambi warrior crossed over to him and ever-so-gently scooped him into his arms, like a father carrying his infant child, and took him back to the cocoon he shared with Aoife. It was the most unlikely and incongruous thing any of them had seen in some time.

The next morning, a new and more muscular Vykers sauntered up to the fire and again asked for food and drink. Though he was still well shy of his normal size and condition, he was beginning to reacquire the menace for which he was famous.

"'Nother day, maybe two," he said. "Then we go huntin'."

"These townsfolk will be sorry to see us go."

"But they'll be glad when we've killed the thing that destroyed their town."

Well, he was probably right. If he and his crew *could kill* the Frog.

"I'm leavin' in the morning," Vykers told Aoife.

"I expected as much," said she, from the half-sleep in which she spent more and more of her time.

"And you?"

"I'll return to my bower."

"I figured." There was so much more he wanted to say, to ask, to discuss. But it seemed she knew his mind, and he, hers, so that conversation was extraneous. They would spend more time together in the future, of that Vykers was certain.

Long & Short, The Fretful Porpentine

He'd been procrastinating, he had to admit. Making excuses of every sort in order to avoid the inevitable conflict with Alheria. But a short while earlier, he'd tried everything he could think of to kill himself; now, he feared being killed.

Make up your mind, old man, Long told himself. *If you've still got one.*

With Short in tow and still disguised as a chicken, Long mingled with strangers in every bar, tavern and inn in Lunessfor, trying to ascertain when and where the Fool might appear next.

He was an entertainer, after all, and the folks at the Fretful Porpentine seemed to know him well, so it stood to reason that he made more or less regular visits to the city's various watering holes.

Of course, folks weren't as forthcoming as they'd been just a day or two earlier, on account of the sudden shortage of Long's Old Peculiar. Some might even say the whole population had become downright surly. Short got a good laugh out of that, though. Crazy old world, when an honest ale made no one happy.

Long persevered, however, because he needed the Fool. The castle had its own onion-layer of spells that kept out hostile magics. Long could attempt to sneak in past the physical barriers, but Alheria's magic would recognize him in an instant, and he would be barred or worse. But if one of Her Majesty's *children* invited Long in...He couldn't finish the thought. He knew what he *hoped* would happen, but hope had never served him particularly well in the past.

"And what'll you do if you *do* get into the castle?" Short challenged.

"One thing at a time," Long snapped. "One thing at a time."

After many long hours of searching, the captain finally found the Fool, acting as judge in a meat pie-eating contest in one of the city's wealthier taverns. When the contest concluded, Long pulled Hoosh aside and said, "Seems an awful waste o' meat, in a town might be under siege soon."

Hoosh threw up his hands. "It's not for me to judge...except when I'm judging."

"Right," Long muttered, unamused. "Last time we spoke, you told an incredible story..."

"All true."

"Right," Long said again. "Have you got any suggestions as to how I'm s'posed to accomplish my task? I mean, how do I get close to 'er Majesty? And then how do I...how do I..."

"Kill 'er," Short clucked.

"Would that I knew," Hoosh answered, eyeing the chicken suspiciously.

"I'm gonna need a little more 'n that. I can feel that castle o' hers keepin' me out. There any way *you* can get me inside?"

"Me?" the Fool laughed in alarm. "The whole point in sharing all this with you was to avoid getting involved myself. If Her Majesty discovers I've spoken with you…"

Long wasn't having any of it. "Which I will guarantee," he said, "unless you help me."

The Fool's face dropped like a corpse on a hangman's gibbet. "You gods," he moaned. "Such bullies."

"We'll talk more about gettin' inside, anon," said Long. "It'll all be moot if there's no way to kill her. What can you tell me?"

Hoosh looked constipated for a moment, and then answered, "You were present at the second battle with Eyatu, were you not? The End-of-All-Things?"

Long knew where this was going. "The invisible dagger?"

"Mmmm. It was forged specifically to kill Alheria. But then you should know that. You made it."

Short broke into a lengthy series of clucks that sounded suspiciously like laughter.

"Your…chicken…" Hoosh began.

"Will be dinner if he don't shut it," Long snapped. He fixed the Fool with his most serious expression. "So, you sneak me into the castle, I find this dagger, and then I stab the Queen with it."

"Easy-peasy," Hoosh responded, in a tone that suggested he felt quite the opposite.

The Fool knew of the perfect entrance, both out-of-the-way and little-used. It had never been popular, especially after the Dead One began using it, so it was unlikely there would be too many witnesses around when Hoosh tried to smuggle Long Pete inside the castle. The guards, for their part, were well-acquainted with the Fool and generally left him to his devices.

But, as the sages have oft noted, some things are too good to be true.

It was late when Long Pete and the Fool approached the door, singing loudly and badly, their arms flung about each other like long-lost drinking buddies reunited. Still in his chicken guise, Short had a tougher challenge in justifying his presence. He only hoped the distraction provided by his companions was enough to do the trick.

No sooner had Long set foot on the door's threshold, however, then the world turned upside down, sending everyone flying like lawn-bowling pins. The guards died instantly, slammed against the stone walls at their backs with such force that their heads exploded on impact. Hoosh tumbled through the air, dazed, and was only saved by the fortuitous placement of an ornamental shrub, upon which he landed with a shocking lack of dignity. Long Pete was not so lucky. The mysterious blast had wrapped him around a stone column, erected in someone's honor and dishonored by the contents of Long's bowels. And yet, he lived. Short was swept along the cobblestones until he came to rest against the base of the building across the avenue.

Despite his injuries, Long still had the presence of mind—or the raw instinct, perhaps—to Jump away with Short before anyone came to investigate.

Qansip, In Nespharia

Qansip was pleased. Although not as beautiful as she imagined Lunessfor to be, Nespharia was nevertheless a vast improvement over life on the march. And, frankly, she'd been getting a bit bored with Mendis. Now she had an entire city to explore and all of the comforts, the luxury, she could wish for.

She'd been given a suite of rooms in the keep that towered high over the city, and she could not have been more delighted. It was almost like being Queen, except for the existence of this Governor Bailis fellow, another native who seemed to have made a successful power grab for himself. Qansip wondered what it was that this Bailis had offered in exchange for such authority, and she meant to find out at her earliest opportunity. There might be a way to wrest some of the man's power away from him, she thought, and she very much wanted to be in charge. She liked the idea of sitting in judgment when peasants appealed to her for justice. She loved the thought of creating new ceremonies and holidays. She adored the notion of inventing and overseeing new fashions. She thrilled at the prospect of endless feasts. Above all, she was beyond excited to preside over executions.

She'd been in Nespharia less than an hour when Governor Bailis arrived outside her suite. He was accompanied by two burly guards, but Qansip suspected they were meant more for Bailis' own safety than any sort of threat against her.

"Welcome," said the Governor. "I'm Governor Bailis, and..."

"What does that mean?" Qansip asked bluntly.

Bailis was momentarily taken aback. "Pardon?"

"What does it mean to be governor of this place?" Qansip repeated slowly, as if talking to a baby.

The warmth Bailis had been trying to exhibit dwindled almost to nothing. He'd seen the girl before and was past the age where outward beauty alone held much sway with him. "It means that I'm in charge of this city," said he. "This city, and this county."

"Oh," said Qansip offhandedly. "And what is my role?"

"Your role?"

"Yes, what am I in charge of? What do I get to manage?"

Bailis said nothing for a moment as he waited for his rising anger to subside. Finally, he said, "You are the Emperor's guest, is that not enough? Shall I tell him you are unhappy with your...situation?"

"Shall I tell him you attempted to rape me?" Qansip shot back softly but fiercely.

Bailis turned briefly to each of his guards, checking to see that they'd heard what he'd heard. "I'll see what I can do," he said at last. "Good day to you."

Qansip watched him go with a feeling of deep satisfaction. She'd won the first bout; she expected a much more agreeable governor the next time they spoke.

Bailis did not return for some time, however, due to the Svarren attack.

...which did not mean that he wasn't thinking about her. Far from it. She'd gone from being an irritant, an inconvenience, to a significant threat—to himself, and, as he saw it, to the Emperor as well. He had never killed a woman before, not intentionally, and he wasn't confident that he could get away with it now, with so many of the Emperor's shapers—wizards—flitting about all the time.

It was in an old enemy, the Svarren, that he found an answer for his newest enemy.

He was touring the recent repairs to the city's outer wall, when a horseman came crashing through the gates, hollering at the top of his lungs about Long Teeth, Svarren. The savages were not wont to attack human settlements in daylight, so, at first, no one took the horseman seriously. Then it started making a strange sort of sense to Bailis: they couldn't hope to defeat the Emperor's main force in a pitched battle, and their constant raids on its flanks were little more than a sometime nuisance. But this! Striking at the Emperor's base of operations and supplies!

Bailis rushed up a flight of stairs near the gate in order to get a better view of the farmlands beyond, and, sure enough, a brownish-grey line of Svarren fighters approached at the edge of vision. Bailis saw them to his left and right, as well. "Man the gates!" he bellowed. "Man the gates!"

A daylight attack. Damned clever, really, when everyone expected the worst at night. The invaders and their new recruits had gotten complacent, almost indolent. They were nowhere near as wary as they ought to have been, and now they'd been caught out. And if Bailis lost the city...

It wouldn't happen. He didn't care how many Svarren were out there, or what they did to the surrounding farmlands. They would never take Nespharia. "To arms!" He yelled. "To arms!"

Men came racing out of the barracks and any and every-where else they'd been occupied, and rushed for their weapons or to man their various stations. One well-trained fellow began ringing the city's great alarm bell, much to Bailis' relief.

The farmers, settlers, tradesmen and others who occupied the lands around Nespharia raced for its gates. At some point, Bailis would have to shut those gates and abandon the stragglers to the Svarren. He dreaded that moment, even as he understood its necessity. The tragedy of it was as nothing, however, to what he was about to do.

"Halfway! Close those gates halfway!" he commanded.

Pausing just long enough to ensure his order was obeyed, he raced over to the archers' platform and said, "Those farmers down there'll start to pile up at the entrance, and those Long Teeth'll take them for easy bait. When they get close enough, I want you men to fire every arrow you've got down their filthy gullets. We'll lose a few farmers, aye, but we'll send hundreds of Long Teeth with 'em!"

The colonel was accustomed to making such choices, hard choices, sacrificing a few so that the many might live. But he never got used to it.

At the gates, the voices of those desperate to squeeze into the city exploded in a cacophony of panicked cries that grew louder and louder as the Svarren drew nearer. Soon, the noise crescendoed in a stark terror that was almost unbearable for those on the gate's opposite side. Bailis wanted to jam his fingers in his ears, but feared it would be seen as a sign of weakness, of cowardice, by his soldiers; so it was with some relief that the next sound he heard was the symphony of bowstrings thrumming at his back as they delivered death to the savages below, who howled and wailed no less frantically than the farmers had but moments earlier.

A soldier ran, panting, to Bailis side. "They're on the far side, too," he gasped. "And, sir, they've got war machines."

Bailis could not have been more shocked if the soldier had stabbed him. Without even stopping to make sure he'd heard what he *thought* he'd heard, the colonel grabbed the still-panting soldier and began to run back the way he'd come. Tired though he was, the younger man soon outpaced the older, so that it was all Bailis could do to wave him onward, whilst he stopped and struggled to catch his breath. *When did I get so old?* He lamented. *And will I have the chance to get older yet?* Underneath his mail shirt, his jerkin was already drenched with sweat, despite the mild weather. *Mahnus, give us a quiet summer!*

It took him far longer to reach the city's far side than he would have hoped, and if his face was red with embarrassment, he knew it could also be taken for exertion.

"Report," he croaked to the first soldier he encountered.

"Never known Svarren to have trebuchets, but they got

'em," the man stammered. "And they're shootin' some foul carcasses our way."

"Tell everyone to stay clear of them!" Bailis barked. "They're like as not diseased! I'll burn the damned things myself."

The new soldier dashed off, just as the previous man had, anxious to convey the commander's message. Bailis nearly grinned. At least his men were well-trained. He stumbled after the man, wishing himself ten years younger and substantially thinner. Or retired to a little fishing village somewhere.

In less time than a horse would have galloped across Nespharia, the whole town was locked up tight. So, too, was it surrounded by the largest gathering of Svarren the governor had ever seen. "I don't understand it," he groused from atop the north wall. "These aren't Svarren tactics. They don't have war machines, and they don't fight in formations."

Yet out in the fields, they gathered around their catapults, trebuchets and arbalests in definite units. Even with all that, Bailis didn't think the Long Teeth could breach the city's walls, but he remained perplexed as to their odd behavior, and this made him question the whole enterprise: what were they after, really?

By late afternoon, the siege had already become routine. The Svarren launched everything that would fit into their machines at Nespharia's walls, but, so far, the damage had all been manageable. Fires were quickly extinguished, corpses were quickly burnt, and anything broken or smashed was quickly repaired.

Naturally, Bailis sent a wizard to inform the Emperor of the Svarren attack, and also of the city's response. Mendis was equally baffled by this turn of events, but did not seem overly concerned, except to inquire whether Qansip was comfortable and safe.

Ah, Qansip.

Bailis assured the wizard that she was probably safer than she'd ever been in her life, and Mendis was glad to hear it. Indeed, he was planning to visit the young woman himself within the next day or two.

Madness.

But Bailis supposed the Emperor had enough wizards alone to quash the Svarren siege in hours, if not sooner, if he felt such a step necessary and never mind the endless legions.

Mendis & Qansip, Nespharia

What Mendis did not mention was the sudden and somehow unsettling effect the local brew was having on some of his men. Oh, they were happy enough and more than so. They were too happy. What kept a man in fighting trim, Mendis believed, was a healthy dose of discontent—not directed at the Empire, of course, but still a very real sense that things were unfair and might be amended through focused violence, in this case, towards the natives. But the more of this new ale his men drank, the less aggressive and more accepting they became.

Mendis' wizards confirmed his suspicions that there was magic in the liquor, but none could identify its nature or determine whether or not it posed a danger to the troops. As a precautionary measure, the Emperor banned its use or possession, which led to an immediate drop in morale. Well, he reasoned, better to have them angry than dead. Except, of course, there had been no evidence that the mysterious ale was dangerous.

The Emperor's ban was, as the old saying went, "more honored in the breach than the observance," and it soon became apparent that he must either enforce it through harsh means or lift it altogether. For once, he couldn't decide which course seemed best, and his thoughts quickly gravitated towards Qansip and whatever escape he could find her in arms.

Yes, Nespharia was under assault by the Svarren, but Mendis had lived there himself for a time and could not imagine a more impregnable fortress. He had forced his way through its wall, but only by virtue of his impossibly superior force. He didn't believe, would not believe that the Svarren could ever mount such a threat. And so, from the citadel above the city, Mendis and Qansip would watch the proceedings and see what there was to see. He had never been a rash or especially overconfident man, but he had no worries about Nespharia's strength or Qansip's safety. The enemy—or enemies—were going to have their little surprises, certainly; that was the nature of conquest, but Mendis believed things were well in hand and saw no reason to change his plans.

Qansip, however, was not quite as pleased to see him as he'd hoped and expected. He felt it immediately, though it was nothing overt. There was simply a distance, call it, that Mendis did not appreciate. He told himself it was due to Qansip's new surroundings, or perhaps to *their* surroundings, namely, the Svarren. She had always been warm, flirtatious and effusive in her praise of him, and he found he'd come to depend upon her sweet, indulgent ministrations. No, *depend* wasn't the right word: he had come to *need* these things. He needed Qansip to be and receive him as she always had. Anything else was... unacceptable.

He tried to draw her out. "Your chambers are not to your liking?"

"Oh," she sighed. "They're wonderful. Really."

He nodded with what he hoped seemed humorous skepticism. "Of course. And they're feeding you well?"

Qansip offered a halfhearted laugh. "Yes, yes, the food is excellent. As always."

Mendis sat on the edge of her bed and watched her as she stood at the window. "I was not aware that these Svarren were planning to attack the city, or I would not have sent you here. I chose it for you—for us—because it is the grandest of my holdings in this land, so far, and I wanted you to be comfortable."

"I'm not bothered by the Svarren," Qansip assured him. "They never managed to penetrate my father's estate, and I'm sure they can't reach me here."

"Then what accounts for your...sadness?"

"I've hardly been able to settle in and now you're here!" she complained. "Before I've got everything just as I want it."

Mendis was flattered. "But I'm not here to see your chambers, sweet. I'm here to see you." Qansip made a dismissive gesture, and the Emperor could see she was still out-of-sorts. Then, out of nowhere, he got the most peculiar idea. "I've come across a new ale I think you'll enjoy."

"You know I prefer wine," Qansip countered.

"O ho!" said Mendis, endeavoring to remain upbeat. "But I think this will change your mind."

He had one of his wizards return to the front and retrieve a generous jug of the stuff, an errand that proved disconcertingly easy given its contraband nature. And, as he'd predicted, Qansip took a liking to it almost instantly. Oh, she put up a little resistance initially, but soon she was downing it like water and swearing wholeheartedly by its virtues. Mendis watched, smitten and bemused. He was glad to see her warming to him again, and she was terribly charming in her inebriated state, but he was also worried that she might fall asleep in her trencher and not awaken 'til sometime the following night. He'd come to spend time with her, after all, and not merely stare at her sleeping form.

...Although there were certainly worse ways to pass the time. He was no poet, but Qansip seemed to him an exotic land all her own, or, better yet, his favorite kingdom. From the crown of her golden-haired head to the exquisitely soft soles of her ever-so-dainty feet, she seemed to contain everything from which he currently derived joy or wonder. There was perfection in her landscape, (normally) temperate weather in her moods, and mystery in the castle-keep of her mind. If he could live in Qansip forever, Mendis thought, he would be happy forever, too. On the periphery of his thoughts, he remembered his wife and children. But they were too, too far away and could in no wise help him or alleviate the burdens of rule as could the young woman beside him.

...Who was now falling-down drunk, which made the Emperor laugh. Qansip was typically so committed to maintaining her equilibrium, to keeping control, that her current condition seemed almost like blessed release. Mendis bent over and scooped Qansip into his arms, shushing her protests and giggling quietly to himself. There would be no love-making this night, but the Emperor would enjoy sharing her bed nonetheless.

One of the peculiar things about this particular ale was that those who drank it tended to remain drunk far longer than normal. In addition, they were never the worse-for-wear once the alcohol wore off. It was truly wonderful stuff...to a point. Mendis worried that it might be habit-forming, even addictive. The fact it was still available in camp despite its having been banned seemed to support this concern. And if it *was* habit-forming, perhaps its appearance in his army was not as coincidental as he'd believed. Perhaps it had been introduced on purpose.

The Emperor summoned a wizard and sent the man back to the front with the message that every possible step should be taken to enforce the ban, and that any locals seen coming or going with kegs should be taken prisoner.

Having settled on a more muscular plan of action, Mendis returned his attention to his still-sleeping consort. In her case, the lingering effects of the liquor were probably advantageous. He certainly hoped so, anyway. His brief experience of a disinterested Qansip had been more than enough—more than he could tolerate, if he was honest, for he cherished the girl's adoration like nothing else, and he understood it to be his own version of magical ale. And probably just as addictive. And so what if it was? He was managing well enough, he thought.

Qansip stirred, saw him, and beamed, still drunk.

"Have a little too much to drink?" Mendis inquired wryly.

"I dunno," Qansip giggled. "Did I?"

Whether her mood was genuine or the result of the native ale, Mendis could not tell and didn't care. She was smiling again, and that was everything to him.

"Shall we go and see these big, bad Svarren?" she cooed.

It was not a bad idea. The Emperor had never seen them up close or in daylight and couldn't imagine what they'd been doing outside his walls for the past two days. "Let's," he said, offering an arm, so her climb out of bed was easier.

It was a warm, blustery day, and the air was ripe with the smell of Svarren. From atop the battlements, the beasts appeared laughably impotent. Governor Bailis had informed the Emperor of the creatures' efforts against the city, but even with the few war machines they'd somehow managed to cobble together, Mendis believed them incapable of doing any real damage to the city or its walls.

"What do you s'pose they're all doing down there?" Qansip slurred ever-so-slightly. "They look so silly."

Mendis put an arm around her waist and pulled her close, even as he kept an eye on the enemy below. "Silly they may look," said he, "but I shudder to think what they'd do to any of our people if they got inside."

And shudder he might, too, for there were eyes amongst the Svarren that watched him and his consort, watched him and planned, planned and waited.

Beesmarch, Eoman & Their Kinfolk, Ahead of the Legions

Beesmarch and his fellows worked day and night to divert all rivers and streams away from the invaders' army. When they could, they built great timber dams fortified with boulders to block and redirect the water's flow. What might have been back-breaking labor for a hundred engineers, was merely a difficult chore for the giants. Still bodies of water posed a greater challenge, but eventually Beesmarch and the others learned to drain the smaller ponds and erect tremendous obstacles between the army and any lakes they might encounter. They fouled the lake-shores with offal and waste and laid traps along the approaches. In short, they used every mean trick they could think of to make the local water unreachable, undrinkable, or both.

And then it was time to do something more about the army's existing water supplies.

"Eoman, what do ye think?" Bees asked.

The former king wanted to snap at his old friend: *You're king now. What do you think?* But that seemed childish to him, petty, and if he was not the largest giant in the world, neither was he small—in any sense of the word. "What do I think?" he said. "I think a mighty hail o' head-sized stones oughta breach their water barrels once and for all."

Beesmarch grinned, grateful that Eoman had spared him

any further unpleasantries, but grateful too for his advice. "Hail o' stones," he repeated. "I like it. We find a ridge somewheres and bombard the bastards with rocks. If we get up high enough, we might even be out o' bow range."

"They'll still have magic," one of the Brothers reminded everyone.

"And I hope I can do something about that," Karrakan pitched in.

"I think if they're expectin' an attack at all, it'll be against their troops, not their water," Eoman opined.

Beesmarch considered all of this and nodded. "Agreed. They'll be lookin' for more of what we done to 'em last time."

Alas, the land ahead was relatively flat for leagues, and a higher perch from which to attack was not to be found. Beesmarch considered the risks and struggled to reach a decision. The mere thought of losing one of his fellows in the action petrified him. Again, Eoman came to his rescue.

"Chances are good one of us will fall to the invaders' magic. There'd be no shame in sitting this one out, if anyone is so inclined."

The ensuing silence spoke of a unity and determination that made Beesmarch proud.

"Good, then," said he. "We'll race as far ahead o' these bastards as we may, gather our stones and wait for 'em."

Giants do not enjoy running, but they can certainly do it when necessary. In a series of short spurts spread out over several hours, they managed to work themselves nearly an hour ahead of the enemy's water wagons. The Emperor's scouting parties, newly increased in size and number, were difficult to elude along the way, but Karrakan's magic made the process somewhat easier. The giants might have waited to attack until nightfall, but they remained convinced the invaders were at their most-prepared after dark—that, and the fact that only a fool would attack such a massive force in daylight, which assumption might make the defenders overconfident, even complaisant.

The exact moment that Bees, Eoman and the others were most hoping to catch the invaders was during a water stop. If they were lucky, they'd be able to crush a few heads along with the water barrels. Ironically, they got their wish during a light rainfall. Horns sounded all along the column, and it slowly ground to a stop. Voices yelled instructions. The giants huddled in a brake. Beesmarch was about to rise and lead the others into action, when Eoman laid a hand across his chest.

"Patience," said he. "Let them gather."

Bees looked over at Karrakan for confirmation, but the shaman was deeply engaged with his magics, attempting to keep the invaders' scouts at bay. Will-o'-wisps darted this way and that like angry fireflies. Bees wiped the rain from his brow with the back of his hand.

"Rain," he grumbled. "I'd hoped we'd seen the last of it for a while."

Eoman only chuckled in response.

Soon enough, though, he poked the bigger giant in the ribs and then pointed at the column: it was time. The giants stood as one, noiselessly, and threw their first volley of stones—little, fist-sized things to them, but fully as big as a man's head to the invaders. If a man could separate their actions from the violence they perpetrated, he might have found humor in a great line of giants popping up and down in the brake like over-curious birds. Heads were smashed, though, and shoulders crushed, and no one was laughing at the sudden rain of stones. No one even had time for astonishment at the giants' range, several times that of a man. Briefly, all was pandemonium, until the invaders adjusted to the situation put their archers and wizards on the attack.

In the brake, Beesmarch was tempted to call a retreat at this point, but Eoman again laid a restraining hand on his chest. "Wait," he urged. "Wait."

A flash of crimson light hit one of the Brothers, and he toppled to the ground like a felled oak, still smoldering from the blow.

"Grab him and let's go!" Beesmarch commanded. If only he'd followed his gut...

They ran. The two brothers who'd remained upright carried

their fallen sibling between them, and Karrakan protected the group's backside as they all vanished into the bush. When they'd distanced themselves enough from the invaders' army, they all plunked themselves down into a circle about their fallen comrade.

"He's dead," said Fendrick, unnecessarily. Everyone could clearly see that for himself.

Beesmarch rose awkwardly and cleared his throat. "I'm sorry. I..."

"Don't apologize, Bees!" Eoman snapped. "Every one of us knew the danger. Every one of us chose to participate. He died doin' the right thing."

The king said nothing, but watched the faces and eyes of the two remaining brothers. They were distressed, aye, but not resentful. Still, Bees didn't think there were so many giants left in the world that the loss of one was insignificant. "Even so," he said.

The rest of the group nodded, one by one, in agreement, and it seemed to Eoman that Bees was slowly growing into his new role, becoming more worthy of his crown.

It had been Karrakan, of course, who'd gone to assess the damage they'd done to their targets. When he returned, he looked as if he'd aged a century.

"Bastards are swarming the area like ants, and their mages are a mite too mighty. We'd best get moving again, if we mean to keep breathing."

The Brothers had a loved one to bury, but it would have to wait.

Once they'd settled again, Karrakan relayed what he'd seen. "We broke about half their barrels and killed a number of their oxen."

"And their soldiers?" Beesmarch inquired.

Karrakan shrugged. "No way to know. They carry them off, just as we've done." He pointed his chin in the direction of the two surviving brothers, who were busy burying the third at the base of a tree. Next, they'd strip the bark and etch runes in the wood in testament to the worthiness of the deceased one's life. It was an old giant custom and stringently observed, no matter the time or place.

"I hope it was worth it," Bees said.

"He thought so," Karrakan answered, still watching the burial.

TEN

Vykers, The Ruined Village

He felt stronger, more himself by the hour, and his muscles seemed to thicken even as he watched. Likewise, his hair and beard came back—slowly at first, like an ever-deepening shadow—until he felt more or less restored.

It was time to find and destroy the Frog.

Hjuest asked him how he planned to do that, but Vykers had merely winked at the Red Knight. He had a plan, and that was enough. His men—and Ona—could only search for answers in each other's eyes, and, finding none, resign themselves once again to following their master in ignorance.

Vykers sat tall in the saddle of his eldritch horse, feeling a certain well-earned smugness and trying not to let it lull him into overconfidence. He had been dead, or as good as, and now he was ready to fight again. Even he was amazed.

He recalled the dreams he'd had whilst lying in his sickbed, the dreams of the myriad injuries he'd sustained over the years, the decades, and, yes, the centuries. His mood grew somber. Legend held that he'd never been cut in battle. Now, he knew differently. He'd been hurt in every way a man can be hurt, and yet he'd always recovered. He studied the skin of his forearms, which showed no evidence of the trauma he'd been through. He ruminated on all the years he'd lived and forgotten and wondered how it could be so. How could he heal as he did? How could he live so long?

What was he, if not a god?

He urged his horse into motion and left the little ruined town behind.

The thing was, he could feel the Frog in the back of his mind, much the same as he'd once felt Arune. Was that because it had vomited all over him? Had it somehow gotten inside him? A lesser man might have been terrified at this turn of events, but Vykers embraced it. He was going to kill the bastard and make him suffer into the bargain. Yes, the Frog had once been a child. Now he was an atrocity, and Vykers owed him a death.

He and his crew had wandered into a fascinating landscape of flat grasslands, pockmarked with enormous hills that seemed to rise straight up out of the plain without any intermediate slope. The ground was flat, and then it wasn't. Vykers decided to climb one of these hills, the better to survey the surrounding territory and perhaps catch a glimpse of the Frog. It was some time, though, before he found a hill that his horse could negotiate. Once he achieved the summit, he again climbed to a standing position in his saddle and slowly turned this way and that. His men and Ona were curious, but knew better than to follow him. He would share whatever needed sharing.

The odd, hilly land stretched in front of him to the very edge of the horizon. The Reaper did not see the Frog, but he did spy a smoke plume some leagues distant that looked promising. He quickly returned to his party and motioned for them to follow.

Once more, the group's miraculous horses raced forward until the world around became a blur of greens, blues and browns. As awed as she was by the experience, Ona could not help wishing for slower travel. She was not convinced that the Reaper was ready for another encounter with the monster he called the Frog. And she was certain that she was not. How in Mahnus' name could they defeat something as large as the surrounding hills? Truly, she thought they might stand a better chance against a hill than the horrible Frog. But Vykers, she knew, would not be deterred. She'd have more luck coaxing the sun from the sky.

It was not so easy to find the Frog, however. When they reached the smoking ruins of his latest rampage, the monster was nowhere to be seen, and no one remained alive for questioning. Worse, there were few bodies left to bury. While his crew scavenged for food and supplies, Vykers rode his horse in an ever-widening spiral around the village. By the time he returned to the group, he'd hit upon an idea.

He jumped from his mount and began grabbing anything that would burn. "Did anyone find tallow, lamp oil, or tar?" Without waiting for a response, he said, "We need to start a fire. A big fire." Then he pointed to one of the distant hills. "On top o' that."

It was the work of two hours or more to get the job done to Vykers' satisfaction, and it required close to a hundred trips between the sad little village and the hill. In the end, the wood pile was bigger than a church.

"If the bastard can't see the fire that comes 'o this, he's blind."

"You vill vait 'til night fall, den?" Hjuest asked.

"Midnight, I'm thinkin'."

Ona was unsure where the actual fight would take place, since the woodpile occupied almost the entire hilltop. "Where are we supposed to stand?"

"We're all gonna be below. The horses need room to run. And anyway," Vykers added, "I want you all to stay outta this."

Hjuest flushed, 'til his face was almost as red as his breast-plate. "If I vant to fight dis ting, I vill fight it! You vill be too busy to stop me."

The Reaper laughed, but it was, for once, a merry and good-natured sound. "Have it your way," said he. "Just don't come whinin' to me when the bastard falls over on your head."

"Or sits on you!" Ona pitched in.

Vykers laughed louder. "Gods, you could wander around in its asshole forever!"

The look of uncomfortable disgust on Hjuest's face sent everyone into gales of laughter.

They were all huddled at the base of the hill, nursing a fire so small, it seemed a spark to the one Vykers was about to light. Nobody spoke whilst he climbed the hill. No one spoke 'til he returned.

"I want two o' you men up top, firing flamin' arrows at the Frog. Keep the fire between him and you, and you should be alright. He's goin' to have other things to worry about."

"And you?" Hjuest asked.

"I'll be ridin' circles around him and takin' chunks out of his hide with my axe."

Hjuest said nothing, but twisted the ends of his moustache nervously.

"I'll not lie, friends. Chances are good we'll all die in this fight."

"Not you," said Ona. She was a little embarrassed for saying it, but it needed saying. She and the others were mortal, to the best of her knowledge. Vykers? Who could say?

"You're right," he said unflinchingly. "I'll probably survive this scrape." He looked everyone in the eye, as was his wont. "But the Frog won't. You can be damned sure o' that."

...Which was good enough for everyone else. The Reaper had been honest with them, and that was all they could ask or hope for.

In minutes the area around the hill grew much brighter, thanks to the bonfire at its summit, and despite their distance from its flames, they could all feel its heat.

"How long do you tink she'll burn?" Hjuest asked.

"Long enough."

And it was true, for it was still burning strong as, one-by-one, Vykers' men fell asleep. Only Ona seemed unfatigued.

"Nervous?" Vykers inquired.

"No. Yes. I don't know *how* to feel, really."

"Nervous is good, so long's you don't get scared. You don't wanna freeze up when the time comes."

"Do you ever get nervous?"

"No."

She needn't have asked.

Suddenly, Vykers and his granddaughter both became aware of a high-pitched squealing scream.

"Wake 'em up," the Reaper commanded. "It's time for a reckoning."

Ona jostled each of the men in turn and was impressed with how quickly they arose and got ready for battle. She'd been with them for weeks now, but this was the first time she'd seen them so grim and determined. Vykers had armored himself in bits and pieces of gear he'd borrowed from the rest of his team, his original armor having been destroyed by the Frog. Still, his arms were largely bare of protection.

"You sure you wouldn't rather borrow someone's mail shirt?" Ona said.

"Nah," Vykers answered. "If he kills me, it won't be 'cause he stabbed me in the side."

It was hard to argue with that.

"Besides," Vykers said, "it's a warm night. I'll be fine."

The screaming squeal sounded again, long, loud and painful to the ears.

"Gods!" Hjuest complained. "What a horrible noise!"

The Reaper smiled and climbed into his saddle, yanking his axe from its tethers as if he meant never to lay it aside again. Ona could see the muscles bunching in his jaw as he clenched his teeth. He might not have fully recovered just yet, but he looked the essence of bad intent nonetheless.

"I'm gonna ride out into the open," he said. "Everyone keep yer distance 'til I've got his attention."

Nobody disagreed.

Vykers and his horse charged away in a blur.

Ona considered the cache of weapons the group had assembled over their travels and landed on a set of javelins as her weapons of choice. They'd belonged to the man the Frog had eaten at their last encounter, and Ona thought it only fitting she brought this little piece of him onto the battlefield. She was just fixing them to the saddle of the dead man's horse when Hjuest walked up and held out a small ceramic jar.

"What's this?"

"De vorst poison dere is," the Red Knight replied. "For your chavelins."

Ona was about to refuse when she thought better of it. "Might as well give it a try."

With the Red Knight's help and taking great care not to touch the greasy substance with her skin, she envenomed the points of each javelin.

"Frog!" Vykers' voice rang out in the dark. "Fraaaaaaawg!"

The monster's roar grew louder, more urgent, and then stopped altogether.

Ona and Hjuest rushed to find positions from which they could see what was happening. At the edge of the fire's radiance, a new hill stood, its tentacles thrashing silently and its pincers snapping.

"Reaper?" came a small, almost boyish voice that was immediately echoed by a chorus of equally odd voices.

"Frog!" the Reaper shouted, now farther off.

"How how how are you alive alive alive alive?"

Suddenly nearby, Vykers yelled, "You can't kill me, boy. I am the bringer of death!" And, just like that, he was gone again, spirited away on his mercurial horse.

The monster shrieked in confusion or fury; no one listening could have said for certain.

"Tonight," the Reaper called out from somewhere to Ona's right, "tonight you die!"

The creature made a new and horrible sound, a scream of pain, Ona hoped. A small wisp of fire appeared high up on its bulk—a flaming arrow, which was rapidly followed by another and another, until the monster was freckled with fire. The arrows seemed to bother him not at all, but at least they defined the general area of his head for those below.

Ona, Hjuest, Ngoro and the rest of Vykers' crew rode out from cover and attempted to position themselves at the Frog's back, the better to attack but also to avoid impeding the Reaper's more-frontal attacks. Vykers appeared in brief flashes, his new axe hacking away at the monster's legs with impossible speed. Was he making any difference though? How does one kill a mountain, exactly?

Ona hurled the first of her javelins at the Frog. A tentacle lashed out, but the javelin streaked past and plunged into a leg with a satisfyingly wet thud. The Frog did not react. Hjuest, Ngoro and the others dodged in and out of the monster's reach, stabbing and slashing as they could and retreating again before any of the Frog's appendages could catch them.

Vykers focused most of his attacks on a particular leg, coming at it from every direction and racing away again before the

Frog could get a fix on his position. Still, the monster was like a windmill, arms and legs flailing away.

Suddenly, one of the men's horses was down, its rider snatched away by an enormous three-fingered claw. The man tried to hack his way free from the claw, but soon he was too far off the ground to escape death by falling. Instead, he hung on, stabbing a finger over and over, hoping to inflict as much damage as he could before his inevitable death. A tentacle wrapped itself about the man's horse and pulled the poor beast into the air, towards one of the Frog's myriad mouths. A second man was instantly impaled by a spear-like appendage that harpooned him and then pulled him towards the monster. Hjuest barely escaped the same fate himself, looking out for Ona.

The Frog vomited at the bonfire, and the archers just beyond its flames howled in agony as they were splashed with the foul acid. The fire did not fare any better, immediately shrinking to a fraction of its original size. Another such effort, and the Frog would extinguish the fire altogether, and fighting him in the dark was the last thing anyone wanted. The archers continued to howl. Ona sank another javelin into a second leg, a leg with the girth of an ancient fir. It was like sticking a sewing needle into the side of a barn—and just about as effective. Still, what other choice was there? Inadvertently, she got too close to the leg and what she had assumed were massive warts turned out to be heads with half-formed faces, some with expressions of malevolence, others, looking woeful or lost. More than a few seemed feeble-minded. With a great heave, she tossed her next javelin directly into one of these faces, whereupon the surrounding ones hissed and snarled at her. Clearly this Frog, a nightmare in and of itself, was also a collection of nightmares.

He vomited a second time, and both the fire and the archers beyond it were snuffed out. The Frog roared in jubilation as the darkness deepened. In the next instant, his tone changed with the unexpected collapse of a leg. Vykers roared back at him, mockingly. But Vykers' crew was rapidly dwindling, and Ona feared the monster would prevail.

Just then, a huge shape shot out of the darkness beyond the hill and hit the creature in the side, knocking him over with a tremendous crash that rattled and shook the ground. Quick as they could, Ona, Hjuest, Ngoro and the few remaining members of Vykers' team backed up and out of the immediate area.

"What in Mahnus' name...?" Vykers grumbled.

It was difficult to see what the new arrival was, but it, too, was huge—not hill-sized, like the Frog, but perhaps cottage-sized. The Frog screamed in rage, his polytonal voice ripping through the darkness, tearing the night into shreds. The new monster roared right back at him, just as Vykers had only seconds earlier. Both creatures thrashed about for purchase in one another's flesh until the Frog at last tossed the smaller one aside. He endeavored to stand again, but his nemesis returned with preternatural speed, leaping onto his back and sinking its teeth and claws into the area near his primary face.

"It's the cat," Vykers said in amazement. "It's that bloody huge cat."

And so it was. The beast yowled and hissed like its diminutive cousins, raking the Frog's chest and side with its claws. But the Frog had multiple arms and legs, a prehensile tongue, and at least one mouth that vomited acid. He also had much greater mass, for all the big cat's size. With a sudden twist, the Frog spun onto his side, pinning the cat between himself and the ground. Vykers recognized that if he didn't get the Frog's attention quickly, the cat would be crushed. He darted in on his mount and took a series of lightning-fast swings at the nearest tentacle, and the Frog responded. He rolled up onto his feet and spat his noxious bile in Vykers' direction. This time, however, the Reaper sat astride his miraculous horse and was gone before the acid arrived. The cat scrambled up and away into the darkness, where it howled in anger, long and low. Now, the Frog was torn: should he pursue the other creature, or stay and deal with the Reaper and his fellows once and for all? While he was attempting to decide, the cat charged back into view and again leapt at the Frog's primary head. Vykers rushed in a second time and continued to hack away at the Frog's tentacles. His arm moved so rapidly those watching were unable to track it. The Reaper began to laugh like a madman, as if every blow brought greater and greater glee.

One of the Frog's arms had gone limp and small pieces of him lay strewn about the battlefield. Still, he fought on, grappling with the cat and striving to locate the Reaper. "Reeeeaaapeeer."

The cat screamed out in pain, stabbed in the shoulder by the same spear-like arm that had killed one of Vykers' men. Yet, the great feline fought on, raking the Frog's head and chest with its long, lethal claws. The Frog's shrieking grew in urgency until, combined with the giant cat's yowling, the noise was almost damaging to the ears. Vykers alone seemed unaffected as he continued to chop away at the Frog. Again the monster managed to throw the cat off, only to have it leap once more into his face.

Ona sensed the momentum of the fight was slowly shifting, so she charged in on her horse and threw her final javelin. She had no difficulty hitting the Frog, colossal as he was, and this time he seemed to feel the blow, for he wheeled in her direction and sought her out. "Reaper?" he said, in a little boy's voice. Never had anything so enormous and menacing seemed so small and vulnerable. Without warning, he began to pitch sideways. His shrieks and the cat's roars subsided, and, for the briefest of instants, Ona could hear the Frog's flesh being rent by the cat, along with the Reaper's lunatic laughter. Then there was an ear-splitting boom, and the Frog was down. The great cat clamped its jaws on some part of the monster, eliciting a terrible, crunching sound, and then all was silent.

Vykers rode out from behind the Frog, where he was met by the cat, which nuzzled him briefly with its enormous snout before limping off into the night.

Mendis, In Camp

As the Emperor had predicted, waves of refugees from the predations of the B'Shar and the Tsundi began arriving in the midlands. The timing was not ideal, what with the Svarren siege of Nespharia and the continued, pernicious drunkenness of entire legions. Thus, Mendis was forced to crack down on his troops by reinforcing the ban on the possession or consumption of any and all alcohol on pain of death—a severe measure by any standard, but he and his forces could ill afford to be caught off-guard when and if the real fighting began, and, at the very least, they needed to present a disciplined and united front to the refugees. He meant for his rule to seem preferable to that of the Virgin Queen, but it would not seem so if his troops were falling-down drunk or asleep.

He was not blind, though, to the fact that he, himself, was using the native ale to control his mistress. None would dare call him hypocrite, but would they think it? Would it become a common understanding amongst his legions? If they could not respect him...

The decision to send Qansip off to Nespharia was looking better by the day.

Mendis entered his pavilion, where he found Lord Commander Dabis waiting for him, as expected.

"Your report?" the Emperor prompted.

"I am rotating the troops, as you requested. Anyone who's the slightest bit drunk is demoted and put on menial labor 'til he recovers. Those wise enough to remain sober have been promoted and pushed to the forefront. I've got them receiving and processing refugees, as well as the usual scouting. Water, however, has become an issue, in that we have too little of it, and it seems in short supply locally. We've even seen evidence of tampering—sabotage, if you will—of local rivers, streams and lakes. Your wizards can extract water from the ground and from plants, of course, but not nearly fast enough to supply our needs."

"And have you found these saboteurs?"

Dabis shook his head. "It is only a matter of time, though."

"Under other circumstances, I'd repeal the ban on alcohol... How do you plan to acquire more water?"

"This tampering seems mostly focused on the lands ahead of us. There's plenty of water behind us."

Mendis considered the Svarren's curious and futile siege of Nespharia, the arrival of the native ale in his camps, and the sabotage of water sources ahead of his army. "They're doing their damnedest to slow us down or even turn us around, whoever they are."

"They'd have more luck preventing the night from falling,"
Dabis replied, which brought a wry smile to Mendis' face.

"You're a good man," the Emperor told his Lord Commander.

"I would like to be."

A great tremblor rattled and jarred the ocean floor, a mere ten
miles from the eastern shore. Anon, the water pulled back from
the shore, going farther out than anyone could remember. Fisher
folk frolicked in the tide flats in celebration of the strange occurrence. They laughed, they danced, they observed the previously
unseen areas of the beach with awe...until the ocean rose up...
and up...and up and came rushing towards them, like the edge
of an eclipse, not to be avoided by man or beast. In their final
moments, the locals were filled with fear and wonder that the
ocean they'd known all their lives should become a mountain
range of water.

The sea surged ashore like an angry god and kept coming
until it had washed miles inland and flooded every farm, village and town in its path. When at last the water retreated, the
sodden land was littered with refuse, with wreckage, and the
bodies of the dead. Men and livestock alike were drowned, broken or crushed by the wave, and those lucky few who'd survived could only ask, over and over, what they'd done to incur
such wrath.

The Imperial army continued to move westward, in spite of the
water shortage, the chaos of arriving refugees, the native ale,
and any and all other obstacles. Once in a while, there were
brief skirmishes with the locals, but on the whole Mendis was
not unduly concerned.

Not until his entire fleet was destroyed in an instant.

He'd been lying in bed with his consort when there came
an urgent knocking at her door. Normally, he would have let
Qansip answer, but there was something about the knocking
that alarmed the Emperor.

He leapt from the bed, wrapped himself in a robe, and
rushed to the door. "Who is it?" he demanded without opening
it.

"Captain Penders, Magnificence."

Mendis opened the door and stepped back, the better to react to any unexpected violence. Captain Penders stood just beyond the open frame.

"There was a wave, Magnificence. The mother of all waves."

"And?" Mendis nearly shouted.

"Everything along the coast has been washed away or ruined."

"The fleet?"

The captain did not have the courage to answer, but Mendis could see it in the man's eyes. "Over how big an area?"

"The whole eastern coast, from the B'Shar to the Tsundi."

"I've never heard of such a thing. Never read of such a thing."

The captain would not contradict his Emperor, but neither would he retract his statement.

"The whole fleet..."

"All of it."

Unless the Emperor abandoned his conquest in order to rebuild the fleet, he and his legions had no way of returning home. He had no way of seeing his wife and children again. Without a word, he shut the door to Qansip's room and went over to sit on the bed. Had he somehow offended the gods? Was he guilty of hubris?

"What was he saying about a wave?" Qansip asked, demonstrating an ever-improving grasp of the Emperor's language.

"Nothing," Mendis lied. It was the first time he'd done so, but he could not bear the thought of appearing weak in her eyes. "Some damage to your native fishing boats."

Qansip did not believe him, but smiled sleepily and reached for a half-empty goblet of ale that sat on her bedside table. The effort caused the blankets to fall off her shoulder, exposing a single, exquisite breast. She looked up and saw Mendis watching her; that he did not respond to her nakedness confirmed her suspicions. She drained the goblet and looked about for the pitcher from which the ale had come. "Have we got any more of this?"

"As much as you'd like," said the Emperor.

"Another goblet, at least, and then a nice, hot bath, I think."

"Of course." Mendis rose and sought out a servant to fetch more ale. "I believe I'll take a walk while you bathe. Get a little fresh air."

Still, she was not fooled: The Emperor was preoccupied this morning—something to do with that wave at the coast. Qansip smiled. He looked so silly when he took things too seriously! She remembered having felt some resentment, even contempt for him, but that was gone now, all gone, thanks to her new favorite beverage. And that was alright with her. Bliss had settled into her muscles and bones, and she had no other ambition than to keep it so, to maintain this serendipitous new happiness for as long as possible.

It made her want to dance, and she knew just the place.

He'd been making a routine circuit of the city walls when he saw her, floating like gossamer on the parapets some quarter mile distant. Suddenly, his heart was in his throat, and he broke into an all-out run in hopes of reaching her before she fell.

"Qansip!" he yelled. "Qansip, get down!"

His warnings seemed to delight her, and she appeared to giggle as she continued to pirouette atop the wall, her gauzy shift fluttering about and behind her in the breeze.

"Qansip, please!" Mendis tried again. "I beg you, get down from there!" He'd closed the gap between them. If he could stall her a moment longer… "If it's dancing you want, I'll throw you a ball!"

She spun around and faced him, beaming. The sun shone in her hair and sparkled in her eyes. His heart ached with her beauty.

"Qansip, come down now!"

He was nearly within reach of her. She spun a final time and stumbled. For an instant, Mendis could not breathe. The few feet between them had become a chasm; he may as well have been back in his palace. Even as he lunged for her, stretching himself to his limit, she drifted outward, off the wall, high above the still-gathered Svarren. He got a hand on the hem of her dress, too late, too late. The fabric snapped through his grasp, and

Qansip fell, gracefully, like a leaf slowly settling to the ground. She was silent the whole time, until she landed amongst the Svarren, who caught her before she hit the ground. And then she began to scream. Oh, how she screamed.

Spirk & Co., Lunessfor

Spirk was in trouble, and he knew it. He needed Long's Old Peculiar like he'd never needed anything in his life, not even his Baa Baa—a small tuft of lamb's fleece he'd kept as a pet and sleeping companion until his father had thrown him out. He doubted Baa Baa could help him now; the burning had gotten too strong, and only the ale could stop it. But Ron wanted him to stop drinking it. In fact, he was becoming kind of a bully, and Spirk wasn't sure he liked him as much, anymore. No one else seemed to give a rip; why should Ron care?

Well, they'd all gone back to their hideout to brew more of the stuff so they could sell it to the invaders, and Spirk thought maybe he could sneak a flask or two into his shirt or his new coat. But Ron was right there to inspect everything the young Shaper touched, which forced Spirk to attempt magical means of deception.

First, he gave Ron a terrible itch in his private areas. Rather than run crazy scratching himself, though, Ron simply stood by his friend's side, twitching and dancing on the balls of his feet, like a child who needs to pee. Perhaps Spirk could encourage that notion. With a subtle wave of his hand, he gave Ron the fullest bladder he'd had in years and stood back, waiting for discomfort to do its job. Ron, however, was made of hardier stuff than even Spirk had imagined and continued to remain at his friend's side. Frustrated, the Shaper snapped his fingers and Ron became terribly sleepy. Mumbling incoherently, the erstwhile archer wandered away in search of his couch. As Kittins, Yendor and Rem continued to prepare for the next trip north, Spirk quickly filled two wineskins and a small jar with his favorite brew and placed them in pockets about his person. His task complete, he grabbed a stein and helped himself to a fresh pint.

And was, of course, rip-roaring drunk when Ron awakened and returned to his side.

"Hells, man!" he griped. "Drunk again? I pray we don't need your services anytime soon!"

Spirk, leaning against a barrel that Kittins and Rem were filling, replied, "But why? I c'n magic with the best of 'em!"

Ron shook his head. There was no point in arguing. But he had to find a way to stop his friend from drinking himself to death. Although Spirk's drinking was driving the friends apart, he was still the most important person in Ron's life. There had to be a way to save him.

Later, the still-wasted Shaper Jumped the group and its cargo back up to their wagons in the north. It took several more attempts than usual, because of Spirk's condition, and one of his errant Jumps sent everyone to a nightmarish landscape that threatened everyone's sanity. Even the normally stolid Kittins looked a shade paler once they'd arrived at their actual destination.

"Fuck was that?" he demanded of Spirk. "Stop yer drinkin', or I'll stop *you*."

Now, it was Spirk's turn to go pale.

The wagons had been stored, oxen and all, in an old abandoned barn that the Shaper had enspelled for safety. The beasts were both hungry and thirsty, but otherwise unharmed. After tending to their needs, Kittins, Yendor, Rem and Ron began loading their freshly filled barrels and kegs onto the wagons, while Spirk pretended to search the area for potential threats. After a half-hour's sweaty labor, the job was done and the group was ready to depart. This time, Kittins grabbed Spirk by the upper arm and slammed him down on the seat next to the captain's.

"Did I do somethin' wrong?" the Shaper wanted to know.

"I want to make sure you don't do anything *else* wrong."

They rode in silence for the longest time, while Spirk slowly became more and more sober and his burning reasserted itself. Eventually, they seemed to exchange moods, as Kittins became lighthearted and Spirk, taciturn. They stopped at one point to relieve themselves, and Yendor asked Spirk, "What's eatin' you?"

"Burning," was all Spirk could manage in response.

Yendor's lone eye widened for a moment and then he looked at the ground. He'd heard about burning, but never given it much thought. Now that he could see its impact on his young friend, he became worried about where it might lead, what it might do to the Shaper. Accordingly, he approached Kittins and said, "What do yer make of our Shaper friend?"

"He's a drunken idiot."

"Speakin' as one myself, he's damned grim for the part."

Kittins studied Spirk. "Maybe he's growing up."

Yendor wasn't so sure. "He says it's the burning."

"So? It's what Shapers do."

"He ain't yer average Shaper, though, is he?"

Kittins rubbed his eyes and growled. "What is it you want me to do?"

"Talk to him. See what's what."

Once they were back on the trail, Kittins spoke without turning to Spirk. "So, you're burning."

"Yeah," said Spirk through clenched teeth.

The captain said nothing for a while, and then suggested, "It's because you haven't been trained, I guess. You were never properly taught how to manage it."

"Yeah."

"But this ale helps."

"Uh-huh."

"And Ron doesn't like you drinkin'."

"Nope."

"What do you think's gonna happen?"

"I dunno," Spirk answered forlornly. "I might essplode?"

Kittins again let the silence grow between them, before he reached into his own coat and produced a flask, which he handed to Spirk. "Guess we'll have to ride the line between drunk and burnin'. I'll make sure you don't drink too much. You make sure you don't explode."

Spirk had never been so grateful for anything in his life. He snatched the flask from Kittins' hand before the big man could change his mind, unstoppered it, and took a goodly swallow, finishing it off with a great sigh of relief.

Kittins flicked the reins and looked away. Maybe they oughta get Spirk some training when they got back to Lunessfor.

They were stopped by a patrol that crept out of the woods like bandits, hastily offloaded their ale, and then snuck back into the trees with their booty as if they'd just committed a crime. And perhaps they had.

"That seem right to you?" Yendor asked Kittins.

"No," said the bigger man. "They had the look o' men breakin' curfew. Or worse."

"Then perhaps our plan is working?" Rem suggested.

"If they're breakin' rules to get their hands on our ale, I'd say so," said Yendor.

Ron spoke up. "How long do we keep this up?"

"I think we'll see interestin' results whether we keep deliverin' or stop altogether."

"Good," said Ron, watching Spirk from the corner of his eye. "'Cause I wanna get back to Lunessfor."

Long Pete, Lunessfor

Long's head hurt like he'd been binging on skent for a week, and for the longest time, he couldn't remember who he was or what he'd been up to. Mercifully, wherever he'd landed was as dark as a tomb and twice as quiet. He rolled from his side, gingerly, onto his back, during which process he determined that he was lying on a thin pile of straw. Under that was cold, damp stone floor.

He was back in the dungeons at House Thornton—as good a place as any for the purpose of sleeping off whatever-it-was that had happened to him. Unfortunately, worry and its cousins doubt and guilt kept him awake. What had become of the Fool? And where was Short Pete?

"Hello?" Long croaked into the darkness.

He was answered by a reciprocal groan. Short was alive and nearby.

It had been stupid of Long, really, to suppose he could just walk into the castle, even in Hoosh Bindy's company. Oh, the captain had been inside before, but that had been back when

Her Majesty thought Mahnus dead. Now, she not only knew him to be alive, but actively seeking her out.

"What a mess," Long sighed.

"Can't you make it light in here?" Short complained.

"Why yes," said Long. "I imagine I can. I'm not ready for that just yet, though."

Short did not contradict him.

Hours passed before either spoke again, and then Long said, "If I can't catch her inside, I'll have to draw her out."

"Sounds easy enough," Short replied sarcastically.

"Doesn't it, though?"

"I figure there's maybe three things she wants: me, Vykers, or the fella in charge o' this invasion."

Short thought about this for a bit, and then said, "Even you are not stupid enough to serve as bait, and I don't think you could ever catch Vykers, so that leaves…"

"Right. I've gotta bring this invader to Lunessfor."

Alheria & Hoosh, Lunessfor

When he opened his eyes, he found his mother standing over him, scowling with such intensity it seemed possible that her face might shatter. And yet, Hoosh found no humor in this. He knew that unless he was able to come up with a plausible excuse for his behavior, he was as good as dead.

"I was delivering the clodpoll into your hands!" he protested.

"I see only one clodpoll," Alheria responded, her voice thick with menace. "And Mahnus is nowhere to be found."

Hoosh looked about. He was on his back in one of the castle's myriad hallways. He might as well have been lying in the desert, for all the difference it made. "Let me make it up to you," he suggested. Pleading would do him little good, he knew, as Her Majesty despised weakness, but she might be willing to negotiate, if he could come up with a sufficiently tempting offer. "I'll find him again and bring him wherever you like."

She smiled, but it was not the kind of smile Hoosh had been hoping for.

"I'll kill him myself!" he offered, with more than a hint of desperation. "If you'll just lend me the dagger."

Alheria bent low over his face. "Oh, I'll give you the dagger," she answered.

"Lend! Lend me the dagger, and I'll finish him!" Hoosh said, nearly yelling now.

"I was having some difficulty deciding which of my children should be the next to go..." Alheria continued. "But you've made the choice so much easier for me..."

The Fool felt a flash of exquisite pain in his belly, and then he collapsed in on himself and was gone.

The witch's hovel was surrounded with bands of great power, great enough that even Alheria was impressed. The Queen surveyed the surrounding swamp, to ensure that her daughter had no hidden allies who might attempt to intervene once the fighting started. Finding none, Alheria called out, "Daughter! You must know I am here! Come out and speak with me."

"I think not," croaked a voice that seemed far older than Alheria's. "I can feel that my brother is dead."

"Yes," Alheria said sadly. "The Fool lived up to his name."

"Diterus is now gone, too."

This was news to Alheria. "I'd almost forgotten about him. When did he die? *How* did he die?"

The witch laughed in her stronghold. "As if you did not know."

Alheria spread her hands. "I wasn't the one who imprisoned him. And the one who did has returned."

More laughter. "I am aware."

The Queen squinted at her daughter's hovel, as if she might penetrate its defenses. "Michere."

"Croonbasket," the witch corrected.

"Come now, that's an idiotic name."

"But freely chosen."

"Be that as it may," Alheria thundered, exasperated, "we cannot both ascend!"

"Then end yourself, and let me rise," Croonbasket quipped.

Alheria pulled the skies down upon her daughter's hovel, smashing it with winds too strong for anything living to endure.

Great sheets of water assaulted the space, even as lightning repeatedly blasted the remains of the structure. The ground beneath it rumbled and shook with unbelievable violence, too, until the whole scene seemed proof that the end of the world had arrived. When at last Alheria's anger subsided, there was nothing of Croonbasket's home but a smoking crater.

The Queen made ready to leave when she was struck between the shoulder blades with a thousand needles of fire and ice, whereupon she lost control of her legs and tottered over onto her side in the mud, squirming helplessly, like some vast amphibian struggling its way out of the ooze. Now, she was the one hit by lightning and clouds of noxious poison, as well. In a trice, she shrank to the size of a flea and then blinked entirely out of sight.

"You were always a clever one," Alheria's voice echoed from the surrounding swamps.

Too clever, it seemed, to take the Queen's bait.

A little green bird watched the proceedings from the relative safety of a distant treetop. A still-invisible Alheria hurled everything she had at the hapless creature and was gratified to hear Croonbasket's wail of despair. The bird fell to the ground, blazing like a fallen star and gradually resolved itself into an old crone, broken and burnt. Alheria returned to her usual form as well and limped over to her daughter, to finish her. Croonbasket looked up at her with eyes full of blood.

"Spare me the lectures," she gasped. "And the pretense of motherly concern."

Alheria shrugged. "As you..."

Croonbasket exploded, not in a mesmerizing shower of sparks, but in a savage, concussive blast, not unlike a volcanic eruption. Alheria tumbled and spun through the air until she landed, face—down, in the swamp.

She found it difficult to extricate herself at first because her left arm was gone.

Vykers & Co, On the Road

The Frog was dead, and no one could say what the killing blow had been. Vykers had been ferocious; for all that, he'd been like a child carving his name on the trunk of an ancient tree. The great cat had fought like a thing possessed, but the Frog was so much bigger that the cat looked like nothing more than a house cat attacking an errant neighbor. The men had shot arrows into the Frog, but even aflame, it was hard to imagine they did much damage. Was it the poison on Ona's javelins? Or had the Frog, finally, decided he no longer wished to live? One thing was certain: his corpse would provide enough carrion for every scavenger, worm and fly on the continent.

Vykers was splashed with the Frog's blood, but otherwise unharmed. The same could not be said of his crew. They'd lost half their number, enough that the Reaper no longer had an excuse for not learning their names. Why bother, though, if they were going to die sooner or later?

Vykers, Hjuest, Ona, Ngoro and three of their fellows returned to the group's original fire. "Get some sleep," the Reaper commanded. "Tomorrow, we'll continue on to the Emperor's homeland."

Sleep was long in coming, however, what with the stench of the Frog's corpse and the disturbing memories of what he'd done to those he'd killed. Each time Ona thought she might drift off, she imagined the monster was not entirely dead and was readying himself for another attack. At some point, Ona rolled into Hjuest's side. The Red Knight put an arm underneath her head, and at last she fell asleep.

At sunrise, Ona rose awkwardly, bidding Hjuest a hasty good morning, stood up to find Vykers brooding by the fire.

"I thought you'd look happier today."

He grunted. "Frog got like he was by eatin' the bodies of magical creatures. And then maybe he was able to keep growing off o' regular creatures."

Ona looked at him: *So?*

"I don't think we can risk letting the local beasties eat the Frog, lest we spawn a whole legion o' similar uglies."

"You're thinking we should burn him?"

"Can't see as there's a better solution."

They spent the day gathering kindling, firewood and

anything else they thought might burn. It was a tedious challenge, since they'd used so much of the local wood in the previous night's bonfire.

"Fat'll burn, no?" Vykers asked Hjuest.

"Ya, but vat are you sinking?"

The Reaper pulled a long knife off his saddle. "I'm gonna go carve that fucker up and toss his fat onto the firewood."

"I help," said the normally taciturn Ngoro.

"Me, too," said Hjuest.

Ona sighed. Getting inside the Frog's skin was the last thing in the world she wanted to be doing, but if it would get the fire going sooner, she was willing to participate. The remaining three members of the crew continued to gather wood, even riding miles out of the way to find what they wanted. Eventually, Vykers and company were able to amass quite a pile of wood and fatty skin to start their fire. They could only hope it was enough.

The Reaper tossed the last few brands from his little campfire onto the Frog's pyre and waited. Slowly, surely, the fat and the drier twigs and sticks ignited the larger branches and logs. Finally, the Frog's skin ignited in a number of places, until the whole of him was engulfed, choking the skies above with thick, black smoke.

"Dunno if he's gonna burn all the way, but I'm not of a mind to hang about and find out," Vykers announced. "We've done what we could." He then returned to his horse and pulled himself up into the saddle. He didn't need to urge his companions to do likewise; they were even more eager to depart than he.

Soon, they were miles removed from the Frog's remains and profoundly grateful to be upwind, even if they still could see the inky column of smoke given off by his burning for hours and hours. Vykers never looked back, though. The Frog had been a bad episode in his life, had almost been the end of it. Now, the Reaper was focused on the Emperor's city and, in particular, his palace, where the ageless warrior hoped to learn his age—and a great deal more, besides.

"Hjuest!" Vykers called out. "How far's this palace?"

Hjuest wasn't sure; he'd never been. But he didn't want to disappoint the Reaper, so he answered, "A veek?"

"A veek," Vykers echoed to himself.

Ona rode up on his far side and said, "I've been thinking about that giant cat..."

The Reaper grinned. "Yeah. We met before. Last time I was over here."

"The same one?"

"The same. I think he's a god."

"What, the god of cats?"

"Yes."

"Why was he fighting for us?"

Vykers half-turned in his saddle and shot her a skeptical look. "I don't know as he was fightin' for us. Prob'ly just wanted to get the Frog outta his lands. He saw an opportunity and took it."

"I wish he'd stayed with us. Might be we could use his help where we're going, especially now that we're down several men."

"The wind and rain do as they list. Why should the god o' cats be any different?" The Reaper turned away again, done with conversation for the time being.

Ona couldn't escape the feeling they'd see the big cat again.

They came across a number of hamlets that had not been destroyed by the Frog, but which, because of their increasing proximity to the Emperor's domain, were nevertheless struggling to survive without their menfolk. Oh, men can't do everything, but a large number of men is worth something, and most of these towns had few or none. The young and the old took up the slack, not knowing when or if their husbands, fathers, brothers or sons would return. Whenever Vykers' crew rode into a new town, the locals stopped whatever they were doing to gawk at the new arrivals. Were they hopeful, afraid or both at the same time?

Vykers let Hjuest do the talking, though the Reaper understood far more than he could reasonably explain. He'd no memory of having been in this strange land prior to rescuing Her Majesty, but, as his recent brush with death had shown him, he had a whole host of experiences he couldn't recall. Perhaps he'd even been mayor of one of these villages.

No, he wasn't the mayor type.

But the locals treated him like one, anyway. They feasted and feted him and his crew everywhere they went. And while none of the locals said as much, Vykers guessed they were desperate for company, or protection, or news of any sort. Hjuest did a fine job of keeping the curious natives appeased, while Vykers made hay with their women. Whether they were drawn to his obvious strength and confidence or to his weirdly boyish skin and hair, he neither knew nor cared. He'd never been so popular with the ladies, and he meant to enjoy himself while he could.

Ona objected, of course; she couldn't bear to witness his womanizing, though from Vykers' perspective, it was none of her business.

"Jealous, girl?" he asked her after her latest reprimand. She made a face of such shock and disgust that Vykers couldn't help laughing. "I meant jealous of *me!*" he clarified.

"I'll never be jealous of them or you. It's disgusting behavior, and a man shouldn't act like that!"

"What do you know about it?" he scoffed in rebuttal. "You ever even been with a man?"

For an instant, her eyes searched for Hjuest and then, finding him, darted away. This told Vykers all he needed to know.

"So you're afraid," he observed mercilessly. "Big, strong girl like you?"

One doesn't tell the Reaper to fuck off, and so Ona said nothing until a thought came to her. "All of this feasting and such is just slowing us down."

It was true, and Vykers had almost forgotten why he'd come to this land in the first place. "Very well. We leave in the morning and keep pushin' forward 'til we reach this Emperor's palace."

Ona wanted to smile, but didn't dare. It was a small victory, but a victory nonetheless.

Trouble at Nespharia

Omeyo was elated. Everything had gone as the Woman had planned and, using her magics, they'd brought the girl down more or less gently into the waiting arms of his warriors. And, best of all, the Invader King had witnessed the whole thing! Oh, the little man had not been happy! Now, perhaps, he had some inkling of how the Svarren felt every day of their lives. Still, an inkling was not enough. Omeyo meant to school the fellow in despair. In order to do that, however, he and his fighters had to survive. Almost as soon as they'd captured the girl, Omeyo sounded the retreat. The Invader wouldn't be long in pursing them, so it was crucial that they get as big a head start as possible. The Woman would focus on obscuring their backtrail, and Omeyo had good cause to believe they'd elude the Invader's forces in the short term. Long term? The Svarren would need more than the giants' help to avoid annihilation.

They might need some help from Her Majesty's army, if it ever returned to the field.

Omeyo barked a command and spurred his horse away from Nespharia's walls. His fighters did not have mounts, but could run remarkably well and for surprisingly long distances. To the northwest, an almost unending scrubland would provide the cover the Svarren needed to break up into smaller groups and head off in different directions. If the Invader King could find his beloved in that maze, well, he was no mere mortal.

As for the girl, she'd been bound, still-dazed, and thrown over the shoulders of one of Omeyo's largest warriors. She'd not been gagged, however, because the old general wanted her to scream, wanted the Invader King to hear her.

The general looked up into the sky; great, heavy clouds had rolled in from the east, but rain seemed unlikely. Too bad. Wet terrain always favored the natives. Soon, a hue and cry arose at the Svarren's back, and Omeyo knew the chase was on. This was a moment for which he and the Woman had spent days in preparation. Rain or no rain, they'd laid enough traps in the scrub to cripple an army.

Then he heard the howling of dogs. Scores of them, by the sound of it. He hadn't been expecting that, but of course the Invader King was no fool, else he could not command his armies as he did. Omeyo cracked his whip and the surrounding Svarren pushed themselves even harder. They, too, had heard the dogs and were not anxious to encounter the beasts until they'd reached favorable ground.

Mendis was a good deal less-armored than usual, but he hadn't a moment to waste if he was going to find and rescue Qansip. If she was even still alive. Gods, if those filthy creatures touched her, if they...he couldn't bear to think about it. He was not accustomed to panic and refused to consider how he'd respond if he began to feel it. He was an Emperor, *the* Emperor, and could not be shaken like some pimply-faced schoolboy. He and his soldiers—and the dogs—would catch up to the Svarren who'd taken Qansip. He would save her and punish them. Perhaps he would have their leader burned alive, or drawn-and-quartered. Something ghastly and painful, certainly.

But even as he rode off in pursuit of Qansip and her abductors, Mendis wrestled with the thousand other things he ought to have been doing. His legions were running out of water. They were also defying his ban on the local ale. Was there a connection? At the same time, he suspected that another visit from Her Majesty might happen at any moment, and he'd made no progress in finding this Long Pete, in kidnapping Wykkerian, or in protecting himself from her wrath. On top of all this, his fleet was in ruins.

And yet, he was charging off into the wild, half-armored and ill-prepared. He wondered if he'd have done the same if the hostage had been his lady wife and mother of his children. He had a daughter just a few years shy of Qansip's age. He...he...

He thought he might go mad. For the first time in his life, his confidence was shaken, and he questioned whether he'd finally bitten off more than he could chew. As quickly as the thought came to mind, he shook it off as unproductive and unworthy. He would get through this, and his empire would endure, if not expand.

But first he had to save Qansip.

The detachment of Svarren who'd made off with the girl vanished into the scrublands without losing a single fighter, and, as Omeyo had hoped, the Invader King had acted impulsively in pursuing them. Once the man and his outriders were well and fully committed, the rest of the Svarren army—those who'd stayed on the far side of Nespharia—redoubled their assault on the city, launching still more piles of disease-ridden offal, bundles of refuse soaked in flaming pitch, or simple heaps of stone. The Woman and two of her sisters summoned clouds of pestilence, too, that floated well above the fray, only to rain sickness and death on Nespharia's people. The city's wizards fought to counter this effort as best they could, but Mendis' most powerful wizards marched with his legions.

Governor Bailis was hard-pressed to keep up with all these developments. Yes, his archers continued to barrage the closest Svarren, but they were of little use against the Svarren siege engines. The colonel pondered a sortie, a quick charge through the best-situated gates in order to destroy some of these catapults and trebuchets. But he had an uneasy feeling the Svarren had prepared for such an action, and that it would therefore result in disaster.

It was that man he'd sometimes glimpsed amongst the enemy, that human warrior. His was quite clearly a trained and experienced military mind. Bailis struggled to place the fellow, but eventually abandoned the effort as counterproductive. He'd no time for such questions with the city under assault. He needed a strategy, a response to the enemy's actions, as soon as possible.

The idea that came to him was sheer insanity.

A hundred men rode with the Emperor, a hundred strong, heavily armed men on exceptional horses. It was a force not meant to overwhelm, but outrun, not crush but extract with surgical precision.

It would not be enough.

From the moment these riders entered the scrublands, it became necessary to divide and divide again. Mendis was uncharacteristically plagued with second thoughts; the only thing he knew for certain was that Qansip's time was running out. Each time the trail split, his force divided even more. Soon, he had but ten men at his back, and he was compelled to wonder if he hadn't rushed into an assassination attempt. After all, he'd been unreachable inside Nespharia's walls. Now? A single spear would...

There were screams somewhere off to his left, human screams of agony. Then, suddenly, to his right he heard the clash of arms. Still, Mendis pushed forward, only to hear prayers and cries for mercy.

The whole thing was a trap, then, and he'd taken the bait. What else could he do, though? Leave his glorious Qansip to her fate? Abruptly, he reined his horse to a stop and stood on his stirrups, the better to see over the sea of bushes surrounding him. Immediately, he wished he hadn't. He and the handful of men who'd followed him were surrounded. The ninety men who'd branched off in other directions were terribly beset, to the point where Mendis could already count them lost. And should he not do the same for himself?

"To me!" he yelled to those who'd followed him. "In a circle."

They didn't have long to wait.

Bailis ordered all the gates opened.

At first, of course, there was widespread resistance to the idea. Once the colonel-now-governor explained his thinking, however, he quickly found converts, and his orders were carried out, whereupon the Svarren attacks ceased and a pregnant silence fell upon the city. Eventually, the savages approached, though. How could they resist? What they found, just inside the gates, were abandoned streets and boarded up windows and doors, as if Nespharia was expecting a storm. Very well: it was storm she would get.

The Svarren raged down the streets, smashing everything within reach and throwing fire at rooftops, so immersed in rapine and destruction that none noticed when the gates closed again and were resealed from the inside and out.

Now, the brutes were well in range, and arrows rained down upon them. The town militia and Imperial Guard, who'd been hiding in the city center, rushed forward with great rage, so that the attackers heard them coming before they appeared.

The Woman, in the back of the throng with her sisters, understood that they'd been tricked. This was no surrender, as she'd hoped, but a hole, a canyon, from which her people might not escape.

When the first Svarren pushed through the bushes, Mendis snarled at them, confident he and his men could beat them back. But as the trickle of creatures became an unrelenting flood, his men and their horses fell, one by one, and the ground beneath them became a bloody mire.

Is this how it ends? Mendis lamented. *The ruler of the greatest empire the world has ever known dies in a thicket, chasing after his mistress? My lady wife will never understand…*

One of the Svarren had a long pole with which, it seemed, he intended to push Mendis off his horse. If that happened…The Emperor batted the pole away with his sword and then made a sweep to his opposite flank. The Svarren were everywhere, swarming about him like ants. Mendis fought like a man possessed, but felt his death fast approaching.

And then he was back with his wizards, shaking with nervous energy and gasping for breath like a man too long underwater. "What?" he asked. "How…?"

"One of our number in Nespharia was concerned for you. It appears he was correct." Newak replied.

Mendis dropped his sword in dirt and fell into an exhausted crouch. "Call everyone to a stop. No more marching today. I would rest and…think."

"As you say."

The carnage inside the city was extreme. Citizens and soldiers alike popped out of houses when least expected and assaulted the Svarren from behind, whilst the main body of troops engaged them in the streets and market square. People died, to be sure. But the Svarren were flat panicked. They fought with great ferocity, like the cornered animals they were, until the Woman ordered them to flee as best they could. Disengaging from the Imperial soldiers and town militia, they stormed out of the city's center and into its most remote and hard-to-reach areas, where they burrowed in like parasites, hoping to avoid detection.

Bailis' plan had worked…to a degree. Between the gates and market square, the streets were littered with Svarren dead.

The townsfolk had suffered losses, but the enemy had been destroyed—destroyed, but not eradicated. Bailis had seen the beasts run off down the alleys and over the rooftops. Now, he and his soldiers would have to hunt them down to the last creature, before they did any more damage, before they killed one more human. Failing that, he had merely to hold Nespharia until reinforcements arrived from the Emperor's main army.

Was the Emperor still alive, though? Bailis had no way of knowing and couldn't afford to dwell on the question. When the opportunity arose, he'd instruct the Emperor's wizards on these matters. For the time being, nothing was more important than the hunt for the remaining Svarren.

Beesmarch & Kin, Western Midlands

With the invaders' search for water becoming more desperate every day, Beesmarch and his fellows were doing more running or fighting than they had in ages. In fact, the King hadn't felt so fit since he'd been a lad. To what end, though? They'd never be enough in number to truly challenge the enemy, and, that being the case, it seemed they were destined to fail in ending the invasion. They hadn't seen their co-conspirators, the Svarren, in days and days, and the Virgin Queen still had not sent her forces into the field. What then was the point in the great and daily risks the giants took on behalf of their absent allies? What more could they do and would any of it matter in the end?

It was time for lunch and, if nothing else, Beesmarch was determined to preserve routine for the sake of normalcy. He called the group to a stop and sat himself down on a fallen log for a few minutes' rest. "Lunch!" said he. Nobody argued. Instead, as was their wont, they all shared whatever they had with each other, so that no one went hungry or felt deprived.

"We'll have to make a more serious effort at finding some game tonight," Beesmarch observed.

"I'm dyin' for some bread and cheese!" Eoman declared.

"Hmph! Unless we find it walkin' about the forest, we'll be stuck with water and meat, and lucky to be so."

Karrakan grinned but said nothing. He could always find

nuts, berries, mushrooms, honey and other edibles to augment any meal. Spring had arrived, and though it was not as bounteous a time as summer, it still offered far more than winter.

The group's scout returned about halfway through the meal, utterly unsurprised to find his friends in this particular location.

"News?" Beesmarch inquired without getting up.

"They've stopped."

"Takin' a break, are they?"

"This looks more than a break," the scout replied. "This looks like they mean to stay a spell."

Beesmarch instinctively glanced Eoman's way.

"Do you mind goin' back at nightfall? And, Kan, would you send some o' your will-o'-wisps? I think we should learn a bit more about what they're planning," Eoman said.

This was something of a breach of protocol, but Bees remembered that his friend had been king for most of his life, and rule and all its habits must have been hard things to unlearn. And, as Beesmarch was still learning the job himself, he wasn't offended in the least. "We may as well make camp ourselves, then. Time to go find some o' that game!" he said.

Several giants stood up immediately and began gathering their hunting tools, whilst others set about starting a fire or building a rustic lean-to in case it rained.

Beesmarch pulled Eoman aside and said, "We both know you're more used to makin' decisions."

Eoman looked at his friend and kept quiet, waiting to hear the rest.

"Just lately, I've been feelin' this whole thing's a fool's errand."

"How so?"

"Well, we're not enough to stop these bastards, are we? We've contrived to slow 'em down, aye, but then what? What've we gained through our efforts?"

"Purpose," said Eoman matter-of-factly. "When's the last time this many of us have gathered to do anything together? And what's the alternative? We go back to our homes and await oblivion?"

"You're gettin' t'be quite the philosopher in yer old age," Beesmarch sighed. "But I'll not gainsay you."

Eoman put a hand on the larger giant's shoulder. "If I die on this adventure, I die amongst my own. That's more than I ever dared dream of, 'til now."

It was a fine sentiment, and Beesmarch couldn't help but agree. "I been meanin' to ask," he said, "where's the crown comes with my title?"

"Oh, I keep it in as safe a place as you could wish for," Eoman winked. "Up my ass. And I hope you'll wait 'til I'm dead to go searchin' for it."

Bees assumed his old friend was having him on, and deservedly so. Still, he walked away wondering if such a thing was even possible.

ELEVEN

Alheria, Lunessfor and Elsewhere

Alheria retired to her library, battered and raw. Things would have been so much easier had she been able to touch her daughter with the dagger. But nothing had ever been easy with that child, to the point that it had been a relief, really, when she'd run away. The Queen had always known where she was, of course, but as long as the girl stayed out from underfoot, Alheria had no qualms with Croonbasket's little show of independence. And what a foolish name she'd chosen for herself! Probably meant to embarrass her mother, but Alheria thought it best to ignore it altogether.

And now she was gone, along with the Fool. And Diterus. She'd dispatched all the others, great and feeble, over the last few years, so that only Mahnus was left. Killing him would not be easy, as evidenced by her previous failure. If only she'd identified his reborn self earlier, before he'd begun to come into his memory and his powers. And to think she'd almost caught him again! His botched attempt to enter her castle was not all good for Alheria, though, for it proved that Mahnus was consciously stalking her now. In a few short months, she'd gone from feeling assured of victory to rattled by the very real possibility of defeat, everything she'd played for for millennia, wasted and undone by her former lover.

She sat, wearily, in her favorite chair and gazed at the sky through the nearest window. It looked like a storm was brewing, and she had the power to disperse it, but was too exhausted from battling with Michere, from summoning the great wave, from keeping her ever-watchful eyes on that idiot Emperor. She had plans for him, oh yes she did. But she had to keep him alive in the meantime.

Rather than chase the storm away, she focused on replacing her missing arm. There were many things in the world that could restore themselves in time; only Mahnus and she could do so in an instant, though even they paid a cost. As soon as her arm was back in its place and fully healed, Alheria felt the irresistible urge to sleep, just as she'd been expecting. The coming sleep would leave her vulnerable, though, so that it had to take place where no one would ever find her.

With a thought, she went elsewhere. Its location could not be found on any map, for only she had ever been there and, if it came to that, only she could ever leave. Elsewhere, she was as safe from Mahnus and Tarmun Vykers as if they'd never existed. Elsewhere, she could sleep for eons in a single moment, or the other way 'round, if she wished. Perhaps, after she was rested, she might use some of her 'extra' time to revisit and revise her plans, to reassure herself. She'd been playing and scheming for thousands of years and, thus far, everything had fallen out just as she'd intended. One could never be too careful, though— especially when the stakes were as high as divinity. Thus, she would trace every possibility to its end, to verify that nothing had changed, that she hadn't missed a single detail.

Sleep swept over her like a dark, heavy blanket, and, for a time, she knew the peace of a dozing child.

Mendis & Long Pete, In Camp

"Magnificence," said General Promartis, "I'm told there is some local bumpkin with a chicken who wishes to speak with you."

Still reeling from Qansip's abduction and the thousand other mishaps he and his legions had endured of late, Mendis could only stare open-mouthed at his general.

"Says his name's Long Pete or some such..."

The Emperor was on his feet in an instant, a look of alarm on his face. "Call my wizards. All of them. And bring the Dread Knights, the lot."

"And this Long Pete?" Promartis asked, somewhat stunned.

"Keep him here. Do whatever it takes. Offer him some of that ale, perhaps."

"The ale that's no longer allowed in camp?"

"That's the stuff."

"As you say, Magnificence."

"Let me know when my wizards have arrived."

In less than five minutes' time, everything was arranged as Mendis had commanded, and he'd had time to brief his wizards on the alleged nature of their visitor. When the Emperor walked out of his pavilion to greet the man, however, he was surprised at what he saw. This Long Pete was as ordinary as a hangnail. Of middle years, gangly build and weathered face, he was nothing like the godlike being he'd expected. The fact he was holding a chicken made him seem more than a little ridiculous.

"You say you're Long Pete..." Mendis began.

"That I am," said Long, clutching his chicken close to his chest.

"You speak the Imperial tongue without accent."

Long broke into a bemused smile. "Funny thing, that..."

"Yes," said Mendis, before drifting into awkward silence. Then: "I hope the ale was to your liking..."

This time, Long laughed. "Oh, yes, we're old friends."

Gradually, Mendis' wizards made their presence known, along with his Dread Knights, as they slowly moved into a circle about their Emperor and his visitor.

"You anticipatin' hostilities?" Long asked, eyeing the new arrivals uncertainly.

"I think it's wise to be prepared for any eventuality. Don't you?"

Long made a face like he hadn't given it much thought, either way. "I've found things tend to happen whether we're ready or not."

If that was a threat, Mendis wasn't having any of it. "Why have you come?"

"Kinda seems like you were expectin' me."

"Actually, no," Mendis admitted. "But I was made aware of

your existence and told to..." He wasn't sure how to finish the sentence.

Long quirked an eyebrow at him. "Told to what?"

"I think I'd like an answer to my question, first."

Apparently, Long squeezed his chicken a little too tightly, for it suddenly said, "Ouch!" and then, rather belatedly and unconvincingly, "Bawk!" Long offered the bird a reproachful look, and then, as if nothing unusual had occurred, said, "I'm here because I want to help you take the capital."

Mendis glanced at the nearest wizard for confirmation that he had in fact heard what he thought he'd heard. "You...wish to help."

"Just so."

"And suppose taking your capital is not amongst my plans."

"Then you'd best rethink your plans."

The man's tone was infuriating! All of a sudden, Mendis had no idea what to do with his hands. He didn't want to seem weak, and he certainly didn't want to appear combative—at least not until he could verify what the Virgin Queen had said about Long Pete. Recalling the many trials of the past few days (and attempting not to dwell, yet, upon Qansip), he finally threw caution to the wind. "I'm told you're a god." Whatever response he'd been expecting was not what he got.

"I dunno. I s'pose so."

"Bawk!"

Mendis tried something else: "You are aware, I imagine, that you don't exactly look like a god..."

Long considered making a crack about the Emperor's height, but decided against it. "Yeah, I know. But about the capital, now..."

Now, it was the Emperor's turn to consider things. For instance, if this fellow was indeed a god with powers similar to the Virgin Queen's, then the Imperial wizards and Dread Knights would pose little resistance if he chose to attack Mendis. Then there was the fact that Queen had insisted Long be captured and killed...but she must have known or suspected that Mendis hadn't the power. What was she after, truly? What was *he* after?

"What are you after?" Mendis demanded.

"This is Her Majesty's land you're marchin' through; these are her people you're killin'. You think she'll let this go on forever?"

"And you believe that attacking her city will somehow forestall her revenge?"

Long lowered his head, seemed to get lost in the feathers atop the chicken's head. "I mean to kill her." *If I can...*

They were quite a contrast in styles, these two gods. Where Alheria had invaded his privacy in an intentionally intimidating display of raw power, Long Pete had arrived like a humble petitioner; where Alheria had made demands, Long Pete was apparently offering allegiance; where hers was a countenance of imperious resolve, his was the face of a farmer. Everything seemed to point in Long Pete's favor; still, Mendis was not one to be deceived by appearances. He needed something beyond assurances; he needed incentives. As it happened, there *was* something he wanted.

"My...consort...has been captured by your Svarren."

"They're not my Svarren," Long corrected.

Without apologizing, Mendis went on, "I'd be much more open to entreaty if she were returned to me."

"You want me to go 'n fetch her."

"Yes."

Suddenly, Long looked a thousand years old and utterly world-weary. "There's always one more errand, ain't there, Short?"

"Bawk."

Kittins, Yendor & Co, Western Midlands

They'd decided on one final run, not because they were getting bored of the job, but because they were running low on regular ale to mix with their magic elixir and skent. And Yendor and Spirk were in favor of saving a large supply for themselves. The mood back in Lunessfor was dour-tending-to-bleak and, even without evidence to support the notion, everyone believed war was coming. Flowers were in bloom throughout the city now, but all anyone could smell was impending death.

The boys simply had to get out of town.

And the truth was, things were simpler in the woods. They rode in the wagons, tended the horses, and made camp whenever necessary. Life in the city required a plan; in the wilds, they had no greater needs than food, water and fire. They took their turns waxing poetic about the surrounding landscape, and even Kittins spoke his piece. There'd been a time, he said, when the forest stretched from the eastern shore to the western, from the southern to the northern. Yendor allowed as it was hard to imagine such a thing, but Kittins assured him it was true. He'd read it in one of the few books he'd ever opened, and if that was all the knowledge he'd retained from the experience, it was good enough. The land had once been a great forest, and then man had changed things.

Kittins thought then of Vykers' A'Shea—or whatever she was. He knew her not at all, but from his few brief encounters, it was clear that she'd chosen nature over civilization and, in fact, seemed to be thriving as a result. Yes, yes, he'd once fantasized about having a small farm with a wife and two or three sons. Hells, he'd have been okay with five daughters and one son. But he'd come to a hard-won understanding that he'd get no children, no wife and no farm. Then, he figured he'd probably die in some asinine and pointless skirmish in a rancid back-alley somewhere…Unless he sought peace in the forest. He was a decent hunter, an accomplished hand at making a fire, and he knew a thing or two about building shelters. Yes, he could make a fair go of it.

Except that he felt an irrational need to test himself against the Reaper. And where in the world was the bastard, anyway? A foreign army had invaded the land, and Vykers was nowhere to be found? Kittins briefly worried the man might be dead and then remembered who he was thinking of. The Reaper was not dead, but instead biding his time for… Mahnus-knew-what.

The question began to eat at Kittins, so that by the time they'd made camp and gathered 'round the fire, he couldn't help bringing it up.

"What do you all reckon the Reaper's been doin' all this time?"

"It's funny," Rem replied, "but I haven't thought about him in weeks."

"Maybe he's dead," said Ron.

"You serious?" Kittins asked.

Yendor took a more philosophical approach. "There's none so glorious but he'll be food and shelter for worms in the fullness o' time, look you, a very worm's desire."

Rem eyed his old friend with renewed appreciation. "I think you missed your calling," said he. "You should have been a poet."

"Indeed? And here I thought I was meant to be a drunkard."

Kittins couldn't help noticing that Spirk reached for his flask at the mention of the word 'drunkard.' Every man's hell's his own, and the captain would not have traded places with the young Shaper for all the gold in Bysvaldia.

Soon, the companions wandered into more frivolous topics and musings, and it wasn't long before they were all asleep.

This time, they were not intercepted by smugglers within the Emperor's army, but by terribly officious soldiers of the same, who seemed to want nothing more than to escort the ale merchants into custody. Before Kittins could lose his temper and begin killing the foreigners, Yendor commanded Spirk to whisk them all away, which the Shaper did.

Yendor should have remembered, however, that Spirk was prone to literality, and, before he knew it, the companions and their would-be captors were all crammed into the gang's hide-out, fumbling in the darkness, tripping over furniture and otherwise struggling to make sense of things.

Rem was first to do so. "Send the invaders away, Spirk! Send them away!" Rem heard a protracted "Oh!" from the young man and the Emperor's men blinked out of the room. Spirk then mumbled something else and the hide-out's candles all bloomed with flame.

When everyone could see, Spirk was amazed to find his friends staring at him—not in rebuke, but in some other emotion he couldn't define. "What?" he asked.

It was Ron would finally spoke up. "You Jumped a whole unit of soldiers in here."

"Without their horses," Yendor added.

"And you Jumped them all away again without sending a single one of us along," Rem added.

"So?" Spirk responded, feeling a bit put upon.

"So?" Yendor echoed. "So? I ain't never heard of a single Shaper could do that."

"I want a drink," said Spirk, self-consciously.

No one was about to argue with him.

Kittins excused himself and instructed the Shaper to deposit him somewhere in the South Shore district. He was overdue in checking in with Her Majesty. Spirk could have Jumped him closer in, but Kittins needed a good walk to assess the city. Last time he'd really studied them, the people of Lunessfor were as surly and irritable as...well, he himself on a typical day. Today, though, they were quiet, and the whole city followed suit. It was a bright, cloudless day, and yet it may as well have been raining for all the activity there was in the streets. Out of curiosity, Kittins wandered over to Market Square and found it as dismal as everywhere else in town. He spied a vintner's booth on the edge of the square and sidled up to its counter, hoping to learn more.

The vintner was as dull and dreary-eyed a fellow as Kittins had encountered in some time, but at least he failed to recoil in fear at the captain's ruined visage.

"Help you?" the vintner asked as if he expected to be slapped.

"Glass o' your best," Kittins said, and tossed a Merchant onto the counter.

The vintner, a short, sallow-faced type with great bags under his bulging eyes reached up and mussed his colorless hair. "'S the most coin I've seen in days."

"Wine's that bad, is it?" Kittins japed.

"No," the man said, taking no offense whatsoever. "It's just that damned ale that everyone's hankerin' for. Town's flat run out of it, and the locals treat anything else like horse piss, not to be drunk fer love or money."

"So they've stopped drinking, then?"

"Some have. Others'll drink anything they can put hand to, but they ain't very appreciative."

Kittins looked about the quiet and mostly-empty market. "Still, business has gotta be done, no?"

The vintner coughed and poured his customer and himself a couple of cups. "Cheers!" said he, as if he didn't understand the word.

The captain tasted his wine and found it improbably palatable. "Wine's good," he lied. "Where is everyone?"

The vintner shrugged and drained his own cup. "Dunno," said he. "I'm just hopin' to hang on until business returns."

Kittins dipped into his profits from selling the aforementioned ale and dropped a Royal on the counter. "Might be this'll help. Stay at it, man. The ale you speak of isn't comin' back, and you heard it from the Dead One."

Her Majesty was nowhere to be found, and Kittins harkened back to the time she'd disappeared for weeks. Then, Bailis had hired him and Long's crew to scout out the Great Eight in search of clues. But Kittins hadn't seen Bailis in ages, and Cindor...well, he was probably dead.

The Alchemist & Cindor, Lunessfor

The Alchemist, as was his wont, sat in the dark, in a chair opposite his captive, smiling the bittersweet smile of a man acknowledging the end of a wonderful experience.

"Nothing more to divulge?" D'Marei asked the misshapen head and torso that were all that remained of Cindor, the Queen's Mage.

"No more," Cindor burbled, happily soused on the Alchemist's elixir.

D'Marei's sad smile fell into an even sadder frown. "Then I have no further use for you."

"No use."

The Alchemist raised a bowl over Cindor's much-abused head and began pouring a thick, syrupy substance all over it.

Cindor giggled—an odd sound, coming from a man who once possessed such gravitas. "What's that?"

"A concoction of my own—you wouldn't recognize most of the ingredients, save quicklime."

Where others would have screamed themselves hoarse, Cindor merely alternated between moaning and short, frightening bursts of laughter.

"Now that is interesting," the Alchemist observed with something like pleasure.

So, the old bitch was Alheria. D'Marei put his head down on his desk and closed his eyes. Alheria! That raised so many questions, the Alchemist didn't know how to begin to decipher all of it. And he'd just killed her closest ally.

It was an odd thing for one as secretive and solitary as himself, but he suddenly felt the need for allies of his own. Who, though? Who in the wide...

Tarmun Vykers.

Yes. D'Marei had done business recently with a girl who'd purported to work for the Reaper. If he could just find that girl...He knew of a place in South Shore where information of all kinds was available—for a price. As it happened, he now had so much of his own to share, thanks to Cindor, that he could make himself rich a hundred times over. If he'd cared for such things. No, saving his own life was his first priority. Everything else would have to be put aside until he'd made himself as safe from Alheria as anyone could.

The object of his quest was a taxidermist who served Lunessfor's wealthy, but the Alchemist rather suspected she did not restrict her work to animals. How she had come by her store of secrets, nobody knew, but Trinta was as well-informed about the city's goings-on as anyone he had ever encountered.

She was also a former lover.

"Well, look what the cat dragged in," she crooned in her snarkiest voice when he came through her door. "I thought you were dead."

"No, you didn't."

"Hoped, then," she quipped. She put down the tool she'd been working with and pushed the dead whatever-it-was away so that she could focus on her guest. "Ah, Dem, you only ever come around when you want something..."

"It's true," he said, rubbing his bald pate, "I'll not gainsay it. But this time I have something to offer in return that will leave you speechless—a condition I'm dying to observe, by the way."

Trinta rinsed her hands in a nearby bowl and, once finished, carried her largest, brightest candle closer to the Alchemist, so she could see how or if his once-familiar countenance had changed. He filled the moment by examining the latest examples of her craft.

"The goat's nice," said he. "Though I can't imagine why anyone would want to preserve it."

"I was thinking the same of you," said she. "But now, what's this glorious secret you're offering?"

"Tsk, tsk!" he said. "That's not how things are done!"

"You do not set terms in my shop."

He looked at her: still the small, mousy woman he'd always known, if there were a few more wrinkles on her face and gray hairs in her head. She looked at him: his round, pale face and hairless scalp above his perennially black attire still made him look like a talking moon, a veritable man-i'-the moon.

D'Marei set his jaw. "Very well. But the secret I offer is worth more than everything you know. I shall expect generous cooperation with my questions once I've shared."

Damn him! He'd piqued her curiosity despite her best efforts to remain aloof. "Fine. What is this secret-of-all-secrets?"

The Alchemist looked around Trinta's one-room shop and raised an eyebrow at her.

"Oh, for Mahnus' sake!" she cried out. "I've got enough magical protections here to keep the very gods from listenin' in."

D'Marei gifted her with his creepiest smile. "It's funny you should say that...I have it on unimpeachable authority that our queen is none other than Alheria, herself."

"Fuck me!" Trinta breathed in shock.

"Maybe some other time," D'Marei countered. "The point

is, she is Alheria, and there is no question about it."

"No question? Who says there's no question?"

"Cindor. I got it from his own lips before I killed him."

The little taxidermist crossed the floor and fell into the room's only chair. "That's two secrets," said she, "each more unbelievable than t'other."

"But true, notwithstanding."

Trinta was quiet for a long time before she responded. "If both are true, then you're in trouble, eh?"

D'Marei rolled his eyes. "Yes. And here's what I would like from you: there was a rather fetching young thing that went about the district this past winter on the Reaper's behalf. I would like to know her name and whereabouts."

This was not what Trinta had been expecting. "Uh...why?"

"Because I am looking for the Reaper."

The taxidermist laughed. "Same old Dem. If you want the Reaper, ask me about the Reaper."

D'Marei hated it when she was right. "Very well," he growled. "Where can I find the Reaper?"

"Nobody knows!" Trinta laughed, picking at the hem of her rather unlovely skirt.

"I should have known better," the Alchemist chided himself.

"Now wait a moment: this means Vykers is either dead, which I suspect you'll agree is unlikely, or he's on the sea somewheres."

"Or *overseas*," D'Marei mused aloud. In the next instant, he turned for the door.

"Where are you off to?"

"I need to find a ship."

"This time, I'm coming with you."

"You're not."

"I am."

"You're aren't."

"I am."

They continued like this whilst she closed her shop, locked it, and followed the Alchemist off into the city.

Vykers & Co, Near the Emperor's Capital

The Emperor's primary domain was atop a long, gradual climb of several days that actually took less than one with the crew's ever-wonderful horses. The capital sat in the center of a vast plateau that stretched for miles in every direction. Up here, it was warmer than Vykers had been expecting, and the air was a touch thinner, too. There was a constant, vigorous breeze that pushed the plateau's grasses and wildflowers every-which-way, but cooled nothing and no one. The scene was at once alien and familiar to Vykers, but he chose not to share these feelings with the others, for he still barely understood them himself.

Vykers pulled a water skin from his saddle and drank deeply, after which he instructed his friends to do likewise. In the heat and altitude, a man who didn't drink enough water was soon fighting for life, and the Reaper didn't have time for that.

The capital was farther away than it looked, and the group passed a number of small farms as it pushed along. How in Mahnus' name did they feed their citizens with such puny farms?

Hjuest seemed to read his mind, for he said, "Every city and town in the empire pays homage to the Emperor, through taxes and foodstuffs. They say he's got a wizard who does nothing all day but ferry these offerings into the city."

"Huh," Vykers grunted. Interesting, but not useful.

They pressed on, and a thin, black line of mounted soldiers appeared in the distance—a welcoming party, Vykers mused. Or an unwelcoming party.

"Do you see dat?" Hjuest pointed at them.

"Yup."

"Vat shall vee do?"

The Reaper ignored the question and kept riding forward, which was answer enough for the Red Knight. Eventually, they came face-to-face with those protecting the city, a contingent of twenty-some men in battered blue armor stippled with yellow stars.

"Who are you and what do you seek?" their leader asked in his native tongue.

Hjuest was about to translate, when Vykers held up a hand and stopped him. "I am the Reaper," he said in the same language, "and I've come to take your city."

The knights had a hearty laugh over that, until their leader looked over at Hjuest and called out, "I recognize your accent. Your people obey the Emperor, do they not? Who is your foolish companion and what does he want?"

Vykers didn't even look Hjuest's way, but waited patiently for what he knew was coming.

"He is the Reaper in truth, and if he says he's come to take your city, den you'd best start running for de gates."

The knights and their leader were not amused by what they assumed was a very poor joke. At the leader's signal, they pulled their weapons and began to fan out around Vykers' much smaller party. The Reaper flashed into their midst too quickly to be seen or avoided, and then the leader was down, his skull cracked open right through his helm, like some enormous egg spilling its yolk onto the ground. Before the two men on either side could adjust, Vykers had cut their throats with a vicious backhand that startled and dismayed the rest of the city's defenders. One of them screamed a retreat, desperate to put as much distance between himself and the Reaper's axe as possible. His comrades scrambled to comply with the order and galloped away from their assailant with all speed...Which was not fast enough, not when running from the Reaper astride an enchanted horse. Soon, he stood over the last of their bodies, smashing and cracking into their armor like a fisherman killing crabs. Just when Ona began to worry that her grandfather meant to make a paste of their remains, a cry atop the city's walls brought him to a stop. She stared at him, drenched in blood and panting like a bull, and had a premonition: worse was coming.

There appeared to be no way into the city. The walls were impressively well made and maintained, and unless Vykers and his friends sprouted wings, there was no going up and over. Nor were there any obvious cracks or chinks that might be widened to admit access. Vykers spent half a day circling the city on his horse and found it as secure as any city or fort he'd ever encountered. Thus, he very much doubted there was any point in attempting to tunnel under the walls, either. If only he'd thought to bring a Shaper along...

They made camp on the plateau, just out of bow-range. There was plenty of dung to be found for a fire and, if they were careful, they had enough water to last several more days. What was Vykers going to do now, Ona wondered. How would he respond to this apparent defeat? For hours and then days, he simply sat and stared at the city's walls.

Long, Mendis & Qansip, the Emperor's Camp

When Long brought her back, she was beyond unresponsive. She was closer to dead, except that her eyes were open and an observant eye would notice her breathing, albeit in a shallow and erratic fashion.

"What's wrong with her?" the Emperor demanded. "Did they...did they...?" He couldn't bring himself to finish the thought.

"What, rape her?" Long asked. "No, strangely enough."

Mendis wanted to rage at the other man's callousness, but the other man was a god, and Mendis was no fool. "Can you... mend her, make her better?"

Long plunked himself down in the closest chair and blew out his cheeks. "Can I? I imagine so." With that, he focused his energies on Qansip and she started to come back to life, as if she'd been frozen and was now thawing out. In time, Mendis ordered that mulled wine be brought for his mistress. It was somewhat out of season, but no one dared say so.

After a while, some color began to return to Qansip's cheeks, and alertness, to her eyes. In another hour, she was almost normal.

Almost.

"Can you talk now, love?" Mendis probed.

"Of course," said she.

"I came as fast as I could. I was nearly killed in the effort."

Often, brown eyes are warm eyes, but in this instance, hers were not. Instead, they were dark, bottomless wells that made no concession to his needs or concern. It was as if she did not know him or did not recognize his station.

"I'm glad we were able to rescue you in the end, though," he added self-consciously. "I don't know what I would have…"

"You'd have thought of something," she said.

Frustrated, Mendis instructed his staff to clear out, to give Qansip some privacy while she rested. He also pulled Long Pete aside, completely forgetting the man's divinity, and demanded, "What is wrong with her?"

"Dunno. I reckon she's shaken up by her little adventure."

"Adventure?" Mendis nearly screamed.

Long yawned, not caring for the Emperor's tone. "I been through worse."

The Emperor fought to maintain his composure. "I want her the way she used to be, the way she's always been." Whilst his back was turned, however, Qansip rose from the cot she'd been laid out upon and began walking away. Mendis shouldered past Long and practically leapt for the young woman's arm as she passed through the curtain dividing this space from the next. He swung her around and deposited her back on the cot more ungently than he'd intended. For a moment, he wanted to apologize. And then again, he didn't. He'd done his damnedest to free her and almost been killed for it. Now that he'd gotten her back, she showed him no affection, no gratitude, nothing but…nothing. It was as if he was a fly on her sleeve. Finally, for want of anything else to say, he asked her, "What do you want?"

His father had always warned him never to ask questions if he was not prepared for their answers. He would come to wish he'd remembered that sage advice just a few seconds earlier.

"I wish to go speak with the Svarren."

Mendis glared then at Long, as if this was all somehow his fault, and then turned back to his mistress. "Never fear, my love. We'll punish them for this!"

Now, her expression changed, from one of aloof disinterest to bewilderment. "Why would you ever do that?"

"Because," Mendis stammered in shock, "they...they hurt you, they frightened you."

"I wish to join them."

"Make her sleep!" the Emperor barked at the god.

Once that was taken care of, Long told the other man, "I came here lookin' for your help, not to be bullied about and yelled at. Might be you've forgotten which of us is the god, here." He watched Mendis close his eyes and lower his head, even as his shoulders drooped and his overall demeanor lost all sense of authority.

"That girl," the Emperor gestured weakly, "has been like a sickness to me, or an addiction."

Long thought of Mardine then and missed her terribly. "And your wife?" he asked with an obvious tinge of judgment in his voice.

For a moment, Mendis seemed enraged, ready to erupt at the old captain. Then the fight went out of him, and he stumbled to Qansip's cot and sat down upon it, next to the sleeping girl. He covered his eyes with the palm of his right hand and massaged his temples with his thumb and fingers. *It might have been better for everyone involved if she'd died in that fall from the parapets,* he thought. No; it might have been better for him. But he would not be so shallow, so weak, so cowardly. With a sigh, he slapped his thighs and stood. Time to change the subject.

"You wish me to take my legions south and attack the capital; by coincidence, Her Majesty has more-or-less commanded me to use my legions to find and kill you."

Long nodded. "I figured it was something like that."

Mendis glanced longingly at his sleeping mistress. "But why should anyone die to resolve a conflict between the two of you?"

"Because," Long replied, "if Her Majesty wins, there'll be a second Great Awakening. Do you understand?"

"I've read my history. The Imperial library is rather well-supplied on that topic. And yet, it seems hard to credit..."

"Then you know of the bloodbath that followed."

Mendis nodded.

"And the loss of culture, of scientific knowledge..."

"Yes."

"Men were little better than Svarren for centuries."

"What would you have me do?"

Omeyo & His Svarren, the Scrublands

Omeyo was beyond merely crestfallen; he was devastated. He and his people had finally wrested order from the chaos of their lot in seizing the Invader King's woman. They had finally gained an enormous advantage with which to barter...and then a strange, rumpled looking fellow appeared out of nowhere, walked unscathed past a host of Svarren fighters, grabbed the city girl on the arm and disappeared. He had to have been a Shaper, of course. But what power!

The Woman would be most displeased.

It was not a complete loss, however, as she and her fighters had resumed their assault on a now-distracted Nespharia. It was even possible, Omeyo imagined, that his mate had found a way inside the city and was even now feasting on the city's frightened inhabitants.

The general expected to hear news of the Woman at any moment.

Bailis, Nespharia

The Imperial soldiers and city guards had cornered the Svarren witch in an apartment down an alley that dead-ended against the base of the causeway. Unless she could burrow or somehow Shape her way through hundreds of feet of stone, she was trapped. She had a lot of fight in her at the moment, but Bailis was certain that fear, exhaustion or hunger would eventually weaken her to the point where she could be captured or killed as opportunity allowed. The Svarren had done horrific damage to the city and its people, and the witch's death would do a great deal of good for morale, if nothing else.

Bailis was not ready to celebrate, though, because the Emperor and his escort had not returned from their rescue mission, and the colonel had a very, very bad feeling about that. What was he to do, for instance, if the Emperor got himself killed? In Bailis' experience, politics required a scapegoat, in case of the worst, and who better than the only native-born member of Mendis' staff? He was sure his appointment has provoked resentment and jealousy amongst his peers. A disaster like the death of the Emperor would provide them the perfect opportunity for revenge. For all he knew, he'd join the Svarren witch in public execution. Unfortunately, local custom called for those slated for execution to be slowly immersed in molten iron. From what Bailis had heard, most victims died by the time they'd sunk in to the kneecaps. He could only pray he was one of those, if it came to that. He couldn't imagine how terrible it might be to survive until the metal reached his mouth...

He shivered violently, despite the rather pleasant spring air. There was no point in getting himself all worked up about what *might* come to pass; he had to survive the present first.

"Orders, sir?" one of the soldiers asked.

"Keep arrows and spears focused on her end of the alley. Let's put the pikemen behind that. And send someone after the city's Shaper. If he's afraid to confront this witch, at least he can throw some fire her way if the need arises."

"Yes sir," the guard said, saluting. Seconds later, he was off about his orders.

Perhaps crushing the Svarren and killing their witch will buy me some leniency, if the Emperor has been killed...

Beesmarch & His Kin, Western Midlands

The giants were elated, at first. It appeared they'd stopped the great army's advance and even managed to turn it around. But that was not the case. Instead, the invading army wheeled a quarter turn and slowly began to reorganize itself in a southern direction, which maneuver took more than a day to accomplish, whereupon it became clear that its new target was the human capital of Lunessfor.

"Humph!" Beesmarch grunted. "Old Moon's Crossing? Whatever for?"

"Haven't the faintest. But let them skirmish a while with

Her Majesty. She'll give 'em what-for, I'll warrant," one of the other giants responded.

Eoman wasn't convinced. "Maybe she will and maybe she won't. The real question is, what'll we do if they smash her city like an anthill?" The other giants fell silent and stared at their former king. "I mean, we've been assumin' she'd sneak up on these bastards and attack them in the open. What happens if they destroy Lunessfor?"

"D'you think it possible?" Beesmarch wanted to know.

"Time was, I'd've said assembling a group of giants was impossible, and yet here we are."

"I suppose the next question is, what's our next move?"

They bandied ideas back and forth for the better part of an afternoon and ultimately decided to head for Nespharia, to see what the Svarren had accomplished on the far end of the invaders' force. Perhaps the giants could help them take the city and, afterward, turn it into a stronghold for those opposing the invaders.

It would be a long journey, but giants are capable of moving great distances when necessary, and none of their group thought they'd be of much help at Lunessfor. It was a well-reasoned decision.

It was also the wrong decision.

Kittins, Lunessfor

The Queen continued to confound her staff with her inexplicable absence, and even Kittins, who normally couldn't give two shits for Her Majesty's comings-and-goings, was beginning to feel frustrated with the situation. Something was coming; he could feel it. Absent further directions, he toured the city walls, more to reassure himself than anything else. To his relief, the guards were all alert and in their proper positions, and the physical changes he'd ordered for the walls and gates had been completed in what he suspected was record time. Next, he paid a visit to the city's barracks and was again pleased to see everything just as he'd specified. At least the guards were taking things seriously. From the barracks, Kittins dropped by the city gaol. There, alas, things were not so well in hand. The constable was drunk at the front desk, and the High Constable was asleep in his office. Two gaolers were playing a game of some sort in the corner, and the Mahnus-cursed floors hadn't even been swept.

Kittins fought to contain his anger, but felt himself slipping, slipping, slipping inexorably back towards his darker, damned self. He grabbed the drunken constable by the back of his head and drove his face into his desk with lethal force. When the High Constable jolted awake and stumbled into the front room to see what had happened, the captain smashed him in the mouth with his big, bony fist. Before the poor man hit the floor, however, Kittins wrenched him back to his feet by the collar. He turned towards the first gate and saw the two gaolers staring at him, slack-jawed.

"Open the fuckin' gate and throw this bastard in the common room."

Well, they weren't going to argue, were they? Both men quickly executed their order and, with the High Constable's screams ringing in their ears, returned to the lobby, where the Dead One immediately promoted them.

"You," he said to the more alert of the two, "are the new High Constable. And you," he said to the second man, "are the new constable. Fuck up in this job, and I'll kill you, too."

The men nodded wordlessly.

"Now call up some more gaolers, and sweep this damned floor."

It was a funny thing, though: although the need to hurt people angered Kittins, he enjoyed the actual hurting. It was something, he felt, that he could continue doing until someone or something stopped him. There was no telling how many folks he might injure or kill before someone got to him. Why did any part of this appeal to him? He wondered. Was he really a monster, after all?

He'd just decided to go to the gang's hideout when he suddenly realized he had no idea how to find it, had no idea how to contact the Shaper in order to make the Jump.

He still had the purloined map of the city's secret tunnels and byways, though. With a renewed sense of purpose, he set about rousting up some torches, tinder and flint...

And quickly discovered that the castle's goblins had been hard at work since his last visit, blocking or barricading the tunnel he'd used previously. As he felt the barricade, though, he believed it might be moved with sufficient force. He took several steps back and ran at the new wall as fast and hard as he could, crashing through like a stone from a catapult, and landing atop the terrified goblin who'd been laboring on the other side.

In the darkness and still-falling dust, he couldn't quite make out the creature's coloring, but he knew it was nothing like his own. The little thing had many of the same features one might find on a bat (save the wings), though its limbs and torso were more dwarf-like. "Don't kill me! Don't kill me!" It squealed under his weight.

Kittins rolled off it and scrambled to his feet, ready to kill the creature anyway, if necessary.

The goblin was slower to rise, having taken the full brunt of the collapsing barricade and Kittins' weight. He made a great show of coughing, slapping the dust off himself, and rolling his shoulders as if setting them back in place.

The captain wanted to ask how it happened to speak his language, but decided he didn't care. It simply did, and that was all that mattered. "What's your life worth to you?" he asked instead.

The goblin seemed stumped by the question. "My life?" he stammered. "Everything?"

Kittins smiled. He drew a knife from his belt, slowly enough so that the goblin couldn't help but notice, and said, "Tell me everything about your people."

In the end, the information wasn't immediately useful, but the captain figured a day might come when he'd need to know all the secrets the goblin had just divulged.

"May I go now?" the goblin asked hopefully.

"No," said Kittins.

"What will you do with me?"

"Dunno. For now, you're my guide."

The goblin looked thoughtful for a moment, perhaps reckoning that being a guide was better than being a slave, and said "My name is…"

"I don't wanna know, little monster. I may have to kill you when all's said and done. Easier if we leave things as they are."

"But I know your name," the goblin protested.

This was a surprise. "Do you, now?"

"You are the Deaddun."

Kittins almost laughed. "So I am. And you're the Little Monster. Now, show me the way out of this city."

Spirk, Yendor & Co, Lunessfor

"The enemy's comin'!" Spirk yelled as he leapt from his couch.

"What?" Yendor asked, still muzzy from sleep.

"The enemy's comin' this way. They're comin' to fight us; I seen it."

"But they were heading west," Rem interjected.

"Well, they ain't now."

It was not welcome news.

Like the giants before them, they fell into a lengthy discussion about what they ought to do next; unlike the giants, they chose to seek divine help.

They were going to visit Long Pete.

Had it not been for Ron's suggestion that Spirk render them all invisible, however, they might've found themselves in dire circumstances. As it was, they were shocked when Spirk's Jump placed them all in the middle of an Imperial tent, surrounded by very important-looking people who were themselves gathered around Long. None of the new arrivals could understand a word that was being said, but they understood the sudden alarm of the foreign Shapers well enough. These men were easily identified by their dark doublets and capes and the variety of oddly-shaped hats on their heads, in direct contrast to the uniforms of the soldiers present. These Shapers stared frantically about the tent and began mouthing words that Spirk had no wish to hear the end of. As quickly as he and his friends had arrived, they Jumped back out to the relative safety of their hide-out. Moments later, Long himself arrived, with a rather harried-looking chicken in tow.

"Long!" the group cried almost in unison.

"What?" he responded in exasperation. "Can't you see I'm workin' on something?"

"Is that...is that..." Spirk stuttered. "Is that Short Pete ya got there?"

While Yendor, Ron and Rem thought Spirk was still drunk, Long merely nodded and the chicken became Very Very Short Pete, who immediately demanded to be set on the floor.

"Yeah," Long shrugged. "It's Short, all right."

"I thought he was dead," said Spirk.

"He was," Long answered, as if that explained everything. "Now what in the infinite hells are you interrupting my meeting for?"

"Wait a minute," said Yendor, "You're with *them?*"

Long plopped himself down on Spirk's dusty old couch. "It's not as simple as that. I've got to kill the Queen."

"Alheria?"

"Yes."

"What?" Rem demanded. "Why?"

"Seems I gotta tell this damned story over 'n over 'til everybody's heard it," Long sighed. "Very well." And once again he relayed everything he knew of the gods' greater design for him and them and everyone else. When he was done, he was amazed to find the young Shaper asleep beside him, though the other three men were wide awake and looking terrified. "Well?" he said when he'd finished.

"I always thought you immortals was s'posed to look after us."

"All I feel's betrayed," Ron added.

"And you, old friend?" Long asked Rem.

"I don't rightly know how I feel," he confessed. "The rug's been pulled out from under me so many times, I've pretty much given up hope of understanding any of this."

Long smiled apologetically and said, "I've got to get back.

Stay safe 'til I see you all again. You may yet have a say in all this." With that, he Jumped away, taking Short with him

"World's a much darker place than I ever imagined," Yendor muttered to himself.

"Aye," said Rem. "It is that."

Vykers & Co, Outside the Imperial Capital

Lately, Vykers had taken to bird-watching, and it seemed to Ona as if he'd lost his mind. All day, every day, she watched him follow birds to and from the city's walls, 'til it got to the point that he claimed he could recognize individual birds and had given them names.

"To what purpose?" Ona demanded.

Vykers just looked over at her and winked.

Unable to get anything more out of her grandfather, Ona turned to Hjuest and Ngoro, hoping they might have seen this behavior from Vykers before, or at least have theories about what was behind it. Somehow, Vykers managed to sneak up behind her and ask, "Can you weave me a basket outta these grasses?" He gestured to the rest of the plateau.

"Why, because I'm a woman?" Ona snapped in response.

Without bothering to answer, the Reaper turned to Hjuest and Ngoro. "Can either o' you make a basket outta these grasses?"

Before they could reply, Ona said, "I can do it!" She resented the question, but also hated the thought of being left out of... whatever-it-was that Vykers was planning.

"Do it," said Vykers. "About so big." And he spread his arms about three feet apart. "Make sure we can close the top, too."

Ona was about to ask if there was anything else, when Vykers walked away, looking for more birds.

It took several hours, and although Ona had no idea how Vykers intended to use the basket, she was proud of her work just the same. When she presented it to him, he quickly popped a live bird inside and fastened the top.

"I did all this for a bird?" she wanted to know.

"Not bird. Birds." Again, he wandered away, looking for more birds.

By evening, they had a basket full of birds. Ona had a head full of questions, too, but answers were not forthcoming.

"You'll see tomorrow," was all the Reaper would say on the subject.

In the morning, Vykers got up, did a lengthy series of exercises with and without weapons, and sat down by the fire to eat the last of the group's foodstuffs with his companions. When he'd finished, he again surprised Ona with an odd request.

"Would you cut off a good length o' your hair for me?"

There was no point in asking why and no point in pretending to resist, either. She pulled her smallest knife from its sheath and carefully sliced through a good rope on the right side of her head. Vykers took it without thanks and started twisting it into tiny braids, five or seven hairs at a time, which he then knotted on both ends. Next, he retrieved his basket of birds—some of which were alarmed and chirping noisily, and others of which seemed almost catatonic—and took out a single bird. He tied one of the miniature braids to its ankle. On the braid's other end, he tied a piece of lichen that he'd dipped into the oil the group used on its leather goods. This, he quickly touched to the fire. The lichen flared up immediately, and Vykers tossed the bird into the air and watched as it frantically flapped its wings in the direction of its home—the city beyond the walls.

"You see?" he asked his team. "Now you do the rest."

When all the birds were gone, Vykers and his crew turned towards the city and watched and waited. It took several minutes, but finally there was a muffled shout of alarm from somewhere inside the city. As the minutes passed, there were more and more such cries, until at last smoke was visible, rising above the walls at several points.

"City's gotta be like kindling in this climate," Vykers explained. "Even if the Emperor left a few Shapers behind, they've got too much area to cover."

"Then what?" Ona inquired.

"They open their gates or die."

Mendis & His Legions, On the March

The Imperial Legions were well on their way to the natives' capital of Lunessfor. It would be a long journey, but now that Mendis had made the decision, he felt unexpectedly relieved. At last, he was acting, instead of reacting, and it felt good to be in charge of his own destiny once more. He was aware that the Virgin Queen might attempt to pop in on him again, but this time he had a god of his own for protection. All in all, he felt stronger and more confident than he had in days, weeks even. Oh, there was still the issue of how best to handle Qansip, but Mendis had no doubt that even that would resolve itself in his favor in time.

And so, he met with his generals and all of his wizards twice a day—after breakfast and again after the evening meal. He was pleased to discover that his troops had embraced the march southward; furthermore, Long Pete had solved the legions' water problems and even rounded up the last of the native ale and turned it over to the Emperor, who kept it under lock and key and surrounded by guards. He did not want his troops drinking any more of the stuff, but neither could he bring himself to destroy what was left. One never knew when it might come in handy...as with Qansip, for instance.

Unable to cajole her from her strange mood, Mendis reluctantly resumed sharing the ale with her. As ever, she relaxed almost as soon as she'd swallowed her first gulp and shortly thereafter became, more or less, the young woman he'd always known.

Except that now she was giggling about the Svarren and rambling on and on about what wonderful people they were! It was maddening, and Mendis was on the verge of making a second appeal to Long Pete, that he might somehow expunge this new Svarren fascination of Qansip's and restore her to her old self. And yet the Emperor was loathe to seem a love-struck fool in front of a god, even if the god in question was as shabby and unassuming as Long Pete.

He should have swallowed his pride and asked anyway, as it turned out, for at the evening meal, Mendis and Qansip were again approached by the girl's father, looking more disheveled and desperate than ever. Mendis was about to explode at the man's temerity, combined with his inexplicable presence in the Emperor's vicinity, when Qansip let loose a guttural growl and planted a large meat fork in the side of Driegan's neck, whereupon he crashed onto the table top, smashing all of the dishes and spilling all of the beverages. Mendis stumbled backwards in shock, only to see Qansip climb up onto her father's still-twitching torso and begin slurping away at the blood that spewed from the man's neck. Mendis grabbed a hold of the girl's shoulders, intending to drag her off and away, when she reared up her head, bared her bloody teeth at him and snarled like a rabid beast. Alarmed, confused and feeling he ought to do something decisive, the Emperor struck her across the face with a closed fist, and she crumpled back into her seat like the near-child she was, unconscious.

Mendis bellowed for his guards, his wizards, his healers, and just about anyone else he thought might be useful at the moment, except for Long Pete. But he would visit the god soon enough; oh, he most certainly would.

And did. But Long was not overly helpful or sympathetic. "What d'you expect me to do about it?" he asked defensively.

"Something!" Mendis shouted. "Anything. If you can't help her, then...then..."

Long had been lying on an extremely comfortable bed of his own creation, with his ersatz chicken lying by his side. Now, he got up from his nap, agitated by Mendis' agitation, "Look," said he, "why not just send her back to Nespharia? Confine her in a tower or some such 'til she's feeling better. I'm sure all she needs is time."

Mendis glanced around Long's "room"—nothing more, really, than a curtained-off corner of the command tent and said, "Would you take her for me? I'm sure you could use a little break from these dreary surroundings."

"I'll take her," said Long. "But I'm no nursemaid. I'll have other things to do and think about than Qansip's comfort."

"Would you ask the Governor to look after her then?"

"What's the governor's name?"

"Bailis."

A sad, not altogether unpleasant smile came to Long's lips then. "I'll do it."

The colonel wasn't comfortable being anywhere else or doing anything other than keeping watch at the alley's open end, waiting, hoping for the final confrontation with the Svarren witch. As a boy, he'd once witnessed a mare giving birth. This experience was similar in some ways—the nervous expectation, the sense that someone or something's life hung in the balance, the fervent desire for a favorable result. That was as far as it went, though, because, in this case, there was no avoiding death. The only question was upon which side it would fall.

Bailis studied the phalanx of men on his end of the alley: they looked good. Rested and ready, if understandably anxious. The witch could not hold out forever; eventually, she would expire from lack of food or water, kill herself, or make one last-ditch attempt to escape through the phalanx. Bailis felt a grim smile stealing across his lips: good, let her try.

Someone handed him a warm hunk of bread with an already melting dollop of butter and honey, and he ate it with gusto, not caring that he was temporarily littering his beard with crumbs. Crumbs were more than that witch had to eat, more than she would ever have, for the rest of her life.

A guard approached from Bailis' left and said, "Milord, the Emperor's consort has returned."

It seemed Mendis had been successful in rescuing her. "And the Emperor?"

"I'm told he's returned to his legions."

Bailis abruptly turned to examine the guard, as if the man might be mad or lying. "What? He's gone back to his army?"

"So I'm told."

The fellow was utterly bland. Even staring directly at him, the colonel couldn't have said what color his hair and eyes were. Grey and grey? Brown and brown? "And who, pray, is telling you this?"

"He calls himself Long Pete. He Jumped right in like a Shaper with the girl in tow. Said he wanted to speak with you."

Long Pete, a Shaper? Now this was an unforeseen development. Bailis cast an eye over the phalanx once more, torn between staying with his men in case the witch emerged and leaving their sides to follow up with Long Pete. After several seconds' thought, he concluded that the Emperor might prefer that he meet with Long Pete.

Naturally, Long had chosen to appear in the keep, at the high end of the great causeway. It was all very well and good for him to pop in and out wherever he pleased, but Bailis had to walk everywhere, and, damn it all, his knees were not happy about it. When he finally stumbled into the keep, he found Long enjoying a lavish meal with only a large green cat for company.

"What's wrong with your cat?"

"He got tired o' bein' a chicken."

Unable to make sense of that, Bailis simply asked, "Mind if I join you?"

"Be my guest!" said Long. "Or, rather, be *your* guest, since I'm told you're the governor around these parts."

"How long have you been a Shaper?"

"Who says I'm a Shaper?" Long countered, as he snapped his fingers and made a cherry pie appear where his trencher had been.

"Funny."

Long dismissed the comment and explained that he'd been directed by the Emperor to deliver a young woman, one Qansip, into the governor's custody. Long understood there'd been an accident recently, but Mendis was quite clear that the girl was to be locked in a tower, given only the special ale to drink (along with whatever food she required) and visited frequently, though always in the presence of several stout guards.

Bailis was surprised and relieved to hear that the Emperor was alive and well, though he confessed some confusion as to the details of Qansip's rescue and Mendis' return to the front.

Alas, Long was unable to enlighten him in that regard, but instead recommended a particularly sharp cheese at the far end of the table.

The governor sampled said cheese and agreed it was delicious and, by the way, could Long do anything about the Svarren witch currently terrifying his men in the town below?

"It seems a fair trade, after all," said he. "You brought me an enchantress, and I give you a witch in return."

Long, his chin smeared with cherry filling, promised to have a look-see as soon as he'd had his afternoon nap.

Bailis was appalled, mortified, incensed...and unable to do anything about it. If his former captain was indeed a Shaper and one trusted by the Emperor, what could Bailis do but shut up and wait?

It was, however, a rather lengthy nap, even for a man named Long. The next morning, he stumbled out into the spring air and said "Where's this witch, then?"

Unfortunately, he'd forgotten to get dressed, and so stood in the keep's courtyard, as naked as milady's newborn. Even his green cat couldn't bear to look upon him.

"You planning to frighten the witch to death?" Bailis inquired.

Only now aware of his nakedness, Long said "P'raps I'm planning to seduce her."

This was a much more whimsical Long Pete than Bailis had ever known, and he wondered if the infamous Shaper's Burning hadn't driven the poor fellow mad. "Even so," said he, "I think the city folk might feel more comfortable if you put your tunic and trousers back on. And maybe you could leave your little feline friend up here while you work."

"Nonsense!" Long exclaimed. "Short goes with me or we both stay here."

Long had never been to Nespharia in all his travels, and he wished he'd come sooner. It was a lovely little city, a Lunessfor in miniature, without the same cosmopolitan air, perhaps, but still lovely. Flowers had begun to appear in window boxes, and homes and storefronts were just getting fresh coats of paint. A lone man with a broom was actually sweeping the streets—and making progress, too!

And yet the city was eerily quiet. Long gathered it had seen more than its share of warfare in recent months—from the Emperor's host and then the Svarren. If confronting and hopefully expelling this witch could bring the city a greater sense of peace, he was all for it. As long as he didn't get hurt in the process. He was now fairly confident that he could not be killed, but was not at all sure he could not be severely injured, mangled, burned.

He found his way to the witch's alley without directions and was amazed at the number of well-armed if bedraggled men arrayed against her. Some were bleeding, others scorched. It seemed she'd made several forays from her den but had been repelled each and every time. One of the lancers even claimed to have impaled her, and still she had not fallen.

Long felt her presence in the same way one feels an ominous and mysterious pain. She was lurking in the building, like a worm i' the bud. Could he compel her to reveal herself? He believed so. Then he thought of Mardine and what her first moments out of the grave must have been like, how terrifying and cruel.

He decided to go to the witch.

With the men of the phalanx fully focused on the far end of the alley, Long Jumped into the darkened little apartment in which the Svarra had holed up. She shrieked in surprise and fury at his sudden appearance, but quickly assumed a stance of guarded quiescence.

"Mahnus," she breathed.

For a god, it was amazing how often Long was caught unawares. He stared at the Svarra for a moment, unsure how to proceed.

"You kill me?"

Long's silence, his almost unbearable awkwardness seemed to stretch into infinity, until he said, "No, I don't think so," and stretched out a hand to the witch. Any number of things could have happened at that point, but, against all expectation, she took his hand in her own, and Long Jumped away.

Alheria, Kittins, Lunessfor

"You look like a dead man when you sleep," Alheria told Kittins from the foot of his bed.

He opened a bleary eye, spotted her, and closed it again. "I wouldn't know the difference, I don't think. Where have you been?"

"Such an impertinent fellow. I might ask you the same."

"'Cept I'm guessing you know, bein' a god and all."

The Queen ignored this quip and said, "The Emperor appears to have reneged on our agreement and is even now leading his armies this direction."

Kittins finally opened both eyes, fixed them on the ceiling directly overhead. "And where is the Queen's army?"

Alheria smiled her usual, cryptic smile. "You needn't worry on that score. But, tell me, is our city secure? Will she withstand a siege?"

Kittins sat up, stretched. "I suppose that rather depends upon your old friend Mahnus." For a moment, he thought he'd finally gone too far, then Her Majesty changed the subject.

"You will have your opportunity to challenge the Reaper," said she. "Though I suspect you won't enjoy it."

Unless you've misread my motivations, he wanted to say. Instead, he said only, "We'll see."

Alheria vanished with an almost-but-not-quite inaudible whoosh. Kittins reached for the pitcher of water on his bedside table and drank directly from it.

Another faint whooshing betokened an arrival. The captain set the pitcher back in its place and looked up to see Spirk Nessno eyeing him expectantly.

"I'm gettin' more traffic lately than bedsheets in a whorehouse," Kittins complained. "What do *you* want?"

"Yendor sent me. He thought you...He wants to know...He asked me to find out what yer doin'."

"Why?"

"Everyone's sayin' the invaders are comin'. Yendor wants to know what we're gonna do."

"You're askin' me?"

"You're the captain, ain'tcha?"

Kittins rubbed the side of his face that could still produce a bit of beard stubble. "Yeah. Yeah, I s'pose I am." He stood. "Let's go."

Alheria found Vykers quite by accident. She'd made a regular habit of watching the Emperor's palace across the sea, curious if his prolonged absence might provoke anyone to usurp his throne, which it had not. But then Vykers showed up with a laughably small band of fellows and camped just outside the city walls. She watched in fascination as he'd taken an interest in the local birds, and, by the time he set about collecting them, she'd figured out just what he planned. If asked, she'd have confessed to a grudging admiration for the man's ingenuity. She'd beaten him at every board or card game they'd ever played together, and yet she couldn't dismiss the possibility that he'd been playing her, as well, that he was far more astute than he let on.

After all, he was meant to be exceptional. The trouble was, in so many ways, he'd been too exceptional. He'd risen above and outlasted all his brethren, and no matter what she, Mahnus or any of the others had thrown at the Reaper down the long millennia, he'd always come through more or less unscathed. And she wasn't allowed to kill him, which galled her no end. He was neither divine nor infernal (regardless of his desires), and it was difficult for Alheria to understand why he should be spared. But rules were rules. Soon enough—and with his help—she would be well beyond caring what he did, thought or wanted.

But for Mendis, well, she would have to pay him a visit soon. Set him straight.

The Imperial legions were now moving with speed towards their destination. Mendis sent messengers to the Tsundi, urging them to extend their new territory southward, to fill in the void left by the Emperor's departure. Likewise, he contacted the B'Shar, asking them to push northward to Lunessfor. The wave that had destroyed his fleet had long since died, but the wave he'd brought ashore was still rolling across the landscape.

Long Pete had not returned from Nespharia, though, and that was worrisome. What could delay a god? Or had he abandoned Mendis just as the Emperor was moving to challenge Alheria? The Imperial wizards reported that they still hadn't found a way to prevent the Virgin Queen from making another visit; indeed, they didn't know how she'd managed it before. Mendis was not a man to give in to nervous conjecture, but everyone had his limits, and the Emperor feared he was fast approaching his own.

To distract himself, he thought of Qansip—not as she was, but as she had been. If he and Long Pete could just find a way to rehabilitate her...which was another reason he wished to see the man (it was difficult, even after all he'd witnessed, to call the fellow a god). What had happened to the girl in the Svarren's company? She'd not been enspelled or raped—his wizards had assured him of that. What had she seen, done or been told that had changed her so thoroughly?

Belatedly—and shamefully so—he thought of his lady wife, his sons and his daughters. Were it not for the Virgin Queen's enigmatic nature, he might have left the rest of the invasion effort to his generals and sailed home to his family. They always adored his stories of new lands, creatures and peoples.

They would not enjoy learning of the Svarren.

Why hadn't he exterminated them as soon as he'd learned of them? Why hadn't he made that his first priority?

Mendis stepped in front of his dressing mirror—one of the many luxuries available to him as Emperor—and examined his face. His hair was as neat, his moustache and beard as well maintained. But his skin had become pallid, and there was something in his hazel eyes—or perhaps *missing* from his eyes—that bothered him. He looked haunted...or hunted. Or both. And that wouldn't do. He was not a large man, but he'd always compensated with confidence, charisma and drive. He needed to show his staff and his legions that he was ready to face whatever came his way.

He summoned one of his officers and commanded that the

legions pick up their pace. Henceforth, he would look eager to engage the enemy.

TWELVE

Vykers & Co, Outside the Imperial Capital

The gates squealed open, and people came boiling out onto the plateau in a bid to escape the still-growing fires that had engulfed parts of their city. These fires would not last, Vykers knew, if the Shapers had their way, but he and his comrades needed only a few seconds to slip past the steady stream of evacuees and into the capital.

Inside, all was chaos, pandemonium. Small clusters of men fought to extinguish individual fires with buckets of water, whilst women, children and less-helpful men raced for the gates through the ever-thickening smoke. There were shouts of alarm, the cries of mothers separated from their children—or children from their mothers—and shrieks from those injured by the flames. Some men were bellowing orders into the thick, choking heat and smoke. Vykers even heard animal screams of terror from a nearby livery stable.

Where were the Shapers?

He took a minute to survey his surroundings and watched his companions do the same. They were clumped together, like rocks protruding from a raging river, as the tumult of panicked citizens swirled past on either side. In the distance, what could only have been the Emperor's palace rose above the hurly-burly as if flames and destruction were too tawdry to warrant a moment's consideration.

Vykers grinned at Ona and the others and drew his long knife.

And the axe.

Beesmarch & Kin, Outside Nespharia

One of their number sighted Nespharia, and Beesmarch barked at them to push even harder to reach it. Their immediate journey was almost over, but they were anxious, one and all, to learn which way the scales had tipped. Had the Svarren assault caused the city to surrender, or was it still in progress? Would the giants' arrival make any difference? If they and the Svarren were able to expel the invaders, would the city's native inhabitants accept their liberation?

From a mile's distance, it was clear something was amiss. There was no sign of Svarren. Their catapults and other machines of war sat abandoned on the plain and, but for bird song, there wasn't a sound to be heard.

The giants slowed to a trot and closed the remaining distance by halves. Once they were within hailing distance of the walls, Beesmarch turned to Eoman and Karrakan.

"What do ye think?"

Eoman, in turn, deferred to the shaman.

"It doesn't feel much like a battle, does it?" Karrakan asked. He sent a small cloud of will-o'-wisps off towards the city and added, "Let's see what we see."

Minutes later, the little creatures returned, spiraling around Karrakan's head, and he announced, "The invaders yet hold the city."

"But where are our *allies*?" Beesmarch wanted to know.

"Many are dead, I think, and others, missing."

"Missing?"

"Gone."

It had been a hard slog, and all for naught, it seemed. Beesmarch sat, perplexed, and the others followed his example.

That was a mistake.

Two columns of armed and mounted knights appeared—one from the city's west side, and one from its east—probably fifty men in all. Beesmarch climbed to his feet again, and Eoman was quick to join him. Separately, they calculated the odds and came to the same conclusion: they could defeat these knights if it came to a fight, but more than one giant was likely to fall as well.

Slowly, the knights began to fan out, hoping to encircle Beesmarch and his fellows. It was too late to run, but there was yet some hope of talking this through.

One of the knights yelled something that none of the giants understood. After a pause, another, heavily-accented voice, yelled, "Drop weapons."

That was not going to happen, and everyone on both sides knew it.

"Drop weapons!" the knight screamed again, louder. "Drop weapons or die!"

It was time to be a king. Beesmarch dropped his own and walked towards the closest knights with open, outstretched hands.

Eoman smashed him over the head with the butt of his axe and Beesmarch went down with a great thud. Whilst the other giants stared at him with a mix of confusion and rage, Eoman dropped his own weapons and walked forward, just as Beesmarch had before him.

"Take care of 'em," he called back to Karrakan. "They're a good lot."

At the last of these words, the knights encircled Eoman and prodded him away from his friends with the ends of their lances. The other giants watched, mouths open in disbelief and despair, fumbling, fuming, struggling to make sense of what had just transpired.

"Let's drag Bees away from here," Karrakan announced. "Let's get well clear of these bastards."

As expected, Beesmarch was furious and all but inconsolable.

But Karrakan understood. "He's been prisoner to these people before," he offered. "And so he's more equipped to deal with them."

"Deal with them?" Beesmarch snapped. "He's a bloody hostage!" He'd never felt such impotent rage and had no idea how to cope with it.

The other giants remained silent, lost in their thoughts,

sullen and dispirited.

Bees rubbed the back of his head, where an enormous lump had risen, painful to the touch. "Son of a bitch about staved my knave's pate in," he muttered to himself. "What are we to do, what are we to do, what are we to do...?"

"Let's walk the perimeter," one of the others said. "Might be we'll somethin' helpful."

What they found was Eoman's bloody head, perched above Nespharia's western gate.

Beesmarch erupted in uncontrollable rage and was like to storm the gate himself, but Karrakan put him to sleep. "Tie him up this time," he ordered, and let's get him as far from this accursed place as we can.

Bailis, Inside Nespharia

"You did *what*?" Bailis roared at his second-in-command, an Imperial officer Mendis had appointed to help the governor.

"I didn't think..." the man stammered.

"You didn't think, all right. You certainly didn't fucking think! We weren't at war with the giants, imbecile! Now...?" His speech rapidly dissolved into an inarticulate growl, whereupon he took to rapid, aggressive pacing, interrupted with frequent bursts of profanity. After nearly an hour had passed, he barked, "Take that head down from the gates and bring it to me. Gently."

It was the same giant, the very same one. As Bailis looked at its head, he sank into a profound depression. What in all hells had he done? How could he have become so misguided? What demon was it that visited him in his sleep and made him betray his own people and the other denizens of his homeland?

He smashed his fist onto the table top, rattling nearby goblets but affecting the giant's head not at all.

"Give me the room," he told the men who'd brought him the grisly token.

Alone at last, save for Eoman's head, Bailis plotted his revenge.

It was well after midnight when he unlocked the door to Qansip's tower. He found her asleep on the floor, naked and befouled with her own shit. The girl had completely lost her mind, magical ale or no.

Bailis pulled her to her feet, waking her in the process, and gestured for her to be quiet. He'd no idea if she'd cooperate, but he was past caring. He found a large cloak and threw it over her, after which he led her out of the tower and down the long causeway into the city below. From there, he dragged her to a particular door in the outer wall, a secret door that very few were aware of. Prying it open with his sword, he pushed the girl out into the night. Only then did he check to see if he'd been seen; it appeared that he had not, and *more's the pity*, he thought. It could all end right now, and he wouldn't have cared.

Long, Omeyo and the Witch, the Scrublands

The Svarren witch and her human mate were an unlikely pair. She was so deformed, it was difficult to look long at her without wanting to look away. She had a hideous mass on her left shoulder; her right arm was considerably longer than her left; her right foot was three times the size of its partner; her long, matted hair was crawling with lice and smelled like a jakes. And but for a rather small loincloth, she was naked. Yet the man looked at her with adoring eyes, as if the woman he saw was not the one seen by everyone else.

Long was baffled.

"And who're you?" he asked the man.

"A tired but grateful old man. You've done me and my people a favor we can never hope to repay."

"Your people?"

The man shrugged. "Adopted."

They stood in a small clearing in a vast sea of bushes that were anywhere from six to ten feet in height. These, Long understood, were the scrublands.

"And before that?" he asked the man.

"Nothing relevant."

But he could not hide his past from Mahnus, and Long knew

where and what the man had been before.

"And you?" the man inquired.

Long didn't see the point in beating about the bush; in their current location, that could last 'til the end of time. "I'm a god, I guess. Mahnus, actually. Leastways, that's what everyone keeps telling me, and I've seen enough to believe it."

If the man was surprised by this, he didn't show it. "And your green cat?"

"He's actually a little man who used to be dead."

Again, the other man seemed unusually unperturbed by these revelations. "And what will you and your little cat-man do now?"

The captain shook his head, as if the question was simply too hard to answer. "I don't even wanna think about that right now." He paused, and then said, "And how about you? Where will you and your adopted folk go from here?"

The other man frowned briefly. "We've lost a terrible number of fighters. But we have many yet to summon from the distant places. We'll have a part to play in this war, yet."

"I don't doubt it, General Omeyo," said Long.

Still, he could not get a rise out of the man.

"And I do not doubt you, Mahnus."

Mendis, Bailis, In Nespharia

Mendis was apoplectic. One of his wizards had delivered news of Qansip's disappearance from Nespharia and of their subsequent inability to locate her. More, Long Pete had still not returned. Coincidence? Or was he responsible for Qansip's disappearance? The Emperor cursed both Mahnus and Alheria and their incessant, treacherous meddling.

He informed his staff that he was returning to Nespharia with all haste and commanded them to maintain his legions' pace and direction. Whatever else transpired, the Imperial army would assault Lunessfor. Promartis, of course, tried to talk him out of leaving at this juncture, but the Emperor would not listen.

Next, Mendis commanded one of his wizards to take him

back to Nespharia, where he intended to find answers and make changes.

When he arrived, the city was quiet and calm prevailed. But why should these folks have calm when his life was in such turmoil? Mendis stormed in upon Bailis whilst he was having his morning meal.

"Explain your failure," he snarled without preamble.

Bailis immediately dropped his utensils and rose to face his Emperor. "She disappeared in the night," he said.

"Did she? A lone, drunken girl escaped from a locked and guarded tower and from thence out of the city? I think not."

Bailis was smart enough to keep his mouth shut, knowing that more was to come.

"And where is Long Pete?" Mendis demanded.

"We had some difficulty with a Svarren witch who'd taken up residence in the town below. Long Pete promised to remove her."

"And himself with her?" Mendis' eyes fell upon a meat fork on Bailis' table and remembered how Qansip had attacked her father. Mendis was tempted to do the same to Bailis. "I am removing you from your office," said he, "and reassigning you to General Promartis' staff. You are going to attack your own capital. Fail in this, and your end will not be merciful."

Bailis was not surprised or even displeased. He was, clearly, not cut out for governing. But he made a special effort to appeared thoroughly cowed by the Emperor's ruling.

"Is there anything else?" Mendis sneered.

The colonel could not help himself. "Your men, Magnificence, have seen fit to butcher one of the local giants. I fear that may have...repercussions."

Mendis struck him across the face: once, twice...and then lost interest. He stalked from the room, found his wizard, and instructed him to take Bailis back to Promartis, to be reassigned however the general wished.

There was a church, below, that would accommodate hundreds. Mendis commanded the nearest officer to round up as many men of good character and loyalty as could be found and have them report to that church as quickly as possible. In less than an hour, the Emperor stood on the dais inside that church, facing a capacity crowd. He needed a scapegoat, but such were easily found.

"I thank you, loyal subjects," he said in a booming, resonant voice, "for all that you have done for the Empire and its newest city, the beautiful Nespharia. Unfortunately, despite its calm exterior, this city remains under assault by our enemies, amongst whom, as you know, are the Svarren and the giants. We must eradicate them by any means necessary."

A loud cheer went up throughout the church.

"Accordingly, I will be personally leading a number of assaults on local Svarren and giant enclaves when and wherever we find them. In addition, I am directing that the city's forges be expanded, for the purpose of increasing weapons production..."

The Emperor spoke for a full hour of his plans to bolster the war effort and, by the end of his speech, those gathered to listen had become a frenzied pro-war mob of zealots, who burst through the church doors anxious to begin the killing of Svarren, giants or anything else that got in their way.

As for Mendis, he had created a plausible front through which he could hunt for Qansip. The soldiers of his Empire were preparing to attack the stronghold of the goddess Alheria, but Mendis cared only about finding and recovering his mistress.

Kittins, Yendor & Co, Lunessfor

It was as if time stood still in the boys' hideout, for each time Kittins or Long came by, the men were arrayed in their usual positions, in their traditional places, drinking. Long Pete had known them all long enough that he should not have been surprised. And yet he was.

"What are you lads doing?" he demanded.

"Drinkin'," said Yendor.

Even Kittins was three sheets to the wind. "Can you think of a better way to celebrate the end of the world?"

Short Pete, back in human form, crawled up onto Spirk's chest and fell asleep, just as if he were still a cat.

"It isn't the end, though; not if I have anything to say about it."

Kittins laughed, spewing ale down his chest and spraying it all over Rem, who sat nearest him. Fortunately, Rem was too drunk to mind. "Yeah?" he said. "And what're you gonna do about it? Thousands of folks are about to die."

Long found a space on Ron's couch and pushed the young man over. "There's only three of us need to, though: Her Majesty and me and...one other," he finished with a sudden edge of despair in his voice.

Drunk or not, this got the group's attention, and they all sat up a bit straighter whilst Long told them everything he knew. When he'd finished, everyone observed a solemn and lengthy silence, except for Spirk, who was of course sobbing like a small child.

"Are you sure?" Rem asked.

Long shot him a look that said he needn't have bothered. Yes, he was sure.

"And I thought I was doomed," Kittins chuckled.

"How can we help?" Yendor asked.

Now, Long choked up, could barely get the words out, so full was he of grief and self-loathing. "I need...I need..." He tried again, "I need you to kill Esmine."

Vykers & Co., Inside the Imperial Capital

Vykers tore through the locals as if he were scything wheat. At one point, the massive façade of a burning business broke free and was about to fall upon him, when a beautiful, dark-skinned woman yelled at him in warning and pushed him out of the way. In the next instant, she was dead, crushed under hundreds if not thousands of pounds of burning wood. Such an odd sacrifice, it seemed, from a woman he would just as easily have cut down himself, and all for naught. The Reaper would never have been hit.

Behind him, Ona, Hjuest, Ngoro and the last two fighters hacked their way through the crowd as well, albeit with a great deal less gusto. This was the thing Vykers was born to, and the others, rough-hewn though they were, had not been.

Up and down the boulevard which led up to the palace, hordes of people were still struggling to get out of their homes and businesses and out to the gates. Vykers, despite his frenzied state, nevertheless noted that there were precious few guards or other city officials. Had they all gone with the Emperor? What fools! What Mahnus-cursed imbeciles!

He brought his axe down on a woman's face, even as his long knife found her heart, then he tossed her corpse aside like so much dead wood.

Where were the Shapers, though? The palace remained untouched by flame, unmoved by the chaos exploding all around it. He surmised the city's magicians could be found there, protecting the throne and the Imperial family.

They meant nothing to him; he wished only to see the rest of the mural from which the Sholdorn fragment had come.

The Giants, In the Wilds

The king of the giants had gone from one extreme, storming and raving for days, to its opposite: stony silence. He was determined, he said, to find and muster the last of their kin, male or female, adult or child, in his intended effort to destroy Nespharia and all those within her walls, regardless of their guilt in Eoman's death. For once, his companions did not disagree or even question his thinking. Eoman had been loved by all, and the atrocity of his murder must be answered for.

Thus, each giant in the group was sent in a different direction, and even the Brothers were separated. They would search every acre of land for others of their kind and meet back in the same spot a month hence. The giants, as a people, were going to war.

As angry as Beesmarch was, though, Karrakan was much, much more distraught. He could not imagine a world without his oldest friend, could not imagine the gods or spirits of nature that would allow his murder.

At a loss for what else he might do, the shaman found a quiet grove and prayed to the Reaper's fey companion, to Aoife.

No one had ever prayed to her before, and she was elated to respond.

Long, Kittins & Co., Lunessfor

"I'll do it," said Kittins, lurching up off Rem's couch before anyone else could respond. When the rest of the group stared at him, he said, "Won't be the first time I've killed a child, so I'm damned anyway. What's the difference?"

Just as Long had figured. "I can...I can drop you just inside her cave. But do it as quickly, as gently as possible. She don't deserve to suffer." He could hardly believe he'd the power to speak such evil words, and if there was suffering to be done, let it be all and only his, forever.

Spirk had heard enough. He staggered up off his own couch, sending Short tumbling through the air, and announced, "I can't let you do it." Fire leapt from his hands, and yet he did not burn.

Kittins scoffed at him. "You heard our old captain: it's her, or it's all of us, forever."

The young Shaper was about to blast the Dead One, when Long put a hand on the bigger man and Jumped away...

Deep into a forest, where it was drizzling lightly on their heads.

"Are you sure you can do this?" Long asked in the voice of a soul in torment.

"You sure you want it done?" the man with the ruined Death's head replied.

Long was afraid to speak, so he nodded instead.

In a gesture so surprising, it even astounded the man making it, Kittins reached out and put a comforting hand on Long's shoulder. "You sure drew the short stick, Captain. Nobody who knows the facts would dare say otherwise. Can't say I envy you, but you've got my respect."

It was cold comfort, but Long was touched that his one-time rival had said anything. "I can put you inside, as I said, and maybe protect you from Zillia's magics..."

"Who, now?"

"Mardine's protector."

"But you'll have to do the rest on your own."

"I figured. Now let's do this before either one of us loses his nerve..."

In this moment of agony, a revelation: he'd never known Kittins capable of such a thing.

Lord Commander Dabis, Approaching Lunessfor

Dabis pushed the legions and their support train into the Virgin Queen's kingdom at last. There was no going back now. She would know of their presence and prepare for it. She might even attack before they came within sight of her city. But he had to have faith in the Emperor's army, the largest the world had ever seen. Goddess she might be, but how could the Virgin Queen hope to counter such numbers, such discipline, especially when she had yet to field an army of her own, according to all the intelligence the Lord Commander had received?

He wished Mendis were with them, though. And then again, he didn't. The Emperor appeared to have lost his mind where this Qansip was concerned, and at the worst possible time. *Well,* Dabis thought, *let him die, if needs must.* Mendis had heirs; the Empire would continue, whatever its current Emperor did. Still, Dabis wished he'd had the girl assassinated. It could have been made to look like an accident, or an act of war from the locals. The Lord Commander very much doubted that the Emperor would ever suspect him. But if the Emperor was no longer right in the head, what difference did it make?

Mendis, In Search of Qansip

He was leading a large contingent of knights back into the scrub-lands. If the Svarren were no longer there, they'd left tracks that could be followed. Mendis would find them and kill every last one of the abominations.

Or so he thought, until the world around him seemed to stop, to hold its breath, and all of his knights and their horses froze in their places, mid-gallop. He knew the genesis of this

frightening phenomenon, of course. It was one thing to understand what caused it, however, and quite another to grasp its
totality. Some of the horses had all four hooves in the air. One or
two of his knights had bounced completely out of their saddles
and hung over their mounts as if fixed there. Even the breeze
had stopped blowing, and there was not a single sound to be
heard.

"Where are you going, little man?" a familiar if hated voice
called out from his right.

He, alone of all his men was able to move. He turned towards
Alheria and said, "Why should you care? Have you come to
threaten me again?"

Like Mendis' horses, she was floating a few feet off the
ground. Decked out in all her royal finery, she answered, "Oh,
no. We are rather beyond that now."

It was a calculated comment, the Emperor knew, and yet he
could not resist responding. "And what, pray tell, is that supposed to mean?"

The Queen said nothing at first, though her eyes beamed an
amused malevolence at him. "I have found the Reaper, you see."

Mendis turned all the way in his saddle, so that he could
face the Queen directly. "If you are going to make me ask, I'll
ask. What about him?"

"You had to bring your enormous fleet to my shores. You
had to kill so many of my sea monsters. But in so doing, you
made it easier for the Reaper to visit your land..."

The Emperor jumped from his saddle and ran to within feet
of the still-hovering goddess.

"What? What is it you're not telling me?"

Alheria smiled, and it might as well have been a dagger to
Mendis' heart. "He's in your palace, as we speak. He's butch-
ered your wife and gutted your children. Because you had to
expand your pathetic empire."

"You lie!" Mendis screamed.

"Would that it were so," Alheria said in false sympathy. "But
your family is dead by Vykers' hand, and your city, in flames."

"All of them?" Mendis wailed. *"He has* no children. *All* my
pretty ones? Did you say *all?"*

"All," Alheria confirmed. "You are the last of the Staurachians."

He felt his face flush crimson and tears begin to well up in his eyes, but daren't let them trip across his lower lids and stream down his face in testament to his utter and absolute defeat. "You might have stopped this!" he howled accusingly.

"Yes," said the Queen, "And so might you."

He had no words.

Ona, Vykers, Inside the Imperial Capital

It had gotten quite hot for a spring day, but perhaps that was due to the series of fires still burning around the city. Or it might have been the heat and exhaustion one feels after battle. Whatever the case, Ona sat on the edge of the well in which she'd been hiding and surveyed the damage. There was not a person left alive within blocks, perhaps anywhere in the city. Even the house pets, horses and smaller livestock had been hacked to pieces, and it looked like some evil spirit had painted every surface with blood.

Ona knew who that evil spirit had been.

She rose from the well, drew some water, washed her face, and quenched her thirst. And promptly vomited.

The air smelled of warm blood, of sweat, of feces. The echoes of screams long silenced rang in her ears, along with the buzzing of very real flies that had descended upon all the fresh meat. Slowly, Ona began moving towards the Emperor's palace, as Vykers had named it. Her muscles hurt, but, more than that, she feared what she might find when she arrived.

And rightly so. Vykers had massacred everyone and everything in his path. Even his own men. Ona wept as she knelt beside Hjuest, his head nearly hacked from his body. His eyes were open and seemed to be asking "Why?" She would ask the Reaper, if she could find him.

But the palace's courtyard was gorier than a rendering plant—bodies and parts of bodies were everywhere, soaked in communal blood. It was all Ona could do to keep her feet, to place one foot in front of the other.

In time, she found Vykers, sitting on an outdoor throne at the back of a plaza. She had to step over the bodies of women and children to approach him, but she needed to understand. When she finally came within speaking distance, she stared at him for the longest time. He appeared to be asleep, but it was hard to see his eyes, because, like everything else, he was red from head to toe, bathed in the blood of the Imperial family. On a sheltered wall some distance behind him and apparently unnoticed by the Reaper was a large mural, missing a few pieces, but one special fragment in particular. She wanted to deface and destroy the accursed mural, to grind its pieces to dust beneath her heel. The butcher before her remained oblivious.

"Vykers," she said quietly, fearfully.

Slowly, he roused himself, dropped the axe he'd been holding in his right hand. It clattered on the stones at his feet, and the noise startled Ona.

"Where are the others?" he asked wearily, as if drunk.

"Where are the others?" Ona repeated, disbelieving. "Where are the others? Dead! They're dead! You killed them!"

She thought Vykers might yell at her, but he did not. In fact, he didn't seem to fully understand what she'd said. "Find Hjuest."

"He's on the ground over there," she pointed. "With his head near shorn off."

"And Ngoro?"

"Dead."

"And..."

"Dead. All Dead. You murdered them all. And everyone else you could find."

Vykers said nothing more, but kept his eyes fixed on his granddaughter.

"What are you?" she finally yelled in anger.

"I...am...the Reaper."

Appendix A

Cast of Characters

Tarmun Vykers, A.K.A, "the Reaper"—a legendary warrior
Mendis Staurachia—Emperor of the invading force
Captain Kittins, A.K.A. the "Dead 'Un"—An officer in Her Majesty's Army
General Omeyo—Eyatu's mortal general
The Woman—His Svarren mate
Ona—Vykers' granddaughter
Aoife—An A'Shea or "Mender"
Qansip—Only child of self-proclaimed "Lord" Deda of Eastcliff
Driegan—Her father
Long, A.K.A, Long Pete—a former captain in Her Majesty's Army
Mardine—His wife, a giantess
Esmine—their child
Eoman Harkin Hainen—King of the Giants
Karrakan—a giant shaman
Beesmarch—a giant
Zillia—a giantess
Yendor Plotz—A drunk and friend to Long
Spirk Nessno—A Shaper and friend to Long
Ron—an archer and friend to Long and Spirk
Remuel Wratch, A.K.A. "Rem,"—a famous actor
Her Majesty, Alheria, A.K. A. "the Virgin Queen"—Ruler of the Central or Midlands Kingdoms, and Goddess of Earth, Nature and life
Cindor—Her First Shaper
D'Marei—An Alchemist
Mahnus—God of Creation and War
Eyatu—the God of Winter
The Historian, A.K.A, "the Ahklatian"—An ancient sage and Shaper

Appendix B

A Guide to Character Name Pronunciation

Author's note: If you've read this far, these are your characters as much as mine. You may imagine their names however you'd like. This list is really for the sticklers amongst us.

Tarmun Vykers = Tahr-muhn Vahy-kurz
Aoife = Ee-fuh
Qansip = Kon-sip
Mardine = Mahr-deen
Omeyo = Oh-mey-oh
Mahnus = Mahn-us
Alheria = Uh-lair-ee-uh
Eoman = Ay-mun
Karrakan = Care-i-cun
Ahklatian = Uh-kley-shuhn

ABOUT THE AUTHOR

Allan Batchelder is a professional actor, educator and former stand up comedian. He has written several plays and screenplays, dialogue for computer games, and online articles about theatre and/or education. *Steel, Blood & Fire* is his first novel, the opening act in a planned series. Allan lives in Washington State with his wife, son, and two cats. And his computer.

Dear Reader:

Thank you for reading *Steel, Blood & Fire*. If you enjoyed it, please consider writing a review on Amazon, Goodreads, or anywhere else books are reviewed. Vykers is one tough bastard, but he can't survive without your support!

For updates and news about sequels, go to:

www.immortaltreachery.com
https://www.facebook.com/SteelBloodFire
And on Twitter at: @TarmunVykers

Immortal Treachery is:

Steel, Blood & Fire
As Flies to Wanton Boys
Corpse Cold
The Abject God
The End of All Things

Curious about other Crossroad Press books?
Stop by our site:
http://store.crossroadpress.com
We offer quality writing
in digital, audio, and print formats.